A TWISTED TALE

BOOK THREE

Fractured

R. PHILLIPS

Fractured

II

Fractured

Copyright © 2023 by R. Phillips

Fractured, A Twisted Tale #3

Edited by: Ellie McLove, My Brother's Editor
Proofread by: Rosa Sharon, My Brother's Editor
Cover design by: Clarissa Kezen - ckbookcoverdesigns.com

ISBN-13: 979-8-9860684-5-9 (Paperback)
ISBN-13: 979-8-9860684-4-2 (Ebook)

www.rphillipswrites.com

Playlist

Swansea by Lemolo (Chapter 1)

Running Up That Hill by Placebo (Chapter 2)

Way down We Go by KALEO (Chapter 3)

Darkside by Neoni (Chapter 6)

Always Remember Us This Way by Lady Gaga (Chapter 8)

Ghost by Justin Bieber (Chapter 9)

Game Of Survival by Ruelle (Chapter 20)

Locksmith by Sadie Jean (Chapter 27)

A Drop In The Ocean by Ron Pope (Chapter 28)

Deeper by Valerie Broussard, Lindsey Stirling (Chapter 33)

Let's You Fly by Bryar (Chapter 36)

Snow On The Beach by Taylor Swift (Chapter 37)

Safe & Sound by Taylor Swift, The Civil Wars (Chapter 41)

Chasing Cars by Tommee Profitt, Fleurie (Chapter 43)

Still Falling For You by Ellie Goulding (Epilogue)

Personally,

I believe the people we love stay with us,

even after they're long gone.

Living on in the piece of themself left in our hearts.

They're the dream of sitting on a park bench,

asking you to look after the girl they left behind.

They're the whispered reminder to never lessen

yourself for the appeasement or love of others.

They're the late-night answer found in a prayer for forgiveness.

So this one's for my ghosts in all their varied forms.

I hear you. I feel you.

I can't wait to laugh with you again one day.

And I know that you are always with me.

Fractured

"There is a tide in the affairs of men."

- Shakespeare, Julius Caesar

Important Notice

This book contains explicit content, profanity, violence, and topics

that may be sensitive to some readers, such as murder/suicide, self-harm,

and sexual assault.

Recommended for 18+

PART ONE

The Breaking

Fractured

Prologue

Jace

Somewhere In Between

What is a life?

A collection of memories? A series of glorious highs and heartrending lows? Is it a purpose, cumulative or singular?

Or is it something more? Something beyond what is tangible or even immaterial?

Something beyond even what is found within us.

Is it a million little touches? A thousand laughing smiles? Hundreds of shed tears and dozens of stolen kisses on a few desperate sighs? Is it the thread of yourself that you leave behind in those around you? The lives you're unknowingly fated to change simply by existing. A single moment of entanglement, forever binding the invisible matter of souls, until you're so much a part of each other that there's no chance of ever being the same. Even if you're fathomless miles apart. Even if one's gone while the other lingers. Even if the very love you hold is the thing that breaks you eternally.

Leaving pieces scattered like notes somewhere among the songs of your life until it's all played together in one crashing crescendo of melody.

I heard the song of my life, lives, when that fire hit. Was thrust back into that haunted place between life and death as I saw Ellie be blown into the water across from me. This horrible place of knowing I've been in once before and somehow forgot.

And all I want is to let go.

It's horrible, this knowing. This heartbreak. The loss of her I've felt thousands of times. This agony of love that we've all been forced to endure over and over again. Even the love and hate that Coop and I have shared in equal measure. The torture of all the times we've been torn apart by the incomparable love we hold for this one girl in her countless forms.

So I try. I feel the fire hit me and this haunted place lay claim to me again… and I try so hard to let go. To leave this pain in my soul behind and set sail for whatever lies beyond this universe in search of something brighter.

But for some reason, I can't.

Maybe because they won't let me escape the fate I'm doomed to endure by the two people I love most in the world.

They never do.

And maybe this time, it's also in punishment for breaking my promise to her. The gods' way of evening the scales for the secret I kept from them both, even if it had been with the best of intentions. Maybe they sentenced me to this purgatory for breaking my word. Or maybe they have something left in store for me, some part I'm still supposed to play in this version of the tragedy.

I see it all, in the most excruciating rush of a macabre melody… with a grieving kind of rage so intense, I'd never experienced anything like it before, flooding me. Tearing into my heart and bleeding a sickening kind of darkness into it. The kind of darkness that people never want to face being capable of because when you do, you find it looking back at you. Terrifying you with the reality of what you could become if you give in.

And it does terrify me, but not enough to not give in.

To see if maybe surrendering to that darkness would finally allow me the escape to somewhere the gods couldn't reach.

But all it does is open my eyes, anchoring me instead of gifting me the freedom from this fate I want so desperately.

Silencing the gods' song of horror with the sight before me as I watch two men push my cousin down to his knees.

I'm not really here.

I know it immediately somehow, and it has little to do with the fact that no one is looking at me and everything to do with the grief in my heart doing battle with the oblivion in my soul.

"Who are you?"

I watch the blood drip from Coop's busted brow into his eyes as he stares up at the man before him. The guy stands out like a fucking flashing road sign in Tommy's ramshackle little beachside apartment. All carefully sculpted salt-and-pepper hair in a suit that's probably worth more than everything inside the four walls he's standing in. But it's the gun in his hand that has me realizing how much of a mistake I might have made in giving in to the darkness inside me because I should be terrified. Terrified of losing my cousin regardless of the fact she picked him... but instead, there's just nothing but that grief and rage and the knowing that I should be doing something more.

He smiles openly down at Coop and takes a step closer to him. "You're a fool, you know?"

I see the same rage poisoning me more by the second reflected in my cousin's face before he tries to jerk out of the hold of the guys holding him.

They react too fast though, tightening their grips as the man lifts the gun.

"You're a fool to think you could get away with this."

His voice is an empty thing, as if it could be any voice in any crowd.

There one second and gone the next.

Coop's lips lift with that fuck-off smirk he's always been so good at. "I already did." He arches a brow. "She's on her way to safety now."

"To Alec, you mean?" The man laughs quietly before looking up and blowing out a breath on a nod. "Yes, an error of judgment was made with that one. Too much mercy was allowed because of his blood." He looks back down to Coop with a small smile. "But don't worry, Cooper. It won't take too long to find him and then…" His voice quiets to a whisper. "Then both of Nadia's children will pay the price they should have all along."

Coop's jaw clenches, eyes narrowing before he grinds out. "We'll see."

The man stares at him for a second longer before the smile slowly falls from his lips. "You mean I'll see."

And the next thing I know, the man fires two bullets in quick succession.

Fires them right into my cousin as I open my mouth to shout, watching him fall to the floor and unable to do anything but be jerked to the side of the girl we're both fated to love more than anything for eternity.

Just in time to see her open her eyes.

**

Take care of our girl, *Jace.*
And tell her *I'll be waiting in the always.*

Chapter One

Wake up, minushka.

My eyes snap open with her voice still ringing through my head, heart frantically thudding against my breastbone and stomach convulsing painfully as I choke on the water filling my mouth. I need to breathe. Breathe, breathe, breathe. It's the demand pounding through every cell in my body with panicked urgency. I can't see anything past it. My lungs are burning, aching with the need to complete the simple act, but when I try to gasp for air, all that happens is the choking that comes as the water flows back down my throat again.

"Get her on her side!"

Who is that?

It's not a familiar voice, the short tone completely foreign to me.

And I can't make out anything more than shadows as I feel two sets of hands roughly roll me onto my side. Allowing the water to pour out of my mouth as my stomach heaves over and over again, ridding my body of the watery death still trying to claim me. Even with the whole world nothing but panic and shadows, the one certainty I have is that I drowned somehow, and I died. It's in every panicked yet still too-slow beat of my heart, as if it's racing faster and faster to escape the remembered stillness. It's in the cold, still lingering in my blood and locking up my bones. The fog in my head and the darkness clouding my vision that just won't let up enough to allow the light to pierce it. The way my clothes are wet and stuck to my skin.

In the knowing that I *need to breathe.*

Maybe it had only been for only a second, that halt of my heart, but I'm sure of it.

There's no other way I could have heard her voice.

Breathe, El. Fucking breathe. Now.

I feel the last of the water fall from my mouth the next moment and gasp, lungs expanding with air that bring with it an instant agony I welcome. Greedy for the pain that's bringing me further back to life. I try to gulp down more air and choke on the feeling of emptiness in my throat as if my body hasn't quite adjusted to the reality of being alive again. Hasn't quite accepted that I've returned to the land of the living. I press my lips together despite the urge to gulp for more air. Gritting my teeth and squeezing my eyes shut before forcing myself to take slow breaths through my nose.

To focus only on the air. To feel the flow of it in a way I had never taken the time to appreciate before.

"That's it, sweetheart. Just breathe."

I still don't know who you are.

Neither side of my now fractured heart called me sweetheart.

I allow myself five more breaths before trying to sort through the disorientation weighing down my mind. It hardly allows me to complete a thought before I lose its trail and have to start all over again. Fighting

9

against the sense of sluggishness and the death that's refusing to go quietly, determined to wage one final battle against the life that's electrifying me. Each little breath forcing the neurons in my head to fire again, bringing them back from the darkness they slipped into that eventually claims us all.

I crack my eyes and focus on the sliver of light that I can now see has a reddish tinge of evening. Trying to remember what happened when I opened my eyes for the first time today. To start at the beginning and work my way forward to somehow figure out how the fuck I ended up here. And most importantly, how I ended up fucking dead.

Jace had been there. There had been his soft press of lips to my head along with his sea-spring scent. But then he had left and... and what happened then? I blink at the hazy red light in answer to the question in my mind. Trying to pull something from the recesses of the mess in my head. What happened after Jace left?

Better question is, why's your heart fractured now, El?

Oh god.

All those pages filled with our poems flash through my mind and a keening kind of noise escapes through my gritted teeth because I remember now what happened next.

I chose.

I made the impossible choice and chose the man that some part of me had always known I'd never be able to rid myself of completely. No matter how hard I might've tried if I had chosen differently. No matter how much

Jace might've wanted me to try anyway. Because Coop had been the one I couldn't bear to lose in the end.

My vision finally starts to clear, and I blink rapidly, tears falling from my eyes until I can eventually make out the red hues of the sun setting over the ocean. The memory of it has my heart seizing up all over again and bleeding with the same color that the water is tinged with. I unclench my teeth enough to gasp for more breath, but there's something acrid in it that sends me coughing again.

And it hits me that I can smell smoke in the air.

"You with us, sweetheart?"

A man leans down in front of me, his face filling my vision and I blink at him a few more times before placing him as the guy who owns a boat docked not too far from Jace's. Not someone I know well though. We had only ever shared a few casual waves of hello whenever he had been on the deck and I'd passed by.

Which means I'm at Jace's.

Because I went to tell him.

And then...

Come on, Princess. Don't tell me you forgot about me that fast.

No. Fucking no.

Coop.

Jace.

The phone call.

The explosion.

No, no, no, no, no—

"Ellie?"

The familiar name has my head turning automatically, wood beneath my cheek scraping as I look up and my eyes flow along the dock I walked down not too long ago. But I know it's not him before my eyes even land on the person who called his name for me. I know it because it's not the teasing, lyrical voice that brought me back to life when I'd been so lost before. That wanted my heart even when I didn't. It's not the person whose heart I broke in return. It's not Jace.

My eyes find a pair of black sneakers first and quickly run up the length of a body that's covered with tattoos before locking onto Zane's face. His face that wears an expression I've never seen on it before. One that has my bleeding heart stilling completely and sends my eyes wildly searching the space behind him with a desperation that's riding me hard now. Already fumbling to push up from the dock when I spy the hand hanging down from the gurney behind him, wrist tilted my way with the point of the tattooed compass on it aimed straight at me. As if even his tattoo knows that the blame for this should be laid directly at my feet.

"Ja-Jace." I cough his name right as my hand slips on the wet wood, and I land hard on my elbow.

"Whoa. Take it easy there, sweetheart."

The guy who's been helping me goes to grab my arm and I manage to jerk it away at the last second. "Don't." At another time, I would give him a warning look, but right now, I won't look away from Jace. I can't. "Don't touch me."

I don't trust anyone right now.

Not even if he's the one who brought me back to life for real this time.

"Okay, well—"

I tune him out and try to push up again, managing to get my hands and feet underneath me this time as Zane walks over.

"Ellie." He makes it to me as I lift up onto my knees and plant one foot, then the other. "What the fuck happened?"

"Don't call me that. Only Jac—"

I cut myself off as a quiet whimper escapes, and he holds out a hand to help me, but I ignore his offer too. My view of the burns marring that beautiful work of art on Jace's arm and the paramedics flitting around him like agitated bees pushing me forward at a frenzied, clumsy pace.

"Ja-Jace!" I yell through another cough, smoke that burns down my throat be damned.

When I make it close to the gurney though, the paramedic closest to me turns and tries to block my path. "Ma'am, we need to check you out—"

He reaches for me, and this time, I scream. "Don't fucking touch me!"

Don't they understand?

Doesn't anyone understand?

His eyes turn wide and worried, quickly moving over my face in an assessing manner as if he's trying to figure out whether I'm crazy or not.

Probably, most likely, but regardless… I don't have time for this.

I could be losing both sides of my heart right at this moment.

I don't have time for any of this.

When the paramedic doesn't move, I push past him with what feels like the last strength my body has to give, shoulder-checking him along the way before the sight of Jace freezes me in place. His shirt is almost completely burned away. The right side of his body littered with splotchy burns and that tattoo I had traced with my eyes, fingers, and lips so many times is nothing but a mess of ink and skin. What parts of his clothes aren't burned away show that they're as wet and stuck to his skin as mine are.

He was in the water with me.

But did he die?

Is he dead?

Movement near his head catches my eye and I look up in time to see another paramedic put an oxygen mask over his nose and mouth.

Not dead then. Breathing. Alive. Just like me.

That's the only reason they use an oxygen mask.

A person has to be breathing for that.

The air bursts from me in relief, carrying his name. "Jace."

I watch his eyes move underneath the lids as if he hears me and feel my throat start to tighten up. And when I spy the blood starting to pool underneath his long, surfer-boy hair on the gurney… it just about locks up completely.

Get it together, El. Bad things are afoot, and you might be the only one left now.

No.

I refuse to accept that they're lost to me... but right now, well, right now, I might be the only one left to do anything about it.

So I clear my throat of the heartbreak and panic trying to dig its claws into me and lift my eyes to the paramedic who put the oxygen mask on him. "Why isn't he awake?" I demand.

She lifts her eyes to mine with what I think is supposed to be a reassuring smile. "We won't know until we get him to the hospital." Her gaze flicks up to my head. "We can check you out in the ambulance on the way."

I look back down at Jace's slack face, so devoid of the usual mischief it always held, even in his sleep, and my own pinches up so tight at the sight that I'm barely able to whisper. "No."

"Excuse me?" the male paramedic who'd tried to stop me before questions at my side.

And even though it rips me to shreds from the inside out, I let my eyes move over Jace's face, trying to memorize every little millimeter of it before repeating. "No."

"Ma'am." He moves closer to me. "We need to check you out. You're bleeding—"

"Zane!" I shout, forcing myself to look away from Jace and over my shoulder to find him already there. Those curious eyes that were a little more hesitant to accept me than others waiting. "Listen to me," I choke out, trying so damn hard to keep it together and force the tears back from my eyes. "You go with Jace. You go with him and you don't leave his side," I order. "Alright, Zane? No matter what, you don't leave his side for anything, okay?"

His gaze narrows on me warily and flicks over my shoulder before coming back to meet mine. "Okay." He nods, voice going low and intense. "How bad is this though?"

I swallow once before forcing out a raspy "Bad." A heavy beat of understanding passes between us, but the panic eating at me more and more with every passing second pushes me to hold out my hand. "Now give me your keys."

"Why?"

"Because mine are probably sitting at the bottom of the ocean."

He hesitates for a second and I can't take it anymore.

Can't take anyone stopping me from getting to the only person who can stop my panic.

"Keys!" I shout.

"Ma'am, I really can't let you leave. You've been through an explosion—"

But it's too late.

Because Zane just dropped his keys in my hand with a look of pained understanding and I'm already sprinting down the dock.

Forcing my wrecked body to endure further damage in the hope of making it to the man I chose above all others before it's too late. Before I'm too late.

Once again, choosing between the two sides of my heart.

Choosing the side, the person, who set my whole world on fire over and over again to make me his. Who burned it down to nothing but ashes and showed me the beauty that came with accepting the ruin. The freedom that came with embracing the darkness in both him and me. The strength that came from choosing to love through my fears. To love him. To love the infinity of us that had been found and built there.

An Eden built among the ashes of tragedy.

And yet with every stride, I hope that the side of my heart that I'm leaving behind doesn't feel my absence. That his heart isn't breaking all over again in his chest.

Chapter Two

My whole body is screaming in agony by the time I make it to Zane's black Dodge Ram, and I don't even have enough control left over my limbs to stop before crashing into the driver's side door. It stuns me for a minute, the pain from another injury. Leaves me breathless as I lean against the cool metal and stare at Franny parked in the space next to his with the lights from the ambulance in the parking lot bouncing off of both of their surfaces. My mind once again in a tailspin until something starts to drip down into my left eye.

I reach up in a daze, my arm heavy like the gravity of the earth has suddenly been amplified, and it takes me longer than it should to bring my hand to the warm, wet substance obscuring my vision. I know that instinctually. And when I draw my fingers away and see them stained red, I know that it's probably because I really am suffering from some kind of injury from the explosion.

Probably a concussion. Maybe a bad one.

Coop, El. Focus.

The reminder of his name jolts me back into motion and I hastily swipe the blood away from my forehead before looking down at the keys in my hand. I press the button to unlock the truck and a harsh beep emits, sounding too loud in my ears. But everything else can wait. I can wait. The only thing that matters right now is getting to him.

I fumble for the door handle twice before forcing myself to slow down enough that I'm able to control my shaky limbs and grab hold of it. Pulling it open while taking a deep breath of the still smoke-laced air and grabbing the steering wheel to haul myself up into the truck. It still takes me another few deep breaths before I'm able to pull the door closed behind me and then another to bring the key to the ignition.

Too slow.

Everything is too slow when I need to be fast.

Thankfully I'm now in a machine that can succeed where my body is currently failing.

Throwing the truck into reverse, I spare a look behind me before backing out and peeling out of the parking lot. My anxiety is a living thing that's only failing in its attempt to strangle me into submission by the hope that I can somehow still get there in time to save him. Although how I plan to do that, I'm not quite sure. I don't even have a phone to call the police, mine lost at the bottom of the ocean along with my keys. And I don't know if they would be much help if I could call them, but it doesn't matter, none of it matters.

I'd rather die trying to save him than sit on the sidelines and live.

Even if that would piss him the fuck off.

I know it would, actually. The same way the secrets he kept did to me.

We've always been two sides of the same insolent coin though, right from the very start.

19

I fly through the first stoplight, uncaring of the fact it's red and hear a car horn blare behind me. Pressing the pedal of the truck down until I'm going a good thirty miles over the speed limit. Faster than anyone has probably ever dared to drive in this little seaside town. The next light is thankfully green, saving me and any stray drivers from possible collision, and then it's only two blocks. Two more blocks and I'll be at Tommy's.

My heart is beating even faster now than when I tried to gasp for that first breath after coming back to life. Hands so sweaty that they ache from the iron grip I have to keep on the steering wheel. All the parts of me held together by nothing more than panic and adrenaline that's either about to finally have an outlet, be it rage or relief, and then fall apart either way.

I come up on the entrance to Tommy's apartment complex and jerk the truck toward it so suddenly that the wheel almost pulls away from me. Sheer determination has me keeping my hold on it though and shooting straight to the apartment I left maybe an hour ago. It takes me a quarter of the time it should have to get here, but is even that quarter too long?

Bringing the truck to a screeching halt in front of the apartment, I go to grab the handle, but the open apartment door catches my eye and makes me pause. My eyes immediately drop to the vibrant color smeared across the concrete landing and sticking there. It's the same red that I can still feel dripping down the side of my face, right there for the world to see. And at the sight of it, that same red that runs through us all... my world stops spinning.

My heart goes still.

My mind completely blanks out.

It's as if someone plucked my consciousness right out of my body and I'm simply looking down at the whole thing from above. Unable to face, to process, what that blood might mean. Incapable of it.

Because he's wrong... he's so terribly wrong.

There's no world for me without *him*.

No universe I want to exist in without *him*.

He is the air in my lungs at this point. No ownership needs to be claimed. I've accepted it.

But if I go into that apartment and... there won't be anything left for me. No mystery or hidden hope like there was when he disappeared before. If I find him dead, there won't be anything at all. To me. For me. He will have taken everything about my future that matters with him into whatever after it is that I just escaped.

Just like there were no words for him, this time, there will be no life left for me.

Because I *chose* him. Over and over again. Despite everything.

He was always the choice I was incapable of not making from that very first night, even though part of me knew I shouldn't. He chose, and I chose.

And we are all bound by our choices.

We bound the fabric of our very souls somehow, I think. If one is gone, the other will inevitably follow. So am I about to lose my soul?

Fear and frenzy begin to riot in me at the possibility and I reach for the door handle suddenly, pushing it open and practically falling out of the truck. He could still be alive. He could be hurt and need me and I wasted those precious seconds dealing with my own fucking damage. I don't bother closing the door behind me, just stumble toward the landing on wobbly feet until I'm standing just outside the doorway. Eyes following that telling trail to where it eventually turns into a large pool that sends me crashing to the ground, hands landing in the same blood that's smeared across the landing.

His blood.

Coop's blood.

And it's so big, that pool. Spread out across the floor like a can of paint I spilled once, little flecks of red sprayed across the ground behind it. It's as large as the one in the crime scene photographs of my mother, the little splatters striking in their familiarity.

I drag my eyes away long enough to scan the rest of the apartment space, the small studio not leaving many places to hide a body. But the bathroom door in the back left corner is closed, and it beckons me. Challenging me to open it with the possibility of salvation if only I'm brave enough to risk the desolation it might hold too.

So I push off the ground with the same determination born of hope that made me choose him in the first place. Forcing myself forward at a steady pace and taking a breath with each step, reminding myself to not let the fear win. Hearing his voice in my head as it repeats the words he used over a year ago to crack my heart open for the first time while I reach out and grasp the door handle, cracking the door in turn. My hand starts to shake around the handle and I tighten my grip on it, pushing the door open and stepping into the room without giving the panic any more time to set in.

And the breath leaves my lungs in one fell whoosh.

I try to take in what I'm seeing, to understand it, but the more I try, the more my eyes seem to unfocus, my brain stuttering to a halt on each random little snippet of the image before me. How the shower curtain is haphazardly thrown back, and the rod is half hanging down. How the rug is bunched in the corner. How the toothbrush holder is shattered on the floor with a single blue toothbrush sitting nestled in the center of all of the brown pieces.

How Tommy's lifeless eyes are staring up at me from the bathtub with his neck twisted at an unnatural angle.

His clothes rumpled.

Red marks still apparent on his arms from where an attacker must have held him.

Chest unmoving.

He's dead.

He's dead and I can't breathe again. Just like he can't anymore.

I can't breathe. I can't breathe. I'm drowning on land this time and I need the person who owns the air in my lungs to put it back there again.

I try to take a step back out of the bathroom, but my foot snags on the edge of the wall and the only thing that keeps me from crashing backward is the painful grip I'm still maintaining on the doorknob. Instead, the door just slams closed and I hold on to it long enough to let myself slowly fall to the floor before rolling over to lean back against it. Unable to stop my eyes from going straight to that pool of blood again, even as my vision starts to go dark around the edges.

Could someone survive that much blood loss? My mother hadn't.

But if he's not dead... then where is he?

Did whoever he was trying to protect me from drag his body off? Making this all that will ever be left of him for me to find? Just some blood on the floor to remind me of the life I could have had?

It can't be. It can't because I need him to make this pain go away.

It's everywhere. All-consuming.

In the random little twitches of my fingers to the way I know my head is about to split right open at any moment. It's in the tears streaming down my face from the burning in my eyes because I can't quite seem to make them blink. In the way my chest fucking *aches* as if it's been beaten on over and over again, each little rapid lift of it driving the excruciating sense deeper. But if it's lifting...

Not drowning then, hyperventilating.

Shame. I think I might have preferred to be drowning if my reality is now a world where I know the truth of us without doubt and still have to face it without him.

To have to tell Jace the cousin I chose over him is dead.

My head starts to spin at the very prospect of it, the room tilting like a seesaw in the shadowed edges of my vision as the pool of blood somehow becomes double the size it was before. I'm going to pass out soon. I know this the same way I know there's nothing I can do about it. I've lost all control of my body, my mind, collapsed here against the door. Guarding the body of the man who was my husband's best friend like some kind of corpse bride.

Who knows? Maybe whoever spilled Coop's blood and killed Tommy will come back for him and find me. Then maybe I'll get to ask them myself what happened here. Maybe they'll kill me too. Maybe that was always the way my story was going to end. Maybe I should have seen it coming.

Why is the story of my life always told through splatters and pools and sprays of blood?

Because you always choose the darkness over the light. Now, wake up, minushka.

I want to, Mama, but I can't. I'm already awake and the nightmare is real.

I'm living it now.

Wake up, minushka. Wake up.

The music of her voice rings through my head again and stuns me into gasping for air. I had almost forgotten what she sounded like after all these years. How honeyed and exotic her voice was, delicate yet a bit lower than most women. It had enchanted me during the day and lulled me to sleep at night with stories of firebirds that had stolen golden apples from kings. It woke me up when I was dead.

Now though, it echoes around like some kind of haunting melody in my head.

And I focus on it, using it to draw deep breaths into my lungs as the room slowly stills. I focus on the already fading sound of her voice and try to wade back from the sea of hysteria that's drowning me. Finally pulling my eyes away from that pool of blood and instead looking at the couch we had fallen on together a few short hours ago. Remembering what it had felt like to have his heart beating under my ear as he drew words of love on my skin. Ran his lips over the ones we vowed to each other.

He can't be dead. He just can't. I would feel it somehow if he were. An emptiness instead of this pain. Even a year ago, when he disappeared… there was never an emptiness. Just pain. It would be different if he was really gone… wouldn't it?

I run my eyes back and forth along the length of the couch a few more times, trying to somehow hold on to the memories from earlier before exhaling a deep breath. Knowing I need to make myself move and figure out what to do next but not wanting to face that step without him… or without Jace.

It's selfish of me. It's fucking atrocious at this point. I should just make sure he's okay and leave him be. Go to Alec's for answers like Coop said, but without the person whose heart I obliterated today. The person who still owns a piece of mine and always will with every sunrise. But right now, I'm a monster grasping for anything to keep me afloat. Any scrap of comfort that can keep me glued together long enough to find my way out of this nightmare.

Shame rises fast in me at what exactly I'm contemplating, no matter how platonic the intentions might be on my end. It'd still either be giving him false hope or forcing him to endure the presence of the person he loves but can't ever have. Not without knowing he wouldn't have been my first choice. I swallow the now constant tightness in my throat and drop my eyes to the base of the couch, hating how fucking weak every part of me feels right now. Hating myself for the very prospect I'm entertaining.

Hating the world or the gods or maybe just fate itself for casting our stones in the pool of the universe for this. For me to love them and all of us to suffer for it.

But none of it really matters right now.

Not until I know what's to become of us today.

I need to check on Jace. Find out what kind of shape he's in, talk to him and then... then I'll go from there. I need to tell someone about Tommy too. He didn't deserve this. He was good and kind and more innocent in this than anyone else who suffered today. He deserved better. A happy life. One that he'll never get now because of... what? I don't even fucking know besides that all of this is because of me.

I can't lose them both because of me.

A sob tries to rise in my throat and I blow it out in a hiccuping breath, locking my arms and pushing up off the floor. Forcing my body to stand despite the heaviness of the pain weighing me down. I don't allow myself to look at the blood again while walking to the couch and giving the apartment one last cursory glance to see if I missed anything. There's nothing though. Nothing besides the bathroom and the blood. The whole apartment looks just the way it did when I left it earlier. Even Coop's black shirt that's still hanging over the arm of the couch. The same one I used to steal all the time in Cahuita.

I stare at the shirt for barely a second before grabbing it and ripping my wet sweatshirt over my head, quickly replacing it with this tiny bit of him. Breathing in his sandalwood scent and pretending that I could still feel some of the lingering heat from his body. Indulging completely in the fantasy because I need him right now and this might be the closest to him I ever—

Don't go there. Don't fucking go there, El.

Because regardless of whether he's alive or dead, I'll find him. Somehow, I'll find him, or whatever remains of him.

But Jace first and then Alec, to face whatever secrets he's keeping.

I take one more deep breath, trying to trap the sandalwood in my lungs before walking out of the apartment without a backward glance.

He chased me around the earth for almost a year before. Now it's my turn.

Chapter Three

I gently press the door of Zane's truck shut in the hospital parking lot and lean my forehead against the cool metal, closing my eyes and letting myself sink into it for just a moment. Every breath is a struggle at this point and with it comes the fight to keep my body from giving out on me. The only part of me that seems insistent on movement is the shaking and twitching in my hands that only stops when I'm clenching something to the point of pain. But I'm all I've got right at this moment. I'm all they've got and if there's anything my sluggishly chaotic mind settled on during the drive to the hospital, it's that there's something much, much bigger at play here than I ever suspected before. My stupid obliviousness gave the devil free rein to quite literally rain fire down on me and those I love.

I should've pushed harder. Should've demanded to know more *now*. Swears and promises be damned.

The anger starts to swirl low in my belly and I reach for it, grasping onto it like a life preserver that will somehow give me the strength to make it through this next step. Because Jace has to be okay too. He has to be the same way Coop does because I can't imagine a world without both of them in it, even if he isn't the one I chose. My world would still go dark without him in it somewhere, even if he hates me. I can take his anger. I understand now what Stef meant by what he said before I came back here. When you love someone, you can take just about anything as long as you know

29

they're okay. But if he's not… I'm not sure my heart could survive that loss either without losing something fundamental to me.

Jace has to be okay and we all have to make it out of this somehow.

I clench my teeth to keep another sob from escaping and the excruciation shoots deeper into my chest in retribution, driving into my heart with a sharp twist that has it faltering in its pace for a moment. Turning my head, I crack my eyes and look at the small, one-story hospital that serves Landing Point and two of the neighboring towns through the shadowy light of the parking lot. It's smaller than my elementary school and the only reason the brown brick building stands out in the dark night is because of the fluorescent light brightening all the windows.

Let's hope the doctors inside actually know what the fuck they're doing.

Don't be a bitch, El. Could be what got you into this in the first place.

I inhale a deep breath and lift my head from the truck, turning to take a step toward the main entrance of the hospital when I notice a figure quickly making its way toward me through the parking lot. I freeze up at the sight, toes digging into the squishy bottoms of my Converse and making me realize how waterlogged they are at exactly the wrong time. Waterlogged shoes aren't good for running, I assume. Part of me wants to just throw myself back into the truck and get the hell out of there, but I won't leave Jace. Can't disappear into the night on him the way Coop did to me. Not without at least giving him an explanation and the option to come along.

But I can be prepared for a fight.

The figure is halfway between me and the hospital when I start to thread Zane's keys between my fingers, making sure to grip them tightly in order to inflict maximum damage if I'm about to be attacked. Blood starting to fill with adrenaline once again from god only knows what reserve as I take in the tall form with light hair glinting in the barely there light. Definitely male. And definitely dangerous by the vibes I'm getting from his quietly powerful strides.

It's five more steps before he's finally close enough that I'm able to catch a glimpse of his features as he passes underneath one of the dim parking lot lights, but I don't loosen my grip on the keys. Not yet, no matter what Coop said. Trust is not something I'm handing out to anyone right now. Not without some answers.

He slows down while approaching that last bit of space, eyes running down the length of me with clinical precision before coming back to mine. Face devoid of any kind of thought or feeling as he comes to a stop a few steps away. His gaze dips back down to the keys I'm clenching and the same cold smirk rises to his lips that he wore sitting across from me once in Costa Rica.

"Well, Helen." He lifts his eyes back to mine and cocks his head. "Don't you look like shit."

"You," I breathe.

"Me." He nods, smirk falling from his lips. "Now what the hell kind of shit show have you gotten yourself into this time and where's Coop?"

31

I open my mouth out of some innate desire to snap something back at him, but nothing comes out. I can't seem to make anything come out. Too shocked by his sudden appearance in a town in which he most definitely does not belong, standing there in head-to-toe black. Too jarred by everything that had happened. I had been so close to my forever.

"What?" He takes another step toward me and I clench the keys tighter in my hand. "Did Helen of Troy finally bring about the destruction I warned of? Did Coop try to kill the cousin or something? From what I just saw in there, he's not that far off."

"Coop—" I suck in a breath, his name sending that knife twisting deeper again in my heart. "Jace."

I can't. I can't. I can't. I can't even muster up enough words of explanation or bravado to armor myself in right now. I'm broken.

His eyes narrow on me for a second and I swear, after a beat, I see something in his face soften. "Helen..." he starts more quietly this time, speaking the nickname I hate. "What happened?"

I swallow once before going right for the question that I need him to answer most. "How are you here?"

Did you play some part in today, Alec? Did you betray your friend somehow?

He isn't supposed to be here.

I watch his jaw slide back and forth as he holds my gaze as if deciding how much he wants to share before shrugging. "Thought you'd be expecting me after Cooper issued his little ultimatum."

"Not for a day or two," I snap, repeating Coop's words, but my tone is all wrong, all empty and confused where it should be strong. "What are you doing here *today*, Alec?" I clear my throat, managing to find some kind of steadiness before digging into his story. "Right now, at this hospital, how the fuck are you here?"

He pauses, pulling back a little and narrowing his eyes even further on mine before snapping back in the short, cold tone that's everything mine is lacking at the moment. "I was already on my way here. Got done with the job I was on early and was almost here to deal with our little ultimatum situation when I got Coop's SOS text." He heaves an irritated breath as if explaining this to me is such a nuisance. "We had a code word on missions we worked in the past together, in case shit ever went south. I got the text a couple hours ago, and when he didn't answer his phone after that, I called the hospital. Found out his cousin was here and here I am."

I don't know whether to believe him or not. Staring into his eyes... they're just so blank. The same as when I met him in Costa Rica. I can't pull any truth from their depths because they're just so fucking cold and my intuition is uncharacteristically silent for once. Maybe it died with some part of me in the water today.

It seems he's grown tired of waiting me out for answers though because the next second he shakes his head and steps right into my space. "Helen. Where the fuck is Monroe?"

I flinch. I can't help it. That name. That damn name that he made sure was mine. That I'll always carry around, even if it's just between the two of us. The name he made me scream to show just how much we belonged to each other has me flinching as if it's a physical blow. It knocks the fucking breath out of me all over again.

And Alec notices. "El." My real name comes out sounding a little unsure on his tongue. Awkward even, as his voice softens further. "Eleanor, where is Coop?"

His eyes drill into mine, and under normal circumstances, I'm sure they'd be intimidating, but right now, I'm just... empty. The adrenaline has faded with his explanation and I'm starting to shut down. "He—" I try to start, but another sob rises, leaving me hiccuping around it as I clench my empty fist.

It's sticky. Fuck. It's sticky.

It's the first time I've noticed, and it sends me plummeting back into the hysteria I just climbed out of. It's sticky with his blood.

"He—" My voice shakes as I look down, opening my hand and staring at the remnants of his life on it. "He's supposed to be dead," I rush out, breath turning choppy as the hyperventilation sets in again.

I'm a mess. All over the fucking place. Exhausted and empty. Panicked and broken. I can't get it together.

Someone should sedate me. I want them to.

Maybe I'll go ask the hospital to sedate me.

The next thing I know, Alec's hand shoots up, gripping my jaw tightly and lifting my head. Bringing his face an inch away from mine as his voice lashes out with the same coldness that chills his eyes. "Who's supposed to be dead, Helen?"

I don't know. Coop never said his name.

"Answer me!"

His shout shocks me in the same way hearing my mother's voice did and has the rest of the story tumbling from my lips in rapid succession. "He said that the man was supposed to be dead. That he killed him. But then they came for him and when I went to the apartment there was blood... so much blood and Tommy." The sob breaks free this time at the reality I'm being forced to face, leaving me no place to hide from it. "Tommy was dead and there was blood on the floor, but no—" I gasp for a breath. "No Coop. Just blood."

His eyes go even more blank if possible, but I know he must be thinking something by the way his breathing picks up a pace that almost matches mine. "They wouldn't have left his body."

"What—"

The hand on my jaw drops to grab my arm with a vicious tug, starting to drag me through the parking lot at just short of a run as my shoes skid and trip over the cement. And he must not realize how bad of shape I'm in, how close I really am to slipping into oblivion, because the next second he actually tries to jerk me into a run. Making me stumble and fall hard onto the ground. Skinning my knees and adding yet another insult to my injury-filled body.

"Get up!" he orders, jerking on my arm again.

I don't even have the energy to fight him, just press my hands into the ground while staring at where the keys are now lying a few feet away. Trying to drag some breath into my lungs as everything starts to tilt and sway again.

"Get the fuck up, Eleanor!" he orders harshly, pulling at me. "We have to leave."

I shake my head once before looking up at him and whispering. "No."

My answer seems to shock him, a taken-aback look flashing across his face before he wipes it clean and barks. "Do you want to die?"

Do I?

It's a valid question at this point. But no, not yet, not until I find Coop… then we'll see.

I give him another single shake of my head in answer, and he nods in return. "Good, then come on. We have to leave."

"Not without Jace."

I won't abandon him.

There's no mistaking the shock on his face this time before he snorts a sardonic sound. "Not without Jace?" He lets go of me, and I barely catch myself from falling face-first into the concrete as he points at the hospital. "Jace is in fucking surgery, getting holes drilled into his skull to try and relieve some of the swelling in his brain!"

"Wh-what?" My voice cracks on the question, eyes immediately filling with tears even as my brain stutters again. Refusing to accept what he's telling me. I knew he was in bad shape but this... I can't comprehend this the same way I can't make sense of what happened to Coop.

"Jace isn't going anywhere, he'll be lucky to ever wake up again." He squats down in front of me, eyes finding mine as his voice goes quiet again. "Coop wasn't the only one they came for today, was he?"

My bottom lip starts to tremble uncontrollably, tears streaming down my face as I shake my head. That last hope that some part of my heart might choose to help me regardless of everything now between us gone in an instant.

"You really are Helen of Troy, aren't you?"

"Don't call me that!" Anger sparks suddenly, driving the words from my mouth even as another sob follows them.

"Good." Alec nods with something like satisfaction. "There's something left of you then." He sighs. "Jace won't be going anywhere for a long time, if ever. What happened to you both?"

"There was an explosion," I choke out. "His boat exploded while I was there."

"They'll be coming to check soon. Probably trying to sort through whether you died in the explosion or were taken to the hospital right now."

"*Who* is?" I rasp, hating the weakness that can be found everywhere, from my body to my voice, but not caring enough to change it.

He eyes me consideringly for a long moment before standing and rolling his shoulders, gaze never leaving mine as he does. "You need to make a choice, Helen. The only thing you do is put Jace at more risk by staying here. They'll leave him alone as long as you're gone and there's nothing you can do for him anyway. The swelling in his brain was substantial from what I overheard and at this point... whether he lives or dies is up to him."

"I can't." I lean back on my heels as an unbearable weight presses in on my chest. Knowing that, explosion or not, I did this to him. If he doesn't wake up... a quiet kind of cry escapes me, and I raise my hands, pressing my palms as hard as I can against my eyes. Head pounding from the pressure as something cracks deep inside of me, the thing that had just started to mend.

"Time to decide," Alec quietly demands. "Live or die?"

Dropping my hands from my eyes, I look up at him and beg for what might be the first time in my life. My voice is coming out as broken as I feel. "Please don't make me leave him."

"I won't make you do anything." He shakes his head. "This is your choice. But if you stay..." A small, uncaring shrug fills the silence before he states bluntly. "Coop's dead." I flinch at his words, but he presses on this time. "Jace's chances of following him are more likely if they find you at his bedside. If you leave, they'll be too busy looking elsewhere to bother with him. It'd be a shame if all of you died, is all I'm saying."

He's right. I know he's right and I hate it. If what he's saying is true, then all I do is put Jace in further danger by staying. If I'm the one they really want. But still... I don't know him. Not really. Not the way I need to.

"Why should I trust you?"

He shrugs again, eyes moving to scan the parking lot while answering. "Coop did."

"And that's supposed to be good enough?"

"It was for him." He brings his gaze back to mine and hesitates for a second. "I'll explain the rest soon."

I turn my head toward the hospital and stare at it, desperately trying to drag some miraculous answer from its depths, but the truth is... there's no right answer here. Nothing to fix this. I stay, and we both possibly die. I leave, and he might live but could wake up to a world where I just abandoned him further. I leave, he lives, I die, and he spends the rest of his life wondering what happened to me and his cousin. I leave, and he dies because I broke his heart and he has no reason *to* wake up.

There's no way out of this.

So I come back to the same thing as earlier. What matters more than anything is that he does live. And if I leave, he stands a better chance than if I stay. That much is certain. At least I hope so.

"Live, Jace," I whisper into the night, uncaring that Alec can hear. "Live to see the sunrise. You promised."

And with tears streaming down my face, I look back to Alec. His gaze narrows on me as if he can't quite figure me out, but I don't care. The only thing I need from him is whatever he knows about what's happening and how I can find out what happened to Coop.

Another beat passes before he holds his hand out to me and I take one of my own before reaching up to grasp it. Hoping like hell I'm not making a mistake by trusting him. He hauls me up and lets go of my hand immediately, as if the contact bothers him for some reason or maybe the unity of the act.

"I'll get you a phone you can use to check on him once we get somewhere safe. One that's harder to track." He clears his throat. "And make sure the police get an anonymous tip about the body in the apartment too."

I give him a nod and he hesitates another second as if he's going to say something else before his brows drop the barest hint and he shakes his head. Turning away from me and setting off across the parking lot again, leaving me with the choice I've already made to follow him into the night. A cool wind picks up as I take those first steps, the dry bite in it hinting at the changing of the seasons that are coming to even a place as far south as Landing Point.

And maybe to me too.

Because for the first time in a long time… there are no stars or sun, neither side of my heart to accompany me on this journey. I'm barren, broken, and utterly alone.

Nothing to light up my universe.

Nothing but the empty sky of me.

Chapter Four

He lied.

Cooper lied to me, or maybe it's just different because I am me.

But I know it as soon as my mind barely begins to stir from the comatose-like sleep I had fallen into not long after getting into Alec's car. Coop lied because there is no moment of blissful ignorance. No peaceful split second of not knowing what nightmare I'm now existing in. No escape where I can pretend that when I open my eyes, everything will be okay.

It's right there.

The first thing I'm aware of even in my sleep, I think. That bruised kind of pain in my chest as if it's about to split the skin right open and pour out the pulpy mess of trauma that my body just can't take anymore. It leaves me absolutely no doubt as to what world I wish I wasn't waking up to.

The sleep has given me a renewed sense of urgency though. And that along with the sense of stillness instead of the steady motion of the car, has me peeling my eyes open to find Alec sprawled out on the couch across from me. Pretty much filling my vision with the bare five feet separating us from where I'm lying on what I'm guessing is a love seat across from him, my head and feet lifted by the arms of it.

The black clothes he's wearing are the same ones as when he appeared in the parking lot, but they're wrinkled now. Jeans that are slimmer at the bottoms and his fitted shirt. His eyes are closed, breathing even and slow without an ounce of tension to be found in his body. Everything about him signals that he's peacefully asleep, harmless, but still, something bugs the ever-loving shit out of me about him, just like the first time I met him. And it bugs me even more that I can't figure out what, exactly, it is.

Is he going to betray me?

He's dangerous, I'm sure of that, but is he dangerous to me? Or just in general? Because I could use him right now if it's the latter and not the former.

And I'm betting this peaceful, innocuous sleep thing is an act he's mastered. Something is telling me that he's the kind who's fully prepared to slit the throat of the person who wakes him. Too bad for him, there's exactly zero self-preservation left to me at the moment. Plus, I need to figure out where the hell he brought me.

I let my eyes run over the room, taking in the old, light wood paneling covering every surface except for the floor which is carpeted in an equally outdated shag. The tan fabric furniture we're lying on is scratchy under my cheek and there's a small brick fireplace sitting empty to our right with an open doorway to our left. There's an empty feeling to the place though. No other furniture in the room besides what we're on and not decoration in sight. Everything about it gives off the vibe that it's a weigh station for people passing through.

I bring my eyes back to him, pausing for a beat to watch his breathing before rasping. "Hey."

No change. No flicker of his eyes or movement of his body. His breaths still slow and even, entirely unaffected by my interruption.

I wait a couple more seconds before trying again. "Hey."

Nothing.

God, he really rubs me the wrong way. Even his breathing irritates me. And he hears me. I know he hears me.

Pushing up off the couch, I raise my voice and call his name. "Alec."

Another long moment passes before he cracks his eyes, staring at me with the same open hostility that I feel for him. "I'm sleeping."

"Obviously." I snort softly. "Where are we?"

He sighs with open irritation before closing his eyes and I'm about to ask again, tired of his shit, when he answers in a bored voice. "Colorado."

Alec's, Princess. 205 East Silver Street, Marble, Colorado. Now repeat it back to me.

I shake my head slowly, trying to dislodge his voice so that I can keep functioning. "Co-colorado?" I splutter incredulously. "That's what? Twenty hours?" Swinging my legs onto the floor, I sit up fast enough to make my head spin. "I slept that long?!"

"Like the dead," he answers through a yawn. "Even checked your pulse a couple times to make sure you hadn't actually died on me."

"That's—You—" I choke on my words, trying to come to grips with the absurdity of it all. "You shouldn't have done that!"

"I think the phrase you're looking for is 'Thank you,'" he mocks, cracking his eyes again and looking up at me only through the slits.

43

"There's some food in the fridge and a phone on the counter. Keep your calls under two minutes." Raising a hand, he flicks his fingers as if to shoo me away while closing his eyes. "Now let me sleep. Some of us didn't get to catch up on our beauty rest on the way here."

Completely dismissing me and leaving me with my mouth hanging open like I've just seen a dick for the first time or something. Which is actually pretty accurate because he is a *dick*. I'm half tempted to go slap him awake, but the temptation of the phone he's offering and the possibility of news has me standing with only a narrowed-eyed look thrown his way.

I hurry across the small room toward the doorway, my assumption that it's the kitchen proving correct as I step into it and the shag gives way to tile that turns cold under my feet. It's a tiny kitchenette as dated as the room I just left with cabinetry that's a shade darker than the walls and a fridge that sounds as if it's about to give out at any moment. The loud whirring noise it's making echoes around the tiny space, its only competition is the faucet that's dripping in a steady trickle below a small window. But the phone is there on the counter next to the kitchen sink as promised and I rush to it, picking it up and cradling it in my hands like the lifeline it is.

I hesitate for a second when I see that it's an iPhone and not the kind of flip phone that Coop always used as a burner, but figure if the fucker in the other room said it's safe then it's his problem. If whatever the big bad is that's after me comes knocking, I'm tripping him so I can make an escape. I quickly swipe the screen up to unlock it and pull up the web browser before searching for the hospital in Landing Point. Holding my breath as I press down on the number and bring the phone to my ear, waiting for someone to answer. Tapping my fingers against the counter with increasing agitation as the ringing seems to go on and on.

"Landing Point General. How can I direct your call?"

The breath leaves me in a giant whoosh and I'm taken off guard because I hadn't thought through this point. "Um…"

"Ma'am?"

Shit. Shit. Shit. They're not going to tell me anything. I'm not family to him…

That's not exactly true though, is it, El?

Still though, I'm nothing to him now.

"Um, yeah." I clear my throat, shuffling through a few possible responses before shooting in the dark. "Can you connect me to Jace Dawson's room, please?"

A pause sounds from the other end of the phone, stretching on before the operator chirps. "Just a moment."

I exhale a breath of relief even as my shoulders tense up with the unknown of what voice might come on the other end of that line. I don't know what I'll even say if it's him, but at the same time… please let it be him. I'd give anything for it to be him.

The ringing isn't long this time though, and the hesitant female voice that answers has me almost hanging up out of a sudden fear of facing her. "Hello?"

She sounds so different already than the overly exuberant girl I met in the parking lot... but then, I guess we all are now.

"Tiff," I breathe, finally forcing her name from my lips.

"El?!" My lips twitch softly as the pitch of her voice rises, even if it's not with the old excitement. "Oh my gosh, where are you? The police came to the bar looking for you last night and Jace is in the hospital. No one can find Coop and then when they went to-to—" She stops suddenly as her voice catches. "Tommy's." I can hear her crying now and I bite down on my lip so hard I can almost feel my teeth meet through the skin. "Tommy's dead, El."

I know that, Tiff. His lifeless eyes are staring back at me from that awkward angle in my mind at this very moment because I saw him. I'll never be able to not see him like that now when all I want to remember is the guy who gave me a smile and broke the awkward silence after everyone found out who I really was.

"El," she continues when I don't respond. "Where are you?"

Not in Alabama anymore, that's for sure.

The reminder of where I am and who I'm with has me pulling the phone away from my ear to see how much time has already passed. And when I see that I'm already over a minute, I bring it back to my ear with a curse.

"Fuck, Tiff." I heave a breath before rushing out. "I'm okay, but right now, I need you to tell me how Jace is."

"But—"

"*Now*, Tiff."

"He's..." She stops for a second before continuing in a quiet voice. "They don't know, El. The doctors have done... his brain was swollen from the explosion, but that's gone down some now—"

"So he's going to be okay?" I interrupt her sharply, *needing* to get this answer before my time runs out.

Her pause echoes over the line in response though, and in that pause, all my worst fears come to life.

"Tiffany," I demand, my heart rate skyrocketing. "He's going to be okay, right?"

"They're not sure." Her open cry sounds over the line. "They said the damage to his brain was substantial and that he'll either wake up in the next week or..."

"Or what?" I push.

"Or he won't wake up at all," she cries. "They asked if he was an organ donor."

Her voice fades away as my mind sticks on that one sentence. On the implications of it. They're going to unplug him. If he doesn't wake up, they're going to unplug him and I'm thousands of miles away, unable to do a damn thing about it.

"You fucking listen to me, Tiffany," I snap into the phone, cutting off whatever she's saying. "I will crucify anyone who even breathes in the direction of that plug. Whatever happens, do not let them unplug him. Do you hear me?"

"El—"

"Swear it to me," I demand, pulling the phone away to see I only have seconds left. "I'll cover whatever costs there are and call you as soon as I can to give you my account info, but I swear to god, Tiff, if anyone unplugs him, I will never forgive them."

"El, the doctors—"

"I don't care what the doctors say!" I shout, knowing I'm being unreasonable, but they don't know what I do. "He'll wake up, Tiff. He promised me." My throat tries to tighten up with tears again, but I swallow them down because I need her to promise me now. "Swear it to me, Tiff. No one unplugs him."

"F-fine," she stutters hesitantly. "I'll do what I can. I swear it."

"Thank you." I sigh in relief. "Now I have to go."

"El!" she yells, stopping me from hanging up. "Where's Coop? Is he with you?"

And this time, that damn tightness wins the battle, only allowing me to choke out. "I don't know. I have to go." I'm already pulling the phone away from my ear, cutting off her response as I finish. "Call you as soon as I can."

I end the call with only seconds to spare and drop it onto the counter with decidedly less care than I picked it up with, the lifeline now a harbinger of only bad tidings. Turning away from it, I begin to open cabinets at random, trying to distract myself enough to avoid falling into the pit of darkness again. Focusing on the motion, the simple task of finding a glass to get some water before facing what comes next.

It doesn't take me long in the tiny kitchen, the third cabinet I open holds a few mismatched glasses and I grab the mason jar one at random before turning back to the sink. Flicking the faucet on carelessly and turning that steady drip into a heavy stream that I shove my glass under. Impatiently waiting the maybe two seconds it takes to fill before pulling the glass up to my lips and taking a large sip. Trying to force all that emotional trauma back down by literally putting something on top of it.

I have to though. If I'm going to survive past this next sip of water and past these next few seconds. If I'm going to do what needs to be done, I have to shove all of this damn *agony* down before it swallows me whole. Leave it to be dealt with or not at another time. After I make it through whatever is necessary to find my answers. Just not now, because the bottom line is I'm no use to anyone like this, including myself.

So I finish my glass of water. Listening to the still-running faucet and slowly shoving it all further and further away until I can see a little more clearly again. Am present enough to actually take in the mountains outside of that small window even if I can't fully appreciate their beauty right now.

Until that agony isn't so much debilitating as it is powerful enough to keep me moving forward.

Tiff will keep her promise, I think, at least for now and what comes after… I don't know yet. That's a problem for tomorrow or the next day, but today, today Jace is safe and I can at least cling to that. Coop, on the other hand… I don't even know where he is. Realistically, I don't even know *if* he is. And that, well, that's my next hurdle to conquer.

So I finish the last of the water in my glass and shove it under the faucet again. Letting it fill right to the brim before pulling it out and reaching up with my free hand to turn the faucet off finally. Watching it ease back into the steady trickle as I take a few deep breaths. In Landing Point, I'd probably need ice for what I'm about to do but not here. Here in Colorado, the water comes out cold enough, no ice needed.

Maybe it has something to do with the mountains or elevation. Temperature lower probably even though it is still summer technically.

Who knows? Who cares. Not me.

I shrug to myself, spilling just a bit on my hand as I turn back to the living room.

Time for me to get some answers.

Chapter Five

"What the fuck?!"

Alec shoots straight up off the couch, face dripping water and platinum hair plastered to his head. His brown eyes more animated than I've ever seen them as he looks down at me with pure fury and I give him a sarcastic smile.

"Rise and shine." I toss out, keeping him in my sights and backing up a couple steps before sitting down on the love seat. "It's truth time, fucker."

I watch his nostrils flare a couple times as he narrows his eyes at me, reaching up to pull his now-wet shirt away from his chest with a couple fingers. "I really don't like you."

"Trust me, it's mutual." I scoff. "But apparently you have the answers I need." I cock my head, narrowing my eyes at him in turn. "And I'd like to know why that is and why you even care whether I live or die for that matter."

"And this couldn't have waited a couple more hours... why?" he drags out.

"Because whatever you know has cost me *everything*."

His eyes search mine for a moment and I make sure to let him see just how much I mean what I've said. How close I am to breaking completely.

And I watch the scorn slowly melt away from his face as he sits back down with a sigh.

We stare at each other for another several seconds, slowly sizing each other up before he asks tonelessly. "What do you want to know?"

"Who is doing all this?" The question leaves me in a single breath, words toppling one over another as I continue. "Who's after me? Why?"

It's the root of the problem. The answer that will lead to all of the others.

His body tenses up, almost imperceptibly, but I'm watching him like the predator some part of me has always known he is and I see his breath still for a moment before he answers. "Nicolai Novikov."

"Who?" My brows drop in confusion as I quickly rack my brain and come up empty. "I don't know anyone by that name."

"You wouldn't." He sighs again, almost with dread this time as he eyes me as closely as I am him. "He isn't directly tied to you—"

"Then why the fuck is he ruining my life?"

A long pause follows my interruption and he narrows his eyes at me in irritation until I eventually shoot him a get-on-with-it look.

"As I was saying." He shoots me an equally pointed look. "Novikov knew your mother before she came to America—"

"My mother?"

"Are you ever going to let me finish?" he snaps, continuing on without waiting for my response. "Novikov met your mother when she was a waitress trying to earn enough money to come to America. At the time, he

52

controlled one of the largest crime syndicates in Eastern Europe. He had risen to power at a young age and essentially put the area in a stranglehold due to the fact he was smarter than his predecessors. Smart enough to stay in the shadows and two steps ahead of the authorities, a large portion of which ended up on his payroll. So you can imagine when he took a liking to Nadia in that restaurant…" he trails off purposefully.

"Yeah." I swallow, knowing the different sides of my mother that I had become familiar with in her journals. "I can imagine."

"She saw her way out." He nods. "But Novikov… for all his charm and money, I don't believe she took into consideration just how ruthless he was. That anyone who became a part of Novikov's life would never be allowed a way out."

And so the firebird stole the golden apples from the king and all the men he sent after her were lost in the forest trying to find her again…

"What happened between them?" I ask hesitantly, fighting the sneaking suspicion that I already knew. That my mother herself had told me the truth through fairy tales.

"She became his lover." He clasps his hands in front of him, breaking our gaze to look into the fireplace. "And for a time, the arrangement worked well for them both, even if it was a toxic one, but then…" I watch his hands tighten around each other as he continues. "Something changed. A complication that neither of them foresaw and I think that might've been what changed the game for Nadia. She wanted out." He looks back at me. "As I said though, *no one* simply walked away from Novikov and his lovers up to this point had only been met with a series of unfortunate ends. But as much as Nadia may not have accounted for his ruthlessness at the start, I don't think Novikov ever realized just how... resourceful she was. Not until the end."

He pauses, finally letting his hands fall apart again and I question. "So did she steal from him?"

"In a sense." He shrugs. "She went to Interpol and cut a deal, ultimately selling him out to the Americans for the drugs he was smuggling into their country. Spent the next six months giving them everything she could on his business dealings and dismantled his entire empire." A small, humorless smirk plays across his face for a second. "He was arrested and she finally got that ticket to America she had always wanted, along with a new identity. Nadia Petras disappeared and she entered America as Nadia Novak, soon to become Delacroix."

"And how..." It takes me a second to force his name out, that pool of blood flashing in my mind. "How did Cooper come into all this? How did Novikov pull this off from a prison cell?"

"I told you," he states bluntly. "Novikov is no ordinary thug, he's cunning. Cunning enough to see his way out when someone from Bainbridge came knocking for information a couple years after he was incarcerated."

"Bainbridge?" I breathe in shock.

"He cut a deal with them." He nods. "Proved he was more resourceful working for them outside of jail than in it and eventually became director of operations himself."

"Fuck." This is so, so bad.

"The person who would have had carte blanche access to Cooper's life in case that wasn't clear." He tacks on sarcastically. "And killed you the moment he became aware of you in retribution for your mother's crimes against him."

A horrible question springs into my head, one that I hate myself for but have to ask. "Did Coop know?" I wave my hand between us. "About all this? When he met me?"

I hold my breath for the beat it takes him to shake his head. "No, Cooper had no idea about any of it until I told him."

"And how exactly…" I narrow my eyes on him with open suspicion. "Do you know all of this?"

His eyes drill into mine a long moment before he clasps his hands again, dropping his eyes to the floor and speaking so low I think it might've just been meant for himself. "Because I'm the complication." He looks back to me, rushing out the next bit in an uncomfortable voice. "Nadia became pregnant with Novikov's child. That's what changed for her. I'm not sure she wanted that life for a child." Quickly looking away, he shakes his head before bringing his eyes back to mine. "Or maybe that's just what I tell myself. So she cut the deal and left the baby at an orphanage in Slovakia on her way to America."

It takes me a few seconds to put the pieces together, but when they finally click into place my mouth pops open and I stare at him in shock. Eyes rolling over his face again and again as I pick it apart bit by bit, noticing that thread of similarity the same way I did the first time we met. His platinum hair that's the exact same shade as mine. The way his lips somehow hold that little bit of attitude even when they're completely relaxed. How his nose is the masculine version of my pert one and how his skin has the exact same underlying golden shade as mine and my mother's.

Holy shit.

Holy shit. Holy shit. Holy shit.

My mother had written in her journals about a *him* she had left behind but never in my wildest dreams would I have imagined it could've been an actual *baby*.

And that means the fucker is my… brother?

It's not uncommon for people from the same region to share similar characteristics… yeah right, my ass.

You always did want a sibling, right, El?

No. No way. That's too weird. I have brothers. Stef, Mac, and Kai are my brothers. I already have a family and he's… well, he might be my brother, but there's nothing between us. Nothing birthed or built. No holidays or funny stories that you get by growing up with someone. No knowledge of each other's inner workings that you learn throughout the years. And by the hostile look he's still giving me, I'm not sure he has any interest in building a relationship.

I'm not sure I do either if I'm being honest.

But still, based on what he's telling me and the little I learned from Coop, it means he must have protected me from his father in some way. Which means he just might be on my side here. It means I might be able to use him to get to his father and find out what happened.

"How did you…" I clear my throat awkwardly, completely ignoring the elephant in the room and hoping he's content to do so too. "How did you end up at Bainbridge? Weren't you adopted?"

Something like relief flashes across his face and he gives me a single nod. "Novikov found me when I was in college. Recruited me then. Thought I could be… useful."

"Oh."

Awkward silence fills the room again and after it's clear he's not going to elaborate any further, I decide to cut straight to the chase. No need to name the elephant if he doesn't feel the need to do so. "Can you help me find him?"

He blinks once at me before hedging. "Who?"

"Novikov."

"You want to find the man who's trying to kill you?"

"Yes." I pause, trying for nice as I ask again. "Can you help me?"

He narrows his eyes at me, and for the first time, it strikes me how similar it is to the way I do. "And can I ask why in the fuck you would want to do that?"

"Because…" It's almost funny how the answer for everything can be found in a single name. "Coop."

His expression clears instantly. "Cooper." He sighs after a long moment, softening his voice, almost imperceptible but there. "Cooper is dead, Eleanor."

I shake my head adamantly. "You don't know that."

"I do." Even his damn eyes thaw a bit, turning me desperate with the pity I find there. "I know Novikov and he—"

"You don't!" I interrupt. "There wasn't a body, only blood—"

"Because the body could have been traced back to Bainbridge, back to him. Tommy couldn't," he interrupts. "He probably chucked Coop in the ocean for the sharks to finish."

"You don't know that."

"I do," he insists. "I know my father, Eleanor. It's why I covered up that you were with Cooper. It's why I broke his phone and had your friends install that software on yours." My head starts to spin from his confession, anger surging in my veins and quickening the pace of my heart as he looks away for a moment. "I thought you deserved to be spared the brutality that he is. He kills those who do him wrong without hesitation, which means…" He looks back at me, speaking in a tone that brokers nothing but finality. "That Cooper is dead."

It takes me a minute to see past the anger that he's the one responsible for Coop not being able to contact me. To realize that arguing about that now... or even whether Coop is still alive or dead will get me nowhere. I have a feeling we could sit here all day arguing back and forth and still be ready to start fresh at it in the morning. Maybe the stubbornness is genetic. But I need him. I need his help with this, which means it's time to switch strategies. He might think my search for Coop is futile, and maybe it is, but revenge... that's something I think he'll understand completely.

I'm empty, broken inside, looking for something to grasp in the absence of the two people I love, and I think I'll let it be this. Let it be fury and revenge to get me through to tomorrow.

"Fine," I snap. "Then I want to hear it from his lips. I want to hear how he killed the man who was supposed to be my forever and then"—best to be up front about it from the start—"I want him to burn for daring to take him from me."

His face tenses and a warning sounds in the back of my mind that I might be pushing too hard, but I don't care. *Nothing* matters but this.

"You want to kill my father?"

"You already helped Coop do it, right?" I push. "Or you thought you did."

"This is different." He scoffs. "He knows what we did and he's gone to ground, most likely home to Europe. I made some discreet inquiries while we were on the way here and no one at Bainbridge even knows he's alive, which means he's using old, personal, loyal resources for this. He's treating this as war now and finding him could take years."

"I don't care."

"Do you even know what you're asking for here?" He cocks his head at me almost mockingly. "What it takes to find someone hiding among the underbelly of the world?"

"I don't care."

The doubt in his expression slowly fades, but he shakes his head. "This isn't what Cooper would have wanted," he argues. "Coop would have wanted me to keep you safe. Stash us away somewhere where Novikov could never find us."

"And spend the rest of my life looking over my shoulder?" I snort. "No thanks." Giving him a sarcastic look, I continue. "Plus, I don't think you want to be stuck with me for the rest of your life either."

"True." He smirks. "But Cooper—"

"Coop's dead, right?" I interrupt, pushing so fucking hard against the bile that comes with the words. Trying to keep my breathing even as I damn my soul a little bit more with my next words, following nothing but instinct. "So do it for me." For your sister, the one you saved, the one you owe.

He knows what I mean, I can see it in the little bit of guilt in his eyes. In that thaw that speaks of feeling. Of an attachment behind all that hostility.

And I'm using it against him shamelessly.

"And Alec, make no mistake," I continue, knowing he needs to see that I mean what I'm saying, and the truth is… I really just might because if this man took Coop from me, fuck, I think I really would happily watch him burn. And if it turns out that he's taken them both from me, I'll become a monster without a second's hesitation. Only to sit in his ashes at the end and see if there's any of my soul left to salvage. Or if I even want to. "When we find him, I *will* end him. Novikov may have struck first, but I will become whatever I need to be to find out what happened in that apartment. I will burn him and anyone else involved. I'll finish this once and for all."

His gaze searches mine for so long that I start to think he's not going to reply when the first true smile I've ever seen from him grows on his face. "Pretty speech, Helen." It's a terrifying display of happiness that sends a flutter of victory through my stomach all the same. "You just might make it out of this with that attitude. We'll rest here for a day or two while I reach out to some contacts overseas and then…" He stands slowly and I do the same, the last two pieces of my mother left in this world, somehow together again. And I swear in that moment, I can feel the earth under me shudder in fear. "We'll start in Berlin."

Chapter Six

Six Months Later

"You know I used to abhor violence?" I sigh tiredly. "I guess you wouldn't. That's a stupid question really. You don't even know who I am." A short laugh leaves me as I flip the knife between my fingers. Looking up at the man duct-taped to the metal chair in the basement of some abandoned farmhouse. The lone light hanging above us casting shadows all around the room.

"But really." I toss the knife into my other hand with a dramatic flourish and lean back, balancing the chair I'm sitting in on its back legs. "Six months ago, I probably would have panicked at the thought of even holding a knife. Thought myself incapable of such a thing, better than it even." Cocking a brow, I start to flip the knife between my fingers again. "Unlucky for you though, a lot can change in half a year."

Like my knife skills and, now apparently, my penchant for villain monologues.

Both things that I'd discovered were highly underrated.

"What the fuck do you want from me?" The heavily accented voice emerges from the bear of a man in front of me with a growl equal to the animal he resembles.

I lean forward, letting the front legs of the chair fall back onto the ground with a smack and bring the knife to a halt. "Tell me, Sergei." Gripping the knife tightly, I reach out, bringing the small blade to the top of his hairy chest and slowly dragging it downward over the protruding gut he's rocking. "Do you know what it's like to lose everything? To become a monster by necessity? To be forced to violence by actions that were not your own? Choices that were taken from you?" I tip my head, giving him my best smirk. No longer quite so bratty, a touch more of Alec found in me day by day now. "I do," I whisper. "And truth be told, I've found I kind of like it."

I see the sweat start to bead on his brow and bring the knife to the top of his pants. "Bluster all you want, Sergei." I push the knife just a hair deeper. "That whorehouse we found you in tells me everything about what matters most to you."

He swallows convulsively a few times before snapping. "What do you want?"

"Where is Nicolai Novikov?"

His face screws up stupidly. "Novikov?"

I narrow my eyes at him, angling the knife downward. "Did I stutter?"

"Piča!" he grunts, face turning an angry shade of red. "I haven't seen Novikov in years."

"Call me a bitch all you want." I drop the knife lower, pressing it against the part of him where his brain clearly resides, even as he starts to squirm. "Facts are facts, and you're lying. Try again."

He looks down at the knife, that protruding belly heaving with great breaths as he growls out. "I did a job for him in America with a crew he set up." His eyes come back to mine with sudden interest. "About six months ago."

Shit.

I mean, he was always going to die. I had learned that pretty early on with Alec. No evidence could be left behind, but still… shit. We hadn't actually *killed* anyone yet.

"And where is he now?" Alec asks, drawing his gaze to where he stands behind me. Probably noticing that he's beginning to get curious like I did.

"I don't fucking know," Sergei grumbles, eyes dropping to the knife again. "He wired me payment when it was done and I haven't heard from him since."

I press the knife harder and feel the fabric of his pants start to tear, desperate for something, anything more he can give me. "You have to know *something*, Sergei. You and Novikov were tight back in the day."

This is our first solid lead in *six months*. Six months of searching and hiding and searching some more have led us to this. Six months of desperation have finally settled into a heavy kind of numbness. He has to know something.

"Novikov never used the same guys too often," he argues, little droplets of spit leaving his mouth and frustration clear even through the heavy accent. "Kept the rats from getting to him."

And this is the problem we keep running into. There's nothing to trace because Novikov left nothing to find. The man is a fucking ghost, and I am so incredibly sick of it by this point.

"What happened on that job, Sergei?" I demand quietly, viciously, barely restrained violence clear in my voice. "What happened in that apartment?"

His eyes roam over my face, clearing enough that I suspect, for the first time since we strapped him to that chair, he really sees past his own dick. "You're her, aren't you?"

"Who?"

"The girl..." His accented voice drags out the two words with more thought than I assumed him capable of. "The girl they were talking about. Nadia's daughter."

"That who was talking about?" I snap, failing in my facade for the first time since we set out tonight. The mere possibility of him sending my heart thumping frantically and my carefully crafted mask crumbling.

"The man," he confirms. "Cooper."

I pause for a beat before forcing out my worst fear and hope all in one. "What happened to him?"

Sergei smiles widely at me. "He died."

"No."

"Yes." He laughs with sick delight. "Pushed him to his knees myself and watched the bullets go into him." Another laugh shakes his protruding belly as he mimes a gun with one of his hands taped to the chair and mocks. "Pow. Pow."

"And what…" I swallow, knowing this is the last question I have to get through. "Happened to his body?"

"The guy in charge had us load it in the van immediately." Sergei shrugs. "After that, it wasn't my problem, piča."

I slowly exhale a breath and pull my knife from his crotch with a small smile. "Thank you, Sergei."

The confusion is clear on his face for a moment before the bluster returns. "Novikov will find you and I can't wait to see all the things he does to you—"

And just like that, his tirade suddenly turns into a scream shriller than I ever would have thought him capable of as I slam my knife down into his left leg, right above his kneecap.

I stand from my chair, twisting the knife and sending his scream reverberating around the room as I bring my lips to his ear. "That was for daring to push the man that I loved to his knees." Ripping the knife from his leg, I stand and jerk my head back to where Alec is leaning against one of the posts in the basement behind me. "But what he's about to do will make you wish you had died instead of him."

I don't move for a few seconds, staring at the blubbering mess of a man wailing pitifully in front of me. Wondering how such a man could have so easily taken one of the two people who mattered most to me. Wondering what they would think if they could see me now.

"You good?"

I startle at the interruption and whip my head to where Alec stands beside me, eyes moving over me assessingly, but after six months with only each other, I can see a little bit more beyond the ice now. The little bit of concern there paired with censure because I didn't notice him walking up behind me.

He's going to kick my ass for that in training tomorrow.

"Yeah." I nod once. "Yeah, I'm good."

"You sure?"

"Yeah." I grip the knife tightly in my hand again. "Stop babying me."

"Right," he snaps, digging his hand into the front pocket of his always-black jeans, pulling out a set of keys and offering them to me. "I can take it from here."

"Right," I echo softly, because as much as I may have changed… I still don't think I want to see what happens next. Better to leave it to these walls to witness that violence.

Snatching the keys from his hand, I shove them into the back pocket of my own black skinny jeans and spin around the next instant. Quickly walking to the staircase leading up from the basement as he yells. "Be careful on the way back!"

I nod my head even though he probably can't see me, fighting against the urge to run and keeping my steps measured up the stairs. Barely making it to the top before the screams start to fill the air again, rattling the wood under my feet. I reach out blindly in the dim light and manage to find the doorknob through my sudden frenzy. Twisting it and ripping the door open as Alec speaks below me. "Sergei, Sergei, Sergei… let's see if there's some more truth under all that skin, shall we?"

I slam the door closed on his voice, knowing what's coming next and running now in search of what I need. My footsteps guided by vague memories of a bathroom toward the front of the house when we scouted this place a few days ago. I push through the doorway and drop to the floor, pulling the lid of the toilet up before emptying the contents of my stomach into it.

All that violence I just committed takes its revenge on me as my stomach heaves painfully. My body calling me out on the truth I'm ignoring. That there's a crack in my facade that just might prove the girl from six months ago isn't gone completely.

It's useless though, that crack. I want no part of it right now.

Especially after what Sergei just told me.

It takes a few minutes for my stomach to settle enough that I can lean back, slowly breathing in and out and vaguely noticing that my hand hurts from the knife I'm still gripping. Eyes immediately going to the blood dripping from it, visible now that I'm upstairs where we turned on a few of the house lights. It's still dark, but not enough to hide the crime I just committed. My stomach tries to rebel against the sight, my body breaking out in a cool sweat, but I swallow the unease back down. It has no place here. Not anymore.

I stand from the floor and turn, dropping the knife into the porcelain sink with a clatter before using my unstained hand to flick the water on. Letting it wash away the evidence from the blade as I scrub my tainted hand clean with harsh movements. Keeping my attention focused on the way the water turns from red to pink and then eventually clear again as if nothing ever happened at all. Only then do I turn the sink off. Allowing myself to try and breathe out some of the adrenaline locking me up as I look up into the mirror.

But what I see steals the breath from my lungs because I barely recognize the girl looking back at me. My features are the same, sure, and I've even put on a little muscle with the training Alec forced me to start when we set out months ago. So I don't look entirely unhealthy, with the exception of the bruised-looking bags under my eyes. The dark-brunette color of my hair still surprises me every time I look in the mirror, but I'd become accustomed to that little jolt months ago. It's necessary to stay under the radar. The color of the hair Alec and I share is too eye-catching, which leaves us both going through at least a box of dye a month.

The thing I can't get past is the emptiness.

And the little bit of satisfaction peeking through the backs of my eyes.

Because while my facade might've cracked, the girl I used to be shocked by what I'd done. The person I'd become to try and save us all reveled in dishing out that little bit of justice. My past and present fighting for me once again, except this time, it's different versions of myself. I blink at the stranger in the mirror once more before quickly looking down to grab the knife out of the sink. Avoiding looking for too long or too deep like I always do now.

There's no need to wonder.

I doubt either of them would recognize me now.

This girl who chose violence in the absence of them.

Chapter Seven

The sky is just starting to lighten into the purple shade of the coming dawn as I pull into the driveway of Alec's safe house outside of Gliwice, Poland. The small house that's set a little ways off of a country road has been our home base for the past six months except when we've been running down leads and it's nice enough. The gray stone one-story with green shutters is a classic example of a countryside European home with three bedrooms and a combination of forest and fields surrounding it. Set far enough away from town that there's no one nearby to ask questions but close enough that a run to the store only takes twenty minutes. Essentially, isolated enough that we'll see anyone coming but still easy to abandon and get the hell out of dodge if we need to. It also borders three of the countries that Novikov used to hold power in, which is essential for what we're doing.

And it's been good to me, in its own way, this house. Kept both me and my pain a secret. It's even prettier now than when we first arrived, with snow littering the roof like something out of a Christmas story. The only thing that's missing is smoke coming from the chimney to complete the picture.

But still, as I bring the car to a stop with ice crushing under its tires, I hesitate to turn it off and go inside.

Dreading what comes next as much as I looked forward to it.

My ritual to end the day, or night really.

Yet another thing that's different now, my nocturnal schedule. It started by accident because of the time change, but it quickly became a habit when I realized that the people we were after tended to only come out to play at night. Easier to just already be on that schedule than try to pull an all-nighter or drag myself out of bed after only a few hours' sleep. So that's what we do now. Wake up as the sun is going down, then eat, train, and shower. Then we either go through what seems to be endless documents looking for leads or leave to run them down, some near and some far away. And apparently if it's a really eventful day like today, we're adding some bloodshed and torture into the mix.

Everything these days is by necessity, it seems, except for my ritual, which is both necessity and indulgence. But today, after what I had just done, I'm not sure I'm ready to face them yet.

I exhale a deep breath and grab my phone from the center console of the car impulsively, debating for a moment over who to call. None of them would be happy to hear from me. Relieved, yes. Happy, no. No one understands what I'm doing. How I just left everyone and disappeared, or why I did it. And I haven't enlightened them, it's safest that way. I've already caused enough tragedy and it will wreck me if I let it touch another person in my life.

The boys are pissed, Mac in particular.

Yvie thinks I've lost my damn mind.

And Tiff... she's the one I'm the most worried about, her voice a little more lost every time I speak to her, which is one of the reasons I call her the most. In a lot of ways, we're in this together, even if she doesn't understand it all like the others. She still knows more than they do though, I haven't been able to skirt around some things with her.

I check the time on the phone, accounting for the time difference before swiping it open and dialing her number. Rolling my eyes at the fact that I actually have people's phone numbers memorized now, thanks to Alec, but I'm not about to fuck around and not follow his rules. All calls are to last under two minutes and never call the same person twice within a week. He's confident in the software he installed on the phone, but still, one could never be too careful when chasing the fucking invisible man.

The line rings for so long that I'm about to hang up, knowing voice mail is coming when she answers. "Hello?"

And there it is, that lost, hesitant tone in her voice that was never there before. It's bugging the shit out of me even though I'm barely holding myself together.

"Hey," I tell her. "It's me."

"Oh." A breath exhales into the phone that almost sounds like relief, but it's wrong, different from how the boys sound when I call. "El."

"Yeah," I answer awkwardly. Already knowing from our past conversations that there really isn't much room for beating around the bush with the time constraints we have. I still can't get past that nagging that something more is going on with her than the obvious though and she... Well, she's Coop's sister, in a way, she's my responsibility now. "You doing okay, Tiff?"

"Uh." I can hear the surprise in her voice at my question, along with the pause. "Yeah, yeah," she hurries. "I'm fine. How are you? Where are you?"

Liar, liar, pants on fire, Tiffany Monroe.

But I leave it alone, in part because I'm thousands of miles away and in part because there's not enough time to drag it out of her.

"Fine," I lie in turn. "Just chasing down more leads." She knows I'm looking for Coop. She knows something bad happened to him, but that's all I would tell her.

"Anything promising?"

And because I can hear how quietly hopeful her voice turns, I lie again. "Maybe."

A long moment passes where both of us say nothing, just quietly hope and commiserate together before she admits. "I miss my brother, El."

"Me too," I force out, clearing my throat to hide the way my voice is trying to crack. Knowing that my time is ticking down and that I need to hurry this up. "How is he, Tiff?"

"He's the same, El," she answers tiredly. "No change."

"Did the doctor I had flown in last week say anything new?" Because that's my other pastime now, researching specialists and flying them to Landing Point.

"No." The hesitation is back in her voice in full force. "Just that the chances of him waking up are pretty much nonexistent. They brought up taking him off—"

"No," I snap.

"El—"

"No, Tiffany!"

The line goes silent as my chest rises and falls rapidly and the memory of Sergei's doing the same flashes through my mind before I start to slow down my breaths.

"I'm sorry," I tell her softly because I shouldn't have snapped at her. None of this is her fault, it's mine. "The account number I gave you is still working to cover the cost of everything, right?" I didn't put it past Yvie and the boys to have me declared dead just so I would have to come home to get funds for Jace.

"Yeah," she answers shortly. Probably as tired of my shit as I am at this point.

"And his dad is still on board, right?"

"Jack will never let go of him." She sighs. "And Coop is his medical power of attorney, so—"

"So nothing happens until I find Coop."

We'd been through this before.

Another beat passes before she continues. "He wouldn't want to live like this, El. You know that."

I can hear the pity in her voice and the worst part is, it doesn't even grate at me anymore because part of me pities myself too. "He'll wake up, Tiff," I tell her confidently. "He will. He promised."

"El—"

"He will," I insist. "Got to go."

Pulling the phone away from my ear, I end the call before she can respond, even though there's a full ten seconds left until I have to. Never thought I would feel guilty over ten seconds, but I do. That's just par for the course these days, I guess though. No matter what I do, what decision I make, even if it's for the right reasons or with the right intentions. Someone gets hurt.

It's a fucked-up kind of existence that left me missing... everything.

I miss the boys and LA.

I miss Tiff and Landing Point even.

I miss Jace as the sun rises and my day ends.

I miss Coop from the moment I wake up with the stars shining above.

I still wouldn't change it though. I wouldn't change loving them. Even with what the outcome appears to be. I can't. To not have loved them is... inconceivable to me, especially now for some reason. It's a mix of self-hatred and confusion that leaves my mind a mess on the best of days, spending them heavy of heart and full of violence, a little less present with each one that passes. Growing that numbness inside of me as I sense them fading further away. Trying so desperately to hold on to whatever is left of them out there that it settles like a weight at the bottom of my heart. So I cling to that heaviness and use it as an anchoring kind of gravity.

And once a day... once a day during my nights filled with the safety of the sunlight, I allow myself to break and face how much I truly miss them. Let myself push away that numbness I'm wielding as a tool of survival and bask in the pain that brings the memory of them to the forefront. To remind myself what I'm doing here. Why I've become this person. What part of myself there might be to find again at the end of this if everything does turn out okay. To try and tether them to me in some way to keep them here.

That's my ritual.

And as the sun starts to rise behind the gray stone house in front of me, I'm spurred into motion at the reminder signaling it's time to begin.

Chapter Eight

I press the button to turn the car off and push open the door, icy air hitting my lungs like a thousand tiny knives and reminding me how much I hate the fucking cold. Stomping my boot-covered feet to get my blood moving, I dig the keys out from my back pocket and lock the car before making a beeline for the front door. Walking as quickly as I can while still being careful to not slip on the icy driveway. The first time that had happened, Alec had chortled mercilessly, then proceeded to play the footage of it from the security camera out front during our training sessions for the next week as *motivation*. Fucker.

My hands are already almost frozen by the time I make it to the landing and have to go through the time-consuming process of unlocking all three dead bolts on the front door. Fingers hurting a little bit more each time I have to turn the key and force the cold metal to give way. All the security is a bitch, but it does let me sleep a little bit more soundly at night. That and the fact that I'm pretty sure Alec will kill anyone who even breathes in the direction of the house. The one delivery guy who had shown up by accident a few months ago really should count his lucky stars that I had been the one to answer the door.

Successfully making my way through the locks, I press the door handle down and throw my shoulder against it to get it past the sticking point like always. Stepping into the house and immediately turning to the alarm that's beeping at me incessantly to type in the code which spells out Helen of Troy on the keypad. Another thing that brought Alec endless amusement. But hey, we both had to get our kicks in somewhere living in such close quarters and I might have *accidentally* nicked him with a knife in training the day after he changed the code.

So fair is fair, I guess.

The beeping ceases from one second to the next as I finish typing the code, making me sigh in relief before I pause to let my eyes scan the house. Making sure nothing is amiss. The short entrance in front of me leads into the main living space that's empty of any furniture and instead filled with workout mats that are covering the floor along with our other training equipment. I walk two more steps into the house before stopping alongside the small entrance table and peeking down the hallway on my left that leads to the bedrooms and bathroom.

When a few more seconds pass without a sound or warning flicker of intuition, I make the call that it's safe enough and drop my keys into the bowl on the table. Clinging to this one ordinary, mundane act even as I pull the black KA-BAR folding blade I always carried now out of my other back pocket and drop it alongside them. The two objects again echoing of my past and present and sending my brows dropping as I stare at them. Knowing that if I didn't find a way to reconcile the two pretty soon, I'm going to have big problems on my hands or bigger problems, I should say. I shake my head to clear it and walk away from the table, leaving that little issue for another day. There are more important things to deal with at this moment anyway.

The floor turns padded under my boots as I walk through the living space before making it to the kitchen. Eyes scanning the large map of Europe that's pinned above the kitchen table like usual as I make my way to the fridge. The map is filled with Post-its and handwritten notes while the table is piled high with papers for all the good it's done us. None of it has gotten me close enough to what I need more than anything.

The sight of the sun cresting over the little hill in the backyard through the window sitting adjacent to the kitchen table snags my attention and I grab a bottle of water from the fridge before walking straight to the back door. Knowing that as soon as this is done I'll be heading straight for part two. I flip the locks on the back door, pulling it open to once again step out into the cold and make my way across the small brick back porch to where it turns into a few steps that lead down into the yard. Sitting down on the top one and setting the water bottle carefully down beside me before wrapping my arms around myself. Pulling my coat tighter as I look out to where the sun is rising beyond the forested hills before me.

I watch the birds just starting to flit about over the tops of the tree branches for a long moment before closing my eyes. Slowing down my breathing and letting my memory pull me to another place. To another sunrise from months ago. One that I witnessed on a boat in the ocean and taught me how to hope. How to heal. I let the memory fill me until it's as if he's sitting right in front of me again and then I open my eyes.

"Hey, Dawson." I sigh, breath steaming up the air in front of me. "You know, it's pretty rude of you to keep me waiting like this." *Wake up, Jace.* "Leaving me to sit in the cold, practically freezing, no coffee in sight." Something like a laugh leaves me, but really, it's the start of it. "I get it though. I do." I blink into the light of the rising sun and feel the first tear escape. "I broke your heart, so maybe this is fair. You keeping me waiting." *Wake up.*

"But Jace, you promised me, remember? To keep chasing that sun regardless of whether it was together or not." I exhale a breath that stutters out visibly in the cold air. "And I'm—" My voice turns choked, going a little bit higher with the cry I'm fighting to keep inside. "I'm holding up my side of the deal and right now, I really need you to do the same." *Wake the fuck up, Jace.* I swallow, needing to speak this next part. To remind him. To will it into being. "Because I know that you always keep your promises and I know that the doctors can go to hell. They don't know you, but I do, and I know you're in there. Fighting to come back to us. To keep your promise to me." I clench my teeth for a second until the sob in my throat passes, quickly turning into tears that run cold down my cheeks. "And I'm going to find him. I promise you that too. I'm going to find him and you're going to have a cousin to come back to, even if it's only to be pissed at him."

Come on, Dawson. You know you want to wake up and flash those pretty eyes at me. At least make me regret my choice a little.

"So anytime you're ready, I am too. I'll fix it between us all somehow." I can't stop the quiet cry this time as the light really begins to fill the sky. "The sun's waiting for you, and so am I." Letting go of my coat, I bring my hands to my cheeks and swipe the tears away with numb fingers. "Come back to us," I whisper. "Wake up."

Wake up, Jace. Wake up.

Wake up, wake up, wake up.

I whisper the words over and over again to the sun in front of me the whole time it's rising. Willing him to hear me even though I'm thousands of miles away. Until not just my hands but my entire body turns numb from the cold. Reminding him that there are so many more sunrises just waiting for him to chase. And even if it's not with me, not the way we pictured, that there's still a whole world filled with possibility for him.

So much left to his story.

I watch the sun set the world on fire and remind myself that there are sunrises still in store for me too. That there's hope no matter how dark things seem. A promise from the universe of better days ahead. I steal a little bit of peace from my memories with him. And then when the sun finally finishes its ascent, turning night to day, I say goodbye to Jace until tomorrow. Then I force my aching limbs to move, standing and turning to walk back toward the house.

Time for part two.

And I'm ready for it now. So, so ready to finally have my stolen moment of release. I can already feel myself beginning to crack as I push open the back door, locking it quickly and heading straight for the hallway that leads to the bathroom.

It always starts this way, with Jace smoothly picking my locks to ease the way for the absolute obliteration that is Coop to pull me under. I shrug my coat off, dropping it inside the open door to my room on the right without stopping on my way to the bathroom. Pulling my black long-sleeve thermal over my head as I step inside and flip the light switch before pulling the door closed behind me. Letting my eyes adjust to the bright fluorescence of the small white bathroom while dropping the shirt on the floor and yanking my sports bra over my head. Carelessly dropping it as well before my pants and underwear follow suit. My need for this little bit of closeness to him nearly consuming me now.

I slide the shower door open and step into the stall, the quiet roll of metal coming to a stop as I close it with an exhale of relief. Pausing for just a moment to appreciate how I'm finally safe. Completely alone in this little cocooned space. And then I clench my teeth together against what's coming, reach out, and turn the knob of the shower. Not flinching one bit as the water suddenly pounds down on me in an icy spray.

I fucking hate the cold.

But this is my reality now. Without them. Until I somehow fix everything.

I lean my back against the wall and sink down to the floor as my body starts to shake. Keeping my teeth clenched to stop them from rattling. Knowing that if I let go right now, when it's still cold, it'll be even worse than if I wait. More painful on me physically in a way that lingers tomorrow. Go on for longer than what surpasses any kind of healthy release. Not that what I'm doing could really be considered healthy anyway.

So I grit my teeth harder, pulling my knees to my chest and wrapping my arms around them while opening myself up to everything that is Coop. Staring at the tile wall in front of me without really seeing it as I imagine that the little droplets of water running down my skin are really his fingers writing words. That the reason my heart is pumping so hard I can feel it against my knees is because he's pissed me off but only because of a fight that's going to end in the best kind of way. Squeezing my eyes shut finally and pretending that really, I'm not even here, just in our shower in Cahuita. Waiting for him to come pull me out of it and drag me back to bed, whispering all kinds of poetry to me as we lose ourselves in each other.

And then, when my jaw feels like it's just about to crack and the water finally turns so hot it's scorching, I unclench my teeth right as the first sob breaks free.

They're unnatural sounding, these sobs. As if they're the tears from thousands of years of agony over his loss. Coming from somewhere deeper in me than I even knew existed as my whole body curls in on itself. Suffering through the onslaught of a kind of utter destruction I never knew was possible. It took me a while to understand that. That part of me might've suspected, even known before, that I would see him again someday. One way or another. That it was easier before when I didn't understand how deep the truth of us was woven.

That there would truly never be any getting past each other.

I squeeze my knees to my chest as tightly as I can, fingers digging into the tops of my arms as my whole body jolts with each gasping cry that leaves me. Missing him in a way that has the heaviness in my heart shifting. As if the pain I'm finally allowing to have free rein is adding to it a bit before it all resettles. Embracing the way the water is burning my skin because, for one stolen moment, it's something like the heat I used to feel from him. Being entranced and broken over and over again with each little memory of him that springs forth in my mind.

The arching brow that mocked mine.

The Princess that was full of nothing but censured demand.

The rare, breathtaking smile that seemed to be only for me when we played.

The love of his that I had chosen.

I cry until the sound turns into something that I can't even describe. Sobbing for what seems like hours until eventually… it stops. Body giving out before my pain does, physically incapable of enduring further assault as endless tears stream down my face. Mixing in with the water to disappear as I gasp, hiccuping breaths while my mind spins, unable to string anything but two words together.

Be alive.

Be alive, be alive, be alive. "Be alive."

I whisper it between the gasps when I can, mind and voice trying to will it into existence. Not believing a word that told me otherwise. It's my secret hope that I won't let go of no matter how much evidence keeps stacking up against it. And eventually, my gasps subside, giving way to shallow breaths that allow me to whisper it like a quiet chant of demand until the water runs cold on my skin again. Sending shivers through my body that signal it's the end for today as the dull ache of emptiness fills me.

I blink slowly, bringing the world back into focus and fighting to pull myself back from the edge. It's always the hardest part, to not just give in to the blissful agony of the memories completely. And I'm intimately aware of how fine a line I'm skating to true insanity these days. So I force my hands to let go of my arms, one finger at a time, knowing that the marks won't fade for hours before standing to turn the shower off. Pushing myself to keep moving now that I'm done because someone still has to fight for all of us.

And somewhere along the way, this became part of the way I fight for them.

To keep them here and tether them to me. To hold them to this plane of existence through sheer force of will. Sacrificing a bit of myself day after day to try and bring them back from whatever edge they themselves are skating.

I slide the shower door open, grabbing my towel from where it hangs on the hook and wrapping myself up in it. Not bothering to dry off before

I step out of the stall and open the bathroom door, walking straight for my room as exhaustion pulls at me with each step. Closing the door behind me and walking to my white bed in the center of it before dropping the towel. I reach down and open up the drawer in the bedside table, pulling out some underwear to step into and turn back to the bed. Quickly snatching up the shirt I'd left on it when I'd woken today.

It's the same shirt I sleep in every night. The same one I'd stolen to sleep in once upon a time in Cahuita. The last little piece of him I cling to religiously even though his sandalwood scent had faded away months ago.

I pull the shirt over my head and collapse onto the bed, knowing that for today, I had at least done my part. And I know that tomorrow will be the same along with every day that follows until I somehow pull them back to me. Every day, the same thing, no matter how hard it is at times. Willing it into being by breaking apart for both of my boys and trying to be the anchor for all of us. Never letting myself falter in the face of everything telling me to give up. Because I can't.

I'll never be able to give up on either of them, they're too deep in my heart. I'll demand them back from whoever I have to. And I swear, in that last second before sleep claims me, I can feel them a little closer to me than before.

Or maybe I'm just already dreaming.

Chapter Nine

Jace

Somewhere In Between

I watch her breathing even out in sleep, as fucking helpless as always. Doomed to watch her put herself through this hell night after night and never be able to tell her that I'm right beside her every step of the way. Or as much as whatever this fucked-up place allows me to be.

At least she'll get a few hours of reprieve now, until the screaming starts. Sometimes I'm grateful to not be here for that part, even though that guilt just feeds the rage inside of me more. But that screaming... it's unbearable, and she doesn't even know that she does it. The first time had been about a month after she got here and would have scared the ever-loving shit out of me if I hadn't already been watching her sleep. Hell, it still did scare the ever-loving shit out of me truthfully.

Her terminator of a brother had crashed into the room with a gun in hand and I'd looked at him as he'd looked at her and seen the slow realization on his face about how bad of shape she's actually in. It was the most emotion I'd ever seen from him, he'd looked almost as wrecked as she clearly was in that moment. And so this guy I'd never even met had become my comrade-in-arms after that, not that he knew it, as we watched her subconscious work through the pain she'd never speak of while awake.

Every night she screams, and every night he comes. Standing in the doorway and watching over her until it eventually subsides and she slides back into what I hope is a sleep of reprieve. At least I assume it's every night, it's hard to gauge here, but I'd say I'm probably around for most of them. No matter how much I wish I wasn't sometimes. Because most of the time, not always but most, she screams *his* name.

I can tell it bothers her brother, but he has no fucking clue what it's like for me. I love her more than anything, and she loves him more than me.

And now… I'm as fucking doomed as she is. Stuck in this place with no end in sight. Just stuck with her screams and pain every night until I fade back into the memories.

It took me a while to figure it out, but eventually I realized that's where I am, stuck in my own memories until whatever this hell she's insisting on putting herself through eventually pulls me to her again. It's the most fucked-up existence beyond anything I could imagine, which makes it clear that this isn't any place I concocted at all. It's all those pieces of shit who got pissed off when their dominoes didn't fall exactly the way they'd planned all those thousands of years ago and decided we get to relive this horrible story until we eventually get it right.

The joke is on them though, because here we are, thousands of years later, and she's still choosing him. Or maybe the joke is on me because even after thousands of years, I've never learned to not love her too.

But even with everything I now know is between us, seeing her still quells some of the rage that seems to whisper in my ear constantly. In just another fucked-up part of all of this, her pain is what gives me a little reprieve of my own. Even if it comes with the reminder that I'll never be to her what she is to me. Because I can't get away from the fact I still love her. As many times as she's broken my heart, I still love her. I'm not sure if that's ever going to change, because it's my doom to fall in love with her all over again the next time they throw us back into this world without ever remembering what came before. What the cost of this love we share for each other is.

I reach out a hand, running my fingers along her hairline to the shell of her ear then back again. Wishing so fucking bad that she could feel my touch and know for just one second that she isn't alone. That even if I don't like it, what she's doing is working.

"I'm right here, Ellie," I tell her softly. "I'm always right here."

Her breath hitches and my hand stops its path as I internally tense, wondering if the screaming is about to start early. When it evens out again a few seconds later though, relief soars over the rage for a moment as I trail my fingers to her cheek.

"Right here and so fucking worried about you."

My hand drops from her face as I work up to what she needs to hear next. Even if she can't, even if speaking the words is useless, maybe it'll sink into her subconscious somehow, like what she's doing every day with me. "I've tried to find him." The rage starts to battle against the balm that's her presence, whispering insidious things I can't even understand in my ear, but I fight it. Needing my head clear. "I've tried to think of him, thinking it might work the same as what you're doing with me would, but there's just... nothing." I watch her face for any reaction but find none. No reason to think that what I'm saying is sinking in, but still, I try. For her, I'd always try, doomed as we were. I'd even try to find him for her, knowing what that would mean for me. "I don't think he's here with me and if he were still with you, I don't know why I wouldn't be able to see him. Even once."

It had happened with my dad a couple times. When he broke down and was missing me. I'd be yanked out of whatever memory I was in and to his side. Tiff a few more and Zane several times when he was drunk... but never Coop, which led me to the one conclusion I hated for both our sakes. Her more so, but me too, because even with everything... I still love him too.

"You might have to let him go, Blondie," I whisper gently, bringing my fingers back to her cheek when I see a tear start to trail down it, but the tear just continues its path. Warning me of what's coming soon. "I'm not sure he's with us anymore. You need to let him go, Ellie."

A quiet moan leaves her lips, almost as if she can hear me, but the next second her face twists and I brace myself for what's coming as her mouth opens with a scream. Ahead of schedule tonight. So I guess maybe she did hear me, and she decided to let me know just how she felt about it.

Fractured

Chapter Ten

"Flip it."

"Not yet."

"You're going to burn it again."

"It needs another—"

"I cannot eat another burned grilled cheese, Helen."

I flick my eyes up to Alec's and narrow them. "Nobody is forcing you."

"Yeah," he scoffs. "You are, by insisting on making them. To toss it would just be…" His eyes drop back down to the pan with a distasteful look before coming back to mine. "Wasteful."

"That sounds like a personal problem to me." I tip my nose up at him haughtily before looking down to wedge the spatula under the sandwich. Awkwardly flipping it over to find that it is, indeed, burned again. Fuck my life.

"For Christ's sake," he grumbles, throwing his hands up in the air. "Why the hell do you keep on doing this to us when you clearly can't cook?"

Because Coop didn't cook, Jace did, but I hadn't chosen him. I had broken his heart and now he wouldn't wake up, so… I had to learn because at least one person in a relationship should know how to cook something beyond grilled meat. And what if Coop *couldn't* cook when I found him? What if he's—

Don't go there, El. You know that rabbit hole has no end.

"Because," I mumble, lifting the pan from the stove as he holds up a plate beside me. "I have to."

His eyes meet mine over the plate as I dump the grilled cheese onto it and a kind of understanding passes between us before he nods. "Fine."

And that's that, understanding without acknowledgment. The basis of Alec's and my entire relationship. In all the months since we came to Europe, we had never discussed the fact that he's my brother. Avoidance of issues appears to be in our genetics to a painful degree.

Those first couple weeks that we were bouncing around setting up fake identities and obtaining other illegal items, things had just been plain awkward between us. Stilted conversations and hard-eyed stares had filled the air between us in Berlin. Then eventually, when we made it into Eastern Europe, the awkwardness had given way to our old hostility. So much so that I sometimes still think it's a miracle we even made it to the safe house in Poland without clawing each other's eyes out.

But then, something shifted between us once we made it to the house. A current of understanding had been unearthed underneath all that hostility. One that I know left us both a little uneasy when we began to discover it. It's different from the twin connection I share with Mac or how Coop is the other side of my coin. This is… something that goes deeper. That originates from those strands of molecules that created us.

It's in the stupid way we both hate any kind of melon and like butter instead of cream cheese on our bagels. It's in the weird way I noticed he sometimes mouths the words he's reading like I do when we're going through documents. It's in the obvious way our thoughts trail one another's, always landing at the same conclusion when we're presented with a challenge in our hunt for Novikov.

Mostly though, it's in the way we fight. Both verbally and physically, like we're living inside the other one's mind. He started training me a little while after we got to the house in Poland, and honestly, I'm grateful to have an outlet for all of the pain that's been pulling me further under since that day in Landing Point. The training has given me a physical outlet for it all. It keeps me moving instead of allowing me to collapse in on myself.

But I'm not sure he or I expected me to be good at it.

Those first few weeks had been filled with bruises and my body begging me to just *stop*, but there was no way I was going to let the fucker win. And eventually, I stopped getting knocked down quite so much. I started to move quicker and hit harder in part because it was him. I'm not sure I would have had it in me to just casually hit someone else, but his constant antagonism made me want to beat him. So much so that it was only two months into our training when I finally managed to knock him on his ass. And it was in that moment, when he had looked up at me from the mat with the wind knocked out of him, that I could tell we both knew.

At our core, what we're made of is the same.

I'll never admit it out loud, but the only reason I managed to knock him on his ass that day was that I'd just *known* somehow that he was about to leave his legs undefended. Some would call it luck, but we had both known in that moment there was a little more to it than that. And then he proceeded to pop up in a showy move using only his legs and beat me silly. Apparently our little quasi-family of two doesn't believe in pulling punches or losing gracefully. Shortly after that, we set a time limit for our daily training sessions because neither one of us understands the meaning of the words "tap out."

"Yours."

I look down to see him holding the plate with half of the freshly cut grilled cheese on it and shake my head to clear the memories. "Thanks."

"Blueberries?" he calls, already turning around to the fridge and opening it as he takes a bite of his half.

I shove a bite of grilled cheese into my mouth and mumble, "Mhmm." Hiding my grimace at the burned taste when he turns back with two protein shakes tucked under his arm and the blueberries in hand.

"Breakfast of champions," he drones mockingly, setting the blueberry container on the counter between us and passing me a shake. "So, what do you feel like for training today?"

"I don't know." I shrug, taking one more bite of the grilled cheese before setting it down on the counter and grabbing for the blueberries. "Knives?"

I had dressed in my favorite training outfit. Might as well get some good action out of it. Although he would probably insist on blunted blades like he had every time since that day I nicked him. Big baby.

"Guns?" he pushes, eating the rest of his half in one bite before picking up my plate.

I roll my eyes. "No." That's the one thing I can't bring myself to train in, which is undoubtedly stupid, but my hang-up with that particular weapon runs a little too deep still.

"Wimp."

"Fucker."

"No knives for you today, stabby," he chides seriously. "Not after that little episode last night. Someone needs to learn to control her emotions."

I turn my head toward him and narrow my eyes, taking the time to pop a couple blueberries into my mouth while watching him finish off my half of the grilled cheese before nodding. "Today might be the day."

He sets my now empty plate down before tilting his head at me. "For what?"

"Your death," I deadpan.

"Ha!" He scoffs, throwing a handful of blueberries into his mouth and grabbing his shake before walking out of the kitchen, calling out over his shoulder. "Hand to hand it is."

I roll my eyes again and sigh. "Whatever."

"And don't forget your shake!" he yells. "Fucking like taking care of a child with you."

"Yeah, yeah," I mumble, picking up the shake he left on the counter and twisting the cap off before taking a swig while pushing off the counter. I walk into the living room and find him already in the center of the mats.

Bouncing on the balls of his feet with his shirt off in a way that tells me he's more than ready to kick my ass. "This is about how you startled me last night, isn't it?"

He shakes his head, bringing an arm across his chest and holding it there to stretch. "I already told you what it's about."

I screw the cap back onto the bottle and set it down at the edge of the mats, mimicking his stretch and walking the short distance to where he's standing. "Clear something up for me."

"What?"

"How come"—I switch arms and cock a brow at him—"it's okay for you to go all torture status on Sergei with your lame 'Let's find some truth under that skin,' but when I merely stab him it's cause for alarm?"

"Because," he starts, reaching down to touch his toes for a second before rising to lift his hands skyward while continuing. "Mine was out of necessity. Yours"—I reach down to touch my toes, knowing what he's about to say and not wanting to hear it, but he pauses. Waiting until I've come back up to mimic his stretch before he lifts his brows and finishes— "was an impulsive reaction to what he said."

I reach down while lifting my leg up to grab my foot, pulling it up to my butt and answering in a bored voice. "I have no idea what you're talking about."

"Right." He narrows his eyes at me, copying my move as I switch legs. "Whatever you say, Helen."

My foot barely has time to touch back down to the ground when he strikes, using the hold he has on his back leg as leverage to suddenly lift it and send a roundhouse kick flying at me. And the fucker is so unnaturally fast that I barely duck in time to miss the hit, body reacting to the sudden threat before my brain can catch up. Adrenaline jolting my system and sending my heart pounding as I realize he really must be pissed. That hit would've knocked me the fuck out for sure.

I pop back up quickly to find him smirking at me as he bounces back to his feet. "Better."

"We were *stretching*." I glare, keeping my feet solidly on the mat and beginning to slide clockwise around him. Knowing better than to get conned into trying to mimic his bullshit bunny rabbit technique. He's still significantly better than me and I need every advantage I can get.

"And yet you still managed to evade the hit." He bounces forward in one stride with a hit aimed for my left kidney, but I drop an arm to block it and send my own fist flying toward his cheekbone. He tilts his head to the side in time to miss the force of my hit, the knuckles on my hand barely meeting his skin before he springs back and we begin to circle again. "Bravo, Helen. Want a gold star?"

I'm unable to keep the grimace of displeasure off my face at the nickname. Hating it as much today as I had the first time he called me it. He knows it too but uses the excuse that it's my codename to keep my real identity safe.

I say that's some utter bullshit.

Right now though, I know he's trying to goad me into an irrational reaction and I've at least learned to keep my feelings under control in this little arena of ours enough to save myself some pain.

So I just keep my arms raised, ignoring the tingling in my left one from where I blocked his hit and smirk. "Actually, I was thinking your liver would do nicely."

"She's funny." He gives me an equally terrifying smile before we come together and exchange a few more hits, parting quickly when neither of us land anything substantial. "I'm shocked. Thought you had left your humor back in America."

"Fucker." I plant my left leg, rotating my hips while lifting my right to send a kick, trying to strike at the point on his thigh I know will deaden the nerve in his leg, but he jumps before I manage to make contact.

His feet hit the mat and we're already moving again. Me ducking to avoid a hit to the face before bringing my knee up to his groin, which he blocks with his own raised knee. He brings his arms around me the next second and I drop like a weight, knowing I'm done for if he manages to really get a hold on me. I slide out of his arms in the nick of time though and spring back while raising my arms up.

"Good." He nods with something like approval as we start to circle again. "Never forget your legs will always hit harder than your arms."

I'd roll my eyes at him, but it'd probably result in a bruise to my face, so I settle for snapping. "I know." He'd only said it about a million times.

"Novikov will hear about Sergei soon. I made sure to leave him somewhere public and linked to him."

"So?" I give him a confused look as we spar without any real heat for a second. "Wasn't that the plan?"

"Just saying." His shoulders shrug with a bounce of his feet. "He'll have confirmation for the first time that we're hunting him. That we're in Europe together. It'll change the game."

I tilt my head at him. "Having doubts about daddy dearest?" Quickly following up the barb with a front kick that's really more to emphasize my point than anything else.

His feet still as he leans back to miss the hit, the annoyance filling his eyes when he comes back up, telling me everything I need to know. "No, Helen." He snorts, that damn bounce back in full force. "Just letting you know that the stakes have been raised since you insisted we try to draw him out."

"It's been months." I dodge a punch aimed for my temple as things start to heat up again. "One of us had to grow some balls and it clearly wasn't going to be you."

"Fucking impulsive—" He cuts himself off and we both still.

"Piča?" I smirk at him. "Don't worry, I've been called worse."

A scoff leaves him. "Still don't like you."

"Same."

He pauses as if debating whether to say something before nodding. "I got an interesting call on the way back from dealing with Sergei."

I immediately go on high alert. "From?"

"A friend from Bainbridge with a potential lead on Novikov."

"I thought you said we couldn't trust anyone from Bainbridge."

"I made the call to her when the leads were really starting to dry up about a month ago before we found Sergei." His expression turns a little more satisfied than usual and I can tell he's fighting a smirk as he continues. "She's someone I trust more than the rest. We've been close from time to time over the years."

It doesn't take me long to understand what he's implying and the horror is real. "Ew!" My nose scrunches up and I give him a disgusted look. "I did not need to know that!"

"Don't be immature."

"Ew!" I shout one more time for good measure. So gross.

"Do you want to know what she said?"

"Maybe after I burn this memory from my mind."

"Helen—"

"Fine." I wiggle my shoulders to rid myself of the weirdness. "What did your booty call have to say?"

He looks up to the ceiling and exhales a deep breath, one of annoyance if I had to guess, before looking back to me. "She found the old Interpol agent who Nadia made her deal with. Thought he might have some interesting insight into Novikov's moves today."

"Oh." That is unexpected.

He laughs dryly. "That was my reaction."

My brows drop at the prospect of meeting the agent who had dealt with our mother. "What'd you tell her?"

"What do you think?"

"That you wanted to make sweet, sweet love to h—"

The hit comes out of nowhere, a flying kick that I don't have a chance of dodging, so caught up in the middle of my taunt to him. Both of his feet hit me in the center of my chest and send me flying backward onto the mats with enough power to knock the air from my lungs. Leaving me gasping for breath as my eyes water and my hands hit the cushioned ground uselessly. Stunned into immobility with pain radiating out from my breastbone bad enough that I know it's going to leave a nasty bruise.

He walks to my side and looks down at me. "I told her to set it up. We leave in the morning to meet him in the Czech Republic." Dropping down onto one knee, he braces an arm on it and leans his head forward till it's directly above mine. "You forgot to set the alarm, Helen." His voice is all quietly threatening and my eyes widen in response because fuck... he's right. I had. "When you got back this morning and went to bed, you forgot to set the alarm. So don't tell me that you didn't go stabby on Sergei because he got to you with what he said about Cooper." I watch his mouth move as if he's resisting the urge to clench his jaw, but for the briefest second, true anger shows on his face. "You have to learn to separate from it. I know how hard that must be, but if you're going to survive Novikov when he's telling you how he shot Coop like a fucking dog"—he closes his eyes with a sharp exhale and a long moment passes before they open to meet mine—"you have to shut it out in order to have clarity." His lips tip up with that same attitude we share. "Because I've now invested way too much time in making you a badass for you to lose this battle. Understood?"

He's alive, Alec. I know he is. He has to be.

I don't argue though, knowing it won't get me anywhere. Plus, after months together, this is the first time he's actually shown that he cares whether I live to see the end of this. It's another shift in our relationship and it might be awkward and violent, but so are we.

So I force myself to stop gasping and slowly nod my head, drawing the air through my nose like he taught me.

"Good." He nods. "And Sergei paid for calling you a bitch. I decided no one gets to do that, not even me."

I cough up a laugh at his words, the first genuine one I'd been able to find in months and it shocks me. The sound of my laughter a foreign thing that immediately fills me with guilt for even attempting it. Leaving the sound to die in the air almost as soon as it leaves my lips.

Alec stands, holding his hand out to me, the knowing clear in his eyes about my sudden silence. "Come on, we'll train for another hour and then try to catch some sleep before leaving in the morning."

I cough once more before reaching up to take his hand. "You know, you definitely made sure I'll never forget that my legs are stronger again."

Chapter Eleven

I'm all out of sorts during the drive, the sudden shift in our nocturnal schedule leaving me restless all night and unable to have my moment of ritual when the sun came up. On top of that, it's strange being out during the day now, everything is too bright, the full sun almost painfully disorienting. I catch myself checking the rearview mirror every two minutes without the cover of darkness that's apparently become my safety blanket at some point. Most people assume the bad things come at night, but I've learned that the monsters can find me in the day just as easily.

Basically, I can't wait to get to Ostrava and get this meeting over with so that I can scurry back to the house and resume our normal routine.

Thankfully, it's only an hour's drive over the border, but that didn't stop me from asking. "How much longer?"

"We're almost there," Alec answers irritably, although whether that stems from my constant repetition of the question or his own unease is debatable.

I turn my head toward where he's sitting in the driver's seat, drumming my fingers against the center console to try and rid myself of some excess energy as we enter the city. "What's this guy's name again?"

"Yakov."

"Right. Yakov," I mutter, dragging out the name and testing it. "And who exactly does he think we are?"

105

He flicks his eyes to me and I'm left with no doubt what the source of his irritation is. "Serena didn't give him our biographies, Helen. Just told him we were some people looking for info on Novikov and offered the man some cash."

"Serena." I choke, mimicking vomiting for good measure and eliciting a long-suffering sigh from him before my brows drop with concern. "Wait, an Interpol agent is willing to accept cash for info?"

"He's retired." Alec shrugs. "But the truth is, in this part of the world, taking a bribe is a pretty commonplace thing."

"Wow." I scoff. "My confidence in this plan right now is overwhelming."

"As is mine." He snorts. "But it's a lead and right now..."

I clear my throat when he trails off, answering softly. "Yeah." We desperately need a lead, any lead. Sergei had been a dead end, and the only other person who might know where Nikolov is would be the man who launders his money for him.

Only problem is, we have no idea *who* that is.

Maybe Yakov could shed some light on that though. Chances are Novikov hasn't switched money men in the past couple of decades because he's been trying to fly under the radar at Bainbridge. He's probably leaving his illegal profits where they are instead of moving them and risking any kind of authorities catching on, friendly or unfriendly. Plus, there've been no rumors of him offing one either, so I'm hopeful if we find the source of the money then we'll have a trail to follow at least.

Alec pulls into a parking lot and I spot a small clock tower with a city square diagonal from us, only a short walk away. It sends my energy skyrocketing again, the drumming of my fingers doing nothing to ease the nerves now that the meeting is actually here. There are so many variables, including the one beside me. We never talked about our mother, avoiders that we are, which leaves me wondering how he's about to react to getting some up close and personal information.

For me, it's different. I know who she was, and sure, my feelings are pretty freaking layered when it comes to her, but I at least still know. Nothing is going to shock me when it comes to her today. But Alec... I don't know what he does or doesn't know and this conversation isn't just going to be about one of his parents but both of them.

He brings the car to a stop in one of the parking spaces on the end while looking around, eyes sharp and scanning every inch of space surrounding us. Immediately making me copy his move. "Do you think it's a setup?"

"I don't know," he answers tensely. "Lots of exit points at least."

"I thought you trusted the booty call?" I poke, unable to help myself as I bring my eyes back to him.

He turns to meet my gaze, stating bluntly. "I don't trust anyone."

The statement hangs heavy in the air between us, almost pulling the question from my lips of whether it applies to me too. But this isn't the time or place and the truth is I'm not sure how I'd feel if he said no. Not after these past months together. We've grown a bit through beating the shit out of each other and if he doesn't trust me like I do him… well, that would kinda suck.

He seems to pick up on the awkward vibe I'm throwing off because he nods toward the other end of the square where a white church sits. "If shit hits the fan and we get split up, wait in the confessional there. I'll come for you."

"And if there's a priest in there?"

"I'm sure you have plenty to atone for."

I narrow my eyes at him and take back every fear I just had about him not trusting me in my head. "Don't like you."

"Don't care." He nods to my side. "Got your knife?"

I pull open the side of my leather jacket to show him the blade safely tucked away in the sheath built into it. A weird, but I suppose equally thoughtful Christmas present from him. "Yep."

It had even made me feel a little guilty that I hadn't gotten him shit.

"Alright." He opens the door and I follow suit. "Let's do this."

We meet at the front of the car and walk side by side through the parking lot. Alec's decked out in all black per usual, but I'm rocking a pair of knee-high boots, jeans, and a burgundy sweater underneath my leather jacket. One of us has to provide a little color to the wardrobe since we are going out during the day and it definitely isn't going to be him saving us from suspicion. The snow starts to fall heavier as we make it into the square and swing a right, walking past the clock tower and a few pastel-painted buildings before coming to a restaurant with outdoor seating that I guess would be pretty if it wasn't cold as shit.

Thankfully, Alec pulls the door open and stands back for me to head inside, but I can see how tense he really is about this meeting in the way his eyes never stop moving. And it makes me pause for just a second, wondering if we're being stupid, but then Coop's face flashes through my head. The memory of one of those rare, breathtaking smiles he gave me when I woke up in Cahuita to find him waiting to say good morning in the language we spoke best.

I step inside without any further hesitation. Anything for him.

Alec steps in behind me, closing the door as I come to a stop and scan the small restaurant that's dim except for the wintery light coming through the front windows. It's narrow and long with tables scattered around and booth seating running along one wall. There's a counter you can sit at in the back with an assortment of coffee-making appliances behind it and two doors on either side. One for the bathrooms and the other labeled staff only. The whole place is a strategic nightmare, I don't need Alec to tell me that. Nowhere to hide and only one exit point, plus we missed the early morning rush, leaving only a few other patrons in the restaurant.

Fuck my life.

Alec comes up beside me and nods his head toward a sixty-something-looking man with brown hair that's just starting to gray sitting at one of the small booth tables. "Yakov," he murmurs quietly.

He's dressed casually in a button-up shirt from what I can see above the table and sipping tea. Some kind of half glasses low on his nose while he reads the newspaper like he's meeting his mom for breakfast and couldn't be more relaxed. And damn, but I hope that's true because right now my intuition is screaming that this is a trap, regardless though we're already here. If this is a trap, then we've sprung it and might as well follow through to see what's waiting at the other end.

Yakov lifts his head from the newspaper, checking his watch before looking up to scan the restaurant and when his eyes land on us, they pause. Quickly flowing over me before moving on to Alec and staying there as he dismisses me as a threat. It rankles me enough that I take the next step toward him without another thought about the logistic nightmare.

Asshole. Just because I have boobs doesn't mean I'm not fucking fierce.

Alec laughs under his breath as if he can read my mind, following behind me as I make my way to the little table in front of the booth with a single chair sitting opposite Yakov. I pull the chair out and slide into it in one move as Alec drags one over from the neighboring table, flipping it around to straddle it before taking his seat. Yakov's eyes move between us as tense silence fills the space and I see a hardened kind of shrewdness fill his eyes when they eventually settle on me.

Much better. Time to play.

I let my lips twitch the barest hint. "Let's cut to the chase, shall we?"

He eyes me for another second before nodding. "What do you want to know?"

The accent in his voice is just as strong as Sergei's, but his speech is a little more refined, albeit still with that rumbling note running through it.

"Everything you can tell me about Nicolai Novikov."

"That would take the whole week." He laughs, the gravelly sound coming out too loud for my liking in the small space. "It will be easier if you narrow it down."

I pause, unsure of which front we should tackle first and which will raise the most suspicion of who we actually are, but Alec intercedes.

"Tell us," he starts slowly, drawing Yakov's attention. "About how he was caught and who was handling his money at the time."

Yakov's eyes harden even more, moving between us again with a spark of curiosity. "Dangerous questions," he muses. "Anything to do with Novikov, especially for two so young."

"We're aware." I smirk. "Tell us anyway."

He picks up his tea, taking a sip before he counters casually. "American?"

"Answer the question, Yakov," Alec interrupts coldly. "You're being paid generously to not ask ones of your own."

His eyes move between us for one more long moment before he nods. "Apologies." He sets his teacup down. "When Novikov was caught, I was on loan to Interpol, working on a task force going up against the beast that was Eastern European. A beast of which Novikov was the head of at the time. He controlled everything coming into and out of Czechia and the surrounding countries, but there was never anything we could stick to him. He was always a step ahead." He sighs. "Witnesses disappeared before they ever came forward. Intel that was supposed to lead to stashes of weapons or drugs instead led to warehouses with nothing but charitable contributions he was making." His face turns a little red with what I'm guessing is remembered anger, head shaking with disgust. "It was an embarrassment to everyone from Interpol to the local police... or the ones who weren't on his payroll."

"Until?" I interrupt, wanting to get on with it.

"Until," he sighs, looking down and pulling his napkin from his lap to set it on the table. "A woman by the name of Nadia Petras found me one day." His eyes come back to mine and I make sure to keep my face perfectly still. "Bumped into me at the supermarket and stuck a note in my pocket somehow, asking me to meet."

"How'd she know who you were?" Alec interrupts, the bored curiosity of his voice hiding what I'm guessing is a whole lot of need to know more about how it all went down. About whether he's the reason she did it.

"She said that Novikov was aware of all of the agents on the task force. That she'd heard their names when he'd had meetings and that I was the one closest to her."

"Makes sense," I interject. "What happened next?"

"Something I could have never predicted." He laughs again and I wince. "The closest person to Novikov turned against him. Said she wanted out and made a deal with me to get as far away from him as possible. I became her envoy with the Americans through Interpol and it was a loss to lose his imprisonment to them, but ultimately"—he shrugs—"worth the price to get him in the end. Only a handful of the charges stuck out of the hundreds he'd committed, but those were still thanks to information Nadia had supplied."

I pause when Novikov finishes that part of his story. Frustrated because it isn't anything we didn't already know. And also because I know what needs to be asked for both personal and investigative reasons next, but it's starting to tread on dangerous territory for both of us if he somehow puts the pieces together.

Fuck it though. We've come here for info and at least one of us should get something out of it. "What can you tell me," I start carefully. "About Nadia's relationship with Novikov? Why did she betray him?"

Or, you know, all the men in her life, but that's a musing for another day.

"Nadia"—Yakov's eyes run over my face again in a way that has alarm bells blaring—"was one of the most interesting people I've ever met."

"Explain," Alec cuts in.

Yakov's eyes move to Alec reluctantly before pausing there, renewed interest blatant in them. "She never said why she betrayed him, and in fact, I think she did care for him, which just made it all the more confusing on my end. I doubted her credibility at times, but she always came through." He pauses, but when neither of us says anything, clearly wanting him to elaborate, he continues. "Novikov, on the other hand, had never let a woman so far into his operations before, which led me to believe that he found her... special in some way, yes?"

His eyes come back to mine and I give him a nod of understanding.

"I'm not sure if it was exactly love between them, but I believe they understood each other to a degree. Perhaps even found an equal in each other at last. Novikov's origins were similar to her own and I think Nadia understood the path he had taken because of that. What someone was capable of when they had experienced such hardship at such a young age. I think some part of her cared for him, even knowing the monster he was." A deep exhale comes from him before he mutters the next part. "Perhaps even in spite of him having made her a monster too."

"What do you mean?" I demand sharply.

"I always had the sense that Novikov had betrayed her somehow and that was what had finally turned her away from him for good." He shrugs. "But those last few months, we communicated only through dead drops, so I never got the chance to ask her. I only knew she made it out after the arrest because the Americans let me know she had made it to their embassy in Slovakia."

Silence fills the table between us all, continuing on past the point of a normal pause in conversation, but I'm struggling to come to terms with what he's telling us. Did my mother love the man who's trying to kill me? Who did... I don't know what to Coop? Or had he just been one of the many? She had loved my father for what he'd given her. She'd loved

Adam Monroe because of what? That he was exciting? Had spoken to her soul? I guess I'd never know because I'd told Coop I didn't want the last journal and who knows where it is now. So had she loved Novikov for his brutality? His ruthlessness that somehow fits what she herself was made of?

The whole parallel hits a little too close to home for me, as all things do when it comes to my mother, but I shake it off. Reminding myself that what Coop and I share isn't the same. That there is no doubt that we love each other more than anything, would sacrifice anything for one another. In our own way, we make each other better versions of ourselves by facing our darker sides and deepest fears together. We shine brighter in the darkness together than we ever would apart in the day. He forces me to be brave. Even today.

That is the truth of it.

That and that my mother had most certainly known how to pick 'em.

"The money?" Alec asks harshly, dragging me back to the present. "Did you ever find out who laundered it for him?"

"Not officially." He shakes his head.

"And unofficially?" I push.

Yakov pauses, as if he's hesitant to say anything more, but Alec taps his finger against the table insistently and he sighs. "I told you that Novikov and Nadia had similar origins. Novikov grew up on the streets and it was rumored that he met another boy at some point and they became like brothers, so much so that Novikov finished off his youth years in the boys' home. That they came up together and could even pass themselves off as blood. Swapping for one another when people hadn't met them before. That it became like a game for them. Some even said Novikov might have been the father's bastard." He throws up his hands. "Bah! Nothing more than a ghost story spread by Novikov himself if you ask me. Few remember it these days."

"Do you have a name?" I snap, so impatient at the prospect of finally having a lead that it's stringing every single one of my nerves more tightly together by the second.

"Only a first."

"What is it?"

"A strange one for these parts." Yakov laughs. "But again, I heard once that one of his parents was British."

"A fucking name, Yakov," Alec spits out.

The name has barely even left his lips when my blood turns cold, heart stopping right along with that first syllable. "Simon."

Chapter Twelve

"Alec," I breathe, shock pulling his name from my lips as a horrible kind of knowing fills me.

His head whips to me, eyes finding mine as my fists clench. "Helen?" He tilts his head at me.

"Alec," I whisper again on a shaky breath and his eyes narrow, understanding passing between us.

"Thank you, Yakov." He stands, grabbing my arm and practically dragging me from my seat, but I don't fight him because my mind is spinning. "That will be all."

He starts to walk us away from the table as Yakov shouts. "What about my money?!"

"It'll be deposited in your account by the end of the day," Alec calls over his shoulder, fingers tight around my arm as he pulls me toward the door and out it. Spinning around to face me as soon as it shuts behind us. "Who is he?"

I open my mouth to answer before snapping it shut quickly. Wondering if I'm grasping here, overreacting even… but it's just too much of a coincidence, the timing of it too perfect.

"Helen," Alec snaps. "Now is not the time to withhold information."

I blow out a shaky breath before starting. "When I was in LA with Coop and Jace over the summer, I met a guy my aunt had started dating at her office one day. Walked in on them actually." I swallow, trying to remember every detail of the interaction. "He introduced himself as Simon."

Alec's eyes flare with surprise for a split second before he wipes his expression clean, back to business. "Did Coop ever meet him?"

"No." I shake my head. "The one time I invited him to dinner, he couldn't come." Sucking in a sharp breath, I ramble the rest off quickly. "But he would be the right age and he—he had a British accent."

He shakes his head. "No, if he grew up here, then he wouldn't have an English accent."

"And if he went back for college?" I counter, pulling my arm from his grip. "Or was faking? It'd sure be easiest to do it in a language you were familiar with."

Alec looks to the side, eyes nearly slits as he works his jaw for a second before giving me a single nod. Confirming that he thinks it's at least a possibility.

"Why would it matter if Coop had met him?"

"Because," he answers tensely, eyes meeting mine again hesitantly. "I think it's just as likely that what Yakov said is true. That it's just a ghost story and that the man you really met was my father."

My eyes widen with further shock that I pretty much thought impossible at this point, shoulders tightening to the point of pain as I whisper. "I need to call Yvie."

"Is she still seeing him?"

"I don't know!" I shout. "I've been on the run with you and haven't really had time for personal conversations during her enraged ranting at me."

Panic starts to pump through me with every beat of my heart and I pull the burner phone out of my back pocket. Looking down to slide my thumb across the screen and unlock it, not even bothering to account for the time change as I pull up the keypad and start to type in Yvie's number.

"Wait." Alec brings his hand back to my elbow, stopping me midnumber as I look up at him in frustration. "You need to be careful," he warns. "Chances are that whether it was Simon or Novikov, they have some kind of bug on her phone."

His words have me trying to slow down my near-frantic brain. Taking a deep breath and forcing myself to some semblance of calm that I'm only able to find because of months of training with him before asking. "What do I do?"

He gives me a nod of approval. "Make it casual, like you're just checking in on her. Valentine's day is just around the corner, so ask if she has any big plans for that."

"And if she does?" I scoff sharply. "With him? What then?"

His jaw shifts again for a second before answering. "We'll deal with that then, but *don't* say anything on the phone, you'll just be putting her at risk."

"Fine." I nod, reluctant and not totally on board with this plan but willing to agree until hearing what Yvie has to say. So I finish typing the last part of her number and bring the phone to my ear, hearing it ring twice, barely enough time for Alec to drop his hand from my arm before she answers.

"Eleanor."

Not Ellie these days. Terms of endearment are reserved for people my aunt is happy with and she's the furthest thing from happy with me.

"Yvie." I breathe in relief. She's still alive. The bogeyman hasn't gotten her yet.

"You rang?" she prods, making sure I don't miss the disapproval in her voice.

"Yeah." I swallow, trying to figure out how the hell I am going to ask about her Valentines plans when she's so freaking mad at me. "How'd you know it was me?" My brows drop as the words pop out of my mouth on instinct, the inner workings of my mind are now permanently altered apparently.

"Not too many people call me from unknown numbers, El." She sighs, clueing me in that she's working herself up to another one of her lectures. "Eleanor—"

"What are you up to?" Don't have time for it right now, Yvie.

"What am I up to?" She repeats back to me irritably. "Why I'm drinking a glass of *your* favorite cabernet on the back porch thinking how I must have utterly failed in raising my niece for her to take off without any explanation as to—"

Fuck. We were never going to get anywhere like this.

"Yvie!" I yell. "Can we please have just one civil conversation?"

"I don't know, Eleanor!" she argues back. "You tell me."

I'm going to have to ask her point blank. Yvie is just as stubborn as me and there's no way we're casually going to happen upon the topic because she won't discuss anything except how she thinks I have utterly lost my mind. I take a few quick breaths while looking into Alec's eyes and it's like he knows I'm about to pull the eject on his plan because he starts to shake his head.

"Please," I tack on quietly, trying to sound as casual as possible, even if it's from a different approach. "Tell me how you and Simon are doing."

"Him." She says scornfully, a pause sounds over the phone that makes me think she's taking a sip of wine. "Only fitting you would ask about him since you two sure do have a lot in common."

My heart stumbles for a beat before I ask carefully. "What do you mean?"

"He up and disappeared about the same time as you. Must have been something in the water," she quips. "Had to go back to England for business and haven't heard from him since."

I lean my head back with a deep sigh of relief. "Oh."

"Yes, 'Oh,' Eleanor," she agrees sarcastically. "You would know these things if you were here where you belong, not doing God knows what—"

"Yvie," I plead, eyes tearing up now that I know she's safe. Or at least as safe as anyone connected to me is at the moment. "Please."

And for once, she stops herself, maybe hearing something in my voice that she can't turn away from. "Fine." She sighs. "Since you seem to care so much about my dating life these days, you should know I've replaced Simon with a better model anyway."

"That's great." I laugh quietly, looking back to Alec in time to see him circling a finger in the air. Reminding me to wrap it up before my time is up. "Listen, I have to go, but I'll call you soon, okay?"

"Fine," she repeats, a little more unhappily this time. "Just tell me you're safe before you go please. I spend my days imagining you drugged up on the street or something."

"No drugs, Yvie." I smile. "I'm in fighting form. I can promise you that."

"If you say so," she mutters with disbelief. "Love you, kid."

"Love you."

I pull the phone away from my ear and look down to end the call as an ache pulses through my heart. A rare one because I didn't normally allow myself to get so emotional outside of my ritual time each day. It leaves me staring at the phone as an immense missing for the people I left behind pierces me so deeply that for a moment, it's hard to breathe.

"Helen." I look up to Alec and see the understanding in his eyes before he sweeps his gaze left then right. "We need to get out of here, regroup and talk about it back at the house."

"Yeah." I nod, forcing myself to focus on the present again and turning to walk back to the parking lot by his side while asking the most important thing. "Do you think she's safe?"

"I think," Alec starts slowly. "That if whoever he is were going to use her to get to you… it would have happened as soon as you disappeared."

"Then what the fuck is he doing?" I snap out, knowing how harsh it sounds and not doing anything to curb it. Everything I thought we knew completely turned on its head, all this time possibly wasted looking for the wrong man.

"Playing the long game." Alec spares me a look with the words as we make it to the parking lot. "Which does nothing but raise the stakes even more."

Chapter Thirteen

Alec shuts the door behind us and I look over my shoulder to keep him in my line of sight. A little bit wary after everything we discovered this morning. Even of him.

At least until we clear a few things up.

He had said himself that he didn't trust anyone, so why shouldn't I do the same?

I watch him shrug his jacket off while walking past me to the kitchen and opt to leave mine on, keeping my knife close as I trail behind him.

"So tell me something," I call out, unable to keep the bite out of my voice. Plus, he'll think it's weird if I'm suddenly nice to him anyway.

"What?" He looks back at me as we make our way through the training area and into the kitchen.

"In all the years you worked with Novikov at Bainbridge"—narrowing my eyes at him, I cock a brow in question—"daddy dearest never mentioned his bestie?"

He comes to a sudden stop and I watch as his body slowly tenses before he turns around carefully, staring back at me through narrowed eyes that are pure ice.

"What are you implying, Helen?"

By the sound of his voice, he's very much aware of what exactly it is that I'm implying.

"Just asking." I lean my head to the side while looking up at him, making sure to keep my hands loose and ready if this goes south, but fuck, I really hope it doesn't, for so many reasons. "Seems weird you would have never heard of him since you are his son, after all."

A beat passes before his strides start to quickly close the space between us. "Really?" he challenges, coming to stand in front of me with nothing but contempt in his gaze. "After I've fucking covered your ass for months. Taught you day after day and dealt with the general bullshit that comes with just being around you. Really?" His voice quiets to a degree that would intimidate most people. "You're going to come at me with this now?"

I don't move an inch, unwilling to back down from my question but unable to help that guilt that stirs with his rebuking as well. Because he's right, I have no real reason to question him, but I'm not wrong either for doing so. He taught me this suspicion that comes so naturally now.

"Right," he scoffs. "If you must know, Novikov wasn't really big on family bonding." The sarcasm hangs so heavy in his voice that I hear a bit more of that slight accent coming out than usual. "He was rarely interested in talking about anything besides how I was ranking at Bainbridge."

We stare at each other silently then, neither of us breaking our gaze as I try to gauge whether he's being real with me. Never wavering in our standoff for so long that I'm pretty sure I'm about to go cross-eyed right before I finally see the smallest bit of hurt hiding in the depths of his brown ones. And it's that hurt that finally sways me.

I look up to the ceiling and heave a breath, hating that circumstances have pushed us this far, before dropping my eyes back to him with the obvious question. "Why then"—my face scrunches up with the same confusion I'm still trying to understand when it comes to him—"why stay if he was such a dick?"

His lips part, and for a second, I think he's about to answer me before he shakes his head, turning around and effectively ending the conversation without giving me an answer.

He walks straight to the kitchen table and opens his laptop that sits among all of our now possibly useless research, leaning over to quickly type away at the keyboard as he asks. "What last name did he give you?"

I don't need him to clarify whose name he's asking for. "Taylor."

His expression hardens with concentration, typing even faster as I walk to the kitchen table and watch his eyes flick around the screen so fast that I don't even know how he's processing anything.

He flips the computer around a second after I make it there. "Is this him?"

My eyes drop to the screen as I take in the picture of the man I met months ago in Yvie's office. Same salt-and-pepper hair. Same nice suit. Same disarming smile. "Yeah." I swallow, scanning the website page and seeing it names him as CEO of an import-export company named Taylor International, based out of the UK and Canada. "Yeah, that's him."

"You were right."

"What?" I tear my eyes away from the screen in time to see Alec's fists clench as he stares at the table.

"You were right." He brings his gaze up to meet mine. "I met him once, Helen. Only once."

It takes me a few tries to get out. "When?"

"He was in Novikov's office one day when I went in to report to him about a mission I had just finished." He shakes his head. "When I asked who he was, Novikov brushed it off, saying he was just a contact from the defense department checking up on the progress of something."

"And you're sure it's him?"

"Without a doubt." He nods, pulling his phone from his back pocket. "No accent when he said hello though."

I snort. "Even more suspicious."

"Agreed," he mutters, looking down at his phone as he types in a number and I bite my tongue in a rare show of restraint. Trying to mend a little bit after our recent stumble by giving him some trust here. Finally shrugging off my jacket and dropping it onto the back of the kitchen chair in front of me as he brings the phone to his ear, lifting his head to give me a look that lets me know he's got *my* number. I give him a small shrug, unwilling to apologize for being what he's made me to some degree and I don't think he'd really want me to anyway.

I'm in the midst of pulling out the chair in front of me when he speaks into the phone and almost makes me topple the thing right over. "Serena."

Barf.

I'm going to barf at his intimate tone and dramatically mimic doing so as I sit in the chair, just to make sure he doesn't miss it. But he just gives me a smile loaded with retribution and continues speaking in such rapid Czech that I can't keep up. Although the words I pick up here and there leave little to the imagination and have me fervently wishing I could plug my ears. That is until I hear him say the name "Simon Taylor." After that, I curb my dramatics slightly so that I can pay better attention and thankfully he switches over to English not too long after.

"Full report, Serena." He pulls the laptop back around to face him and looks down at it. "I want anything you can dig up. Financials, background, associates, business, all of it. He's CEO of a company, so the surface-level stuff won't be difficult, but I want to know what he's hiding. Don't use Bainbridge, it needs to be off books but go deep."

He smirks openly at whatever *Serena* says in response to his last words before muttering a quick goodbye to her in Czech and hanging up.

"That was mean," I grumble, petulance in full force.

"Serena's one of the best computer hackers I've ever met." He shrugs, walking away from the table and into the kitchen. "Even better than me. She's who you want on this."

"So where does this leave us?" I turn in my chair, watching him walk to the fridge and reach up to open the cabinet above it that I'm sure we don't keep shit in before pulling out something that has my mouth popping open.

"Drinking."

He holds the bottle in the air along with two shot glasses while walking back to the table, leaving my still speechless ass staring at it like it's a fucking life preserver.

Alec didn't allow alcohol in the house. It had been one of his first ground rules, and no matter how many times I tried to sneak it in the grocery cart, he just snuck it right back out before checkout. Every damn time. Saying how it isn't good for training. It poisons your body. It clouds the mind. It— "You fucking liar!"

He shrugs, placing the bottle on the table between us and taking the seat across from me. "I thought it was best at the time."

"Oh?" I scoff, full of attitude again. "You thought it was best?"

"Yep." He doesn't even bother sparing me a glance as he twists the top off the half-empty vodka bottle and pours us both a shot. "Do I really need to elaborate?"

The protests die in my throat at the not-so-subtle dig because he's right. Fucking asshole fucker, but still... he's right. I was a fucking mess when we got here and probably would have tried to drown it all out nightly if he hadn't put me literally in prohibition.

So I reach out to take the shot glass sitting on the table without another word, lifting it to my lips and taking a small sip that has me fighting the urge to cough. Fucking vodka, should've known that would be his drink of choice. Bet there is no good tequila hiding in the back of that cupboard.

"So." He throws back his shot, slamming the glass back down onto the table with clear frustration before grasping his hands behind his head. "Throw all of this out the window."

"Throw what out?"

"This…" He nods down at the table and the multitude of papers we have scattered around it. "Throw it all out and think this through from square one with me."

I take another small sip while coming to terms with what he's asking, staring down at all the work that's now meaningless. "Disregard everything we thought we knew."

I look back up as he nods and reaches out to grab the bottle, filling his glass again. "Exactly."

And I do as he asks, putting every assumption based on what we thought we knew out of my mind and thinking it through from the very start. Quickly arriving at the first and most obvious question based on the sequence of events. "Did he die?"

"That is the question," he agrees quietly, eyes narrowed at some point over my shoulder.

"You and Coop saw him that night, right?" I question carefully. "Coop was sure he'd shot him."

Alec jerks his eyes back to me, face distant and carefully blank as he gives me a single nod. "We both were until all this shit went down."

"Then maybe…" I trail off, finishing off my shot, needing the burn to take the edge off my anger at the whole fucking world over how wrong we might have been here. "Maybe it feels like we've been chasing the invisible man because we have. Maybe he really did die that night and it's been Simon pulling the strings ever since."

"The man behind the curtain."

"Right." I nod, reaching out for the bottle to refill my own glass. "But to what end? That's what I don't get. He could have easily killed me in LA."

"Not without drawing a shit ton of attention." He shakes his head. "Not with your life there, much easier to just let you disappear trying to hide and then do it quietly later."

My hand stills at his insinuation, glass held midair as unease fills me. "So you're saying we're playing into his hand?"

He looks down at the table, twisting his shot glass around for a long moment before countering. "I'm saying this might not be about you at all." His eyes come back to mine as he continues. "Novikov's grudge against you might or might not extend to Simon... but if what Yakov said is true and my father and Simon really were like brothers, then—"

"Coop," I breathe, not needing him to continue the trail of thought because I'm already there and it's even more terrifying than if it were me. "Then it would've been about Coop to him. Maybe me too by association or cause, but really it would've been about Coop and—"

"Me." He nods, cutting me off quietly.

We stare at each other for another beat before I throw back my shot, coughing up a loud "Fuck!" as I drop my glass back down on the table with only slightly less force than he did before. "Fuck," I breathe again. "What do we do now?"

"Now," he starts slowly, lifting his glass into the air. "We wait for Serena to get back to me with information on him and"—the glass in the air dips toward me in cheers—"we drink because this has been one fucked-up day and I think you might finally be able to take it without offing yourself."

"Thanks." I snort, watching him down the shot. "I wouldn't have offed myself, just so you know, too much left to do."

"Right." The disbelief is clear in his voice as he reaches for the bottle, pouring us both another round.

"Seriously," I argue. "I need to know what happened to him. To fix it all somehow."

"Helen." He sets the bottle down softly, pausing for a second before bringing his eyes back to mine. "You know what happened to him."

I could argue. He could argue back. We could go back and forth for an hour over it, with neither of us backing down from our point of view, but the truth is the game has changed. We don't really know what Simon wants here if it is him, and it gives me more hope than I've had in months, regardless of anything he might say.

"Right," I toss out with a bratty smirk, feeling a little nostalgic from the alcohol. "Of course."

Fucker is giving me vodka, so I guess I'll say the words even if we both know I don't mean them.

He snarks a laugh, letting me know I got that one right before throwing back another shot, setting the glass down on the table and looking down at it while rolling his shoulders. Kind of like I do when I'm stressed sometimes. The sense of weirdness that comes from yet another reminder of what exactly we are to each other has me looking down at my own glass. Brows dropping as I wonder whether we're ever actually going to talk about the elephant in the room. But even if I did bring it up, what the hell am I supposed to do then? Invite him for Christmas next year when we're hopefully not on the run?

Not that I'd mind him being there, I guess. It's actually going to be a little weird whenever all this comes to an end and we aren't tied at the hip anymore. But I don't know how to get to that... other place with him either, and we both are clearly awkward as fuck and suck at it. Not to mention his bullshit "I don't trust anyone" thing.

I'm so lost in thought about our weird unacknowledged-sibling relationship that I jolt in my seat when he speaks, looking up at him as he brings up the very person responsible for it. "Tell me about our—" He stops, clearing his throat. "Tell me about Nadia, what you remember about her."

And I'm so freaking shocked by the fact he actually brought her up, plus a little buzzed after all my time here in prohibition Antarctica, that I just stare at him like he's grown two heads.

"Please," he tacks on formally.

The icy tone of his voice jolts me again, this time into actually opening my mouth.

"Oh, uh—" Bet that tone is covering up about as much awkwardness as I'm now sinking in like quicksand, or snow, more accurately. "Well, I was really young when she—"

"Just…" He exhales a tight breath. "Anything you remember will do."

Right. Okay.

"Okay." I nod, speaking the word out loud this time. Anything I can remember, except for the part where she was having an affair with my husband's dad. At least I'm guessing he doesn't want to hear the breakdown of that story. "Okay."

Think happy thoughts, El. Happy thoughts.

I look down at the table, bringing my shot glass to my lips and taking a sip while wading to the very back of my memories. "She, uh…" I try to start awkwardly again, biting my lip and setting the shot glass back down. Continuing to stare at it so I can make it through this, both the trip down memory lane and sharing something so precious and intimate that I had guarded it even from myself at times.

The things I'd nearly let myself block out until that day.

"She used to bake," I finally start, not looking at him and pretending I'm only talking to myself to make it easier. "All the time. I remember no matter what time of day it was, the house always smelled like cinnamon and sugar. A steady supply of baked goods ready to be snagged off the counter come rain or shine." I'm surprised when my lips lift, letting myself remember what she looked like when she laughed. What it was like when she played with me. How happy I was once. "She had this… irresistible quality to her. No matter how mad I was because she'd scolded me about something, she'd always come and tickle me after and it was hard to stay angry. She was just so free in those moments with me that it was impossible to not join in."

I swallow down the sudden tightness in my throat, admitting something that maybe only he would ever get. "She wasn't perfect by any means. She fucked up in some of the worst ways and had a shit ton of faults, don't get me wrong." A breath snags in my throat and it takes me a second to blow it out. "But even with everything she did, I didn't realize till recently that I never for one moment of my life doubted that she loved me." I make myself look up to meet his gaze. *Needing* someone else, someone tied to me but set apart in a way to understand. All of a sudden finding it as necessary to know these memories have been heard as my next breath. "So that's what I try to remember about her now."

I give him a sad smile. "I used to be so angry at her, Alec. At both of them really, but now… well, now I'm still not sure how exactly I feel about who she was as a person. But right now I'm trying to remember that there were as many smiles and fairy tales for every mistake she may have made. That we're all imperfect and maybe that's okay. That maybe expecting her to have been was a childish wish that damns her for things I'll never really understand." I sigh, bringing the glass to my lips and taking a sip before finishing. "That maybe it's okay to be a little like her because, at the end of the day, she was my mom and she loved me. And the truth is part of me will always love her." I can see a world of thoughts peeking through the icy expression on his face, so I give him more. "After all this, you know, she did what she had to do to survive for a long time and with what I've gone through these past months... I can respect that."

Our eyes don't leave each other for a moment before he looks down, spinning the shot glass rapidly as he clears his throat. "Thank you, Eleanor."

And it's the use of my real name that lets me know how much he really means it.

"Don't mention it." I swallow down the rest of the tightness in my throat, brows dropping and trying to work up the nerve to ask him the question I've been wanting to for months, but he did bring her up, so... "Can you translate something for me?" He looks back up to me and I rush out. "I've tried to listen for the word since we've been here but haven't heard it—"

"Of course." He jerks a nod. "What is it?"

"Minushka," I tell him softly. "She used to call me that, I think."

His expression tenses before he answers. "It means uh, my soul, or precious darling loosely." His face goes blank again the next second. "It's a term of endearment found in some parts here."

I blink rapidly and nod, the kernel of warmth inside of me from his words a fierce thing. Equally as fierce as the conflict I now see playing out in his eyes. The one he's trying to hide with that blank, cold look. "I'm sorry." The words pop out of my mouth before I can censor them. "That you never got to know her. Tha-that she left you."

A beat passes between us before he shrugs. "It doesn't matter." He reaches out to snag the bottle off the table, giving it a shake in the air. "Feel like getting a little drunk with me?" I snort a laugh and he lifts his brows. "Pretty sure we've earned it."

"Sounds good to me." I watch him bypass his shot glass, taking a swig right from the bottle and that act alone lets me know just how much it really does matter to him. "When should we hear back from your booty call?"

He passes me the bottle. "Hopefully by the time we make it through this."

Chapter Fourteen

"You know the part I don't get?"

Alec slides the vodka bottle back to me across the workout mats. We had abandoned the kitchen table about an hour ago, opting to sit on the mats in the living room and watch the sun go down through the back windows. "What's that?"

I pick up the bottle that's substantially lighter now than when we began while turning my head toward him. "The boat."

He groans, letting himself fall back onto the mats. "Not this again."

"It's the one part that's never made sense."

He reaches up, laying his forearm over his eyes as if that's going to block me out somehow. "Yes, it does."

"No, it doesn't," I insist. "Why blow up a boat if there was no sure bet I'd be there?"

"Worth the risk if you want to kill someone badly enough."

"Maybe." I take a sip of the vodka and turn his words over slowly, the alcohol reducing my reasoning capabilities to a sluggish pace. Apparently, I'm something of a lightweight after six months of sobriety. "Maybe if you're Novikov." Looking back out the window and seeing the last of the light is just starting to leave the sky, I add. "But not Simon, he's the man behind the curtain, right?"

A beat passes before he replies. "Tell me more."

I turn back to look at him and find he's pulled his arm up to rest on his forehead and is looking at me with real consideration in his eyes for once.

Holy shit. The fucker thought I might actually be onto something.

"Simon." Work brain, work. "He's been all about staying under the radar, reasons currently unknown, right?"

"Right," Alec agrees, holding a finger in the air as he continues. "Although it's probable that's just because he's incredibly successful and has managed to stay that way by staying under the radar."

"Right," I echo, giving him a nod. "But no matter the reason, it doesn't really follow that he would then blow up a boat on the off chance I'd be there, right?" His silence has me plowing forward. "Plus, like you said, this could not even be about me to him, it could be about the people who killed Novikov."

"Or." He pauses for a second, eyes narrowing on my face. "It could be about making the people who killed Novikov pay in a different way."

The meaning of his words hits me and would probably scare me a little more if not for the amount of vodka in my system, right now though, it actually has me fighting a laugh. The irony is just too much. No matter which way I turn or which guy I'm with, I'm always in someone's crosshairs.

It's a miracle I've survived this long really.

Alec's eyes narrow even further on me. "Are you smiling?"

"No," I answer quickly, biting my cheek to correct the inappropriate reaction before going straight for distraction. "Even if that is the case though, it still doesn't make sense that he would blow me up *and* kill Coop. Plus Jace never did anything to him, that's a lot of collateral for a very slight chance of a payoff."

He looks up to the ceiling, silent for so long that I look back to the window, thinking he's dismissing me yet again before he sighs. "You're right." My head whips around to find his eyes are back on me as he continues. "It doesn't make sense." I can't help the victorious grin that pulls at my lips, that is, until he holds up that finger again. "Yet."

"Come on!" The protest bursts from me, but he just answers with a short laugh. "Seriously! I can't win with you."

"Helen, as far as I know, the only enemies your boyfriend had were locked up tight, so unless he was into some other shady shit." He shrugs against the mats. "Simon or Novikov are the only ones that make sense."

I narrow my eyes at him, trying to find any possible error in his argument, but quickly come up empty. Jace didn't have enemies outside of the Morrisons. Everyone loved him. I still love him. His argument is as valid as mine and that right there pisses me off to no end.

So I settle for tipping my nose up at him. "I don't like you."

He laughs shortly again. "I don't care."

"Right back at you." I roll my eyes and turn back to the window, still not sure whether we both mean what we say or not or whether maybe it's both. Trust and mistrust, avoidance and confrontation. Understanding that's never acknowledged.

A fucking shit show, but… a shit show that has grown on me.

"No change with him, right?"

I shake my head while bringing the bottle to my lips immediately. "Nope."

He brings his arm down to tap my leg and I pass him the bottle without looking away from the window. Leaving me completely caught off guard when he speaks a moment later.

"Do you think you'll go back to him?" His voice holds a detached kind of curiosity and I know he doesn't mean to hurt me by asking it, but still…

The question cuts deep.

"If he ever wakes up?" He continues. "Do you think you would go back to him?"

I suck in a breath, setting my eyes on the trees and counting each leaf that I can barely make out while tossing back. "What's with the twenty questions today?"

"Just interested." He pauses and I can feel his eyes picking apart my body language, taking my temperature to make sure I'm okay in his own weird way. "This will all be over one day and then what happens for you?"

Coop.

A tiny shack of a house on the beach in Cahuita.

After I make sure Jace is okay somehow, that he has a chance at a happy life. The one that I get the sense I robbed him of day after day. After I somehow fix that and find Coop… I want to go back to that little slice of paradise and figure out where we go from there.

That day in Landing Point and every one since cuts through everything, leaving me knowing that none of the rest of it matters without the other half I chose. Not the present or the past, certainly not the future. I'd just been too selfishly focused on my own damage all along to realize it until his blood was on the floor before me.

So I tell him the truth, or at least the part I know he'll accept, laying another brick in the foundation that's building between us.

"No," I whisper, that one quiet word filling the air of the room until it's almost as if it's pressing back down against my skin. "No, I won't go back to him in that way."

A beat passes before he questions, this time with open curiosity. "Really?"

"Really."

"Why?"

I press my lips together for a moment, counting those leaves to ground myself before answering. "You know"—I blow out a slow breath with the start of my explanation—"at least once a week, I have to fight the urge to just get on a plane back to Alabama so I can just lie with him. Try to coax him back to consciousness. To just be with him. He…" My voice catches, but I try to cover it up by pulling my knees up and wrapping my arms around them. "He's innate to me in some ways, always will be, because he put me back together and became my safe place. And the truth is, he'd probably take me back." I blink hard, turning my head to look at him while dropping my cheek onto a knee. "Because he's so much fucking better

142

than any of us, than me, and I'll always love him for that." He lifts his brows at my statement and I shrug. "Coop knew it."

"Bet he loved that." He smirks.

My lips twitch up the tiniest bit because... "Yeah."

"Still not seeing the problem here."

"Alec," I snort softly. "Imagine spending the rest of your life *knowing* you weren't someone's first choice. That's..." Even the thought of doing it to him has me closing my eyes for a second, blocking out that horrible path before opening them and finding his gaze again. "It would be unspeakably cruel, I think, to do that to him. Even if he disagreed. I'd be sentencing him to a life of always having the choice I'd made that wasn't him right there between us. A daily reminder that would eat at us until maybe there was nothing left. So no." I shake my head against the skin and bone it's lying on. "No, I made my choice and I won't go back on that."

His eyes narrow on mine for a moment before his lips lift a hint. "I'm almost impressed, Helen."

"Don't be," I scoff. "There's nothing impressive about being the breaking point between two men. Not really. It's nothing but a tragedy that's romanticized so that we can justify the fallout."

Alway so *dramatic, El. It's exhausting honestly.*

"Now I'm really impressed." He laughs.

"I should have left them both there in Landing Point and never looked back, but I just..." I trail off.

"You loved them," he finishes and I nod once as he lifts up onto his forearms, giving me his full attention. "Stop being so hard on yourself. Sure, it was an, uh, interesting situation, but a triangle involves more than one and a lot of what happened wasn't even on the three of you. It was just… fate, I suppose."

"Fuck fate," I let loose a sigh before narrowing my own eyes at him. "Since we're apparently sharing. You going to tell me why you kept working for Novikov even after it was clear he wasn't looking to join the family for Thanksgiving?" I cock a brow at him. "Or is this the part of the night where we move on to braiding each other's hair?"

"Oh, Helen," he drones, dropping his head back on the mats. "I only play with Serena's hair." I roll my eyes and he looks down at me in time to catch it. "I will tell you this because I think you need to hear it though."

"What's that?"

"You search the shadows long enough and they start to play games with you." His chest rises with a breath as he looks up to the ceiling and away from me. "Tricking you into playing a game you can't win before you even realize you're participating."

I run my eyes over him, looking for any kind of clue as to what might be going on in his head, but he's got that detached expression firmly in place. Making me think I probably already know the answer when I ask him softly. "Is that what happened to you?"

A beat passes before he answers quietly. "Something like that."

His words have a trickle of fear running down my spine and needing to know more so that maybe I can change how it ends for me. "Did you find what you were looking for?"

"Yes."

"Did you like it?"

"My life has never allowed me the freedom to like or dislike something, it's always been about whether something was useful. If it kept me alive for another day." He looks back at me finally. "And being a monster like him has proved useful."

My brows drop at his declaration, eyes darting between his as I start to truly *understand* him for the first time, I think. And as I search his blank gaze, I remember how he always finishes the shit food I make. Every day. No matter how burned or undercooked it is, like he really can't let it go to waste. I remember where he spent his formative years and how he probably went with Novikov in search of some kind of biological connection. Only to find one to the most brutal part of himself that had been born out of necessity to survive before he'd even been able to form proper thoughts. And that dormant anger for my mother burns bright with the reminder of how she left him to what I'm guessing were some harsh fucking conditions in that orphanage before she fled to a country thousands of miles away.

Why? Why would she leave him when she loved me? Yvie had said once that I was possibly the only person my mother truly cared for, so why wouldn't that hold true for Alec too?

I clamp down on the anger though, reminding myself that we all sometimes make decisions others don't understand for reasons only known to us. That I don't know where she was at when she made that choice, just like my own family doesn't know why I'm doing what I am right now. That I had left someone so incredibly precious to me at the worst possible moment too.

So I blow out a deep breath, hoping the anger will go with it, and lift my head off my knees to respond. "Alec—"

The sound of a phone ringing pierces the air, cutting me off and leaving us staring at each other for a beat as anticipation threads the space between us.

Alec looks away and sits up quickly, grabbing the phone from where it lies on the ground beside him and swiping his finger across it as he brings it to his ear. "Cau."

The sound of a female voice on the other end of the phone speaking rapidly has me locking my arms around my legs, fighting the urge to grab the phone right out of his hands. Needing to know if this is finally the break we've been waiting for to a physical degree that has my shoulders tightening up to the point of pain. Alec darts his eyes back to mine and the flash of hesitation in them has me immediately mouthing the question of, "What?" but he just shakes his head. I listen to him volley phrases in hurried Czech over the next couple of minutes, picking up words of agreement along with a couple questions about a time and identities, I think. My nerves are just about raw because I can't translate the sentences completely when he's talking so fast and I'm about to demand he switches to English when he pulls the phone away from his ear with a muttered goodbye, looking down as he hangs up.

"What did she say?"

But he doesn't look up, just keeps staring at the phone blankly and my heart immediately starts to race in my chest.

"Alec!" I demand. "What did she say?"

He raises his head slowly, meeting my eyes with a single blink. "He's in Montreal, was seen as recently as two days ago going into his main office there."

"And?" I press, waving my hand in the air for him to hurry it up.

"It appears Yakov was telling the truth and his ghost story is very much real." His eyes drop for a second as he clears his throat before raising them back to mine. "Serena said that on the surface, Simon's business seemed completely legit, but there were several things that set off alarm bells with her. One of the most important being that he did grow up in the same area as Novikov before going back to London for university. That right there is suspicious enough," he scoffs. "But when you add to it that she could find no reason, business or otherwise, for him to be in California at any time, it shot him right up there to prime suspect material. Then there was the little issue that Serena couldn't get a deeper look into the inner workings of his business because"—his jaw moves for a second, letting me know how truly pissed off he must be before he spits out—"he has a fucking firewall she and I designed for *Bainbridge* hardwired into all of his systems. We made the fucking thing damn near impenetrable and there's only one way he got his hands on that."

"Oh, shit."

"Pretty much." He nods. "We'll have to find one of the computers linked to the system and hardwire into it if we want a closer look at things, but she was able to pull everyone who works for him and is running them now. At least the ones who are in public records." His eyes dip from mine again before he continues. "Last thing, about a year and a half ago, he had four graves dug on his property and one had a coffin buried in it immediately."

"Your father?" I guess.

"That's what I'm thinking." An irritated noise bursts from him. "Never thought to ask Bainbridge what happened to the body."

He's still staring at the ground though, refusing to bring his eyes back to mine and I know in my bones that whatever he's holding out on is either my worst fear… or my salvation.

Simon had dug four graves, one for his oldest friend, possibly even his brother and the other three for his enemies. One had been filled in.

"Alec," I call softly, worried that if I speak the words too loudly, I might jinx it or something. "Alec, were any of the other graves filled in?"

He finally lifts his eyes back to mine and after a moment in which I swear I can feel the whole world holding its breath right along with me, he shakes his head. "Not that she could find."

I'm immediately fighting the urge to sob in relief as true hope fills me for the first time in months. "But that could—"

"Helen…"

"Don't 'Helen' me!" I snap. "It could mean he's alive, Alec."

"It could mean a lot of things," he cautions, eyes and voice going hard. "Don't get your hopes up only to put yourself through a trauma you've already survived once."

The urge to argue back is strong, but I want to get on with this and find out what our next move is too bad to get into it with him right now. So I swallow the words even though they go down like sandpaper and shoot back. "What's our next step then?"

A sound leaves him that's part laugh and part disbelief before he answers. "Serena booked us on a flight to Montreal under one of the fake identities we picked up in Berlin. We leave in an hour." His eyes meet mine again as I jump up, wobbling just a bit when my head goes dizzy from the vodka and he shakes his. "Go pack your bags."

Normally I would take the time to toss back some witty retort, letting him know that I very much do not appreciate him ordering me around. But the hope that has each beat of my heart feeling lighter, along with our earlier conversation, has my brows dropping as an urge fills me. Making me pause as I look down at him and think about how he probably wasn't hugged a whole lot for those first years of his life.

Fuck it. We could unacknowledge all day long, but I'm too happy right now to deny myself anything. Plus, we've already established I have bigger balls than him.

I kneel down before I can second-guess it and enfold him in a tight hug, surprising the shit out of him and kind of myself too. His body immediately goes still under my arms at the contact and he makes no move to return the gesture as I whisper. "If there's anything I've learned lately, it's that sometimes it's okay to be a monster for the people you love. Maybe that makes us unforgivable, but Alec"—I squeeze my arms tighter around his neck—"I'm really glad you're my monster."

I end the hug as suddenly as it started then, popping back up onto my feet and having to fight the urge to giggle because his eyes are slightly wider than usual with a clearly awkward expression on his face. So I throw him a bone to ease his obvious discomfort, quickly falling back into our routine.

"Still don't like you," I toss out, not waiting for his response before starting to practically skip from the room. It takes longer than usual and I'm already in the hallway by the time his shout reaches me, the sound of it immediately making my lips twitch.

"Still don't care!"

Chapter Fifteen

I'm a bundle of nerves by the time the plane touches down in Canada. All that hope dissolved into nothing but a sick kind of pit in my stomach that had me slowly sipping my water for the second half of the flight while my mind went down every dark rabbit hole possible. Because I'd realized something somewhere over the Atlantic, locked in that hunk of metal hurtling through the air with no escape. I'd realized that if Coop really was alive like I'd willed him to be all this time. What had he gone through these past six months?

And for a split second, I'd hoped that he was dead instead.

Because I'd heard the kind of screams Sergei made when Alec had barely started with him. I couldn't imagine what would be left of Coop after six months at Simon's hands. It was sickening, and truth be told, I'd never considered it too much before. I'd been so locked into this tunnel vision of needing him to be alive that I hadn't considered *what* being alive meant for him. I'd had to fight hard against the urge to run to the bathroom and vomit for a good hour after I had. After that, I'd swallowed the excess saliva filling my mouth with each new method of torture that popped into my mind and washed it down with water. All of it leaving the baggy white hoodie I'd dressed in damp by the time the plane landed.

Even with all those horrible imaginings circling around my head though, I still can't help the quiet chant in my head for him to be alive as my feet cross over from the plane and onto Canadian soil. Trying to convince myself that all is not lost. That I can find him, fix Jace, and that everyone will be okay if they just fucking listen to me and stay alive.

"You good?" Alec's voice interrupts next to me.

"Mhmm," I drag out, shooting him an irritated look as we walk up the long tunnel leading into the airport. "Tell me something. Do you get a power trip from babying me or something?"

"Aren't you in a pissy mood today." He snorts, rolling his eyes at me. "Care to share with the team?"

"It's my birthday in three days," I mutter, latching on to the first thing that pops into my head because I don't want him to know how sick I am over the mere thought of torture. Fucker would probably bench me.

"And?" he drones. "What? Did you expect me to plan a party?"

"No," I snap. "But his birthday was New Year's Eve. Mine is in three days."

"Helen…" He sighs.

"We never got to spend our birthdays together." I grip the straps of the backpack I'm wearing as we enter the terminal, pulling it up higher on my back. "I'm sick of us missing out on all these things." He comes to a stop, tilting his head at me and I drop my eyes to the ground, finishing quietly. "Christmases, New Year's, birthdays, a normal life together. All of it."

A beat passes before he snarks. "So happy to see you took my advice to not get your hopes up."

I lift my eyes back to his with a smirk and shrug one shoulder. "Well, you give shit advice, so…"

He shakes his head, turning to walk down the long terminal and I stay by his side as we follow the signs pointing to customs. "Well here's some more shit advice." He lowers his voice and I watch his eyes scan the people surrounding us. "We've been through a few customs checkpoints before, so you know the drill. Stay calm, act casual, show them your docs and we'll be good."

"I know."

"Name?"

I roll my eyes at him. "Morgan Mitchell. I also know my birth date, address, and place of fake occupation. Stop worrying."

He shoots me an are-you-serious look and I barely keep from wincing because he is kind of right. I am a bit of a magnet, but we've been through this rodeo a few times now and never once ran into a snag getting by. It would actually shock me if it wasn't for the fact that I know Alec only uses the best forgers. I'd met the one in Berlin and despite the fact he'd answered the door in only his underwear, holding a gaming controller, he'd been compulsive when it came to his work. So I have no doubts that Morgan Mitchell will reenter her home country today and return to her life as a barista after a getaway to Poland.

Alec, well, I always make sure to put a few people between me and him. He passes off the casual vibe pretty well, but one can never be too careful with guilt by association and all that. Plus, I certainly have more confidence in him escaping the authorities than in me. Fuck, Yvie and the guys probably have alerts set up if anyone actually runs my prints and I'll be whisked back to LA before I can even utter a word of protest.

And true to form, an hour later, when I pass through customs without a problem, I make sure to toss a wink back at Alec that has his eyes icing over with irritation. The whole thing would make me giggle if it weren't for that sick pit in my stomach that churns as I step onto the escalator, heading down to baggage claim without waiting for him to catch up. It'll probably piss him off, but the dark imaginings of the rabbit hole are still lingering in the back of my head, right there and more than ready to launch me from impulsive to reckless.

Maybe it's time for a little recklessness though. The shadows have certainly gained us nothing, so maybe it's time for a little more of a direct approach. Definitely something worth mulling over once we get to our new safe house. No matter how much Alec might detest the idea.

I scan the signs lit up above the baggage carousels, quickly spotting the one with Warsaw on it and heading in that direction. Already scoping out the people around the carousel I'm heading to and missing the knife I had to leave at the house in Gliwice. Couldn't really pack that for travel though, so I have to take solace in the fact that I'll get a new one here which immediately makes me question the kind of person I've become. That is, until I remind myself of something, I've become a survivor. So fuck anyone who doesn't approve of that, even my subconscious.

I'm three steps away from the carousel when a voice calls out behind me. "Eleanor Delacroix?"

My feet stop of their own accord, the shock of hearing my real name, along with the years of automatic reaction taking over and rendering me useless. Mind blanking out for precious seconds until it fires back with the knowledge that I'm already screwed because I've given myself away. If I keep walking now, it will just look suspicious. Better to try and play off whatever this is before resorting to extreme measures.

Maybe it's just someone I know. Someone who recognizes me.

So I turn my head, looking over my shoulder to locate the source of the voice while bracing myself to run if need be. Quickly finding a guy a little younger than me dressed in a nice suit and smiling harmlessly at me while holding a pristinely wrapped present in his hands. The gift is covered in bright-red paper with a large bow on top, its burst of color standing out sharply in the airport and drawing the eyes of people passing by.

What the actual fuck?

My brows drop in suspicion as he takes a step closer and questions again. "Are you Eleanor Delacroix? Your hair is different than the picture, so—"

"Who's asking?" I demand. Fuck not drawing attention, right now I'd happily take a police officer approaching because this is weird as shit. I'd expected a hit man or customs officer. Not future business leaders of America here.

And where the hell is Alec?

His smile widens. "My boss asked me to drop this off to you." He holds the present out to me with a shrug. "Been waiting a couple hours just to make sure I didn't miss you. He said it was important and this internship factors into my grade."

Don't take that present, El. Walk the fuck away while you still can.

My brows pull down sharply as I stare at the large, perfectly square box, already knowing the answer to the question I'm about to ask but needing to hear it. "Who's your boss?"

"Simon Taylor." The guy's face turns a little annoyed. "Listen, can you please just take it?"

And I am going to take it. Even knowing that I shouldn't and that there is, without a doubt, nothing good in there. Despite the fact I know that I should be running to find Alec and let him know that Simon somehow knows we're here.

But he sent a present, not a death squad which means he wants to play. It's an invitation. One that I'm incapable of turning down because I've always liked to play too, and he's holding the only person who's ever beaten me at my own game. The first one to truly checkmate me. Jace hadn't been the same. He won by letting me win, but Coop... there is no denying that he won my heart by beating me, and then he won it again by giving me his and mine back again.

So I reach out for the present slowly, keeping my breathing steady even as my heart hammers away and sweat starts to break out on my skin. Fingers closing around the box with a featherlight touch and lifting it from his hands, my shoulders giving a painful twitch as if even my body wants no part of the gift.

"Helen!"

The shout echoes through baggage claim, but I can't tear my eyes away from the gift. Considering what a box of that size could hold, each horrible idea that springs to mind is quickly followed by an even worse one. My breathing, that I've so far managed to keep even, halts completely as I realize that a human head could fit in there.

"What the fuck are you doing?" Alec snags my arm hard enough to jolt me into looking up at him, my eyes quickly landing on the bruise forming on his left cheekbone. "Who was that?"

I inhale sharply, kick-starting my lungs again before asking. "What happened to you?"

"Move." He pushes at my arm until I start walking toward the exit. "I got jumped when I stopped to take a piss. Fucking should've known not to leave you alone."

"What about our bags?"

"Fuck the bags." He flicks his eyes to me. "You have all the important shit in your backpack, right?"

Coop's shirt is in it and I have my leather jacket on, everything else can be replaced.

I nod as the sliding glass doors open, engulfing me in what feels like yet another icy tundra. "He knows we're here."

"No shit!" Alec shouts, the outburst making me stop at what I would've thought before now was an impossibility from him. He lets go of my arm quickly, looking down at the present I'm still holding and lowering his voice again. "Open it now because that thing is not coming one step further with us."

I look down at the present, bringing my finger up and running it along the edge of the box top with the pretty bow wrapped around it. Not ready to open it in the slightest, but there's no way I'm leaving it here either. So I close my fingers around the lid and flip it, hearing it clatter softly onto the concrete beside me as my eyes land on the note inside.

Eleanor,

I found out you were coming to town through a friend that I stumbled into and knew I had to send you a welcoming gift. I hope this read proves as illuminating for you as it did for me. So much so that I've hardly been able to put it down for the past six months.

Here's hoping that Montreal proves memorable.

Looking forward to seeing you again,

Simon.

Every sound fades away as my eyes run over the note, flicking between it and what it's lying on top of every few words. So much so that when I make it to the end, I have to restart back at the beginning, barely taking in a word of it until I read it again.

And again.

That featherlight touch I've maintained on the box quickly becomes a thing of the past as my fingers tighten around it with each beat of my heart. The sick pit in my stomach and the nerves, even that little trickle of fear that's still there over what I found myself capable of when it comes to the people I love… all of it completely dissolves as my arms start to shake. Not from fear though.

It's rage.

Pure, undiluted rage that grows and grows with each of his words until it drowns out everything in me and gives free rein to a reckless kind of monster. The kind that is capable of damn near anything to win the game. That is free of fear of self and has a scream of nothing but raw, volatile, feminine fury working its way up my throat.

Even with everything that had happened, I hadn't felt it yet.

I hadn't let myself go completely.

But now, with his taunt lying right there on top of the thing that brought *us* back together again. On top of Coop's journal. I decide I'll bother with finding the goodness in my soul again when this is done because right now, I would happily cut him up the way Alec did to Sergei in that basement.

The way he's probably done to Coop over these past six months.

Using everything precious about us while he did it.

I'm not sure I meant it when Alec and I had set out all those months ago, but now I know. Simon Taylor will burn for this.

A hand grips my chin and jerks my head to the side so fast that I fight it for a moment before realizing it's Alec.

"Rein it in," he orders, eyes moving over my face in quick assessment. "Pull yourself together and rein it in."

"Fuck you," I snarl, ripping my chin from his grip. "With your bullshit about hiding and pushing the feelings away." Reaching into the box, I grab the journal, letting everything else fall to the ground as I hold it up. "Look at where it's gotten us!"

His hand shoots up to close around my arm, hard enough to bruise. "Where I've gotten us is alive. Now bitch all you want, but you agreed with each and every plan."

"Because I thought you knew better!"

"I do!" he shouts. "Just like I know that doing this out here in the open where he probably already has eyes on us is the worst possible scenario right now." A beat passes between us and I barely resist the urge to do him physical harm from the sheer frustration his words spark before he continues more quietly. "Now, we need to get the fuck out of here and regroup. As much as you may want to, you cannot march down to his office and slit his throat. You'd send yourself to jail and what a shame that would be if Coop is alive."

A vicious kind of laugh leaves me and I open my mouth to tell him what an idiot he is for still questioning it at this point, but he digs his fingers into my arm. "He's. Playing. With. You." Each harsh word is spoken through clenched teeth, his mouth barely opening until he continues. "You know he is because you and I share the same fucked-up need to win the game. I've seen it when we train, just like you have. Now, are you going to let him win?"

His words finally pierce some of the rage I'm drowning in, pulling me up just enough to gasp a breath and give him a single shake of my head.

I should've known better. That whatever he would choose to put in that box would be chosen because it would inflict the maximum amount of pain.

"Good." He nods. "Now get in the taxi."

He pushes me toward the line of cars and I walk to the nearest one quickly while dragging the icy air into my lungs. Trying to regain enough control to think clearly but still not letting go of that rage. That, I'm not about to let go anywhere. I'm going to channel it into everything I need to be to end this once and for all. Grabbing the handle on the door, I jerk it open and slide in, barely sparing the driver a glance as I scoot over to make room for Alec to follow me.

Leave it to him to make sure the guy isn't a hit man.

And if he is, I'd be happy to deal with it right now.

Alec shuts the door and the driver asks in a friendly voice. "Where to?"

"Just drive," he tells him curtly. "I'll have a destination for you soon."

That snags my attention enough to look at him. "What's wrong with the previous plan?" No need to use the word safe house in front of the cabby.

"The friend," he starts quietly, looking out the window. "That he said he stumbled into in the note. I'm guessing it was Serena."

My lips part in surprise and I lower my own voice. "Willingly?"

"Or not." He looks back at me and I can see his own anger tightening up every one of the muscles in his face. "If they have access to that firewall, they could have access to other things we designed to backtrack any kind of ping off their network. I should have foreseen it. Either way." His shoulders jerk up with what I think is supposed to be a shrug. "We have to assume they got info on us from her and adjust."

"That's fine." I look down at the journal I'm clutching in my lap as an impulsive kind of plan starts to unfurl in the back of my mind. "I already know where we're going."

"Care to share?" He scoffs.

"We're changing the game." I raise my eyes back to him with a smirk that I really hope is as terrifying as some of his are before calling out to the driver, "Take us to the Ritz-Carlton."

Chapter Sixteen

I drop my backpack on the green velvet couch sitting in front of the fireplace in the cream-colored room and walk to the window, pushing back the curtains and letting in all the wintery sunlight Montreal has to offer. Along with giving anyone watching an unobstructed view of me standing in the main living room of the royal suite. The check-in girl had given me a dubious look when I'd requested the over-the-top three-bedroom penthouse, but after one look at Alec she'd seemed happy enough to play along. And when the card number I'd given her went through, her attitude had quickly changed to overly accommodating, at least where he was concerned. I give the surrounding buildings a cursory glance before smirking and flipping my middle finger to the window for good measure, turning around to find Alec's wide eyes on me with a look of sheer panic for the first time since I met him.

"I was wrong to give you the vodka," he states seriously. "You do still want to die."

I roll my eyes at him and head to the phone sitting on the little table beside the couch, scanning the list of numbers on it before picking it up while muttering. "No, I don't."

"Then, please." A short, humorless laugh leaves him as I press five for room service. "Explain this."

I hold up one finger to him as the other line picks up and a polite voice greets me. "Room service. How can I help you today?"

"Hi," I answer brightly. "Eleanor Delacroix here. Can I have an order of waffles with strawberries and whipped cream?"

"Of course, ma'am. Anything else?"

"Yeah." My lips twitch. "I'll also have two orders of bacon and eggs. One side of freshly cut fruit with yogurt and granola. And let's throw in a couple croissants too. Do you think you can melt some chocolate to go with those?"

"Uh—" the operator stutters for a second before quickly agreeing. "Of course."

"Perfect," I chirp, continuing without pause. "Coffee is a must of course. Some freshly squeezed orange juice never goes amiss. Oh and what the hell, might as well add a bottle of Dom with a caviar spread too. Thanks so much!"

I drop the phone into the cradle without waiting for her to respond and look up to see Alec staring at me as if I really have lost my damn mind, which I most definitely have. But right now, there's a reason in the madness, or at least I hope there is or else we're all screwed.

"Simon wouldn't touch me in LA," I start, not needing him to voice the question again. "He wouldn't touch me in LA because, like we suspect, he's the man behind the curtain and the last thing he wants is my death somehow linked to him. I was too public there, splashy, surrounded by people that would care if something happened."

A flicker of understanding sparks in his eyes, but he shakes his head. "It's still a bullshit plan. He could poison you. Have someone mug you and make it look like an accident. A million things could happen—"

"*I don't care!*" My shout echoes between us in the suite, the same words I told him all those months ago and the air between us instantly turns hostile.

"Cooper would care." His quiet words hit me like a well-placed strike and I barely stop myself from flinching. "Cooper didn't save you only for you to jump off the deep end now and get yourself killed."

"You don't understand." I shake my head. "I'm done playing hide-and-seek in the dark."

"I understand," he emphasizes. "I will not help you get yourself killed. I won't help you if you continue on this idiotic path, either you listen and we play this smart or you can count me out."

"Fine." I shrug, voice empty and clinging to that reckless rage, trying to not feel the words. "Then I'll finish it without you. Like I said, I don't care."

His eyes narrow on mine, nostrils flaring as the first truly furious expression I've ever seen on him slowly overtakes his face. "Did it ever occur to you that *I care*?!" The sudden shout is even louder than mine, his anger exploding into the space with a boom as he continues. "That I didn't just agree to kill my father and babysit your ass for the past six months for fun? That I didn't teach you everything I know so that you could go off by yourself on some suicide mission?" He takes another step toward me, pausing with his mouth open before he continues hesitantly. "Did you ever think about what it would do to me if my little sister *died*?"

My chest tightens up instantly, breath stuttering to a panicked halt as the elephant in the room is finally acknowledged because it somehow means everything to me to finally be claimed as his family. That the only other part of my mother in this world wants me, even as messed up as I may be, but that only makes it worse too, because I can't do what he wants. Not this time.

So I have to make him understand.

"I can feel him."

"What?"

"I can feel him," I repeat the words quietly and yet somehow they sound louder than any of our shouts. "I know it sounds crazy." Something like a laugh escapes my lips at actually hearing how insane the words are, but he has to understand why I'm acting the way I am. Why I'm willing to risk everything. "It's why I never believed you when you said he was dead because I can—" I choke on the air for a second as the words that I've hidden, never spoken out loud, slowly unearth themselves from the depths of my soul. Each one making their way up through my heart with a pang before tumbling out of my lips.

"I can fucking feel him out there, Alec. It's like this steady pull at my cells. At first, I think I was too shocked to realize it, but in the weeks that followed, I started to feel it. First it was right there in the center of my chest." I bring a hand up to rest on the spot, the ache in it growing the more

I speak and making my face pinch up. "Right there in the heart or soul, whatever the hell you want to call it. And then," I scoff softly. "Then when I shut that down so I could still fucking function when I needed to, it settled into my skin. This thrum of knowledge that he's still out there, but now..." My voice breaks, throat tightening up so quickly that it damn near closes off. As if even my body doesn't want to acknowledge the dread that's been slowly circling around at the back of my mind the past couple weeks.

"It's like I can feel him slipping away a little more each day," I rasp out finally.

His face tightens up at my words. "Helen..."

"No." I shake my head, pushing forward because he has to understand. "I gave up on him, Alec. When I left Cahuita before it was..." The memory of it has me pressing my lips together, trying to hold in the cry fighting to escape as I tear my heart open. Letting him see the shame that's driving me to what he thinks is insanity. "If you make me stop or slow down. If you make me play it safe and something happens to him. If he dies and I didn't do everything possible in my power to find him, then it won't matter whether I'm alive or dead." I give him a helpless shrug, blinking rapidly to rid my eyes of the tears filling them, but they only fall onto my cheeks. "Not really. At that point, you might as well let me go because I'd hate myself forever. Even if I was here physically, I'd be nothing but a shell filled with guilt and hate because whatever part anyone else may have played, I failed him before."

I bring both my hands up to swipe at the tears on my cheeks and take a step toward him. "And if he dies now, right before I could have found him. If Jace slips away. It means all of this…" An empty laugh leaves me and I look away, gasping a few quick breaths. "All the pain we went through was for nothing," I finally tell him, looking back and swallowing another cry. "It makes everything that happened between us nothing more than a fucking tragedy if we don't all make it through this somehow. So please, help me." My voice cracks with each word as I plead softly. "Don't ask me to give up on him when he's never once given up on me."

His eyes drill into mine for a moment, unknowable thoughts flying behind them before he sucks in a sharp breath and breaks our gaze to look out the window. "You know, he used to say the same thing."

"What?" My head pulls back with the hushed word because he can't mean…

"That he could feel you." He shakes his head, looking back at me. "When he spent that year tracking you down, I'd help him whenever I could and he'd always spout off about how close you were." A short sound of disbelief leaves him as he begins to imitate Coop. "'She feels closer today. We're on the right track' or 'We're looking in the wrong place. I know it. Can barely feel her now.'"

His words have my breath turning choppy, heart that I've just torn open expanding in my chest to the point of agony at hearing someone else's memories of him. At the validation that what I feel doesn't exist only in my head. It's blinding relief followed immediately by a gutting of this new knowledge of us, of him. This precious knowledge of our love that I took for granted before.

"I've never been one to believe in love or soul mates," Alec continues quietly. "Or I don't even fucking know what it is between you two. I don't know if you can classify something like that with words. But you two…" His head tips to the side, eyes moving over my face as he looks down at me. "You two make me believe in something greater than everything we know and understand. So if you can really feel him out there, Helen. If you feel him slipping. Then I'll help you with your flashy bullshit plan." My lips twitch even as fresh tears fall onto my cheeks and he nods once, holding up a finger. "With one condition."

"What's that?" I quip raspily.

His eyes narrow on mine with a no-bullshit look. "You're going to start carrying a gun if we go into any serious situations because I'd prefer if you didn't die before we finish this." My stomach flips with unease at his request and it's on the tip of my tongue to argue as he presses. "Deal, little sister?"

Well, fuck. How the hell am I supposed to say no to that? The fucker cares. I can see it in the backs of his eyes. How nervous he is about going along with this but he's doing it for me. So maybe this is the least I can do for him.

"Deal." I give him with another twitch of my lips. "Although we're seriously lacking in the weapons department right now, so it's not like I'm giving you much there."

He slides his backpack off, lowering it to the ground next to one of the cream damask chairs sitting adjacent to the couch and leaning down to unzip it.

"That…" he states like it's a deadly sin or something while pulling out his laptop. "Is something that I plan to fix immediately." I watch him walk to the small butler's bar behind the chairs, working up the nerve to tell him the next part of my plan as he slides onto one of the barstools. "Along with finding out every possible thing we can about Simon that's not hiding behind his firewall." He sets the laptop on the bar, quickly opening it and pressing the button to power it up. "Doesn't really matter how many alarms we trip now that you're determined to shove our presence in his face."

"Yeah." I clear my throat nervously as he begins to type away on the keyboard, darting my eyes to the ground and scuffing the toe of my Converse on the marble floor. "So about that presence."

"What's that?"

"Nothing major." I force a small laugh, trying to keep it light and casual. "It just might be about to grow by, like… say, three people?"

The sound of typing comes to a halt and you could hear a pin drop in the beat that passes before his sharp voice fills the air. "Why?"

"Well." I look up finally to find his eyes narrowed on me to the point that they look like slits. "You know that card number I gave the receptionist?" He doesn't bother with a nod when I pause, leaving me to continue filling him in on part two as I walk to the area behind the bar.

Suddenly really in need of a drink with what I know is coming. "It's my personal one, and it's the first time it's been used in six months, so I'm guessing alerts just went out all around and they're already on their way to the airport." I glance at the clock on the wall before giving him a small smile. "Brace yourself, I'd guess we're at about six hours and counting."

Chapter Seventeen

Knock, knock, knock.

Right on time, I close Coop's journal with a sigh and set it down on the glass table in front of me, resigning myself to end the torture session I've been putting myself through by leafing through the pages and reading random bits. Having my heart torn out over and over again as I grasp at the memories of him and our time together.

I look at Alec, who's lying back on the couch, typing away at his computer as if I'm not here like he has been ever since his temper tantrum about the second part of my plan. Totally giving me the silent treatment. Big brother did not approve of my idea even if he had eventually admitted its merit, only the slightest bit of merit though, his words, not mine. What I'm beginning to suspect is that he's secretly nervous about how it will change our dynamics. How it might alter the rhythm we've found over the past months and the very new aspect of acknowledgment of caring in it.

Not that the fucker would ever admit it.

Knock, knock, knock.

When he doesn't look up or stop typing, I roll my eyes, tossing out sarcastically. "Don't worry, I'll get it."

Standing from my chair, I make sure to walk the long way out of the main room around the glass table in the center of the space so that I can give his outstretched leg a well-placed kick. Looking down to see that he doesn't even falter in his typing, which has me rolling my eyes again and letting out a quiet snort. I shake my head at his antics while walking to the hallway that leads to the main door, my stomach suddenly filling with nerves at the prospect of finally seeing them.

Which girl will they be facing though, El? The old you or the new and improved?

And that right there is the problem.

I've longed for them these past months, in those moments when I wake up to stare at the dusk feeling so fucking lost. But the thing is... those moments when I've been so terribly alone, with only the exception being someone who antagonizes me and beats me down to make me stronger. Those moments when I'd been truly alone for the first time in my life. When there's been nothing but me and the darkness trying to pull me under, in a way, that's when I really unearthed what I'm made of. In those moments I discovered how to keep pushing, keep getting up, to keep fighting against that darkness because of the people who need me.

In the midst of all that survival, I've found someone there underneath the party girl, beyond the searcher, a contradiction to the girl who'd been so scared she blocked out the connections the world offered her at times. Someone deeper with more metal to them.

And the truth is... I think I kind of love that girl now too. The one who spouts villain monologues and gets a little stabby when you hurt the people she loves. She scares me sometimes, sure, but I'm also grateful to have discovered her because she's stronger than I ever thought I could be.

So I really hope they love her too.

"You would. You're a survivor."

I trip on the air as Jace's voice rings through my head, the memory of when he spoke those words to me on the boat bottoming out my heart and making me gasp for a breath.

"You good?" Alec's sardonic voice calls from the living space.

"Yeah!" I shake my head, trying to dislodge the weird sense of déjà vu as I answer him. "Fine. Just tripped over my own feet."

I can hear his snort all the way in the hallway and it makes me want to roll my eyes at him yet again, but I'm quickly distracted when the sound of voices on the other side of the door a few feet away starts to filter through.

"I just fucking heard her. Two more seconds and I'm going to bust that door down."

"Patience, Macallan. We'll get a key card if need be."

"Do you think he actually could kick it in? I might pay for the damages just to see if he can."

A wide smile breaks free on my face, nerves momentarily forgotten at the familiar bickering and making me take those last two steps, closing my hand around the doorknob and pulling it open quickly.

"So." I cock a brow at their stunned faces. "What's this I hear about kicking a door down?" Letting my hand drop from the knob, I give the solid door a knock. "Because I definitely want to get in on that bet."

It's almost comical, the way all of their mouths part slightly in shock and their eyes move over me assessingly, doing a simultaneous double take of my dyed-dark-brown hair. Mac is in his typical white V-neck but in sweater form this time because of the cold weather, paired with fitted chinos and some kind of fancy boot. Kai in a baggy pair of black skinny jeans and a large Seether tee peeking out from under a gray zip-up hoodie that has me doing my own double take as I eye it, trying to figure out if he stole it from my closet. And Stef, looking more disheveled than I've ever seen him in jeans and a wrinkled brown Henley, concentrating on me so hard it's as if he thinks I'm about to disappear.

"I mean, it's no party, but…" I jerk a nod over my shoulder, unable to wipe the smile from my face even if I wanted to. "Feel like coming in?"

My vision is filled with bronze skin and black clothing the next instant as Kai launches himself at me, snagging me around my middle and lifting me into the air as he squeezes the breath out of me.

"Fucking hell, Els," he curses roughly, the turpentine smell clinging to him even after a six-hour flight and filling my nose. "Don't ever do that again."

"I'm sorry." I wrap my arms around his neck and squeeze him as hard as I can back. "I know it's been hell for you guys."

"I'm more worried about you." He sets me down and leans back to look at me with those whiskey eyes.

"Yeah." My lips lift with a small smile, trying to ease his concern before breaking our gaze to look past him at Stef and Mac. "There's a lot of catching up to do."

Stef steps over the threshold into the suite as Kai moves back, making room in the tiny hallway for him to walk that last step toward me. His eyes never leave mine as he raises a hand up to cup my face. "You scared me, cara."

I nod against his hand, leaning into the familiar touch and rasping a quiet. "I know." Blinking hard as my eyes try to start filling with tears again and see him do the same before he clears his throat, dipping his head to press a soft kiss to the top of my head. I close my eyes, allowing myself one blissful moment to bask in the familiar comfort I've deprived myself of for months before opening them when his hand drops from my face.

Stef steps back then, moving further down the hallway while clearing his throat a couple more times and leaving me staring at my twin. The one who hasn't moved or taken one step toward me. Who's looking at me like he's as pissed as grateful to see me again, chest rising and falling rapidly as his hands clench and unclench. The sense of betrayal pouring off him in a way that lets me know I'm going to have to be the one to take the first step to mend this.

I give him a shrug, unable to stop the couple tears that escape. "Guess I was a little longer than a couple weeks, huh?"

An angry breath leaves him, those sapphire eyes looking up to the ceiling for a second before dropping back to mine. "You're such a fucking bitch."

And at those words, I can't help the laugh that escapes me, hiding the cry underneath as I close the distance between us in two quick steps and jump into his arms. Soothing a little bit of that hurt between us and clinging to him as tightly as he does me.

"You don't have to forgive me this time," I whisper. "At least not yet."

"Shut the fuck up," he orders, carrying me into the suite. "But I don't want to hear shit when your arm is hurting like a bitch from the LoJack I'm having implanted tonight."

Another burst of laughter leaves me with a few more tears, but I don't try to brush these ones away because, for the first time in months, they're not all pain. "Deal," I agree as he drops me to the ground, not letting go completely and looking down at me with some of that hurt betrayal still. It has me repeating his words from when I came back to LA, trying to give him something to ease it. "I fucking missed you, Macallan."

"Missed you too, Els." He sighs, sliding an arm around my neck and jostling me playfully as we turn to walk down the hallway. "You have some serious explain—"

"Who the fuck are you?"

Kai's outburst has my eyes widening with the realization that he and Stef must have found Alec.

"Shit," I mutter, walking more quickly and grabbing Mac's hand as his arm falls from my shoulder to pull him along. "Shit. Shit. Shit."

I definitely needed to be there for these introductions.

"Oh." Alec's smirking face comes into view as I round the corner to find him still laid out on the couch, eyes on his computer screen. "Just someone with a mutual interest in the girl you just flew to another country to find."

Mac stops so abruptly that I'm jerked back, falling into his shoulder before righting myself and glancing back to find him looking like he's seen a ghost. I quickly dart my eyes to Stef and Kai, finding they too, have gone completely still, all eyes on Alec as he types away like he doesn't have a care in the world.

Apparently they remember him.

"I know you," Mac growls out behind me. "Your voice."

"Aren't you a smart one," Alec retorts dryly. "But we're all on the same side here. Right, Helen?"

The guys' eyes snap to me and I cringe before giving them what I'm hoping is a believable smile. "Yep."

"Speaking of..." Alec shuts his laptop and stands all in one move, casting his eyes over the guys before casually dismissing them and looking at me. "I just had a contact pull through for weapons."

"Really?" I perk up. "That's good."

"Weapons?" Stef and Kai's voices echo over each other with equal shock.

"Um—" I look over at them to find their eyes still on Alec, animosity clear on their faces before the man in question speaks again, drawing my attention back to him.

"I'm going to go pick them up." He lifts his brows at me. "You good to go over what I found out about Simon when I get back?" A smirk lifts the edges of his lips. "Figure that gives you time to play catch-up with the three musketeers."

"Uh, yep, yeah," I stutter, the air in the room turning drenched with a level of violent testosterone I hadn't had to navigate for half a year now. Still, priorities of life first. "You going to be okay going alone?"

"Don't worry about me." He sets the laptop on the table and walks around to ruffle my hair with a show of affection he's most definitely never displayed before. Letting me know I'm definitely fucking right about him being a little worried about our newfound dynamics changing. "Don't you know by now I'm invulnerable, little sister?"

My mouth pops open at the outing of our relationship, but he only snarks a laugh while walking from the room, leaving me to deal with the shitstorm he's stirred up. So much for easing the three other people I consider family down the fucked-up catch-up path of my life. I can feel their eyes burning into my skin with questions as the door closes, making me finally look back at them with another cringe.

"So yeah," I drawl awkwardly. "The fucker is my brother." A weary sigh leaves me and I collapse into the nearest chair. "And honestly, that's not even the worst of it."

Fractured

Chapter Eighteen

"Are you sure he hasn't been holding you hostage?"

"For the millionth time, Mac," I groan. "No."

"This isn't some form of Stockholm syndrome?" he presses, face so freakishly serious from where he sits next to me on the couch that I can't help but laugh despite the heavy story I just told them all.

"No."

"More importantly"—Stef shoots him a pointed look from where he sits in one of the chairs across from us—"to summarize, the Simon who was dating Yvie is now out for revenge against you and your, uh…" His face twists as if he's tasted something bitter before he continues, "Alec, and is most likely holding Cooper somewhere?"

"Pretty much." I shrug. "We'll find out what Alec was able to dig up when he gets back."

"With the weapons," Kai confirms, looking at me like I've been taken by body snatchers.

"Yep." I cock a brow at him teasingly. "Be careful pissing me off these days, Kaison. My hand to hand is pretty solid, but where I really excel is the knives."

Stef narrows his eyes on me. "*Cara.*"

"Stefano." I drag out his name playfully and see his lips lift just a bit.

"You don't like violence," he finishes.

"Well." I clear my throat and look down to pull one of the decorative pillows on the couch into my lap, a bit of that unease rising again. "You know, after everything went down, I wasn't doing too good for a while. Wasn't much use to anyone, including myself." I start to play with the tassels on the pillow, going straight down the edge one right after another while unearthing those memories. "I was scattered. A mess. Would sleep for what felt like days sometimes and then not go to sleep for way too long at other times when we had leads. It wasn't any kind of healthy." Blowing out a breath, I look up to find all of them eyeing me intently. "But when Alec started the training, it helped. Gave me a reason to get up every day, to stay on a schedule. It gave me somewhere to channel…" I trail off, trying to find the right word to describe the thing sitting at the bottom of my stomach that's only dulled by action, constantly waiting for another spark to ignite it again. "All of it."

Their silence has my stomach flipping with nerves again and I shoot them a small smile. "So, I still don't like guns. Don't get me wrong. And yeah, any kind of blood still makes my stomach turn. Unless it's Alec's because he's pissed me off." A quiet laugh leaves me and I see Mac's lips lift beside me. "I just felt so fucking helpless after everything went down. I wanted to make someone pay," I admit, looking down to the pillow again. "But I had no way of doing that. So when the training started, I realized it gave me something back. Some measure of control. Some kind of—"

"Power." Stef's quiet word fills the air and I look up at him to see the dawning realization in his eyes. "It gave you power."

A long pause passes before I nod. "Yes." His words force my own acknowledgment of it. "Yeah, it did, and I needed it. Not only against others, but I needed that power over myself too."

"Well," he answers, that secret smile playing over his face. "The only part of that I'm mad about is that we weren't there to teach you to kick ass ourselves."

A huge breath of relief leaves me at his words, at the automatic acceptance of whatever person I've become that I find in their answering smiles. Even as the truth of it rings through me too. That I might have never become this person had I been with them. They would have coddled me, all of them, even Mac in his own way, and I might have just crawled under the covers and never come out if I hadn't had someone pushing me. Sometimes it takes being without anything familiar, anyone familiar, to force you to grow past what you've ever expected from yourself.

To find out the extent of what you can survive.

"Have you told Yvie?" Stef continues. "Asked her about him?"

"No." I give him a sharp shake of my head. "And I have no intention of telling her. I don't want any of this touching her, Stef."

"So why'd you finally let us know where you were?" Kai pipes up, flicking that tongue ring between his teeth nervously. "Not that I'm complaining."

"Because," I tell him with a smile. "I need you."

"Me?" That shit-eating grin grows on his face. "You rethinking that marriage proposal, Els?"

"No." I snort before looking at Mac beside me. "Actually, I needed you specifically, but I figured we wouldn't leave the other two out."

Because out of all of us, Mac's name holds the most political clout. The Astors are American royalty, their name traces back to the Mayflower itself and they've even had a president or two since then. If something ever happens to him, or anyone he's with, especially in a foreign country… well, that news story would never rest.

"Me?" I can see the confusion in his eyes, but the door to the suite opens before he can get another word out, effectively ending our little round of catch-up. "Don't forget the safe word if you want to escape." He mutters under his breath, making me elbow him, trying to hide a laugh as Alec walks into the room carrying a duffel bag.

A very heavily loaded duffel bag, by the looks of it.

Alec pauses at the sight of us, cold eyes doing a single sweep over everyone before walking in a few more steps and unzipping the duffel. He pulls out almost an exact replica of my KA-BAR folding blade I'd had to leave in Poland and tosses it to me.

"For you."

I snag the blade out of the air, flipping it open to examine the edge while singsonging. "Thank you."

More than happy to have my favorite form of protection again now that I'm about to be flashing my presence around the town that Simon lives in.

"It's perfect." I close the blade and look up to see him nod in return before Kai's loud groan draws both of our gazes.

"This is…" He huffs. "I don't think I'm comfortable with this."

I cock a brow at him. "Why's that?"

"Because," he grumbles sullenly. "You waving blades around makes me feel things that weird me out."

Mac and Stef start to chuckle as my lips twitch and I tease him. "That sounds like a problem for your therapist, Kaison."

"You are my therapist," he complains.

"And on that note," Alec interrupts, giving Kai a hard look before bringing his eyes back to mine. "Want to know what I found out?"

He breaks our gaze without waiting for an answer, heading past the butler's bar and into the dining room that sits to the side of the main living area. I hear him drop the duffel bag onto the wooden table with a thunk and roll my eyes, getting up to follow after as the guys rise to do the same. The tension between everyone is not quite as thick as before, but still without a doubt there and it has my shoulders tightening up as I step into the room. Eyes going straight for the selection of handguns he's lining up on the table and instinctually coming to a stop before I push through it to keep walking.

"Really hope he put the *do not disturb* sign out," Mac whispers. Loudly.

I shoot him a warning look before pulling out a chair and asking. "So what did you find out?"

"It appears..." he starts as I sit down, Mac taking the seat to my immediate left with Stef and Kai rounding out the other end of the table. "That Simon is one of the largest import and export businessmen in Canada and Britain, with some business in America as well and a larger portion than even I expected in Eastern Europe." I lift my brows in question at his words and he continues. "He also has the reputation of being a choirboy. Now in my experience"—he chuckles coldly—"these two things cannot coexist, which means that he without a doubt used his connection to Novikov to hide his sins."

"Which are?"

He pauses in the process of unloading the weapons, bracing his hands on the table and looking at me. "Not even a speeding ticket as far as the public is concerned."

"Any hint of where he could be keeping Coop?"

"No." He shakes his head. "The number of buildings he either owns or rents in Montreal alone would take at least two weeks to work through."

"Then enlighten me," I scoff in frustration. "I can flash my presence to the whole of Montreal to distract him and make sure I'm too public a target for him to take down with these three." I jerk my head toward the guys before asking him. "But how do we narrow it down? How do we find Coop?"

He pauses, looking down at the table and I can see him working it through, jaw moving before he exhales a deep breath. "It's back to the original problem." His eyes come back to mine. "I need access to his network. There are always tells, shipments of certain necessities when you're holding someone, but I'm blind without access."

"And you know this from experience?" Stef's quiet question has my shoulders immediately tightening another notch and they lock up completely as Alec answers plainly.

"Yes."

"Okay," I interrupt, not needing them to go further down *that* path right now. There would be a time and a place for them to work through whatever they dislike about each other, preferably when I'm not around to witness it, but that time is not now. "What do you need to gain access to his network?"

Alec shrugs. "Just need to plug my laptop into one of the computers linked into it and create a back door. I could do it in twenty minutes probably, but all those computers are locked up tight in his central offices and I guarantee we're on the do-not-welcome list there."

I look down, sliding my fingers back and forth against the rich grain of the cherrywood table and thinking through the problem. Those long hours I'd witnessed Yvie work at her own high-powered job come to mind and a light bulb goes off in my head. "You take the work home with you," I mutter to myself before looking up at Alec. "What are the chances he has a home computer linked to the network?"

He pauses, eyes narrowing on mine before conceding. "High."

"I bet it'd be easier to get in there when the house is empty."

"Doubtful." He shakes his head, looking down at the table himself as if he doesn't want to tell me something.

"What, Alec?" I snap.

"When I was looking into him, I saw that he's hosting an endorsement party for a local politician at his house tomorrow night." He brings his eyes back to mine. "It would be an opportunity."

"Party crashing?" Kai laughs. "Now that's more my speed."

"No." Alec shoots him down. "They'd turn us all away at the door. The plan would have to be one part stealth, one part distraction."

"I'm the distraction."

My announcement is followed immediately by a kind of silence that lets me know every single one of them is about to argue against it if I don't prove my point quickly.

"He sent the gift to me, Alec," I press, sucking in a breath at just how uncomfortable what I'm about to say makes me. "The taunt was for me. For some reason, he wants to play… with me."

Alec snorts. "Which is exactly why you won't be walking in there alone and declaring it open season."

"Agreed." Stef nods, totally teaming up against me. Asshole.

"I never said I'd be going alone," I argue back. "I'm not a total idiot, but it'd be a public setting. He wouldn't touch me there and it'd throw him for such a fucking loop that I'm betting you could do whatever you needed to."

"No." Alec gives me a hard shake of his head. "We don't know him, Helen. Don't know everything he's capable of yet."

"Please." The reminder to him leaves me with a soft word. "Remember what I told you, we can't let this chance pass. Plus," I add. "What's all that training been for if I never get to put it to use?"

His face tightens up and I can tell he wants to argue against the idea some more, but he doesn't. He also doesn't confirm he's on board, but when it comes to him, I'll take that silence and run with it.

"Who would you take, *cara*?" Stef asks from the other end of the table, drawing my gaze to his disapproving face.

And I know he wants it to be him, but it's not his name I need to get through the door tomorrow.

So I look at Mac beside me and smirk. "No one ever turns away an Astor, right?"

That troublemaker smile slowly spreads before he answers happily. "That they don't, Els." He raises both hands to the back of his head, leaning back in his chair with a smug look. "That they don't."

Chapter Nineteen

Jace

Somewhere In Between

I open my eyes to see Ellie thrashing in bed, Mac trying to shake her awake as she screams my name before falling back into quietly moaning for Coop.

"What the fuck?!" Mac shouts. "Els, wake up!"

I'm glad to see him with her but really wish he would stop, it just makes it worse and he seems to realize that a second later when she starts to scream at the top of her lungs again. He jerks his hands back from her and I turn in a circle, eyes moving over the room and realizing she's in a new place. The large white silk bed paired with some tiny little couch at the end, along with the fireplace built into one wall, reminds me more of her home in LA. Everything is plush and over the top. The door to the room flies open and I look up to see her other two boys standing there, Stef and Kai, both out of breath.

"*Cara*!" Stef shouts, walking quickly to the bed as Mac warns. "Don't touch her!"

"What?!" Kai steps closer. "Why the fuck not?! Wake her up!"

"I tried!" Mac answers quickly. "It only made it worse."

My eyes go to her brother slowly walking in, drink in hand and face tensed up as he stares at her. "Leave her be," he calls out quietly, barely loud enough to be heard over her cries that have now fallen back into Coop's name. "It'll pass soon."

All of them swing their heads toward him and Stef marches across the floor. "What do you mean, it will pass soon?"

Alec lifts his drink, motioning to her with a rough look. "She does this." He throws the rest of it back before finishing. "Every night."

A long moment passes then, Ellie's boys all exchanging heavy looks, silent communication flowing between them as Alec continues in a weary voice. "I thought you all being here might help." He blows out a deep breath. "But apparently not."

"And you've tried to wake her?" Kai questions sharply.

"Once." Alec scoffs, waving a hand at Mac. "Went about as well as I'm sure it did for ponyboy there."

I look back to the bed then, seeing how Mac is on his knees and looking down at her with absolute terror on his face. "We have to find him," he calls out roughly. "Tomorrow night has to work and we have to find him. She can't, she can't—"

His words end suddenly and Alec answers in a somber voice. "I know."

"This piece-of-shit Simon can't have done this to her," Mac continues. "He can't have left her to a life like this. We have to find Satan and fix this—"

"We will, Macallan," Stef interrupts. "We will."

191

He walks to the bed and sits down on the couch at the end before starting to speak soft words in Italian to her that I can't understand. Alec's and my silent vigil growing by three until her screams pass an hour later and she eventually falls back into a silent sleep. So Coop is alive, that's why the change in location and the additions that she's never allowed before. She must've found some evidence that he's alive and whoever this Simon person is must be responsible. Probably the guy I had seen that day in the apartment. But if that's the case, why can't I find him? Why has he never reached out to me?

Where the hell are you, Coop?

Chapter Twenty

The town car we ordered for the night drives through the wrought-iron gates of Simon's estate right as Alec's voice blasts through my ear.

"Remember the plan, Helen," he orders. "No deviations. No going lone wolf. Got it?"

"Got it." I mutter, giving Mac a shake of my head and reaching up to tap my earbud where it's hidden underneath a draping of curls pulled to one side of my head, making him smirk.

We were all wired up with little earbuds for the evening, thanks to Alec's recent acquisition. Although Mac's is tucked safely away in his jacket for now since he couldn't exactly get away with hiding it under long hair. The plan we'd devised all day yesterday is fairly simple. Mac and I go in the front door via the invitation secured by way of one very painful call to his father while the rest of the guys sneak in the back, posing as members of the catering crew. Then while I'm making a fuss over how good it is to see my aunt's old boyfriend Simon again to everyone within earshot, Alec finds his office and sets up the back door into his network.

What could go wrong, right?

Um. Hate to point this out, El, but your head could be served on a silver platter for the toast tonight instead of the champagne.

True, true.

There is always the possibility that I'm wrong, that Simon will have no problem chopping me into tiny bits regardless of the crowd that will be there tonight. But I have to rely on the facts, and the facts are telling me he cares too much about his public image to sully it in a fit of temper. Novikov had lived in the shadows his whole life, it would mean little to him to lash out and then slink back into them, but Simon is a different animal. He's playing the long game for multiple reasons, one known and the others a mystery.

And so we'll play.

It has that rage pumping all kinds of excitement into my veins because tonight will truly be my first move, and hopefully… it's a brilliant one. Hopefully, it will be the one that leads me to Coop. I just hope it doesn't end up costing me more than I bargained for in the end. That I haven't miscalculated and am about to damn us all.

The car slows as it circles the drive and I peek out the window past Mac, taking in the sprawling gray stone estate with its windows lit up and bright-copper roof glinting in the moonlight. Snow falling thickly through the night sky and making the whole scene look like a whimsical winter wonderland to anyone who doesn't know better. A pretty castle with a ruler hiding behind the mask of a choirboy.

Everyone wears masks. Coop himself had been the first person to teach me that.

So what is Simon's mask hiding?

One man stands by the front door, checking the invitation of the couple who just arrived before us, with another at the base of the stairs leading up to it, opening the car doors of whoever comes next. Waiting to so willingly let in the girl who's planning to burn down the whole fucking kingdom.

Mac lifts a hand, checking the cuff link on his suit as our car pulls up while throwing out nonchalantly. "Ready to show this piece of shit he fucked with the wrong girl?"

He holds out a hand to me when the car comes to a stop, the door opening as my lips twitch and I answer. "Abso-fucking-lutely."

A full-on smile flashes across his face before he steps out of the car, keeping his hand in mine as I slide across the seat and follow. Stomach twisting with sick anticipation as the cold air hits me and he pulls my hand up to tuck it in the crook of his arm. This is the other reason I picked Mac, because I knew some part of my twin would delight in this plan, just like me. Alec would be too hard, Stef would be too protective, Kai would be too worried, but Mac, he would put on a hell of a show with me because he reveled in it.

I give the young valet holding the door open a loaded smile and his eyes widen, dropping briefly to my dress before he snaps them back up with a guilty look. No doubt worried that Mac is about to catch him and get pissed. A quiet laugh leaves me as I look away from him toward the front door, taking that first step up the staircase and finding the doorman there with his mouth slightly parted. Eyes running down the length of me for a second as we make our way to him until Mac clears his throat and he seems to catch himself.

But really, I can't blame them.

I am the distraction, and I've made sure to dress every bit the part.

The dress I ordered for tonight is from a place called Château Nadia and it'd made me laugh out loud at the irony. It was delivered to the hotel today and is something straight out of an old Hollywood glamour movie. Crushed blood-red velvet that wraps around my body with a sweetheart neckline and flows out around my knees in a mermaid cut. Matching red gloves that come up almost to the tops of my arms paired with a white faux-fur shrug draped around my arms. I also spent the majority of the day in the bathroom of my room in the suite, stripping all that brown dye out of my hair and almost getting it back to its normal platinum. Just a touch more bronze in it than usual. The light eye and blood-red lip only add to the look along with the black pumps I ordered. But to put it simply, I've made sure I'm quite literally waving the red flag in front of the bull. Everything about the outfit is bright and bold, designed to grab your attention and not let go.

Appropriate for the occasion in design but not with the attitude I'm wearing it with.

Mac hands our invitation to the doorman and he looks it over before nodding and offering a polite "Thank you, sir." He opens the door and the sounds of classical music, along with light conversation, fill the air. "Enjoy your evening."

I can't help but smirk at the way he's pointedly avoiding looking at me again as Mac nods back before leading us through the doorway. The chilled air changes instantly to an almost oppressive heat and my eyes sweep the space, finding a cream-and-gray marble staircase that leads up the second floor past the foyer we're standing in with a large hallway beside it. A door far at the end of the hall opens, giving me a peek at all of the staff members bustling around in what I'm guessing is the kitchen before it closes again. My gaze drifts to the left then, where one of the largest living spaces I've ever seen sits with a fire roaring in the insanely large fireplace that's built into the wall, seating for those in attendance situated in the first half of the room with classical musicians beyond that and a small area for dancing.

I scan the people within the room quickly before coming up empty and turning my head to check out the space to my right. Finding a slightly smaller dining room with waiters carrying trays of champagne and hors d'oeuvres, circling around people as they chat away. The floor in this room is different, a black-and-white checkerboard marble, while the walls and ceiling are done in the same dark wood as the rest of the house.

And right there, standing at the center of all that bustle, is Simon Taylor himself.

He's dressed almost the same as the day I met him in my aunt's office. The elegant suit just a touch dressier tonight with a steel-colored handkerchief folded perfectly in his pocket and gleaming underneath the chandelier lighting up the room. As if he picked it out to highlight his salt-

and-pepper hair. He laughs at something someone in the small circle he's standing in says before replying with something that makes them laugh harder in turn. His entire disposition is open and I can see how easily he's putting everyone around him at ease, from the body language that mirrors theirs to that disarming smile.

It's the perfect mask, the perfect ruse, and I had fallen for it completely. Blaming any suspicion I'd had on my own recent misadventures in the department of men. It has that rage sparking in my stomach with a twist as I grip Mac's arm tightly to stop my hand from shaking. The fury trying to pull me under and seduce me into doing something impulsive with the reminder of how this man had played everyone in my life and then stolen the person I couldn't live without. It leaves me having to force a few slow breaths through my nose, tamping down the urge to do harm and taming it with the reminder that I'm about to return his audacity with my own.

That I just have to make it through this and I'll be one step closer to Coop.

One step closer to finally fixing all of us. Everything. Somehow.

"There he is," I murmur to Mac under my breath, nodding to where he stands in the dining room.

His eyes follow in that direction before narrowing. "Piece of shit," he mutters in turn.

"We're in place."

Alec's low voice blasts in my ear and I barely catch myself from jumping before nodding to Mac. "Ready?"

One side of his mouth tips up. "Do you really need to ask?"

"No." I laugh under my breath and turn, taking that first step into the dining room.

And I immediately catch how the heads of those near us turn, taking in the new arrivals. Stopping for a second longer than appropriate on the girl dressed in red before I meet their curious gazes with a small, knowing smile of my own. Each new person we pass has the same reaction. The head turn, followed by a second of surprise that gives way to appreciation or envy before they politely look away.

Fucking unforgettable, thank you very much. Goal not only achieved but surpassed.

We're maybe ten feet from Simon when he notices us for the first time, drink held to his lips as he takes a sip of what I'm guessing is a pricey scotch or brandy. His eyes meet mine, flashing with surprise and I let the rage out to play on my lips. Allowing them to twitch up just a bit higher, more toward the vicious side I've learned from Alec these months. I snag a glass of champagne from a passing waiter without taking my eyes off of him, tipping it toward him in salute on our final approach and I swear something like excitement, or maybe respect, fills his eyes for a second. As if he's pleased.

It has my stomach giving a twist as equally vicious as the smirk on my lips, making me swallow hard while stepping right through the small circle of people surrounding him with a giddy. "Simon!"

And then I pull my arm from Mac's, walking those two more steps and immediately wrapping them around the man I want to make pay as surely as the world spins.

I don't stop. I don't falter.

I keep my body loose and my breathing even in a way that Alec should be applauding me for later. Letting the hug last for just the appropriate amount of time before pulling back and looking up at him with the airiest smile I can pull off.

"It's so good to see you!" I practically squeal, holding on to his shoulders, still not paying attention to any of the other people as his eyes narrow almost an imperceptible amount.

Trying to figure out what the fuck I'm playing at, aren't you now, buddy?

Doesn't feel too good, does it?

I nod over my shoulder to Mac, who's doing at least a mildly decent job of looking like he doesn't want to murder him before gushing. "I was up in Banff skiing with my best friend Mac." I giggle. "You know Macallan *Astor*, right? I can't remember, did you meet him when you were in LA?" Letting my hands drop from his shoulders because I physically can't make myself hold them there a second longer, I take a step back and wave one in the air. "Oh, I guess it doesn't matter. You're meeting him now!"

Mac nods in greeting, garnering the eyes of the curious onlookers for a moment and Simon opens his mouth to say something, but I just can't let that happen yet. "Anyway!" I cut him off with another giggle. "We were up in Banff skiing and I told Mac we just had to come down and say hi to you! Especially after that gift you sent me." I wink and cock a brow at him conspiratorially. "It was simply *to die for*, you always did have such good taste."

I finally stop to catch my breath, seeing the tiniest spark of anger in his eyes before he looks around the small circle of people whose curiosity is tangible in the air. Letting my eyes follow his as if I hadn't even noticed them myself, I force another giggle and bring a hand to my chest.

"Oh my gosh!" I gush, leaning so heavily on the airhead act that it makes me inwardly cringe. "Where are my manners?" Dropping the hand from my chest, I hold it out to the man directly to Simon's left. "Eleanor Delacroix," I tell him, loud enough to be heard throughout the increasingly quiet room. "Simon used to date my aunt."

Nail. Hammer. Coffin.

How's it feel, you piece of shit?

"Eleanor," Simon interrupts right when the man opens his mouth to return my greeting. No trace of the accent that had surely made Yvie swoon to be found in his voice. "I wasn't expecting you tonight." I look back to him in time to see that disarming smile fall firmly into place again. "What a pleasant surprise."

"Like I said." I shrug happily. "I just couldn't come to Canada and not see you. All it took was Mac calling his dad to get the invite. Did you know his great-granddaddy was a president?" I whisper loudly, seeing his eyes spark with that anger again. "And your gift was such a nice surprise, I wanted to return the favor!"

Now where the fuck is Coop?

"Well, mission accomplished." He laughs good-naturedly, scanning the group as they immediately join in. Then he pauses, only for a split second, but it's long enough that my lips twitch for real this time as I watch him realize just how fucked he is now. "Let me introduce you to…"

And so the night begins, with me standing in a blood-red gown, making the first move on the black-and-white chessboard under our feet.

Chapter Twenty-One

"I'm going to need longer than I thought."

I bring the champagne glass up to hide my mouth before murmuring. "Why?"

"Because." Alec's voice fills my ear again. "It's not a simple password protection I can crack, there's an underlying firewall and if I try to bypass it, the whole hard drive will corrupt itself. It won't take that much longer. Just tack on an extra ten minutes."

Thirty minutes then. Thirty more minutes and we'll be in the clear.

I can stomach thirty more minutes.

It isn't an option, I have to.

I'd already stomached the introduction to the mayor and city officials, whose names I'd actually made a point of remembering thanks to Alec's near-obsessive training. I had stomached the polite conversation while feeling his eyes come back to me again and again. I had stomached not taking my knife out from where it was tucked into a sheath on my ankle and stabbing him in the heart right then and there. I had listened in while Alec had taken the stairs at the back of the house up to the second floor before finally finding Simon's office up there.

And where I had flagged, Mac had picked up the slack, talking proudly about his family political line when I knew for a fact he couldn't stand the lot of them.

"Nothing suspicious on our end," Stef answers quietly from where he's stationed in the kitchen.

Kai's now keeping watch at the base of the stairs while Stef is playing some kind of waiter and helping out in the kitchen. On any other day, I would have paid good money to see that, but today I just hope all those cooking lessons Nona has given him are helping him pass himself off as part of the crew.

"Thirty more minutes," I repeat out loud and Mac nods in understanding.

Then I can get the fuck out of here before I do something that's actually stupid. Like announcing what a murderous manipulator he is to the whole room. I enjoyed it at first, throwing my presence in his face, but after that initial surge, it faded to nothing more than a dull rage. Each time he'd opened his mouth, speaking in that weirdly blank, accentless tone, saying all the right words to those around him, all my brain did was dredge up images of him doing things to Coop that had my stomach twisting worse by the minute.

"Take a breath," Mac soothes under his breath. "Drink your champagne. Thirty more minutes and we're out of here."

"I know." I manage to lift my lips just a bit and he nods toward the fireplace.

"Doesn't look like he's going anywhere."

"No." I flick my eyes to where Simon is standing, talking to some new guest and have to bite my tongue to hold myself in check. "I fucking hate him." The words leave me in a shallow gasp, quiet and barely audible enough to be heard with all the noise around.

"Els…"

Blinking hard, I look back to Mac. "He's taken everything from me."

"Not everything," he murmurs softly, dipping his head closer to mine. "Only what you're willing to give. You taught me that." The champagne in my hand disappears the next instant as he passes it off to a waiter nearby. "Now come dance with me to keep him guessing."

My lips twitch at his effort. "You hate to dance."

"True." He winds his fingers through mine. "But I love you." I shake my head at him as he leads us over to the small dance floor and tacks on, "Plus, after you get Coop back… Satan will probably never let anyone else dance with you again."

I can't help the open laughter that pours from my mouth as he pulls me in to dance, despite the seriousness of the situation, because he's not too far off probably. Hopefully. He answers with that troublemaker smile, leading us in the dance with maybe not the same grace as Coop but with every bit of the perfect form to make up for it.

"You know, I actually think he didn't hate you too much." I tease him.

A sound of disbelief leaves him. "That wasn't the impression I got."

"I know him better."

His head pulls back, eyes on mine and filled with a question, mouth even opening a bit before he stops himself and shakes his head.

I narrow my eyes at him. "What?"

"Just," he starts right as my spine tingles in warning and I sense that horrible pair of eyes on me again. "Why did you pick him? Instead of Jace?"

The question catches me completely off guard because it's the last thing I would've expected him to ask, considering the circumstances and it sends a sharp pang through both parts of my heart that the men he's asking about live in. But this is Mac asking, so I swallow hard as he turns us, ready to answer when movement over his shoulder by the fireplace catches my eye and I see Simon start to walk from the room. His hand is on the shoulder of another one of the male guests, probably another businessman if I had to guess and he's leading him from the room with both a drink and cigar in hand.

No, no, no, no.

I come to a sudden stop, watching him walk a little ways and willing him to just take him into the dining room. Hell, I'd settle for any room downstairs. Just please don't go near the stairs.

"Els?" Mac questions when I fail to move, but right then, Simon comes to a stop at the entrance of the room and points toward the direction of the staircase.

"Fuck!"

My curse draws looks from a few of the other dancers, but I'm already moving, Mac automatically trailing one step behind.

"Alec," I call softly. "Simon is trying to go upstairs. I don't know if it's to his office or not but we can't risk it. I'm going to distract him."

"No, *cara*," Stef answers firmly. "Find another way."

"Agreed," Kai and Alec chime in simultaneously.

"There is no other way!" I argue under my breath, holding out a hand for Mac to stop and hang back as I approach the entrance to the foyer. "It's either this or any chance we have at finding Coop goes right out the window."

Stop being irrational, El. Come back tomorrow. Sneak in, something else.

No. He could be gone by then, I can feel it.

I dart around the corner just as Mac reaches out a hand to grab me, barely escaping his fingertips as they skim the back of my arm and he comes to a screeching halt, muttering a curse at the same time I call out breathlessly.

"Simon!"

He stops with one foot on the staircase, turning his head slowly to look at me with a flash of irritation. "Eleanor." The businessman beside him gives me an indulgent smile as he continues. "What can I do for you?"

"I'm so sorry to interrupt." I take a step forward, pulling my lips up into a wide smile and digging deep to keep up this bullshit act at this point. Someone better have a fucking Oscar ready for me at the end of this, or better yet, some tequila. My acting skills have surpassed anything I've ever been able to pull off tonight, but then again, I'm playing for a different reason now. "But I have a rather delicate issue I need to discuss with you and my date wants to leave soon." Tilting my head at him, I widen my eyes and blink once to play up the picture of ditzy innocence. "Would it be terribly rude of me to steal you away for a minute?"

The businessman at his side starts to chuckle. "We can discuss this after you help the lady with whatever she needs, Taylor."

Simon pauses for a moment, eyes narrowing the slightest bit even as he returns my smile with one of his own. "Of course." His gaze drifts up the second floor before he looks back to me, holding a hand out to the left of the staircase. "We can talk in the library."

I nod once, ignoring the adrenaline that's starting to pump through my veins, urging me to fucking run and taking a step forward instead. "Perfect."

Alec's voice comes through the bud in my ear as I follow Simon, quickly spouting off with that quiet anger of his. "Macallan, do you have that fucking earbud in?"

"Yes," Mac's tight voice responds. "My eyes are on her now."

I peek over my shoulder to see Mac is now leaning against the wall just inside the foyer, face fuming but still keeping his distance like I ordered.

"Listen to me, Helen," Alec orders. "I just got into the computer. Twenty minutes and we'll have you out of there. I'm going as fast as I can, so you just keep him talking."

Simon comes to a halt at the first door to our left, just past the dining room, and pushes it open before stepping back. Brown eyes meet mine with a clear order in them. If we're going to continue with this little charade, then I'm going to have to be the one to take the first step into the room. I dip my head at him with a look of understanding before forcing myself forward, passing over the threshold and into a room that's entire walls are covered in floor-to-ceiling bookshelves. It reminds me of Coop instantly, making me pause as anger overcomes the sick feeling in my stomach while I take in the space.

There's another fireplace in this room, logs within it roaring with a small leather couch and two oversized chairs in front of it. The floor is covered in a large cream-and-black oriental rug, an oversized desk at the back of the room with a tray on it filled with an assortment of liquor decanters and a crystal ashtray set beside it. One window lies in the back wall behind the desk with curtains draped artfully over it and several lamps are littered throughout the space casting the room in low light.

And as the door behind me closes with a snick, every single cell, breath, and thump of the heart in my body is begging me to turn around and escape.

But I can't. I won't.

The decision resounds in my head even as Simon pauses behind me, lingering there for a moment and leaving me fighting against the urge to lash out at him. Skin crawling as the breath stalls in my lungs and I try to hold it there, knowing Alec would berate me for the tell, but I can't help it. It's the only way I manage to stay perfectly still until he steps around me.

"You impressed me tonight, Eleanor." He starts casually while walking toward the desk.

I take advantage of his back being to me and finally blow out the breath I'm holding in a quiet stream, somehow managing to make myself take a few more steps into the room.

"What?" He looks up at me as he rounds the desk, grabbing one of the decanters to refill his glass. "Nothing to say now that you're not putting on a show?"

"Just waiting for you to elaborate." I shrug, the simple act holding all the fuck-you attitude I've been hiding tonight. "There're so many things about me that are impressive."

"Ha!" The humorless laugh leaves him as he raises the glass to his lips, quickly downing the contents before looking down to set it gently on the desk. "There's the girl I met in LA." He looks up and the sudden change to his face has me halting instantly. "Confident little bitch, just like your mother."

It happens that fast.

Gone is the charming businessman, the choirboy, and in his place is a man looking at me like something he'd like to dissect. I'd use the word predator if I didn't think that would be doing the lion a disservice because even they hunt to eat. And the way he's staring at me, the intensity of it holds me still even though at the core of his gaze, it's nothing but intrigued indifference. No feeling to be found there. Vacant almost. As if he's lost in his own head, idly wondering how many limbs he could pull off of me before I died.

It's a different kind of evil than I've ever seen.

And it has my heart thumping so fucking hard in my chest that I barely manage to get out. "You knew my mother?"

"Oh, yes." A short sound of irritation leaves him as he looks down to fill his drink again. "Nadia was the one thing Nicolai and I never agreed on. A point of contention between us until the end, if you must know." He takes a seat at the chair behind the desk. "I was proved right when she sold him out, but truthfully"—lifting his drink, he swirls the liquid while leaning his head to the side to stare at me—"I'm not sure he really would have killed you for what she did. He may never have said it, may have played hard about it in front of his bastard, but Nadia was always his weak spot and you, my dear, could be her twin." He rights his head suddenly. "But that's neither here nor there now."

"And you?" I swallow hard, reminding myself that this is all about buying time. "Why are you doing this? What's in it for you?"

"You mean besides the fact that they killed the only person in the world I had an attachment to?"

"Yeah." I scoff. "Besides that, because I'm getting the feeling now that might not be enough for you to go to these lengths."

"I need a replacement."

His words have my brows dropping in confusion. "Excuse me?" Because... what?

"Your boys really screwed me over, Eleanor." He sighs tiredly. "Nicolai and I had a good thing. I maintained the public image, he played the brutal overlord at my direction, and both of us benefited immensely."

A horrible kind of realization starts to take hold of me as he raises a hand and continues. "At first, I admit, I was pissed when he was killed. After I figured out who was really behind it, I went to LA and waited. Knowing you would show up and bring them right to me since I assumed they had done it to keep you safe. After that, I went to Landing Point as soon as you were away from prying eyes and put two bullets in Cooper. But then..." A pleased expression comes over his face that's... horrifying, truthfully. "As he was bleeding out there on the floor, I noticed that journal on the couch, picked it up out of curiosity, and that's when I had an epiphany."

"It was always you," I guess quietly. Sickly. "Wasn't it?"

"In charge?" He leans his head to the side, staring at me in that horrible kind of way again. "Mostly. Nicolai branched off a bit after our falling out over Nadia and then Bainbridge, but he still knew who to turn to when he needed to figure his way out of a problem."

The man behind the curtain.

"And now"—I shake my head at him in disbelief—"what? You expect Alec to fall in line?"

"And Cooper." He nods. "Two for the price of one."

I walk to the desk suddenly, steps fueled by the confirmation I've been waiting for before bracing my hands on the desk and lashing out with every bit of that rage pumping through me. "Where is he?"

"No, Eleanor." He smiles blankly, eyes sparking with delight and making my skin start to sweat under the velvet of my dress. "That's not how this game is played."

"What the fuck are you talking about?!" I shout, chest heaving and edging closer to that line of hysteria. Losing a little bit of that edge I'd acquired all these months as reason falls to the wayside.

Because I understand, but at the same time, I don't, not completely, and I need to understand what kind of game he's playing.

He leans back in his chair, eyeing me for a beat before musing. "Cooper has proved uncooperative so far and I'm guessing Alec would prove even more so." His lips lift. "But like I told you, that journal was my moment of epiphany."

"No way," I snort, shaking my head because I know them both and they would never be puppets for anyone, much less this piece of shit. "They won't do it."

"But they will." He laughs quietly. "Because I have you."

His words shock me enough that I pause for a beat before laughing right back in his face. "Try again." I rise up from the desk with a smirk. "You can't lay a fucking hand on me after what I did tonight without having a shitstorm land in your lap."

"Oh, Eleanor," he intones, voice nothing but condescending as he reaches for the cigar in the tray. "You're missing it." He lifts the cigar to his lips, flicking the lighter while bringing it to the end before inhaling sharply and blowing the smoke out at me. "You've damned yourself as much as them."

"What?" I breathe, stomach dropping right down to the floor with dread.

"You love them." He sits back up, moving closer to the desk. "As much as they love you, which means I own you."

My spine locks up at his words, tingling in warning and making the hair on the back of my neck stand up. Quickly clenching my fists to hide how my fingers are starting to shake, the fear finally winning out over the fury in me.

"Get out of there, *cara.*"

Stef's voice whispers through the mic in my ear, but I don't respond. I can't.

"What?" He questions, brows lifting as he takes another puff of his cigar. "Did you not consider that angle?" The taunt is quiet, his eyes moving over my face. "And to think you started the night out so strong. Such a bold move to walk through my front door. Now, though…" The smoke leaves his mouth as his eyes run down my body, making bile immediately surge up my throat. "You seem a little lacking."

"Get the fuck out of there, *cara.*"

"Let's see if you can impress me in some other way." Simon lifts the glass to his lips, taking a sip. "You see, Eleanor, there's so many things you can do to someone that won't even leave a mark."

"Helen, I'm stopping. Get out of there."

"N-No." I shake my head with the stuttered response, both to the voices in my ear and the evil in front of me. Telling him just that. "You're a fucking psychopath."

Keep going, Alec. We're so close.

"You're just now catching on to that?" He tips his drink at me in a mockery of how I saluted him earlier. "Strip."

I don't move. I can't move.

His simple order has me completely frozen because out of all the things I've imagined and feared could happen tonight, it's never been this.

Death, sure.

Killing, maybe.

But not... this.

Not this violation.

Stupid. So, so very stupid of me.

"Let me make something clear," he continues with a little bit of impatience in his voice, as if I'm wasting his time by not getting a move on. "Either you take off that fucking dress, or I go put a bullet in Cooper's head right now, and there's no doctor that can save him from that like before." That small, idle smile spreads slowly on his face. "Don't forget, I have three more graves ready and waiting out back if anyone ever gets too brave."

Mac's pissed-off voice pours through my earbud. "I'm getting her out of there."

"*No*," I order, sucking in a sharp breath and speaking more to the people I love in my ear than anyone in the room with me. "That would be unforgivable."

I would never forgive anyone who got Coop killed. Including myself.

"More unforgivable than letting him die?" His eyes narrow on me with that intrigued look. "Strip. Now."

He has me. He fucking has me and he knows it. It's the checkmate to my queen, literally stripping me of all the power I've found over the past months.

He knows exactly how to get all of us to do what he wants. The only one outside of his grip right now is Alec and that's only because he doesn't know he's right upstairs. He's choosing to play with me tonight in retribution for what I did in coming here and there's no bargaining with someone who is incapable of feeling. He has me because he knows I'd do anything for Coop. Anything to keep him alive.

He got a firsthand account of our love story.

So I clench my jaw, swallowing down all that bile fighting to escape and let my shrug fall to the floor before reaching a shaking hand up to where the zipper rests under my arm. Ignoring the way my stomach is rolling again and again. Ignoring how everything in me is revolting at what I'm doing as I pull the zipper down slowly, trying to keep this part of me, that should only be given willingly for just a little bit longer while still cooperating enough to save the person I chose. Choosing him again as I bring my hands up to my chest quickly, holding the dress there for a moment more as my eyes fill with tears that I fucking hate. So fucking angry at how weak I feel in this moment. Willingly, cooperatively, weak.

And then I lower my hands, letting that blood-red dress I'd worn so boldly to make my first move drop to the floor, feeling something inside of me break. Something that I'd never even known was there before. Something that had been singularly mine, never even Coop's or Jace's. Only mine.

Until this moment, when I broke it by obeying.

The silence that follows is a painful thing.

I watch his eyes run over my body, detached in their perusal of it as he lifts his drink to his lips. Starting at the top and running the length of my shoulders before dropping to my bare breasts. I'm not wearing a bra tonight, figuring it pointless since the dress basically has a built-in corset, but now, as his eyes linger on my nipples that are pebbling in the air... That seems just as much of a gross misjudgment as my oversight of what you could do to a person without ever touching them. His eyes drop lower, gliding over my stomach and my body tenses even more, muscles quaking from how tightly I'm keeping myself in check. And when they land on my seamless nude underwear with a look of mild irritation, I start to fold in on myself. Whispering internal words to myself in an attempt to pull away from what's happening as he drops the cigar into the ashtray, pushing back and standing from the desk. Trying desperately to save some part of me as he slowly walks to me.

Just make it through this. Just make it through this.

Hearing Mac's voice in my head saying he can't take anything I'm not willing to give. But I am, that's the problem. I'm giving this willingly. I'm choosing this. So how am I supposed to reconcile that?

When his hand closes around the underwear at my hip, I close my eyes and try to think of sunrises and stars. Unable to stop the tears leaking onto my cheeks as I'm filled with guilt and shame that crumbles that part of me that's only mine into dust.

"This is how I win the game," he whispers sickeningly, breath fanning against my ear. "And this is how you lose."

And then he yanks violently, ripping the underwear off my skin and sending me tumbling to the ground painfully.

Chapter Twenty-Two

Jace

Somewhere In Between

What the fuck is happening?

One minute I'd been in a memory of me and Ellie playing on the beach in LA and the next, I'd been pulled to some library. Staring in horror as I watch a man expose her to him. A man I've seen before. The one who shot Coop in Tommy's apartment that day. I don't hesitate for a second, already rushing toward him as she crashes to the ground. This has to be the guy they were talking about the night before. The one they think is holding Coop now.

But where the fuck are her boys? Where is that terminator brother of hers?

What the fuck is happening?

I try to push the fucker to the ground on instinct, not about to let him get any closer to her, but my hands pass an inch through him before I remember that I'm not really here. That I can't do anything. That my worst nightmare is about to play out in front of me and all I can do is watch.

It has my hands going to rip at my own hair, true feeling taking over for the first time since I opened my eyes in this place. I quickly change direction and go straight to her side, needing to be able to do *something*.

"Ellie, baby." I kneel, not understanding why the fuck she isn't getting up. Fighting. Trying to run from the room. "You've got to get up. You have to get out of here."

My girl is a fighter. She'd never go down meekly like this. She has a fucking knife strapped to her ankle, for fuck's sake. Why isn't she gutting him like a fish? None of this makes any sense.

"Ellie!" I shout, reaching out to try and touch her face. Willing her to hear me harder than I ever have as the man starts to walk toward her. "Eleanor, open your eyes. Please."

The man kneels down next to her and I watch her squeeze her eyes more tightly shut. Watch as he looks down at the knife on her ankle and laughs before reaching up to caress the tattoo under her left breast. Watch her flinch from it. It makes me fucking sick. Completely blocks out everything *other* about the place I'm in and brings me solidly into the here and now.

"The other piece," the man murmurs in that terrible fucking voice I'd heard right before he put two bullets in my cousin. "I'll be sure to tell him I've seen the matched set now."

"Ellie," I plead, watching the tears fall down her cheeks. "I know you're thinking about me somewhere in there, so please *hear me*." I whisper the demand, trying to dredge up anything inside of myself to make it true. "Open your eyes and get up."

"Don't worry." The man trails his hand down over her stomach. "We won't go too far today. I do have guests waiting. But remember, Eleanor, I hold all the cards here." His fingers slide lower then and something in my chest tightens up severely. "Coop will do anything to keep you safe once he knows how you'll debase yourself to keep him alive." He pauses, trailing his hand back up and I can't keep the wrecked sound inside of me any longer. "I'm guessing Alec will feel the same." His hand starts to come to the bottom of her breast and her face crumbles.

And it's that crumbling of her face that does it for me because I can't, I can't. This can't be happening.

"I look forward to all the visits we'll undoubtedly have in the future."

She cries out then, a horrible sound of helplessness I've never heard from her before, even in the midst of all her nightly screams. It has that poisonous, dark rage that whispers in my ear day after day, engulfing me in an instant. Right there, living side by side with all of the wrecked feelings pumping through me and somehow turning my body hot as I shout, "No!"

The sound seems to reverberate around the room, surprising the hell out of me as the fire roars in the fireplace and makes the man stand instantly. I stare at the fireplace with as much shock as him, not knowing what the hell just happened but so fucking thankful that it had. The door to the room flies open the next instant, banging hard against the wall and

I smile as Mac steps into the room. His eyes immediately go to where Ellie lies on the ground and turn murderous right before he flies at the man.

Leaving me to exhale in relief before falling back into my memories.

Chapter Twenty-Three

"I'm done! I'm done! Get her out!"

Alec's panicked voice shouts desperately through my ear, barely a second before I hear the door crash open and my eyes fly wide in time to see Mac going straight for Simon. That possessed look in his eyes letting me know he's good and gone from the sight of me. Not thinking straight at all as his fist comes crashing down on Simon's face and blood spurts right onto that immaculate oriental rug.

I'm jolted into motion by the hit, mind coming out from its hiding place a mess but focused solely on where my dress lies on the floor a few feet away. I scramble over to it in the commotion, grabbing it and rising up onto my knees right as what looks like two security guards come running through the door. They descend on Mac immediately, each grabbing one of his arms while I pull the dress to my body in an attempt to cover up.

"Are you okay, sir?" one of them asks Simon with obvious concern.

I watch Mac fight in their arms, his chest heaving and face red as Simon replies.

"Of course." He holds up a hand to reassure them, mask firmly in place again as he gives a little laugh. "Ms. Delacroix just had a little misunderstanding about my intentions toward her and her boyfriend did not react kindly to it."

So that's how it's going to be.

I'm the whore.

The security guard's eyes move to me and I see the automatic judgment in the one's on the right, condemnation there right along with the barest pity. The one on the left looks a little suspicious, his eyes dropping to the small knife strapped to my ankle, but not by much. Not enough to do anything about it or ask any questions at least. And even though it shouldn't, it still makes that shame rise so fiercely that it swallows me up. Eyes dropping to the floor as more tears track down my cheeks, making me hate myself even more for being so weak. For not being able to hold their eyes and give them that bratty smirk like I have every other person who judged me in my life.

But that part of me, it's not here right now.

It fell somewhere on the floor, along with my dress, I think.

"No need to make a scene, gentleman," Simon continues calmly. "Please escort Ms. Delacroix and Mr. Astor from the party after she manages to find her clothes again."

And just like that, he leaves with soft footsteps on the floor that would never tell of the evil that lies within. As if nothing ever happened here and he didn't just make me violate myself to save the man I love.

I can't look up, can't make myself drag my eyes up from the floor even after he shuts the door behind him. All I can do is stare at that spot marked with his blood as my breath sounds in my ears. It's like my mind can't process what just happened, so overcome with confusion that it's rendering me incapable of making sense of it. Leaving me suspended in time as I try and try but still can't work through it.

Violation, yes. Not the worst kind, yes.

But where does that leave me? I'm not sure.

I'm not sure of anything except the taint that's sticking to my skin.

That shame that's locking me up.

I'm not sure of anything except that I don't want to feel this way.

"Els." Mac squats down in front of me and my head jerks up, eyes finding his as my chest rises and falls against my hands. "Can you get dressed?"

It takes me a few seconds to nod and then a few more before answering.

"Y-yeah." I nod again, swallowing to try and rid my mouth of that lingering bile, stomach nothing but an aching, empty pit now. "Yeah." Repeating the word more to myself as my eyes drift to the security guards over his shoulder, finding the one who was mildly suspicious earlier now looking a little concerned. "Can you stand in front of me?"

"Of course." He stands immediately, turning around and growling, "Turn the fuck around and give her some privacy!"

I take a few breaths, trying to muster up the will to finally move again before standing and quickly stepping into the dress. Keeping my eyes solidly on Mac's back as I do to remind myself that it's over now. That he's gone and someone I trust is here. That everything is going to be fine. Our plan will work. We'll find Coop now and then figure out a way to be rid of Simon. I'll even let Alec kill him if he wants. It can be my belated

Christmas present to him because I'm not sure I can ever stomach being in the same room as that psychopath again.

No. That's not true.

I want to at least see what happens to him so that I can know he suffered, but I don't think I want to kill him myself, shockingly. The problem with it being I never want to feel his skin against mine again.

I dart over to grab one of my shoes that fell off during it all, calling out over my shoulder to Mac. "I'm done."

He turns back to me and I walk quickly to his side, watching his worried eyes move all over my face as if he's not quite sure where to look. "Els…"

"Don't," I snap, more sharply than he deserves, but I can't take him asking the question I know he wants to in front of these strangers. "Let's go."

He gives me a tight nod, turning and walking with me as we leave the library without waiting for the guards to escort us. Moving as quickly as I can in my heels and not looking at a soul while walking down the hallway toward the front door. Definitely not hearing Simon's casual laughter in the other room that no one seems to be able to tell is all wrong. Why do people never recognize the monsters right in front of them?

I'll never understand it, but then again, I'd been stupid tonight too. I'd thought the monster in me might be able to outsmart him.

I grasp the handle of the front door like it's a lifeline, pulling it open and practically throwing myself back into the cold. Sucking the air into my lungs greedily even though it hurts. Walking down the stairs as all that strength I'd found over the past months surviving in the dark collapses further with each breath, falling from me just like the snowflakes in the air.

"Els." Mac steps around me, my name a command as he moves in and reaches up to hold my shoulders. "Els. Look at me." My eyes slowly focus on him, finding that his brows are pulled down with a tight expression on his face that's all barely restrained feeling. "You remember that first time I snuck in when we were in junior high? It must've been what? Eighth grade? About a year after we met."

I give him a small nod, the memory overtaking the mess in my mind and pushing out some of what just happened.

"My dad had gone on a rampage that night because I embarrassed him and mouthed off at a campaign dinner. He was drunk, remember?" He pushes and I nod again. "It was always the worst when he was drunk." A pained laugh leaves him and I reach up, putting my hands on his out of instinct born over the years. "I was so scared." He admits quietly. "I was always so fucking scared when he lost it like that. So after a few hits, I ran to my room and locked the door. Snuck out my window and ran the whole five miles to your place."

"I remember," I rasp, picturing perfectly how I had snuck him in. How he had finally confessed as to why he was always dodging my questions and blaming his bruises on sports. How Yvie had just about come out of her skin when she found him in my bed the next morning. "I remember."

"Do you remember what you told me?"

I shake my head and his lips pull up into a sad smile. "I told you earlier." One of his hands comes up to the side of my face and I can't help the little hiccuping cry that escapes. "You told me that for every hit, I should tuck away a little bit more of myself somewhere he could never reach. Use the fear to build myself up stronger. That way, he could never take anything I wasn't willing to give." He drops his forehead to mine as fresh tears fall onto my cheeks. "You became my twin that night because you were everything I wanted to be. Fearless. Defiant. Strong." My shoulders start to shake and I gasp through a cry as he wraps an arm around me. "Don't give that piece of shit a single part of you. Don't let him win." He drops a hand to my chest. "Don't let him steal anything in here. Use tonight just like you set out to. Use it to take back everything he's stolen from you."

I nod against his forehead, his words giving me more in this moment than any kind of vengeance could while breathing in and smelling nothing but his familiar skin. I wrap my arms around his neck finally, holding on tight and dropping my head to his shoulder, pressing the side of my face against his jacket. Letting him return the hug as my body softly shakes against him, though whether it's from the cold or fading adrenaline, I'm not quite sure.

It's a few minutes later when Alec's tight voice comes through the bud in my ear. "Helen, we're out. I—"

"See you at the hotel," I interrupt. Not wanting to talk anymore for a minute.

Slowly trying to tuck all those pieces of me inside to heal, scavenging what I could to steal back from the evil inside just like I'm stealing this moment in the snow with my twin.

Hoping that tonight would be worth it.

Chapter Twenty-Four

I can see it on all of their faces when we walk into the living room of the suite, in the near-murderous concern on Stef's face when his pacing comes to a quick halt at the sight of me. In the way Kai is looking off at nothing like someone just ran over his puppy before his gaze snaps to mine. In the way Alec's back is to me where he stands looking out the window, body not moving at all as we enter the room even though I'm sure he heard me before the others.

"So," I start with a weak smile, trying to change the mood of the room into what I want. Something, *anything* else than this. "Did we peek into that network yet?"

"*Cara...*" The quiet pain in Stef's voice, along with the way Kai's face twists, has me shaking my head.

"No, guys," I dismiss them, walking past the butler's bar. "We're not going to do this."

I had my moment with Mac. I'm not going to do it a second time tonight.

I can't.

"Els," Kai protests, drawing my eyes to his and seeing that rare violence there now.

"No, Kaison," I snap. "Not right now."

Alec's quiet scoff has my head whipping around to him. "What?" And the word holds all the sharpness from the shattered glass feeling inside of me still.

He doesn't respond, doesn't move, and the fact he doesn't bother to finally sparks some anger in me again.

"What?" I demand, marching over to where he stands and crossing my arms while coming alongside him. "Do you have something to add?"

Still, he doesn't move.

I run my eyes over him then, trying to figure out what the fuck his problem is and taking in the short, shallow pace of his breaths. The way the veins in his neck are standing out, body completely still and unmoving as he stares out the window. And as much as I hate it, I hear Simon's voice in my head saying how he loved me, would do anything to keep me safe, the same as Coop. I remember how he pushed caution again and again and didn't want me going tonight at all. How he's an avoider just like me, but this is one elephant he won't ignore because he does love me. Because he heard the whole thing play out.

"Alec," I try again softly, gathering my courage against the fear that's kept me from saying the words. The fear of loving another person only to lose them. "Big brother."

His head turns to me instantly, the ice in his eyes melting enough to let me see the surprise.

"Listen to me," I sigh, exhaustion pulling at me hard as I reach out to grab a couple of his fingers. Ignoring the way he flinches at the contact since he's making me bring up the one thing I didn't want to. "Tonight was not your fault."

His face tightens up and he jerks his head back around to look out the window, chest collapsing suddenly as I squeeze his fingers.

"It's not your fault," I repeat, reaching up to grip his chin like he does to me when he's pissed and I'm being irrational. Pulling at it until he cooperates. Forcing him to look me in the eyes as I tell him truthfully. "You are my brother and even if we want to beat the shit out of each other half the time... I love you." My lips twitch up a bit as I watch him swallow hard. "Tonight was not your fault, Alec. I made my own choices."

"Helen..." he whispers roughly.

"No," I retort adamantly, sweeping my eyes across the rest of them in warning before bringing them back to him. "I'm not going to hear anything more about this." Letting go of his chin, I muster up enough of myself to cock a brow. "Now, don't you have a husband of mine to find?"

He jerks a nod and I step back, starting to walk left toward where all of our rooms are, my shoulders drooping farther by the second. Stopping for only long enough to toss back over my shoulder absently, "Oh, and big brother?"

Alec looks up to me from where he's digging his laptop out of his backpack.

"I think now that we're officially family... you have to start calling me El."

That smirk of his that matches mine flashes for a second before he snorts. "Never."

***

I walk out of the bathroom wearing Coop's shirt to see Mac waiting for me already, sitting on the edge of the bed in a pair of sweatpants with those tattooed wings peeking over the edge of his shoulders. His gaze jumps up to me from the floor immediately, expression a little unsure and eyes a little lost as they meet mine. Like he's half expecting me to freak out and kick him out of the room we've been sharing.

No matter how old we get, he always looks so adorably the same when he's pushed out of his emotional comfort zone and my lips twitch up at the sight of it. "What?"

"Nothing." He shrugs, the move a little less smooth than usual. "Just wasn't sure if you wanted to share tonight or if you wanted space."

I roll my eyes, shaking my head at him as I walk to the bed and push at his shoulder. "Shut the fuck up and move over."

He humphs, quickly scooting over to his side while complaining. "You're always so mean."

"And you're always such a little bitch," I shoot back, smirking as we both lie down and roll to face each other. It immediately reminds me of the memory he spoke of tonight from when we were young and my brows drop as recent events start to take over again.

I hadn't done my ritual tonight. It's the first time I've willingly chosen to break the habit in almost six months. But when I'd gotten in the bathroom, all I'd wanted was to scorch every trace of Simon from my skin. So that's what I did.

I'd waited until the water was nearly boiling before stepping under it with my dress still on. Just standing there for a while before peeling it from my skin and scrubbing myself raw. Over and over again. Until I'd used all the hotel soaps and shampoos and had lost count of how many times I'd washed. Only then had I felt a little bit more like myself.

"You're going to have to talk about it," Mac interrupts, snapping me out of it and making my face pinch up with distaste.

"Not yet," I answer quietly. "We already talked tonight anyway."

"I know." He nods with equal quiet. "Just saying, you and I both know that one day what happened is going to seep through no matter how hard you push it away and act like it didn't happen—"

"I'm not—"

"You are," he pushes carefully. "And that's okay for a while because that's what we're good at. It's how we learned to survive, but eventually, when you're ready, and it won't be ignored anymore. I'm here. We all are."

It takes me a couple seconds and one long sigh before grumbling. "Fine."

"Good."

"Good." I narrow my eyes at him. "What the fuck is this newfound emotional intelligence though?"

"Don't worry." He chuckles, sapphire eyes turning amused for the first time in hours. "It's not emotional intelligence. It's just twin-telligence. I'm still a fucking mess when it comes to myself."

"Well, at least some things never change." I give him a small grin before nodding to the door. "How's it going out there?"

"Oh, you know," he answers casually. "Kai had to tackle Stef to keep him from calling his dad to hire a hit man while your brother threatened to shoot them both without looking up from his computer."

"So great then," I surmise seriously.

"Exactly." He laughs. "The Alec thing is weird, but I like him."

I pull a disbelieving face. "Seriously?"

He pauses before admitting hesitantly. "You scream."

"What?"

"You scream," he repeats. "Every night, and it's fucking terrifying honestly."

My lips part, brain struggling to believe what he's telling me and all I can do is ask. "What?"

"And every night," he continues. "He comes and stands at the door, watching until you stop to make sure you're okay. Told us himself last night when we were all freaking the fuck out over it." He shrugs the shoulder not pressed against the bed. "So that makes him okay in my book."

"Oh." Well that's just fucking great. No wonder he babied me. "Why doesn't he wake me up?"

"Said he tried once and it just made it worse."

"Oh," I echo, not quite sure what the hell to do with this little revelation and more than a little embarrassed. "Do I say anything?"

"Coop. You scream for Coop, sometimes Jace, but mostly"—he sighs—"just Coop's name."

And then I breathe out for a third time, face pulling in with the word. "Oh." Because what else is there to say?

Guess that explains why I never feel like I get enough sleep.

Pretty sure a therapist warned you about this at some point, El.

I can see the questions, the worry, swirling around in Mac's eyes and try to find some way to explain.

"You asked before—" My heart twists in my chest and I suck in a quick breath before trying again. "You asked why I chose Coop instead of Jace." He gives me a slow nod and I clear my throat. "It's not a simple answer and the truth is… I loved them both desperately. And if you asked me why I loved one of them more than the other, I wouldn't have one for you," I admit, rolling on my back to look up to the ceiling for a second as he asks.

"How then?"

"Because," I breathe out shakily. "I think sometimes we keep coming back to the same person. The one that's always right there, lingering in the back of our mind. The one who some part of us is screaming out for deep inside." I turn my head and give him a sad smile. "And I realized that as happy as I would have been with Jace when I thought Coop didn't want me or disappeared... I'd never be able to live in a world where I knew he was out there. Wanting me as much as some part of me was screaming out for him." My voice cracks and I blink rapidly to keep from crying again. "He said once that no matter what, he would haunt me for eternity and I think that's true. I never would have been able to escape that. Him." I fight against the tremble of my bottom lip. "I think there's a reason why we keep coming back to someone, good or bad. They get too deep, all tangled up in our cells until... it's just them. Always them. So really," I choke out with a weak smile, finishing, "I never stood a chance. I knew in a split second, reading nothing more than a few words on a page, that he would always be the choice I made. The one I came back to in the end."

His eyes search mine for a long moment before he finally responds softly, "Well, that's something, I guess."

"Yeah," I whisper back. "Yeah, it is."

We just stare at each other then, taking comfort in each other's gaze that's as familiar as our own. Old memories and new confessions flowing between us until my eyelids grow heavy and eventually close.

***

A loud crash jolts me awake and I shoot up in bed, Mac doing the same beside me as my blurry eyes immediately land on Alec where he stands in the doorway. The door to our room in one hand and holding his computer aloft in the other, chest lifting with rapid breaths. Not a trace of that usual ice to be found in his expression as he swallows again and again, like he can't quite get the words out.

"Alec?" I rasp, voice rough from sleep and the hope that I'm trying to keep from unfurling in my chest. So incredibly scared that maybe I'm wrong.

"Happy birthday, little sister." He looks down at his computer, blinking once before meeting my eyes again and with three simple words and nine letters, everything changes for me once again. "I found him."

PART TWO

The Remaking

Chapter Twenty-Five

Coop

Six Months Ago

Air floods down my throat as my eyes open, pain exploding into my mind with the sense of my chest being ripped apart and dug into with a meat cleaver.

"Hello, Cooper."

I try to move my eyes toward the voice of the man that shot me. Try to reconcile the fact that I'm alive when I should be dead through the scattered mess of agony in my head. Finally plucking out the realization that it probably isn't for any good reason if I'm still with him.

"You don't know me really," he continues and I finally force my eyes to move, finding him sitting neatly in a chair beside me in a shabby concrete room. "But I know you." His hand lifts, holding something aloft for me to see and I recognize the item in it immediately because it's the thing containing almost every precious memory I have of her. "This"—he pauses, voice becoming sick with delight—"proved to be the thing that saved your life." A quiet laugh leaves him. "It appears Nadia's daughter is as alluring as she herself was."

My hands twitch at what he's saying, hot anger winding up through the pain, but I keep my mouth shut because to say anything would just be giving him more than what he already has.

His eyes drop to the move though, the close perception making something in the back of my mind shout a warning as he smiles blandly. "Yes, this will work out quite well."

His gaze comes back to mine as he continues. "There's a shift that happens when someone is contemplating betrayal. Did you know that, Cooper?" And again, I don't reply, this time making sure my body doesn't move either, although the pain living inside of me won't allow for much, even if I want to. "I felt that shift only once with Novikov, who, just to clarify for you"— eyes narrow on me—"was my oldest and only friend. My ally and business partner." He drags his gaze away and sighs, crossing one leg over the other. "Still, I felt it from him once. Not long after Nadia came into his life and that just wouldn't do."

This is news to me. My whole perception of the story tilts even as the room starts to spin in earnest because my lungs are struggling under the onslaught of pain. But I fight it. Fight to drag some air into my lungs as he continues.

"I told Nadia that she would die if she kept trying to pull him away, but she didn't believe me"—he smiles, bringing his eyes back to mine—"at first." A shrug leaves him. "And when I made clear exactly how serious I was, she went to Novikov, but he wouldn't believe her. Not his oldest friend, he wouldn't harm her." My stomach convulses then but whether it's from ripping sense in my chest or what he's saying... who knows? Probably both. "And then she turned traitor, solving all of our problems." Another sigh leaves him and he lifts the journal. "Or so I thought."

Silence falls then as he waits me out with a detached look, leaving me the time I need to work past the pain enough to decide that I have to know what he wants with her, what he wants from all of us. Barely being able to cough up those exact words.

"Wh-what"—my jaw snaps shut, body seizing for a second before I force out—"do you want?"

He still doesn't answer me for a minute, prolonging my disadvantage like a bastard. "I want what you and Alec took from me."

"A frien—" I try to spit out the insult, but the pain stops before I can finish and he smiles, making my stomach fill with bile, knowing I should have controlled myself better.

"No." He stands. "You and Alec will take over for me as Novikov's replacements at Bainbridge, ensuring that my business continues without issue and that I have two men with connections to the highest reaches of the underworld." I don't say anything this time, despite his fucking delusional wish, but he must see some of the thoughts in my body or eyes because he takes a step closer and lifts the journal higher. "And if you both do not cooperate... I will find the girl you love so much and do unspeakable things to her." And even that pain in my heart comes to a stop at his words, fury quickly taking over, pumping thickly through my veins. "It would be no hardship considering that she's Nadia's daughter after all."

He lowers his head closer to me with that detached smile wide on his face. "And have you seen her?" The whisper comes as he drops a bit more. "I would so enjoy making sure you could feel everything I'd done to her with your cock if you ever got her back one day."

My mind snaps and I lose it completely. Vision clouding with black around the edges as I reach for his neck with the full intention of snapping it. Knowing he needs to be stopped before this can spiral more out of control. Knowing that I'll die inside if she ever has to go through that because of me and what I brought into her life.

But my body has other plans.

Arms jerking to a stop even as they come up off the bed, that cracked feeling in my chest stopping them midlift.

He laughs then, this horrible sound of glee and I know what I have to do. Know what I'm probably about to have to endure. Had gone through the training for situations just like this, first in the Navy and then with Bainbridge. So the pain, I could take the pain and foresee most of it already…. What I can't take is hearing him talk about her.

Hearing the name of the person I'm supposed to keep safe and cherished coming out of his sick fucking lips.

"There it is," he continues with quiet contemplation and I drag my eyes to the ceiling in preparation. "Exactly what this journal told me." Dragging a memory of her to the forefront of my mind. "That you would do anything to keep her safe, which means all I have to do is find her and I'll get exactly what I want from the both of you."

I picture her face. That first morning after we got married, staring down at me with the smallest smile I'd ever seen on her face. As if she was terrified to let herself really embrace the happiness we were claiming. As if she somehow knew that the universe was about to take it away.

"There's no reason we can't go ahead and get started though." I see him take a seat in the chair again out of the corner of my eye. "Tell me about Eleanor."

She's everything.

"The things that aren't in this journal, her everyday habits."

She could probably drink me under the table when it comes to tequila and she tips her chin up at me when she's arguing a point. She's the first thing I think about in the morning and the last thing before I close my eyes every night. Thinking back now, I'm pretty sure I fell a little bit in love with her when I was telling her a fairy tale on that fucking horrible night. Maybe that's why I still like to watch her sleep sometimes.

"Tell me about Alec."

He'll protect her.

"Where would they go, Cooper?"

I lose myself in memories of her then, going so deep in my head that nothing exists but her. Not even his voice. Not these concrete walls or the pain in my chest. I go so deep that the sun is warming my skin and her laugh is echoing in my head, lips brushing together with the softest kiss.

There will be a point where I'll break though. No matter how much training you have for it or how much pain you can take, everyone breaks eventually. I know that. And if that point ever comes for me, well, I'll make sure there is no way I can tell her secrets.

Until then though… I'll live in my head, basking in everything she is to me.

Chapter Twenty-Six

Everyone is running around the suite like it's a fire drill two hours later because I'm not about to let another day pass with Coop in whatever cage Simon is keeping him in. I had marched into the living room after Alec's words, yelled until everyone woke up and proceeded to tell them we were leaving right the fuck now. And if they didn't want to get on board, I'd damn well go by myself. To which Alec had snarked that it'd be a little bit hard to do without the location he was still holding in his hands. I had then replied by grabbing a knife from the duffel and throwing it at him. Problem solved.

"No," Stef retorts to whatever the person on the other end of the phone said while tossing his charger into his bag. "I don't need the house two days from now. I need it *now*."

He's been put in charge of finding us all a new location within a reasonable driving distance from where Coop is being held in some type of warehouse building on the outskirts of Ottawa. Alec says if we're really doing this, we should go in hard and then disappear to regroup. And since my plan with Simon had gone more than a little bit off track, I'm happy to let him make the calls this time, outside of the fact that we're doing this right the fuck now.

Kai darts through the room in his underwear, running to the couch to snag his sweatpants and already has one leg in when Alec walks in the room carrying the duffel and shakes his head at him. "No." Kai stops, looking up in confusion and Alec drops the bag on the floor, reaching down to unzip it as he speaks. "Go put some jeans on. You're coming in with me."

Stef closes his phone with a snap. "Got a cabin on Lake Rosseau. It was a bit farther than I—" He comes to a stop as he looks up and sees Kai's shocked face staring at Alec. "What?"

"Uh," Kai scoffs. "Jason Bourne here just recruited me to the big leagues."

"You too." Alec jerks his head at Stef, pulling two semiautomatic pistols out of the duffel and walking over to where he stands before holding one out. "You with me, Corleonesi?"

A heavy beat passes between them before Stef flashes a hard smile at him. "Figured you were the friend."

Leaving Alec to retort as he takes the gun from him. "Wasn't about to let Helen here go traipsing across Europe with three guys without doing my homework."

"You know, guys," Kai starts lamely. "What do you think the chances are that we'll actually have to uh—"

"High," Alec cuts him off with a short reply. "We're going in blind, so assume the worst possible circumstances."

"Right." Kai nods as Alec walks over and presses the other gun into his hand. "Great. Sounds like a party."

He turns to me then and I hold out my hands with a winning smile, having known this moment was coming and too far gone to fight about it. The truth is, if another second passes without us hitting the road, I'm going to come out of my skin. Alec shakes his head at me, rolling his eyes as he walks behind me to the bar and leans down to grab something from below the counter.

When he comes back up it's with what looks like a glass of vodka that he passes to me with a serious look. "We need to talk before heading out." I look down at the glass and open my mouth to protest, but he continues over me. "You're going to need it."

"Fine," I snap, quickly picking the drink up and throwing it back in one swig, my whole body giving a little shake and cringing from the taste before pulling a sarcastic face. "Happy?"

"Yes." He smirks. "Thank you."

"You're welcome." I roll my eyes back at him. "So what is it?"

"We need to talk about how I found Cooper."

My brows drop with confusion and I give him a questioning look. "Through Simon's network, right?"

"Yeah." He nods. "But—"

"It's those items he talked about before, *cara*," Stef's voice cuts him off, drawing my gaze to where he stands behind me and at the sight of his face, I start to get that pit in my stomach again. "The ones that are typically associated with a hostage."

"Oh." I nod. "Okay." Looking back at Alec, I see him eyeing Stef with a warning look and push. "Alec, just tell me. What is it?"

He drags his eyes back to me with a sigh. "You need to brace yourself for what kind of shape he might be in."

All those methods rush through my mind, stomach rolling and making me feel sick, dizzy almost as I nod again. "I know." My body starts to grow hot and I cough at the burning still in my throat. "I'll be fine. I'll handle it. It's nothing I haven't thought up a thousand times since knowing for sure that he was alive."

"Thinking and seeing are two different things."

"I know," I repeat harshly, fear and impatience riding me hard. "Now come on, give me a gun and let's get going. It'll be dawn by the time we get there now."

"Fine." Alec agrees, walking around from behind the bar and heading to the duffel.

Something about his sudden easy compliance has alarm bells ringing in my head though and I scan the room. Quickly finding Stef's eyes trained on me and Kai sitting on the couch with only one pant leg still on. Kai's eyes drop to the floor when I meet his gaze and another sliver of unease works its way up my spine. Something isn't right here.

He holds out the gun to me and I shake my shoulders, trying to rid myself of the unease and chalking it up to just being on edge. Starting to take a step toward him only to find my foot stumbling over nothing almost the second it lifts into the air. Suddenly hit by the sense that I have no control over my own limbs.

I reach out for the barstool, struggling to grab on to it for support as the room starts to blur and my eyes go straight to Alec. "What—" I blink slowly, his face doubling as speech becomes hard. "What did you do?"

The hand holding the gun drops to his side. "I'm sorry, little sister, but there's no way I'm letting you get anywhere near Simon again." He takes a step closer to me as I sink to my knees, trying desperately to hold on to the chair and stay awake, to ignore the black spots starting to fill my vision. "Mac'll wake you up when we're close, but you're nothing but a liability there."

It hits me then. Mac isn't in the room.

He isn't in the room because—

My grip on the chair finally gives out and I brace myself to hit the floor, but the hit never comes because I'm somehow suddenly looking up into the torn sapphire gaze of my twin.

"They knew you'd see it in me if I was here," he whispers. "Sleep now, Els."

"Mac—" I slur.

"When you wake up, he'll be here."

And then everything goes black as the panic sucks me under with a different voice in my head whispering, "*Faster.*"

***

I wake with a jolt, eyes flying open and body coming alive with a rancid smell in my nose. Head pounding with the most terrible kind of panicked confusion pumping through me. Something is wrong. Something is terribly wrong. It's pulling at my gut insistently. I blink fast and realize that I'm lying down, but what I'm looking out of has to be a car window because I'm seeing nothing but trees. Trying to remember when I had fallen asleep and what had happened. I was on my way to Coop—

Coop. Fuck.

It takes me two tries before I finally manage to get my now jittery limbs to cooperate enough to push up in my seat, head turning to see Mac's guilty face looking down at me.

"What the fuck did you do?" I lash out, tongue still heavy, but that's the least of my concerns right now. "What the actual fuck did you all do?!"

"Els." He sighs.

"No!" I shout, eyes flicking rapidly around and searching our surroundings, desperate for any kind of clue as to where he's taken me. "Macallan, you take me there right now!" There's nothing but snow-covered trees though, trees, trees, and more trees and the dirt road our SUV is on. All of it lit by that first bit of dawn that's filling the sky. No clues and my still foggy brain can't make out a sense of direction. "Right the fuck now!"

"No can do, Els." He sighs again, drawing my gaze back to him and I see the resolution in his eyes. "Think it through. You know this is the smart move."

"No!" I shout again, hysteria edging in on my voice as it fills the car harshly. "No, I most certainly do not." Grabbing the handle of my door, I push it open while tossing out at him viciously. "If anything happens to him and I wasn't there, I will *never* forgive you for this!"

I let myself drop down from the SUV and slam the door closed as hard as I can, the panic and betrayal overwhelming me to the point that I almost can't breathe. The cold air hitting me just as it seems like my chest is about to collapse from knowing that something is so, so wrong. I need to be there. I need to be there and it all needs to be faster. He's slipping away. I can feel it in the painful itch of my skin. In the way my fucking cells are screaming as if all of me is trying to break apart to make it to him before it's too late.

"Els!" Mac's shout spurs me into motion and I gasp for a breath before starting to march down the road.

I'll fucking walk there if I have to.

"Where are they, Macallan?!" I call out over my shoulder, hearing him right behind me now. "How far are we?"

"Only a couple miles." He snags my elbow, bringing me to a halt and swinging me around to look at him. "Stop. Fucking stop and listen to me!"

"No!" I scream in his face, chest heaving as my eyes start to fill. "No! I should have been there!"

"To what?!" he shouts right back. "Distract them from saving him?!"

"I could have helped!"

"Maybe." He gives me a clipped nod. "But ultimately you would have been a liability because everyone there would have been more concerned with making sure you were safe than saving Coop."

His words rattle around inside of my head until it's like they're going to explode right out. Until they do nothing but hurt and make me want to lash out.

"Fuck you!" I jerk my arm from his hold and whip back around, looking down the road that suddenly seems endless as he continues.

"They're going in right now and will call as soon as they have him. That's why I woke you up." He tries to place a hand on my shoulder and I shrug it off immediately. "They promised."

I'm not going to make it there in time. Even if I run, they'll already be in the thick of it by the time I get there. So now, not only will I not be there for Coop, three of the other people I care about most in the world are walking into danger because of me. Without me even being there to make sure they're okay and have their back.

"Fuck you," I whisper again, folding over and grabbing for my knees, pulling deep breaths into my lungs to ward off the sense of dizziness that's trying to creep in. That voice in my head again, sending my panic skyrocketing with each whisper of *faster, faster, faster.*

I need to distract myself. Give myself something else to focus on, or else I'm going to scream. I know it. And if I lose him when he's so close, right before I see him again, I'll never stop screaming.

I hold a hand out behind me to Mac and demand sharply. "Give me your phone."

"My phone?" he questions, but I can hear him already moving to dig it out and give it to me.

"Yes, Macallan, your phone."

He presses the phone into my hand and I bring it around, swiping up and typing in his code as he continues hesitantly. "They're already in there, Els. You're not going to be able to—"

"I'm not calling them," I mutter, cutting him off while typing the number in. "I'm calling Tiff."

"Who?"

I toss him a bitchy look over my shoulder while standing and bringing the phone to my ear. "Coop's sister."

Holding my breath as the phone rings once, twice, four times before her tired voice answers. "Hello?"

And then I answer, breathing out on a rushed exhale what I've been waiting to tell her for months. "I found him."

A beat passes before her voice wobbles over the phone. "Coop?"

"Yeah." I nod to myself even though she can't see it. "Yeah, my—" Cutting myself off because she doesn't know who Alec is yet, I finish simply. "He's being rescued right now."

"Oh my god," she cries softly. "Oh my god, El. Thank you. I'm so sorry for all the shit I gave—" Her words are cut off by the sound of a voice in the room, speaking softly and I listen in, trying to figure out who it is. "Yeah, I'm fine. Thank you."

Her polite response is followed by silence, and in it, the sound of soft beeping hits my ears, mechanical and steady, like the sounds of a hospital.

Like it's someone's heart beating.

And it sends my own thundering as I close my eyes, already knowing but needing to hear it for some part of me to believe it still. To believe the reality I've never seen with my own eyes.

"Where are you?" I gasp softly.

Her answer takes a long time to come, and when it does, it's filled with nothing but sadness. "I'm at the hospital"—she pauses before finishing even more quietly—"with him."

I open my eyes to the sky that's continuing to lighten and have to clench my teeth together to keep the sudden sob inside. Overcome with guilt that tears at my heart like it's determined to leave it in nothing but shreds as punishment for not being there with him. Staring at the darkness and light that's playing together across the universe for this brief moment in time, seeing nothing but us as the miracle of it all hits me hard enough to leave me gasping for the words I need to ask.

"Can I talk to him?"

Chapter Twenty-Seven

Jace & El

I sweep my eyes across the room I've been pulled to. Wondering where the fuck I am for probably the hundredth time. Mild annoyance flowing underneath all that constant, never-ending rage as I take in the concrete walls of the small space. Not finding a window in the place, only a dim light coming from a sliver of space under the door giving me anything to work with. I can barely see a thing. It's all shadows and dark corners and has a disbelieving sound leaving me. Not that anyone hears it, or maybe they do. I'm not really sure about how this place works, especially after that mindfuck with the fireplace the other day, but I guess night vision isn't a perk of being wherever the hell I am.

"Little cousin."

I freeze completely at the sound of his voice, not believing it for a second until he continues.

"I tried so hard."

Spinning on my heel, I search for the direction his voice is coming from, barely making out the shadowy form of a body in one of the corners.

"To be strong. To hold on."

I step toward the sound of his voice and hear him struggle for a breath. The quiet sound tamping down that rage inside me.

"And I was." He scoffs a low laugh. "Never told him a fucking thing about her or Alec, no matter what he did."

I finally come close enough that I can make him out, am almost on top of him when what I'm seeing finally clicks and brings me to a stop.

"Went so deep into my head that nothing existed but her." He inhales a deep breath. "And honestly, it was a hell of a place to be. Wouldn't have wanted to spend the last of my life anywhere else." His voice weakens, roughens and I can hear how each word is becoming a struggle for him. "I can feel myself starting to break though. Those walls in my head that I built out of pieces of her are starting to crumble, Jace."

My eyes dip, landing on a jagged piece of metal in his hand that's covered in blood.

"And I won't let him use me to get to her." His head lolls to the side, eyes drooping just a bit. "So here's my last confession, little cousin. Hoping maybe you can hear me somewhere out there."

And maybe it's because I've been here for so long, figured out how to push beyond the rage somewhat, but fear surges in me as I whisper in horror. "What the fuck did you do, Coop?"

***

"Hey, Dawson."

I feel Mac's eyes drilling into my back with curiosity as I speak his name through the phone, but I ignore him. I ignore everything. Blocking the world out as I suck in a breath and speak to him from that place where he lives in my heart. The one that will always hurt a little now.

"I miss you," I whisper, giving voice to that brokenness as the sound catches on the air. "I miss you so fucking much and I'm so, so sorry." Because it's time to make good. To hope that some part of him can hear me. "I'm so sorry because I never should have dragged you into this and I knew that." I jerk a nod, face falling as my eyes start to spill the tears filling them. "I knew I should've turned you away because I'd never be able to give you that part of me I had already given to him." I press my lips together, not wanting him to hear the cry that fills my mouth, words nothing but a few cracks when I finally admit. "But I couldn't."

Something between a sob and a laugh finally breaks free and I close my eyes as every memory of us flashes through my mind. "I couldn't because you came into my life with sunrises and teasing and damn firework eyes right when I needed it most. I couldn't because I *needed* you, Jace. In that moment of my life, I needed you more than anything." I inhale a quick breath through my nose, crying all the ugliness out now. Heart twisting and twisting in my chest until I'm not sure I'll ever be able to unravel it again as I choke out. "And then I fell for you." Forcing my eyes open, I continue softly. "I fell so incredibly in love with you."

***

"You stupid fucking idiot," I grind out, dropping down onto my knees and squinting. Trying to make out how much blood has pooled onto the ground around him as he gasps roughly again. "So fucking stupid."

There's too much blood. Too much fucking blood and more pouring from the jagged slices on his wrists by the second.

"I always knew wanting her was wrong," he confesses. "I always knew you still wondered about her. Wanted her." A weak cough leaves him. "Loved her." I look up in time to see his lips lift for a split second. "Even if you didn't realize it, I did."

I look down when he pauses, the breath leaving him rattling the air in the small space and it hits me that there's not a fucking thing I can do.

There's nothing I can do. Fuck, there's nothing I can do.

Nothing, nothing— "Goddammit, Coop." I gasp. "You don't get to do this."

"But like I told her and you, I was too selfish, and when I found her," He gasps right along with me this time. "I finally found a home. She became my home. And so I took one from you." I watch him slide farther down the wall before he continues on jagged breaths. "I wanted to tell you how sorry I am for that. Stealing your home from you."

"Fuck!" I shout. "Listen to me, it doesn't matt—"

"Not that much longer now though." His eyes close for a long second and it's like my comatose heart stops in my chest until they open again. "I'm giving her back to you."

***

"It was probably the most selfish thing I've ever done," I confess, staring down that road. "Unforgivable." My voice breaks on the word of truth, but I push through it because I need him to hear me right now. "And I'm okay with that. I'm okay with being unforgivable. If you need someone to hate." I swallow hard. "Hate me. You always said you couldn't, but if that's what it takes for you to wake up—" Another cry tries to escape, cutting me off and I gasp, bending over to brace a hand on my knees again. "Fucking hate me so hard that it rattles you awake. You have to wake up now, Jace," I plead. "You have to wake up because I found him."

I stare at the ground for a long moment, forcing myself to face how fucking terrible I really am in this moment before forcing the words out. "And I'm coming to you selfishly again because I can't have him coming back to a world that you won't wake up to because of what I did to you." The sob finally breaks free, leaving me gasping and crying the words I'm trying to speak. "I can't live—" Mac's hand lands on my back and this time I don't shrug it off as I beg. "How am I supposed to be happy with him without you here too?"

***

"No!" I get right up in his face as his eyes droop again. "You fucking listen to me, Coop."

I see him smile for real and it stops me for a second. "She doesn't even realize it, you know? The things that make her special." He scoffs weakly. "'Course you do."

"You don't get to *give her back*." My head shakes with the objection. "Doesn't work that way. And guess what?" I will him to hear my words with everything in me. To hold on just a little bit longer. To call for the help I can't give. To do anything. "She's out there right now looking for you."

"Sure, she plays on the pretty thing." Another weak laugh leaves him, the sound barely making it to me. "The other stuff though, the important stuff, she's oblivious to because it's as natural as breathing to her." His lips fall, brows tightening with pain. "Once you finally crack that wall of hers." He looks up to the ceiling. "She loves so fucking hard that she'd do anything for you." I see the tears start to slide down his cheeks as his eyes close. "She was the best part of my life, Jace."

"Not was, Coop," I call out over him. "Is, she fucking is."

His eyes open and I swear it's like he can actually see me. "And I can't be sorry for that because as much as you're her sun, when I met her that night… she saved me, little cousin. Saved me when I didn't even realize how bad I needed saving."

"Then let her save you now," I plead. "Fucking hear me, Coop. You don't know what she's gone through to find you. All you gotta do is hold on a little longer."

"She saved me even here."

***

"That's the worst part." The next sob comes from somewhere so deep that it forces me to my heels and I drop down to the ground, cold working its way through me until it numbs everything but the pain locking me up. "That I need you out there somewhere so that I can go on being fucking happy." I bring a hand up to wipe roughly at the cold wetness covering my overheated face before whispering. "That I needed you, until I didn't, but really still do." I close my eyes with the confession. "I need you living out there, seeing every sunrise that I do because as much as I love him... I will never stop loving you too."

My whole body starts to shake from the force of the cries I can feel everywhere, head pounding in tune as I drop the phone from my ear for a moment. Gasping over and over again and trying to gain enough control to continue. Finally, I raise my head to keep my eyes right there on that light in the sky while bringing the phone back to my ear. Trying to swallow down the hysteria that's finally showing its face to the world, but I can't seem to force it through the tightness in my throat any more than I can deny that it's my face in this moment of truth.

So I just keep speaking, words barely understandable but being spoken regardless because they need to be said. "Coop said once that the piece of my heart that's yours was his punishment." I try to swallow convulsively again. "But I don't think that's true anymore." My cries finally turn softer as I admit, "I think it's mine for being so selfish in loving you."

***

"You fucking hold on for her!" I shout the order at him and stand, looking around and knowing I can't just let this happen. Desperate to be able to do anything to save him for us both now because, as fucking pissed as I am at him… he's still my cousin. Is the person that's been there for as long as I can remember.

"He used to taunt me with our poems sometimes." His words are so weak that I can barely hear them as I pace the confines of the room. "But they were my air, each little piece of her kept me going. Those memories—" I stop as his words suddenly turn slow, slurred. "She, us, kept me going."

"No, no, no!" I shout while walking to him and dropping to my knees again in time to see his eyes close. "Don't you fucking dare, Coop!"

"I told—" His head lolls farther to the side with a heavy breath. "Told her I'd love her forever."

"You fucking bastard!"

"Meant to tell you too."

***

"The thing is—" I lean back into Mac's hand for steadiness, forcing myself to start again. "I never deserved you." My tears finally start to slow and I smile sadly at the absolute truth of it. "You are the best of us, Jace. I never deserved you for a second and truthfully." A scoff of a laugh leaves me and I tell him, "You deserved better than me from day one too." Bringing my legs up, I wrap an arm around them as my body starts to shiver from the cold. "I was never whole, Jace, and you deserve someone who has their whole heart to give you. Someone who—"

I rack my brain for the words, trying to make him understand as if he's really listening.

And then the reality of where I am, what I'm sitting here waiting for, hits me hard. "Someone who doesn't turn your world upside down"—I remind him softly of his words to me—"but sets it on fucking fire and leaves you knowing that you wouldn't have it any other way because, without them, the world doesn't matter." I shake my head. "I was never that person for you." And then I correct myself, because we're being honest here. "To you."

My voice breaks on every word as I tell him, "And I'm so incredibly sorry I couldn't give that to you." I press my lips together again and look straight at the rising sun before forcing out. "As sorry as I am for loving you"—my eyes drop from the sky with the horrible admission—"but I will always treasure what you gave me too. You made me believe again." I gasp. "So I guess I'm calling to tell you—"

***

"Coop!" I shout at the top of my lungs, trying to hit the wall beside his head, but nothing happens. Nothing ever happens except for that one time with her.

Why could I save her but not him too?

"She fucking chose you!" I yell at him, standing as my chest gasps for air that's not even really there. "She chose you! She's still choosing you!" I bring my hands to the back of my head as a rough sob leaves me. "You don't get to die now when *she fucking chose you*!"

Sudden light floods the small space and my head whips toward it, the sight of Alec's face making me collapse to the floor with relief. "Thank fuck." I sob roughly again.

"Fuck." Alec's curse echoes as he rushes to my cousin's side and quickly checks his pulse, face filling with relief for a split second at the confirmation he's still alive before he reaches down and lifts his arms into the air. "Always have to be the goddamn hero, don't you, Coop?" He looks back over his shoulder and shouts. "Get in here!"

And just as two other forms rush into the room, I feel a tug pulling me somewhere else as Alec's words echo around me. "Call her *now*."

***

"Hate me forever if it makes you wake up, forget about me, whatever you want to do." I look back to the sky that's almost completely lit up now. "But even if you forget about me, I'll never stop cherishing the pain that lives in my heart from you. Because your love made me so much better than I ever would have been without you."

Chapter Twenty-Eight

The phone rings almost as soon as I end the call and the sight of Stef's name has me immediately swiping my finger across it, bringing it to my ear and choking out. "Do you have him?"

"Yeah," he answers shortly and I hear Alec shouting something unintelligible in the background. "Tell Mac to get here now."

The phone goes silent the next instant and I swing my head around to Mac, gasping for a second before I can get the words out. "They got him." My twisted heart is about to explode in my chest as it really hits me, and I cry, "They got him." So shaken as what I've held on to all these months becomes a reality. "Stef said to come now." I laugh through the fresh tears.

He returns my smile with a wide one of his own, eyes filling with relief as he stands and holds out a hand to me. "Let's go get your man."

I grab his hand, using it to jump up and quickly throw my arms around his neck. Squeezing tight and whispering raspily, "Thank you so much for coming when I needed you."

"We are who we choose." He brings his arms around me. "And we made ours years ago."

Unable to wait another moment, I drop my arms and quip with a smirk, "No take-backs." Tossing out over my shoulder while running to the SUV. "Even if I am a massive bitch sometimes!"

I see a hint of a smile play across his face as he follows me to the car, both of us quickly hopping in before he shoots down the road. Not even bothering with our seat belts. It would be useless for me right now anyway. I can't even sit still in my seat, fidgeting and bouncing all over with every muscle in my body on edge. Hand ready to shoot to that door handle the second we get there. Needing to lay my eyes on him and hear his voice more than anything in my entire life.

I don't even care what kind of shape he's in. I know it's going to be bad, but as long as he's here. That's all I need. Just to feel his skin against mine while his heart beats under my ear again. Every morning and night and noon, forever. I don't think I'll ever stop needing that sound after this.

The dirt road finally comes to an end and Mac swings right onto a long stretch of freeway that's mostly empty, besides a few low-slung industrial buildings dotting the space here and there. I can hear my heart hammering in my ears, adrenaline pounding through it with each increasingly chaotic beat. Nearly frantic and about to ask him how much farther when he makes a sharp right turn into the parking lot of a particularly shabby looking one. He drives right through the metal gate that's clearly been cut open and continues to the back of the lot behind the building.

I'm already grabbing the handle before the car even stops and am throwing myself out of it the second it seems steady enough. Chest heaving like I've run a marathon as I sprint toward the open doorway before skidding to a stop at the sight of them. Stef and Kai carry a body that's bare except for a pair of black underwear, while Alec's hands are wrapped like vises around the wrists. Wrists that are dripping a steady stream of blood despite the hold he's got on them. And that body, that body that's covered in bruises and scars that weren't there before with hair shaggier than when I met him and a face is covered in heavy scruff. That body that's dripping the same blood that haunts my dreams and sends me screaming at night. That body that brings my chaotic pulse to a stop and is my beautiful tragedy come to life is… Coop. My eyes take it all in a second before Alec looks up, meeting mine with a look of apology that automatically makes me just want to scream at him.

He opens up his mouth as if he knows what's coming though, and shouts, "Open up the trunk and get the seats down!"

Effectively cutting me off and spurring me into motion as I race to the back of the SUV, pushing the trunk door up with everything I've got while Mac hops into the back seat. Quickly working with him to get the seats down and bags pushed to the sides as the guys bring Coop to the back. I scoot toward the front to give them as much room as possible and Alec jumps in first, still holding on to Coop's wrists as Stef hauls his upper body into the car before sliding in to pull him the rest of the way. Kai spares a moment to make sure his legs are clear before he slams the trunk door closed and sprints to the front to join Mac.

All of it happens in a few seconds and I know I should be moving, doing something more to help, but I just can't take my eyes off of him. Rattled into shock by the fact that he's here. He's here with a long scar shooting straight down the center of his chest, our words covered in blood that's spilling from his wrist onto the fabric of the car and telling me that I was right because Coop would never take his own life. Not unless he was well and truly broken or saw no other way out. No other option.

I can't have come this far to lose him. I can't, I can't have come this far to—

"Eleanor!"

My eyes snap to Alec's at his shout and I realize it must not have been the first time he called me. "Wh-what?"

"Pass me the red bag behind you." He looks to Stef as I turn to grab the bag and I hear him ask. "What blood type are you?"

"*A* positive," Stef answers quietly, voice tight with concern. "Is he—"

"I'm *O* positive," I interrupt, hauling the bag into my lap as we hit a bump in the road that jostles us all. "Universal donor." Pulling the zipper on the bag open, I see all the medical supplies within and dart my eyes up to his, straight up fucking demanding some kind of calm from every part of me as I ask. "What do you need?" Because I *did not* come all this way to lose him.

"Saline bottle first." He nods in appreciation. "Then gauze and sutures." I start to dig through the bag for the saline as he continues. "We need to get this bleeding stopped and then we'll see if he needs blood."

I find the bottle and hold it out to him, unable to help the question that pops out. "Can you do this?" Because as much as we need to hide right now, to run, if it's a matter of Coop's life—

"You mean am I qualified?" He snarks a humorless laugh. "Probably not." My stomach turns as he drops Coop's wrists to the floor of the car, quickly spraying the saline all over them and giving me a look at the jagged slices on them. "But we'll see if I can manage. Emergency medical training was part of the Bainbridge curriculum."

I give him a quick nod, tearing my eyes away from Coop's wrists to look out the window and hide the tears in my eyes. Exhaling a stuttering breath in the sudden silence before looking back down to find the gauze and suture kit, whatever the hell that's supposed to look like. It only takes me a few seconds before I locate the gauze and pass it to him without looking up and then a couple more before I take a guess at the suture kit. I look up to ask if I got it right, but he's already looking at me with the gauze now held tight around Coop's wrists.

"Talk to him," he tells me right as we hit another bump and Mac curses.

"Fuck!" He clears his throat. "Sorry, it should be smoother now. We're on the main stretch."

"Talk to him," he repeats the quiet order and lifts a hand to take the kit from me. "I'm betting he's wanted to hear your voice as bad as you've wanted to hear his. So talk to him." I look up at the ceiling as my face crumbles, futilely trying to keep the tears in now and he finishes with rare gentleness. "Let him know you're here."

So I blow out another shaky breath before looking back down with a nod and scooting in closer to where Coop's sprawled. Starting to lean down before pausing to shoot Alec a look, suddenly unsure if it's okay to even touch him.

"Go ahead," he encourages, resituating himself to pull one of Coop's wrists into his lap and hold the gauze tightly over that speaking wound again.

I look down at him, taking in the marks all over his body and my throat starts to close up with how scared I am. Scared for him and what he went through. Scared that if I touch him, I'm going to hurt him more. Scared that if I don't, he won't know that I'm here. Won't know that it's okay to wake up now because he's safe. Scared into motionless at the thought that he's going to be in a bed right beside Jace, both of them forever asleep. Frozen by the fear that he'll never know how sorry I am for not finding him sooner. Terrified into inaction until my eyes go to his closed ones and I hear his voice in my head, reminding me to not let the fear win.

My lips twitch despite everything, remembering that first time he'd called me out on my shit. And I hold on to that, his voice, those memories as I slowly lay my head down on his chest, right over that long scar, as carefully as I can. Breathing out relief from the depths of my fucking soul as I hear that steady thump under my ear that calms my own. Looking up at him and tracing those beautiful lines of his face with my eyes as I start to speak to him.

"Hey, baby." My breath fans out over him and I see the goose bumps erupt even with how cool his skin is. "I know, it's fucking cold here." I laugh softly, bringing a hand up to wipe the tears from my face before they can land on him. "And you'd be bitching about me calling you baby if you were awake." My voice breaks and I suck in a breath before finishing. "But you're not awake yet, and we're a long way from any kind of warmth, so I'm taking some liberties."

I stare at him for a minute then, wanting nothing more than just to silently soak him up since we both know I've never been great at the talking thing. But if there's any chance that my talking will help him and let him know I'm here, that it will give him something to fight for... then I'd talk to him forever. So I leaf through our memories in my mind, quickly going to my favorites and my lips lift against his skin as I start again.

"Remember our first dance that definitely did count in that bar in San Jose?" I remind him, a smile growing with the memory in my mind, heart lifting for the first time in months. "It was to that stupid, overplayed 'Drop In The Ocean' song that every TV show uses and every English-speaking person in the bar was singing right along with it?" A trembling kind of laugh leaves me because these memories, they're the ones that I didn't let myself think of for so long after that summer because they were always the most precious to me. "And then, out of nowhere, you started practically shouting the song right along with them and baby"—another laugh escapes that has me sucking back in the cry trying to escape—"I almost walked away right then because as sexy and poetic as you are, you can't sing for shit."

I hear Stef's and Mac's quiet laughter join mine and blink hard a few times, giving up on trying to keep the tears off of him as they slide down my face. Let them soak into his skin and let him know I'm here too.

"But you were so happy," I continue softly. "And I thought it was impossible at that point, but I looked at you then and fell a little bit more in love with you." My lips twitch. "Terrible singing and all, I knew you were mine and I'd never been happier."

The next words come easier then, locked in this little bubble of memories with him. "Remember our last night together in Cahuita? When we imagined that life together over and over again?" I press a kiss to his chest, breathing him in despite the dirt and grime I can feel on his skin. "We named them that night, the kids we'd have one day. Maddoc for a boy and Stella for a girl. And I made you promise we'd live within walking distance to Stef's so that I could send what will most certainly be the little tyrants to his house for manual labor whenever they get all diabolical on me—"

And I tell him every precious memory. Giving him all of my favorites in the hope that they're his too. Pouring our whole story out onto his skin with my laughter and tears. Reminding him the whole drive that he's the one I always come back to.

***

"Why hasn't he woken up yet?" I snap, eyes never leaving Coop's face where he's lying in the burgundy-and-wood bed.

"Give it time," Alec consoles, checking the bandages on his wrists again. "He lost a lot of blood, but he'll come around."

"We've been here all day now! He should be awake," I argue. "Give him some of mine."

He shakes his head, rolling his eyes at me. "I'd rather not have to rig that kind of transfusion if I don't have to." I watch him walk around to where I'm sitting in a chair beside the bed out of the corner of my eye and hear him sigh as he ruffles my hair. "Just give him time." I don't bother with a response and he scoffs quietly before I hear his footsteps slowly fade, the door to the room closing a second later.

I know I should be more grateful to him after everything he's done today. Everything he's done for months. But I'm a fucking mess. It's dark out now and we've been at the cabin for hours. He should be awake. He should have moved. *Something* should have happened. There's not even a trace of that ever-present tension in his brow. There's just… nothing.

The wind gusts against the cabin again like it's been doing since we got here, sending the wood creaking and ice hitting the large window in the room that overlooks the lake. And I'm sure it's beautiful in a cold, frigid kingdom kind of way if I bothered to look. At another time I might've even grabbed my camera to snap a few shots, admiring the peace of the moment. Right now though… my impatience is stringing me so tight that it's shooting these painful little tingles through my shoulders and my eyes are burning because I refuse to blink until I absolutely have to. Scared I'm going to miss the moment he finally opens his.

My eyes trace the lines of his face for probably the millionth time today and it makes my heart twist up impossibly more even as it fills. All of me so raw that I want nothing more than to just slide into the bed beside him and sleep for days, but I can't until he wakes up. Not until I know for sure that he's going to be okay.

"Okay." I blow out a weary breath, bringing my eyes back to his closed ones and tossing out, "We're going to try this again and don't you dare hold out on me, Cooper Monroe." Making sure my voice is full of that haughty note that always used to get a reaction from him. "Remember that last argument we had in Costa Rica before I left for my trip?" I whisper, suddenly scared to even say the words out loud. As if the universe will hear and automatically wreak havoc on it because, well, I'm me and he's him. "If you wake up, I'll let you win."

I wait a couple minutes to see if anything happens, but he doesn't even bother with any motion under his eyelids to let me know he's in there. "Come on, Coop," I press, reaching out to take his hand, enclosing it in both of mine as that burn in my eyes turns to tears. "I'm pulling out the big guns here."

Nothing, nothing, and more nothing.

I scoff at Alec's idiotic advice to talk to him and look up to the ceiling, trying to keep the tears from falling and continuing out of habit at this point. "I've thought about that fight a lot these past months. Regretted it, what I said. The truth is, I was scared." I suck in a breath. "So if you wake up, you win, okay? You win—"

"Hey, Princess."

The words catch in my throat, air stilling in my lungs for one resounding beat of my heart before I drop my eyes back to him. And when my eyes lock with his night-forest ones, the ones I cried for day after day, I know I didn't imagine that rough whisper. A long moment passes before I see his lips ghost up, little flecks of dark in his eyes sparking with amusement, but I still don't say anything because I'm almost scared to believe it. Scared that if I speak or move I'll somehow break the spell and realize that I'm just dreaming.

He arches a weak brow at me and the next words come out even rougher than the last. "So what did I win?"

The air leaves me in a whoosh and I laugh, bringing his hand up and pressing a kiss to it with the tears falling from my eyes. "Everything," I tell him, voice breaking into a quiet cry and standing just enough to finally slide onto that bed beside him. Dropping my forehead to his and looking into those night-forest eyes that I never want to look away from again, repeating through the smiling sob that comes next. "Everything."

Chapter Twenty-Nine

The stillness is jolting.

It's been two days since I finally got Coop back and I still can't get over it. Can't adjust. After all those months of searching, moving, fighting with that ever-present little bit of panic somewhere inside of me… the stillness is the part that's throwing me off now. It has my grip tightening around the mug of coffee I'm holding with every passing minute, some part of me just waiting for the bottom to fall out again. Unable to let myself relax fully despite the fact that we're safe and together again.

You're not really safe yet though. Are you, El?

No, no, I'm not. And that doesn't help any.

Neither does the fact that this is the first time I've really taken my eyes off of him for those entire two days. He's slept for most of it and I've lain there and watched him for all of it. I've seen each time his body has tightened up before he gasps and flinches. Each time he jolts in his sleep before his eyes fly open and it takes him a minute to realize where he is again. And every time it happens, my heart turns itself inside out for him all over again. Hurting so deeply for what he's gone through that I have to fight to keep the tears from my eyes each time he wakes up searching for me.

Yesterday, when he'd finally been awake for longer than a few minutes, I'd finally worked up the courage to ask about the slices on his wrists.

He'd looked at me for a long moment, then twined his fingers through mine and answered simply that he'd felt himself slipping and wouldn't be used as a pawn against me and Alec. I'd then opened my mouth to tell him what utter bullshit that was and that I'd be happier having him used against me than not here at all, but he'd closed his eyes the next second, sliding back into sleep before I could ream him out properly. Leaving me to bottle up that little speech for a time when he's in better shape to take it because, as grateful as I am to have him back... I'm still pissed at him for almost leaving me, again.

This morning though, when we'd finally woken together and he'd traced endless I love yous on my skin while we stared at that blanket of white snow out the window... I hadn't had it in me to bring it up again and ruin the moment. The first of what would hopefully be all of our moments now. So instead, I'd opted to just press my lips against his chest, which was finally as hot as I remembered and tried to commit the whole thing to memory with each little letter of love.

I'd almost had it then, the peace I was waiting for, but there was still so much unsaid. The things I hadn't worked up the courage to speak out loud yet.

Like Jace.

It was there in every one of my breaths, the truth I needed to tell him about Jace, but I had just gotten him back and I'd wanted a couple days before crashing reality down on us again. It had been hard enough to tell him about Tommy but Jace... I couldn't make myself face that conversation yet. So I'd stuck myself in this almost peaceful in-between where I'd soaked up every bit of him, putting off the inevitable for a little bit longer. But then, after two hours of the closest I'd come to that peace this morning, he'd said that he was feeling better, wanted to shower and shave and all that jazz. Which was great, it was good... but then he'd asked if I wanted to join him.

And I'd fucking frozen.

Frozen like all those icicles hanging just outside the window.

It was ridiculous. I knew it was Coop. Coop who would never hurt me. Coop who I loved more than anyone else on this earth and had wanted to an excruciating degree for months now. Still though, when he'd asked, my mind had automatically flashed to the last time I'd taken my clothes off in front of a man... and it had made my stomach roll so bad that when I'd eventually recovered, I'd just muttered something about getting us coffee before bolting from the room.

I had always been able to deal with my damage, in some way shape or form, but this... this I didn't know what the fuck to do with. It was the one area I'd never struggled in. The area that Coop and I had always excelled in. It was the language we'd spoken from day one, so to have that suddenly ripped away left me floundering. It'd become clear my suspicion that Simon hadn't had the time to tell him about what happened between us before he was rescued was correct when he'd asked me that.

And I didn't see any reason to clue him in at the moment. The one thing I was sure of was that I didn't want him to know right now. He'd been through hell and I just... didn't want him to know. Not yet.

That little bit of shame starts to trail its way slowly around my stomach as if it's enjoying playing with me just like Simon had and it makes my fingers tighten around the mug even more. The storm inside me a perfect reflection of the blizzard outside the living room windows I'm looking out.

Maybe not ever.

Tut, tut, tut. Have you learned nothing about the downfall of secrets yet, El?

Shut the fuck up. At least I hadn't screamed whenever I'd passed out for a few hours here and there. *That*, I definitely would have had to explain to him.

"*Cara.*"

I jolt at the sudden intrusion, hands jerking around the mug and spilling coffee all over them as a curse slips from my lips. "Shit." Looking behind me, I see Stef at the foot of the stairs, next to the stone fireplace that sits to the right of the master bedroom I had claimed. Its beautiful stonework visible all the way up to the roof in the open living room of the large cabin he'd rented on Lake Rosseau.

He lifts his brows at me and I cringe, muttering a quick. "Sorry."

"A little tense, are we?" he jokes, that secret smile playing across his face as he walks through the living room and into the large, clearly renovated kitchen that's upscale rustic, if that is such a thing.

"Just a bit." I scoff, making my way to the kitchen as he grabs a few paper towels from the roll by the sink and holds them out over the butcher block island to me.

His expression turns considering, eyes sweeping over my face as I step between the barstools and set my mug down, taking the paper towels from him. "And here I thought you'd be all happy and relaxed."

"Yeah." I dart my eyes away from him, looking down to wipe my hands. "Yeah, you would think."

"Breakfast?"

I look back up at the question, pointedly ignoring the knowing look in his eyes. "Sounds great." Clearing my throat, I set the paper towels down on the counter. "Where is everyone?"

"Mac and Kai"—he drones their names while turning to the retro-looking brown-and-gold fridge beside the stove and opening it—"are still sleeping off the hangover from the well-earned stupor they drank themselves into last night as a reward for… playing *Rambo*? I think that's what they said." A small puff of laughter escapes me as he sets down eggs, cheese, bacon and onion on the counter before looking back to me. "Your brother"—he lifts his brows pointedly and pulls a bottle of champagne out along with some orange juice, before closing the fridge and turning back to the island—"was staring at his computer like the rest of the world didn't exist and gave me some kind of grunt when I mentioned breakfast, so I'm assuming that means he'll be down shortly."

"Yeah." I laugh again, more openly this time. "Yeah, he does that."

He holds the champagne up, eyes flicking over my shoulder quickly before coming back to mine. "Mimosa?"

"Uh," I drag out, jolted yet again by the normalcy of breakfast and mimosas with Stef before giving him a slow nod. "Sure."

A pair of arms wrap around my waist the next instant, making me immediately go tense before his voice whispers in my ear. "I've missed that sound."

The air leaves me with a burst of relief and I laugh, trying to cover it up and turning my head to look up into his night-forest eyes. "What sound?" I tease, continuing before he can answer at the sight of his newly buzzed head and clean-shaven face. "You shaved."

I reach up to cup his face, running my fingers over that dark-olive skin that's finally back to the right color again and he drops his forehead down to rest on mine. "You, laughing." He breathes roughly, eyes staring so deeply into mine it's like having my soul on display. "If it's not too much to ask, I think I'd like to hear it every day from here on out."

My lips twitch even as I lift up to brush them against his with my answer. "I think we can manage that."

He reaches a hand up, cupping my cheek and I pull back a bit, just enough to see his brow tense a second before I feel that thumb on my cheek with the question. "Why'd you run, Princess?"

"I didn't." My reply is too quick though, too fast, practically overlapping with his name for me and we both know it's bullshit. "I didn't." I try again, sighing and offering up a different truth than the one I'm avoiding. "I just, we need to talk about—"

"Jace," he finishes for me, brows dropping even more as those ridiculously full lips tighten for a beat. "Where is he?"

For a long moment, I just stare into his eyes, wondering what he's expecting to hear and knowing that it's definitely not what I'm about to have to tell him before I take a step back, breaking our gaze while quietly answering. "Not here."

I slide onto one of the barstools and he steps with me, dropping his hands onto either side of the chair with an equally quiet "Princess."

And the love I can hear in that one word, the concern, the care right along with the demand, it's as real as the sounds of Stef moving around the kitchen. So fucking real it's tangible in the air. The purity of it knocks me on my ass all over again, like I'm seeing him again for the first time and I realize then I might not ever get over this sense that everything about us, from the singular to the plural, from the silent looks to the words spoken and the I love yous written on my skin are all so infinitely precious now. It has my throat tightening with pain even as my heart swells with joy.

I bring my eyes slowly back to his, seeing the sharp worry in them and exhale shakily at the memories I'm having to face. "When Simon took you from Landing Point"—my eyes drop to the scar on his chest, so fucking long and deep that it makes my stomach twist and sends my eyes snapping back up to his—"there was an explosion." I suck in a breath this time as his expression turns stunned, but that worry in his eyes, it's a living thing now and has me continuing quickly. "Jace's boat exploded and he and I got knocked around pretty good. I—" I didn't matter here. "I made it out okay, but Jace, he had some swelling in his brain." He opens his mouth but pauses and I know he doesn't want to ask the question, so I finish for him. "He's in a coma, Coop. Has been since the explosion."

"Fuck." His head drops with the rough curse, chest heaving, and I reach up to wrap my arms around his neck, breathing in the comfort of his sandalwood scent even as his pain radiates against me. "What do the doctors say?"

"It doesn't matter what they say," I tell him fiercely. "He'll wake up. I know it."

A beat passes before he pulls back, eyes raking my face and coming back to mine, but the shadows of fear I see there send unease shooting straight up my spine. "What—"

"Well, well, well," Alec's sardonic voice calls and I look over my shoulder to see him jogging down the stairs. "Look who finally decided to roll out of bed."

When I turn back, Coop's eyes are still on me and he drops his forehead to mine, voice going rough. "Nothing that can't wait until later." He sighs. "But we do need to talk about it later because no more secrets, right?"

"Right," I mutter, ignoring the guilt in my stomach as he drops his lips to mine.

He rises up as Alec approaches and I turn in time to see the smirk they exchange before folding each other in one of those weird guy-hug things. Alec grabs his shoulders when they pull back, giving him a little shake. "You fucking idiot."

"Agreed." I snort.

Coop's head turns to me and I give him my best bratty smirk, not backing down an inch and seeing him fighting against the twitch of his own before looking back to Alec.

"Thank you." Coop nods at him, suddenly serious. "Thank you for keeping her safe. For finding me."

Alec's eyes flick to mine and I see the question in them, making me give him the slightest shake of my head.

No, Alec, he does not know exactly everything that went down to get here.

"Of course." He clears his throat, looking back to Coop. "Although if it was up to me, you'd probably be dead right now," A smirk pulls at his lips and he dips his head my way. "She was the one who refused to stop scouring the earth for you."

I watch Coop's eyes flare with surprise as Alec drops his hands, walking back around us to the kitchen and giving Stef what sounds like a grudging hello. Coop turns slowly back around toward me and I look up at him, batting my lashes dramatically and making his lips ghost up.

He steps back into my space and cages me in again, dropping his voice low. "Princess."

I tip my nose up at him. "Yes?"

"Thank you," he tells me, making those two simple words sound unbelievably intimate and sending my stomach flipping with desire.

Well, thank fuck. At least that hasn't changed. Now I just need to get all the parts of my conscience over what happened with Simon.

"Don't mention it." I shrug one shoulder, dipping my head toward it at the same time like it's no big deal. "Figured it was about time I returned the favor."

"Hmm." He drops his head closer, bringing us a breath away as his eyes devour mine. "Thank you, Eleanor Monroe, for saving me my whole damn life."

My lips part in surprise at his words and he takes advantage of it, finally closing the distance between us and sweeping his tongue into my mouth. Kissing me with that slow kind of demand that's always left me breathless, working my heart and body over with each little unbelievably intimate meeting of our lips. I reach up, wrapping my arms around him and running my fingers over the back of his freshly buzzed head as he drags my bottom lip through his teeth before breaking long enough to whisper. "Even when you didn't know you were."

I open my eyes and choke out. "Always, Cooper Monroe." Pressing my lips hard against his for a quick moment. "There's nothing in the world I'd rather be doing."

"Little sister!" Alec snaps, sending my lips up into an open smile because I know what's coming. "As you would say, fucking gross."

A quiet laugh leaves Coop as he lifts up, arching that brow at Alec. "Little sister, huh?"

His eyes come back to mine and I give him a shrug, tossing out with mock indifference. "In our good moments."

"Understandable." He nods seriously.

I turn in my seat, a burst of laughter leaving me at the suddenly sour expression on Alec's face and I dart my eyes to Stef's amused ones as he holds up the champagne. "On that note"—he looks to Coop—"I'm happy we found you, Monroe, for *my* sister's sake." I roll my eyes at his not-so-subtle pissing on me as Alec's expression turns even more sour, leaving me trying to cover up my next laugh with a cough. "And I know that there's still a lot to overcome here for everyone." His eyes find mine and the laughter dies in my throat at the knowing look there. "But if I've learned anything, it's to celebrate the little victories, and this is a victory that definitely deserves to be honored."

"Agreed, Stefano," I murmur quietly.

He gives me a decisive nod before quickly popping the cork on the champagne and pouring it into the glasses he set out on the counter in front of him. Each of us grabbing one before I clear my throat and lift mine into the air, finding each person in our little group's eyes and saving Coop's for last as I steal Stef's words for the cheers. "To the little victories."

His lips twitch as he clinks his glass against mine, echoing me. "The little victories."

I take a sip of my champagne, watching him do the same before setting my glass down on the counter as he slides into the barstool next to me with a deep breath that automatically makes me worry.

I narrow my eyes at him. "You doing okay?"

"Yeah." He nods. "Just a little more worn down than usual is all." A shrug leaves him and I open my mouth to order him back to bed as he adds. "Nothing I can't deal with."

"Good," Alec interrupts, making me turn to him with a death glare that he completely ignores by keeping his eyes on Coop. "Because we need to talk about blowback."

"Simon," Coop grits out, the name sounding like a curse and holding all sorts of dark notes. "Needs to die."

I whip my head back toward him, finding his jaw clenched and eyes on where he's tightly gripping his hands together on the counter. I mean, I agree, I wholeheartedly agree after the condition we'd found him in, whatever Simon did to me aside. But the last thing I want is for Coop to go putting himself in danger again. Not when I just got him back.

"Yes," Alec agrees, that icy voice coming out to play. "But it has to be done... Carefully."

Coop's eyes lift to his and I see his chest rise then still for a second before he exhales a breath. "Carefully." He nods, giving me the sense that there's some understanding between them that I'm missing. "And planned."

"And in the meantime," Alec starts again. "There are certain things, people, we need to address."

"Yvie," Stef interjects, drawing my gaze as surprise runs through me for a second, quickly followed by fear. "It makes sense," he tacks on, that calculating look in his eyes letting me know how capable he is of playing on the same level as the two other men in the room.

I look at Alec, a full-on freak-out starting to set in. "You said Yvie was safe."

"She was"—he sighs—"before, when he didn't need additional leverage."

"Before you rescued me," Coop continues the trail of thought, drawing my gaze for a beat before I turn back to ask the room.

"So what do we do?"

"I still doubt he would go after her with how high profile she is there." Alec muses. "But you can never—"

"It's handled," Stef interrupts, gaining all of our attention as he gives me that small smile. "Kai and I have flights booked back to LA tomorrow, we'll stay with Yvie for the time being and give her a roundabout version of the story to explain."

And I'm suddenly so fucking grateful for him that it takes me a second to simply say his name. "Stef."

"I'll even call in additional security if need be." He dips the glass of champagne in his hand toward me. "Don't worry about Yvie. I've got her."

I have to clear my throat to get the next words out. "Thank you."

"Look at you, Corleonesi," Alec jokes shortly, face turning sour again because he apparently played with others most of the time even worse than I did. Coop being the exception of course. "Making all kinds of bold moves."

"The thought struck and it was necessary. Plus, we have the club to get back to." Stef shrugs. "But I'm leaving Macallan with you because it's doubtful I could drag him away for the foreseeable future anyway."

"True." I laugh softly, sliding off my barstool and walking around the island to scoot between him and Alec. Wrapping my arms around his neck and squeezing him tight as he returns my hug with equal measure. "Thank you, Stefano," I whisper. "I love you and I promise I'll be home as soon as I can, with the exception of a little detour I plan to take for a month or two."

His laughter rumbles out through his body as he answers back quietly. "Of course, but I do expect an invitation on this little trip."

"Deal," I agree, pulling back to joke. "But a mile or two down the beach, yeah?"

"Deal." He nods, that secret smile flashing again at the inside joke. "Love you too, *cara*."

"Question," Coop interrupts, causing all of us to turn to him as he continues thoughtfully. "Not that I'm not grateful, but how did you all finally find me, by the way?"

All of us go still, the silence that follows his question resounding as if we've just been caught in a lie because I most definitely am hiding something and making every person in this house besides Coop my unwilling accomplice.

Coop's eyes narrow, swinging back and forth across us as he demands. "What is it?"

"Nothing," I answer quickly, forcing a smile. "It's nothing, Alec just did some magical computer bullshit and we were finally able to break into Simon's network after we put the pieces together and figured out it was him." Alec's silence next to me lasts a beat too long and I lift my foot as discreetly as possible before digging my heel down into the top of his foot.

"Right." He nods finally, voice maybe a touch higher than usual, but I'd take it. "He had a Bainbridge firewall, but we were able to find a way in."

Fucking bastard, leaving it all open-ended like that.

Coop's eyes narrow even further and I can see the pieces he's trying to put together as they move between us. "How?" he demands. "What was the way in?"

"Simon had a party at his house," Stef supplies because, apparently, he too is a deserting bastard. "We used it as a distraction and Alec snuck in to uplink into the network."

292

Okay, okay. Never mind, I still love him. He's all the goodness that Italy and Hollywood have to offer, all rolled into one handsome package. I really should make sure to get him a badass Christmas present this year.

Coop's not buying it though, I can see it in the way his eyes are still darting between us like he's searching for a weak link and it has Alec's heel pressing down on my foot this time, silently encouraging me to tell him.

But I can't. I can't bring myself to say the words.

"You two"—Coop's eyes finally settle on Alec and me, moving back and forth slowly—"are hiding something."

I muster up all of that old bravado that I can and force a laugh. "No, we're not."

"Eleanor," Coop warns gently. "You are. It's the same as the time you two met."

"No." I cock a challenging brow at him. "We're not."

He arches one right back at me and I see the tiny bit of anger spark in his eyes. "Thought we didn't keep secrets anymore, Princess?"

I blanch, mouth opening, but no words coming out because he's right. We didn't, shouldn't. I shouldn't be doing this and I don't want to. I don't want this hurt between us when I've just gotten him back, but I can't make myself say the fucking words.

And why is that, El? Worried he'll look at you differently? Worried it will finally make it real? Make you face it?

Yes. Yes to all of it. I don't want to see it in his eyes every time he looks at me like I still do with the rest of them. I don't want him to be hesitant to touch me, worried I might break, even though what happened sent me running from the room. I don't want that precious intimacy between us to become tainted.

"Coop." Alec sighs next to me. "It's nothing. El and Mac went in as a distraction while I hacked into his network. We just didn't want you to get all worked up about her being around Simon before you got all your blood volume back."

I watch Coop's eyes fill with shadows, turning about a hundred shades darker before they fly to mine. "You're okay though?"

"Mhmm." I nod slowly before scoffing up a bit of truth. "He is a piece of work though. Made me want to break my knife out and get all stabby as Alec likes to say."

Distract, distract, distract.

"You?" His brows drop down sharply. "Stabby?"

"Oh, yeah." Alec scoffs, a near-perfect imitation of mine as he draws his attention. "I've managed to turn your little Princess here into somewhat of a deadly weapon these past months."

Okay, okay. No need to get *that* into it, Alec. Try to avoid talk of me stabbing men in cellars.

And why oh why are you continuing to hide things, El?

I fight against the pull of my own brow as Coop's lips finally ghost up, his eyes coming back to me and raking my face with all kinds of new questions in them. "Now that's something I want to see."

"Deal." I shoot him a wink before spinning around to open the fridge, grabbing for some more champagne we definitely don't need yet and ignoring the way I can feel his eyes drilling into me still. Ignoring the clock I can feel ticking down on my secrets because he's right, we don't keep them anymore. And he never even let me keep secrets in the first place.

But this time, these secrets, they're mine... And I finally understand how hard it can be to work up the courage to tell the person you love most about them.

Chapter Thirty

I'm standing in the living room the next morning, waiting for Stef and Kai to come down so I can tell them goodbye before Alec takes them to the airport and mulling over whether to just hop in the car and join them as a means of escape. Coop's about to push, I can feel it in the ever-thickening tension in the air between us. He'd let it go for a while after breakfast yesterday, but then I'd started to feel those night-forest eyes coming back to me with increasing frequency throughout the rest of the day. And I know it's because he can sense I'm holding out on him and is searching for all the new parts of me I'm trying to hide.

That he can sense just like I can that the secret of what Simon had done is driving a silent wedge between us. It doesn't help that I somehow have it all tangled up into who I've become without him too. I figured that part out last night at least, having lain there awake for hours after he had finally drifted off from exhaustion. Somehow, I've started to associate the badass, stabby girl with the shamed girl and once again, I'm not sure what the fuck to do with it. And now I'm worried about if he would—

Fuck. I need to get it together before my self-destructive side takes over and does some serious damage.

Self-awareness is great and all, but I'd sure as shit take some ready-made answers to my problems over it any day of the week.

The thing is, I've never been great at talking to begin with, as evidenced by pretty much my entire life. Sometimes I'd just stare at a therapist or two growing up just to see what they would do. And Coop, while he used to be an exception to that rule to a degree, that's before we'd been apart these past months. Now though, it's like we're meeting all over again in so many ways. Knowing we love each other more than anything but not fully understanding who we've become apart this time.

Because this time, the change had been dramatic. At least on my half of the equation and on his…. Well, I'm still trying to figure that out too.

It all had a ball of nerves flitting around my stomach as soon as I opened my eyes this morning, once again sending me from the room before Coop could wake up and push like I knew he was going to. Leaving me pacing in the living room without any hope of an appetite, contemplating whether to run and buy myself a few more hours or just word vomit the truth all over him despite how much it fucking scared me.

"Els."

I look up and find Kai coming down the stairs with his duffel thrown over his shoulder, the shit-eating grin on his face faltering a bit when he gets a good look at me.

"Kaison." I sigh, unable to do anything but return his grin with a small one of my own. Always seeing him as a little brother despite how much he hates it.

"So." He drops his bag at the base of the stairs before sauntering over to me and wrapping me in a bear hug, swinging us side to side as he continues. "You going to be able to survive with these fuckers without me?"

A small laugh escapes me. "I think I'll manage."

He flashes me that grin again while stepping back and flicking his tongue ring between his teeth, eyes searching mine for a minute before looking down. "So listen," he sighs. "We all picked up on the weird vibe yesterday."

A beat passes before I scoff quietly. "Great." Just what I needed, further confirmation that I'm completely screwed. "Freaking perfect."

He looks back up with an amused grin before tipping his head at me, expression turning openly curious. "Why are you hiding it from him, Els?"

I shrug. "I don't know." Even though I do.

A long moment passes where his eyes continue to search mine before he finally seems to come to terms with something and sighs. "You remember when Hannah and I broke up?"

"Of course." I snort at the reference to the only girlfriend any of them had ever had. "It was a clusterfuck."

Probably hadn't helped that I didn't like her from the start too.

Hannah had been his stepsister and a prima donna bitch, in my not-so-humble opinion. To say we hadn't exactly gotten along is putting it lightly. And to say their parents hadn't approved when it had finally come out would pretty much be the understatement of the century.

"Yeah." A short, humorless laugh leaves him and he looks down for a beat before repeating. "Yeah it was." His hand floats around to pull a beanie from his back pocket and he plays with it for a moment before looking back up to me. "The thing is, as weird as what we had was, I loved her."

I drop my eyes to the beanie in his hands again, suddenly suspicious of the item and tell him softly. "I know that, Kaison."

"You know what hurt the most about it all?"

I pause for a second, knowing that I'm not going to like where he's taking this, unable to do anything but eventually ask. "What?"

"We were going through something when she took off." He looks down at that beanie again, clearing his throat. "Something more than the obvious and what hurt the most was that she didn't let me be there to help her through it in the end." His eyes come back up to mine again as he drives the point home. "She shut me out and took off. Didn't trust or want me to be there for her and I don't think the hurt from that will ever go away completely."

"Kai—" My voice breaks on his name, cutting me off and I bite down hard on my bottom lip. Wanting to offer him comfort but unable to do so without breaking down myself.

He takes a step back in and folds his arms around me again, quietly murmuring. "Let him in, Els, because nothing will hurt him like knowing you didn't trust him enough to be there for you."

I jerk a nod against his shoulder, releasing my lip to suck in a quick breath and let go of him as the sound of footsteps coming down the stairs hit me.

"For me…" Clearing my throat, I hurry to tell him before the others come down far enough to hear. "It's not about a lack of trust. Not really. So I don't know, maybe it wasn't for Hannah either," I finish with a small shrug, trying to give him something to ease what I know has to still be a deep wound.

"Thanks, Els." He gives me a nod, flashing that shit-eating grin while pulling the beanie onto his head. "I'll keep that in mind."

"Or not," I joke hopefully as the others finally trail into the room. "She was still a bitch."

He lifts his brows at me with a pointed look as Mac walks up, chiming in. "Who's a bitch? Els?"

I roll my eyes at them both, grumbling. "Point taken."

Now I just need to find some of that old armor again to face what's next.

***

I've been staring at him sleeping for an hour now since the guys left, still in my pajamas as Kai's words echo in my ears, eyes continuing to come back to how that tension is heavy in his brow again. Stomach churning because I know I'm a big part of the reason for it, but he hasn't exactly opened up yet about what he'd gone through with Simon either. Even though I felt him jerk awake numerous times during the night and I knew it had to be atrocious by the way his body was littered with scars that had never been there before.

Can I really expect that of him though? Full disclosure when I haven't yet given it to him? Doesn't really seem fair to me.

I need to tell him.

This isn't how it's supposed to be. How we're supposed to be. Not after everything.

It all just feels so wrong now and I have no one to blame for it but myself.

It's only been three days, but it's obvious what it's doing to us. We'd passed the point in our relationship where secrets could sit when he'd shown up on a boat that no longer existed in Landing Point months ago. The more tightly I hold on to them now, the worse the damage will be, and that… I just can't do that to us. Can't hurt him the way Kai had laid it out to me. Can't be responsible for the destruction of the most precious thing in my world.

I'm just so fucking scared… because I'm not sure I can be the girl he fell in love with in Costa Rica ever again. Not really. Not after everything I've gone through without him. And I've never factored that in.

My eyes run down his face to where that long scar sits on his chest and I raise a hand to it, tracing my finger down the length of the jagged flesh as his heart gives me answering beats underneath. I reach the bottom of it and let my eyes trail lower, over his taut abdomen to where his arm is lying on top of it, the left one with our words winding around it. And I run my eyes over those letters again and again for what feels like forever before I bring a finger to them too and start to trace there as well. As if I could somehow make them deeper, last through whatever is about to come and into forever with a simple brush of my skin on his.

I know the second he wakes up, but I don't look up and he doesn't interrupt me either. No communication passing between us besides the kind you don't need words for. The kind where you understand someone so deeply that anything verbal almost does a disservice to the way you just know what the other person needs. Even before they might. And right now, Coop knows that I need to stay silent for a little bit longer even if it goes against the grain for him. He does it because he knows I need it and it makes my heart crack open, breath hitching as I fall impossibly more in love with him again. Ratcheting my terror up even more as I breathe him in while tracing words on his skin for once.

We stay that way for another hour at least until I eventually lay my head down on his stomach, looking up into his waiting eyes and seeing the knowledge there. The intensity of his gaze on mine only softened by the soft ghost of his lips as he brings his hand up to rest on the side of my face and starts to speak.

"Did you know…" His thumb brushes back and forth across my cheek with each word, eyes following the movement—"that when Jace and I were in the hospital after his accident"—I watch his chest fall with an exhale and my brows do the same because this is definitely not what I had been expecting—"he told me that he never wanted to live like that?" His eyes come back to mine as shock runs through me. "He made me swear to him that I'd never let him live that way. In a coma forever. He said he couldn't remember much, but he knew he hadn't liked wherever he'd been."

A heavy silence fills the air, lasting for a long minute before I finally unlock my mouth to ask. "What are you saying?" I almost choke on the next words, even more terrified than I was at the start of this. "Are you going to unplug him?"

"No." He shakes his head with the quiet word. "But I did think you needed to know." His face screws up a little, brows dropping to mirror my own. "What *he* wanted."

"Don't fucking do this," I snap softly, the terror suddenly clawing its way through my body for a whole different reason. "I don't—can't hear this." A short, horrible kind of laugh leaves me. "I just spent the better part of the past year fighting for both of you and you know what I care about?" I pause for only a split second before finishing. "He promised me and *I know* he'll come back."

A beat passes between us, his eyes never leaving mine before he answers simply. "Okay."

I narrow my eyes at him and question. "Okay?" Because *nothing* is simple now.

Not after the bomb he just dropped. How am I supposed to keep fighting for someone who doesn't want to be fought for? He promised me. I need him.

"Okay." Coop nods with confirmation. "I'm not going to unplug him until you're ready. You'd never forgive me, so if you make me choose, I'll always choose you."

And suddenly I can't stand that thumb on my cheek. I can't stand how much he understands me. I can't, I can't—

"Fuck off," I snap, sitting up quickly and batting his hand away. Looking out the window while trying to drag enough breath into my lungs. The weight of what he just dropped on me too much to bear, ripping me right down the middle. I can't lose him. I can't save him. I can't do what he wants and I can't not. I can't be the reason he chooses to never wake up, just like I can't be the same girl Coop fell in love with once. *I can't do anything.*

Coop knows exactly what he's doing putting this on me and for a second, I hate him as much as I love him too.

"What is this, Eleanor?" he finally asks, voice going low and when I look back to him, he swallows hard. "Do you wish you had chosen him?"

I shake my head, unable to keep the irritation from my voice. "Don't ask me that, I will always choose you."

He pushes up onto his elbows in bed, narrowing his eyes. "What am I supposed to think"—the frustration is clear in his voice and it pulls at me—"when I can see that you're holding on to something so hard it's making you a fucking mess?"

"And you're not?" I toss out, suddenly desperate to avoid it all and acting on a pissed-off impulse. "I'm not the only one holding on to secrets here, Coop. What happened with Simon all those months?"

"What do you want to know?" He sits up completely, eyes going dark as his anger suddenly fills the room. So palpable I can almost feel it, like that heat that's always radiating from his skin. "What do you want to know, Eleanor?" He grinds the question out, voice dropping to a violent note as he continues. "Want to know how he liked to electrocute me every couple of weeks?" His hand comes up to wave roughly at those mirror scars on his pecks. "Or how he liked to have his guys beat me while he droned on in the corner about how good I would have it if I just gave in?" He throws out, chest heaving as an expression of true anguish rolls over his face. "Or how he outlined to me, in detail, all the things he would do to you if I didn't cooperate whenever he eventually got his hands on you?" I scoot off the bed, already shaking my head and trying to hide the way I'm gasping for breath as he holds his hands out on either side of himself. "So tell me what the fuck you want to know, Eleanor." He waves one at me. "Because I'll tell you whatever that is."

I turn away from him, greedily gulping for air as the terror starts to take over, whispering my worst fear. "What if we don't work anymore?"

His sudden silence eats at me, going on so long that I look back to find his jaw clenched so hard it shows through every part of his face.

"What the fuck did you just say?" he snaps back roughly.

305

I gulp a few more breaths before repeating quietly, "What if we don't work anymore?" What if you don't want me anymore?

His eyes drill into mine for a minute before he whips back the covers, standing in nothing but his boxer briefs and closing the distance between us with powerful strides. That pissed-off energy pouring out of him and practically pushing at my skin with demand as he comes to stand before me.

"Why are you doing this?" His eyes dart between mine. "Why the fuck are you pushing me away so damn hard again when we finally made our way back to each other again?" He drops his head closer to mine, invading my space and I can hear the restraint in his voice to keep from shouting. "What has you so twisted up that you'd be willing to sacrifice *us*?"

"Nothing!" I finally explode, his eyes widening on me in an instant. "Fucking nothing! That's the problem. I can't—fuck." I bring a hand to my chest, head spinning at my inability to get enough air in as I force the words out. "I'm so fucking terrified of losing you again that I can't *breathe*, Cooper." My voice breaks on his name, eyes filling with tears and I scoff. "And I'm sorry, but you picked my flavor of damage, so you want to know what I'm doing?" I wave a hand at myself shortly. "I'm pushing at you because I'm so fucking scared you might not want me anymore that it's like imagining living in a nightmare."

His brows drop down sharply, eyes still searching mine for the piece he's missing as he raises a hand to my cheek. "There is no world that exists where I don't want you, Eleanor," he whispers. "You should know that by now."

I reach up, grabbing his hand on my cheek and whispering back brokenly. "You don't know that." My face pinches up, tears spilling onto my cheeks as I try to explain. "That girl who you met in Costa Rica, who stripped off her"—a gasp cuts me off, the reality of it all crashing down on me—"fuck, I've done things, I can't—fuck, I can't."

And finally the weight of it all becomes too much, a sob breaking free that would send me collapsing to the floor if not for his arms catching me. Pulling me into his lap as he sets us both down gently and wraps the heat of his body around me. Bringing a hand to the back of my head as I continue to sob.

"I-I don't need y-you to haunt me for eternity," I force out, bringing a hand to his chest and reassuring myself with the steady thump there. "I need you right here."

"Then why don't you give me the chance to be?" He brings his hand to my chin the next moment, tipping my head back gently and forcing me to look him in the eyes. "You said when I woke up that I won everything, so whatever this is... let me in, Princess."

I nod once in his hand, looking down to try and order my thoughts with a few steadying breaths. Digging deeper than ever before into my damage and unearthing the most vulnerable parts of myself as I meet his eyes again.

"When I lost you and Jace, I think, in a way, it was like losing my parents all over again." My words start out slow and shaky, making me suck in another breath. "Except this time, I was old enough to do something about it." I look away, trying to choose the right words to explain. "So I did. I went with Alec and he—we, it—" Fuck would I ever stop sucking at this? "It turned out that I shared a predisposition for certain skills like him, which he kind of already told you." I blow out a breath, knowing I'm dragging it all on.

Sometime today, El.

I bring my eyes back to his, telling him point blank. "I stabbed one of the guys who was involved with taking you. Fucking drove a knife into his knee when he said you were dead and then I left him for Alec to torture."

His lips part slightly, eyes flashing with surprise and I have to swallow down my fear to finish.

"And I never regretted it," I admit tightly. "Not once and at the time I even got some sort of… I don't know, satisfaction from it."

Breaking our gaze, I look down again, pulling my chin from his hand as I continue rawly.

"I've lost so much, Coop. So I became who I needed to be to find you because I couldn't live in a world where I lost you too. The thing is"—my throat tries to close up and I bite my lip for a second, using the pain to keep another sob at bay before giving voice to my worst fear—"I'm terrified now because of what I went through, what I've done, who I became—" I force myself to look back up, seeing the dawning of understanding in those night-forest ones I love so much as they lock with mine. "What if the person I became to find you is too far from the girl you fell in love with?"

"Eleanor Monroe." He drops his forehead to mine with a low laugh before continuing in a quiet voice. "Do you know why I fell in love with you?"

I shake my head against his, seeing those flecks of dark spark in his eyes.

"Because you were so fucking defiant in the face of the world, you made me feel alive for the first time. So strong despite everything that life had thrown at you and fuck"—his voice turns rough—"when you finally let someone in enough to love them, it's with the same recklessness that lives in your soul. Almost to a fault. You love so hard and I could see it, even if you didn't want me to. Didn't want anyone to…" He pauses, tears filling his own eyes as we breathe the same air. "There is nothing you wouldn't do for those that make it past your walls. No depth or darkness that you wouldn't delve into. And that…" I feel his hands on my cheeks a second later, holding me tight as he finishes. "That is why I fell in love with you." A soft sob leaves me even as he brushes his lips against mine. "And I will continue to love every version of you, whether it's the girl I fell for on the beach or the woman that I love even more today, because you are still all of those things. Broken parts fitting mine with every version of you amazing me."

I wrap my arms around him, clutching him and tucking my face into his neck as I sob openly. Each cry purges some of the fear as I finally start to find some kind of middle ground, some peace between those two versions of myself again. Fitting some of those pieces of me that Simon had knocked to the ground that night back into place as I work up the courage to speak of it. Hating that I have to after he taunted Coop with the possibilities... but I have to, for both of us.

So that we can finally start to heal in both the singular and plural sense.

"There's something else," I choke out, swallowing my cries and pushing back from him enough to look up into his eyes. "Simon—" The words die in my throat as the memory flashes through my mind, making my stomach twist sharply and I see Coop's eyes go hard. His brows drop as my silence continues and I look away, exhaling a stuttering breath before continuing. "The night we were there. He was headed up to his office when Alec was hacking into his computer and we needed a distraction," I tell him, voice empty and keeping my eyes down. Trying to detach myself from it enough to get through it. "So I stopped him. Told him we needed to talk. And he, we went into his library—" Fuck, I'm choking. Choking on air and words and it's not working. It's like everything about that moment is strangling me all over again.

"Eleanor." And I can hear it, that he already knows in the gravelly tone. So full of feeling I have to press my lips together to keep another sob in. Another beat passing before his hands come to my cheeks again with a barely there touch, so incredibly careful that it breaks me a little. "What happened in that room?"

"Nothing." I shake my head. "I mean, not nothing, but other people go through—"

"Eleanor," he interrupts, voice demanding my eyes as he nudges my head up gently. And when I finally look up and our eyes lock, I see nothing but pain and love and dark fury. All of it beating through the tight pulse of his body against mine. "What happened?"

It takes me a moment to open my mouth, like my body is fighting against forcing the reality I don't want to acknowledge from my lips. "He made me strip. Told me he'd put a bullet in you if I didn't, so I—" My face crumbles as I suck in a breath, knowing I'm about to break his heart and mine but that there's no other option. "I did what I had to, to keep you alive."

His jaw clenches again for a long moment, hands giving a single tremble against my cheeks before he breathes roughly. "What else?"

"Nothing, really." I break our gaze, looking down again. "Pushed me to the ground and felt me up a little is all." Stomach turning sick with the confession before I shake my head. "Like I said, other people have—"

"Don't you dare do that," he orders quietly, drawing my eyes back up in surprise. "*Don't you dare* make what you went through seem small. Yes, other people have suffered worse but don't compare your pain to theirs. No assault should be minimized." His nostrils flare, voice almost breathless as he finishes. "What he did to you is real and horrible and deserves to be acknowledged so that you can be proud that you survived it." He drops his forehead to mine, eyes squeezing shut as pain blankets his face for a moment before he opens them back up to lock with mine. "And I swear to god, Princess, I will make him pay for what he did to you. Anything you want done to him, I will—"

"Coop," I cut him off softly, bringing my hands back to his and twining my fingers between them. "I'm not opposed to the idea, but I have you back. That's all I ever wanted and as long as he's no longer a threat to us in the end... the rest doesn't matter. Not as long as we're safe." A small shrug leaves me because suddenly, it's so very true. All that pain and fury leaks out of me a bit, my soul giving a little sigh. "I just needed you to know so that you could understand why I ran when you asked me to—"

"Fuck." He shakes his head with the curse. "I'm so sorr—"

"Don't apologize. Don't do that," I tell him, finding some strength in it. In expressing what I need. "I don't want you to treat me like I'm made of glass. I'm okay. I *will* be okay. I just need to figure out my way through this and that's always been our language, so—"

"So we grow," he finishes for me, lips twitching the barest hint. "We grow stronger."

My lips twitch in answer to his even as fresh tears fall onto my cheeks, that distance between us closing as I stare into his eyes, a resounding pulse echoing between us as our souls fully tangle together again.

"We grow together," I repeat softly.

"And in the meantime," That thumb runs along the curve of my cheek and I watch his eyes track the movement before he exhales deeply, meeting my gaze again. "Tell me everything. Everything about our time apart. I don't want to miss out on one memory or part of you."

A breath passes from me to him before I smile through the tears and close the distance between us. Pressing my lips to his and knowing somehow that everything is going to be okay now. That we're going to make it out of this. Heal. Thrive. As long as we keep coming back to this. And that's what we do all day, hardly moving from that spot on the floor as we grow together. Talking and kissing and crying and laughing. No longer twisted up by the secrets.

Finding our way back to an even better version of us through a whole new language.

Chapter Thirty-One

"So." I grab some pasta off the shelf and throw it into the grocery cart, debating how to broach this topic with Mac whistling a merry tune at my side as we restock at the local mom-and-pop grocery store.

It had been two weeks since me and Coop spent that day on the floor and I had never felt closer to him. We had never focused so much on the emotional well-being of our relationship before and truthfully, looking back now, we probably should have. Might have even saved us some trouble. We had talked about what he went through with Simon in more detail. We had talked about how I screamed for him at night while wearing his shirt to bed. I had even walked him through my ritual, much to his apparent horror.

And eventually, we talked about Jace, deciding to leave that decision for after we finally dealt with Simon and could talk to the doctors in person. Fly a couple more specialists in for a twentieth and twenty-first opinion I deemed as necessary. But regardless, that decision would wait because no matter what it was… there's no way either of us would let him go without saying goodbye.

And I still wasn't sure I could make the decision Jace wanted, selfishly needing him to open his eyes because I love him too much to let him go.

Just like I had with Coop.

So it's been two weeks of talking and talking and talking some more. He's never once pressed for more and while I'm grateful to him for it, happy we've had this time together… I have now spent the past two days staring at his frequently shirtless body, pretty much constantly fantasizing about having his cock inside of me and it's just plain embarrassing at this point. I'm pretty sure Alec had even caught me when I'd been staring at him over my wineglass last night if the disgusted look he had shot me was any indication. And this morning when he'd come out of the bathroom with only a towel wrapped around his waist, freshly showered with *fucking water droplets* running down his skin… I'd literally had to change my panties after he left the room.

Needless to say, I need to get laid about six different ways to Sunday.

I'm just at a fucking loss as to how to approach it. Worrying that I'll suddenly get cold feet or that it will feel tainted. Different. When all I want is to just feel us again, coming together in that singular way we always do. Just me and him without any part of what Simon did between us.

Mac rounds the corner of the aisle, seemingly having forgotten I ever started to speak and I decide to just cut to the chase. For both mine and my vagina's sake.

"I need to get laid," I blurt out.

His whistling suddenly cuts off and he shoots me a distinctly awkward look. "Uh, okay." He looks both ways down the aisle before squinting his eyes at me. "Is this something that can wait until we finish shopping, or are you saying we need to leave now…"

I roll my eyes at him as he drags the question out and huff. "No, we don't need to leave now."

"Then I'm confused." He squints further, tilting his head. "I'm sure you can shoot your man a text and he'll be ready and waiting—"

"Oh my god!" I snap, walking a few more paces down the aisle and leaving him to trail behind, hopefully with my embarrassment as I mutter. "Please shut up."

It's moments like this when it would be really useful to have a girlfriend here. Not that I really have a lot of them, or any, but I'd take Tiff for this mortifying conversation if not for the fact she'd probably be equally embarrassed.

"Don't get mad at me because you're all horny!" He fails to whisper, picking up the pace to follow me and drawing the scandalized eyes of the poor elderly man we pass by. "I mean, sure you both have—" His words die midsentence, along with the sound of the grocery cart, before he exclaims loudly, "Holy shit, you haven't done it yet!"

My eyes just about bug out of my head and I whip around toward him. "Shut up!"

"Holy shit," he mutters again, shocked eyes matching mine.

I dart my eyes to the people on the aisle that are openly staring at us before giving him a glare. "*Macallan.*"

Another second passes and he shakes his head. "Okay, okay." He pushes the cart the rest of the way toward me. "I can do this." His eyes close and he blows out what I think is supposed to be a zen breath before opening them and looking at me seriously. "Sex therapist mode initiated. What seems to be the problem?"

I narrow my eyes, really having to tamp down the urge to smack him with the reminder that there're witnesses and instead turn around while grumbling. "Never mind."

"Stop." He laughs out loud, making me glance over my shoulder, watching him throw some peanut butter and jelly into the cart because our five-year-old palates were also twins. "Just trying to lighten the mood a little." He makes it to my side and gives me a small smile. "I never really thought about it once we got him back but thinking about it now, I can guess, uh, the why of your problem."

"You think?" I pull a sarcastic face at him, grabbing a bag of donuts off the shelf and opening them right there in the store. Maybe the sugar would calm my nerves, and at the very least, I fucking deserved it. Reaching into the bag, I grab one of the donuts and plop the whole thing into my mouth, talking around it as we start to walk again. "Sex has just always been so natural to me. I never felt any shame or struggled with it in any way. It was just a part of being alive for me. One of the best parts too." I dip my head toward him and he nods in agreement. "But now…" Swallowing the donut down, I promptly grab another and start the process all over again as Mac gives me a judgy look that I choose to ignore. "I mean, I feel better. Not so sick over it anymore. Hell, I even walked through the room in my underwear yesterday without even thinking about it." I stop and turn toward him, grabbing another donut out of the bag in preparation for its necessity. "But what if it's different now? What if I freak out or something? What if I never get past what he did and have to go through life without—"

"Shut up." He plucks the donut bag out of my hands the next instant, dropping it into the cart and shaking his head at me with a disapproving look. "And when we get back, jump Satan for both our sakes."

My mouth pops open, donuts and all, as I stare at him in shock for a moment before popping off. "Excuse me?"

"Bang it out." He nods at me. "You obviously need it."

Completely incompetent as he turns to push the cart around the corner of the next aisle, leaving me shoving my last donut into my mouth before running to catch up.

"That's your advice? Really?" I snap. "'Bang it out'? Did you not hear anything I just said?"

"Oh, I did." He scoffs, turning to me. "And I get it, Els. I really do. But the more you think about it, the crazier it's going to drive you." A sigh leaves him and his face softens a bit. "Like a self-fulfilling prophecy. If you expect to freak out, you're going to. So you need to stop thinking about it and just do it."

I let his words rattle around in my head for a minute, face pulling tight because the truth is I'm not sure what I think about them. They make sense, but at the same time, they don't. So finally, I just snag my donuts back out of the cart, tossing out over my shoulder while walking ahead of him. "You suck."

"So glad I could help," he tosses back, pushing the cart to catch up.

"Whatever," I mumble. "I'm trading you in for a girl."

We finish up our shopping quickly then, him whistling a merry tune and me scarfing down the donuts to try and quell my growing anxiety. Heading to the checkout and paying cash like I've become accustomed to so that we can't be tracked by credit card transactions. It had been hard enough to get by Coop with only Mac in tow, but I had needed to have that very unhelpful conversation, so I had practically raced out while yelling where I was going over my shoulder. Regardless though, I'm still making sure to mind the necessary rules for all of our sakes.

Mac's whistling tune changes as we exit the store and my brows drop as I try to place the sound I know somehow. It hits me then that he's switched it up to "Let's Get It On" and I open my mouth to snap at him again, but the sight of someone sitting on the hood of our SUV stops me short. Or, more accurately, a tall, leggy girl with heavy makeup and black hair that's dyed red underneath, dressed head to toe in leather. Smirking at me while tossing freaking Sour Patch Kids into her mouth.

Mac clearly notices her too, because his whistling comes to a stop, letting me know that at least I'm not hallucinating from sugar and stress. She raises a hand, waving her fingers at me in a motion to come closer and I narrow my eyes back, shaking my head with a clear message. No way am I going near that fucking car now that some strange, candy-eating girl has planted herself on it. I dart my eyes quickly around the parking lot, looking for anything else out of place, but come up empty. Nothing seems to be amiss besides, well, the obvious, and I look back to her, deciding that I disliked her even more for the candy. I need some fucking candy today. She clearly doesn't, if the growing smile on her face is any indication.

She gives me a nod, sliding off the hood of the car at the same time Mac mutters. "What do you want to do?"

"Wait and see." I shrug, letting my hand drift inside my leather jacket to grasp the knife there tightly. "It's two against one, at least from the looks of it."

She saunters over confidently, stopping probably five feet away from me before the smile on her face turns almost maniacal. "Well this explains so much."

I give her an annoyed look, narrowing my eyes again and retorting sharply. "Can I help you with something?"

"And there it is." She laughs, pointing at my face with a Sour Patch Kid. "Right there around the eyes and in that fucking superior tone." Tossing the candy into her mouth, she finishes while chewing. "So obvious."

I take a step toward her out of impulse, her demeanor pissing me off and making me grip the knife in my jacket even more tightly. "Who the fuck are you?"

"Serena," she answers casually. "And you"—her eyes run over my face again assessingly as she takes a step closer to me—"are Alec's sister."

I fight against the surprise trying to work its way into my face, staying silent and neither confirming nor denying her guess.

"It's okay," she whispers conspiratorially. "No need to say anything. I'm good at guessing these kinds of things." Her hand comes up, covering her mouth as she speaks out of the side of it. "Plus, you kind of look alike, in case no one has mentioned it yet."

"Good for you." I make sure the sarcasm is dripping from my voice, letting my own smirk out to play. "Now let me repeat it since you obviously didn't get that part the first time." Emphasizing every word that follows. "Can. I. Help. You. With. Something?"

"And touchy just like him too." She laughs. "That's why I decided to wait and approach someone else that he was shacking up with. He probably would have shot me first and then taken the time to figure out whether I was still on his side or not. Would have preferred Coop but..." That fucking Sour Patch Kid comes up and she circles it around my face in the air. "Little did I know the treat I'd be in for in finding you! It all makes sense now."

And with that, my limit is reached because this is quite literally the last shit I need today.

"Start talking fast, Serena." I take another step toward her, coming within swiping distance and flash her the knife inside my jacket. "Because the last I heard, you had run into Simon, and yes, *my brother* didn't know whether you were dead or alive." That smirk on my face turns as vicious as his and I finish quietly. "And it turns out I don't mind being as deadly as him, so cut the bullshit."

The smile is gone from her face in an instant, and she answers back with equal quiet, "Careful, little girl. You're playing outside of your depth."

"Oh." I tip my head to the side with a scoff. "Right about now, I'd be willing to take my chances."

She stares into my eyes for another beat before sighing. "Fine." Stuffing the candy into her jacket, she brings up her hands, brushing the sugar from them before talking. "After I looked into Simon for Alec, he managed to trace the hack back to me, but only because I underestimated him." She holds up a finger. "Not through any lack of my own skills. I hadn't been properly prepared for the fucking monster you two were awakening." Another dramatic sigh leaves her as she shakes her head. "Needless to say, after I had to pull the cord on my babies because he was having himself a wonderful little stroll through all of my files, I decided, fuck Alec," A shrug leaves her with his name. "If he wasn't going to be straight with me about where he had gone or why then I was going to pull in the right people to make sure that my ass wasn't the one taking the heat."

I make it there as soon as she finishes talking, guessing softly. "You went to Bainbridge."

"I did." She nods. "Right to the top, and they were not happy campers when I told them that their software was being used outside of the company."

"So what?" My brows drop with the question, trying to figure out her angle here. "They want to come in and save the day now?"

"Not exactly." She shakes her head. "But they do have some information and want to talk."

"To Alec?" I guess again.

"And Coop, if he'd be will—"

"No," I cut her off sharply, even knowing he wouldn't want me to. That he would talk to them in an instant if it meant taking Simon down, but I can't deal with that. Not yet. "That's out of the question."

That crazed smile grows on her face again. "Interesting."

"Yeah, well," I bite out, tipping my chin up at her. "Get uninterested."

"Fine. Fine." She holds her hands up in surrender. "Just pass my message along to your brother." Walking back a few steps, she laughs again. "He'll know how to get in touch with me." Her eyes move to Mac at my side and she flashes him a wink. "And don't think I forgot about you, handsome. Might have to run into you again sometime soon under more friendly circumstances." She raises a hand, flitting her fingers at us in some sort of flashy bullshit wave before turning on her heel and walking away.

Trudging through the ice and snow like it's no big deal and making me hate her a little bit more, if that's even possible. Okay, maybe it isn't complete hate yet, but under the circumstances, it's a strong possibility. Plus, she is screwing my brother periodically and practically just propositioned my twin. *Not* that I'm judging… but gross.

I should make that a rule. If you're going to be someone who comes around, you can only screw one of my family members at a time.

Pretty sure that goes something like pot meet kettle, whose name is El.

"I think I'm in love."

My head whips to Mac at his soft proclamation and I take in the slightly dazed look on his face.

"Oh my god," I snap in frustration. "Get in the fucking car, or I swear to god I really will trade you in for a girl."

Chapter Thirty-Two

By the time we get back from the store, my irritation with pretty much everyone and everything has been driven to even greater heights. In part because of the sheer number of times I've caught Mac staring off dazedly, muttering about how it's been too long since he got laid too. So when I walk into the living room and see that the space has been cleared of furniture to make room for Coop and Alec to duke it out in hand to hand, and neither of them notices me or comes to a stop at my presence, I'm more than a little annoyed by it.

My eyes go to Coop's, yet again shirtless body, covered in nothing but a pair of loose sweatpants and I can't help but think about how I used to be the hot girl eating candy on cars. Okay, maybe not on cars, but still. Now I'm just pounding the donuts to deal with the fact that I'm scared to get laid. It's atrocious and Mac is right, I will not fucking allow it.

Yes, I might never be the girl who strips naked on the beach again. Maybe. But I've come so much further than she ever wanted or dreamed of in so many other ways. I've grown up. I've grown stronger. I'm still fucking hot and I'm going to have an orgasm today, or so help me, somebody, not excluding myself, will pay.

And with that thought, I drop the grocery bags in my hands onto the floor with a crash, bringing them both to a sudden stop as I announce with fake cheer. "I just got ambushed by the fucking booty call."

Coop cocks his head at me in confusion, chest heaving as he asks, "Who?" while Alec mutters, "Shit."

"Oh ho ho." I laugh mockingly. "Shit would be right, big brother."

Mac walks in behind me then, arms weighed down by the bulk of the groceries as he sighs again. "I think I'm in love with your fuck buddy, Alec."

"Oh my god." I throw my hands up into the air, turning on him. "You are not in love, Macallan."

"How do you know?"

"Because you and that girl would be a fucking train wreck," I state bluntly, turning back around to see Alec fighting a smirk while Coop isn't even trying to hide his amusement. "Oh, fuck this shit." Reaching down, I start to pull off my boots while griping out the rest. "Serena said to contact her, Alec. Bainbridge isn't happy about Simon and they might want to cut a deal or"—I toss one of the oversized winter boots to the side before grabbing for the other—"I don't know, some other type of bullshit." Exhaling some of my irritation, I toss the next boot over my shoulder, maybe or maybe not purposefully in Mac's direction, hearing a curse escape him behind me as I yank my socks off. "It was kind of hard to discern between her"—I wave my socks in the air before finishing sarcastically—"everything."

A smirk flashes across Coop's face, that damn amusement even clearer in his voice as he confirms. "You met Serena?"

Uh, no. Don't like that look one bit.

"Be very careful right now, Cooper Monroe"—I let the socks drop to the floor and hold up a finger to him in warning—"because I cannot be held responsible for my actions if I find out your cock went anywhere near that Sour Patch–eating—"

Alec's sudden burst of laughter cuts me off and I look at him in surprise, the sound so genuine and rare it shocks me a little.

"Sorry." He stops himself as if realizing what he's doing and thinking it's wrong or something. "It's just you sounded like such a"—he lifts his brows at me—"wife."

A beat passes between us before I practically growl at him. "Ugh!" I shrug my jacket off and let it fall to the floor, leaving myself standing in leggings and the old Aerosmith tee Stef had shipped to me last week. Not exactly a sparring outfit, but under the current circumstances, I'll make it work. At least I'm wearing a sports bra already.

Narrowing my eyes at them both, I take a casual step their way. "I'm suddenly feeling a little violent." I cock a brow and let my lips twitch in invitation. "So who feels like getting their ass beat?"

"Right." Alec snorts. "Someone hide the knives before she comes at me."

I open my mouth to pop back that it's too late for that, but Coop's eyes snag mine, stopping me with the dark flash of desire I see there and sending my stomach flipping. The air between us turns thick as our gaze holds and I lift my brow a little higher at him in challenge, fighting against the smirk that wants to answer the one growing on his face. He takes that first step while arching a brow right back, eyes never leaving mine as he walks slowly toward me. The desire between us ramping up so suddenly and severely that I'm left trying to hide the fact that I'm fucking breathless from the force of it.

He comes to stand in front of me and pauses for a second, eyes raking my face before he takes yet another step toward me. Putting us at that nearly touching point that has me having to fight against the urge to lean in and close the distance. His eyes come back to mine, and this time, I don't even try to hide the lift of my lips, that pull between us as palpable as the light sheen of sweat on his chest. He dips his head slowly, keeping our eyes locked and giving me time to process exactly what he's doing as he brings his lips to my ear.

"Oh, Princess." His voice comes out a little rough and all kinds of intimate. "I thought you'd never ask."

My lips part, breath hitching and pussy clenching instantly with a pounding kind of need that has my mind going blank.

His head lifts a little when my silence continues and I can hear the teasing arrogance in it as he pushes. "Or are you scared? Don't want to be embarrassed?"

Narrowing my eyes at him, I tip my chin up and bring our faces back closer together again, making damn sure he can hear exactly how breathy my voice is. "Oh, Coop." I go up on my toes and bring my lips to his ear, echoing his words. "I thought you'd never ask." Dropping back down, I watch his pupils dilate with an open need that's answering mine and give him my best bratty smirk. "Let's play, big boy."

That savage smirk spreads slowly on his face for the first time since I got him back and another piece of my heart heals with it. Both of us, under each other's spell, are left unable to move and getting pulled further into the black hole of our gravity by the second until Alec's sardonic voice interrupts.

"Well, this is awkward."

Coop's eyes never leave mine as he shoots back with a low laugh. "We are married, Alec."

"Doesn't change the fact that it's still fucking weird." He snorts, walking to the stairs while continuing. "I'm going to contact Serena. At the very least, we need to know how she found us."

Mac sighs again dramatically, dropping his groceries to the ground beside mine. "Don't forget to put these up whenever you're done—" He cuts himself off. "Uh, sparring." Although the word sparring sounds very much like something else as he heads for the stairs too, muttering under his breath. "I'm really starting to hate Canada."

"So." I tip my head to the side with the quiet word, heart pounding with excitement and anticipation. Not quite realizing how much I've missed our particular brand of play until this very moment. "What do you feel like? Knives?" Bringing my lips closer to his as every cell in my body fires with new life, I lower my voice even more. "Or something a little more physical?"

He brushes his lips against mine in answer. "Is that even a question?"

I pull away and walk past him with a grin, tossing out over my shoulder. "Like I said, let's play a game."

A beat passes before his footsteps start to trail after me into the cleared living space, amused voice calling out. "You want to play a game, Princess?"

"Well." I look back at him over my shoulder while reaching my hands up into the air with a stretch. "That first one did end so well." A small shrug leaves me before I reach down for my toes while tacking on. "Even if I'm not as partial to stripping naked in public these days."

I watch his feet come closer through the space between my legs and lift up when he comes to a stop behind me, loving the tight anticipation of having him at my back again.

"You are perfect"—his breath fans out against my lower neck with the quiet word before trailing up to my ear with that damn barely there touch—"for me." His fingertips touch the tips of mine as goose bumps erupt pretty much over my entire body. "Faults, damage, and all."

I'm just about ready to turn around and say to hell with it then, blood pounding through my body with demand, but he takes a step back and orders. "Let's see what you've learned."

It takes me a beat to catch up, but I eventually blow out a deep breath and force my body to focus on the now instead of what's hopefully going to happen because... Well, I really do want to play this game with him.

That smirk when he said Serena's name nagging at some part of my feminine intuition.

"Fine." I spin around, rolling my shoulders. "Rules are, if you make contact, you get to ask a question."

His lips twitch, eyes running down the length of me as I take up a fighting pose and he backs up a couple more steps. "Look at how far you've come."

"Watch yourself," I warn, narrowing my eyes at the amused note in his voice. "Do we have a deal?"

"We have a deal." He nods.

A beat passes between us then and I know in that instant that I could very possibly have this fight in the bag. Not because I'm better than him, although give me a few years and I just might be. It's because hidden underneath all that desire and strength and night-forest shadows in his eyes… I can see it, that little bit of unsureness. As if he doesn't know where to strike first or how to approach me and it's because what's happening is in direct opposition to his core when it comes to me. Where Alec has no problem beating the shit out of me to get his point across when it comes to physical defense, Coop would never actually hurt me. The idea more abhorrent to him than any kind of pain he could suffer himself. Even if it's to make me better, stronger, he'll always hold back. I can already see it in the way he's holding his body, too tight and in check. And while I don't exactly want to hurt him either, I have no qualms about using his hesitancy to my advantage.

"Hey, Coop," I call out with a soft smile.

His eyes narrow on mine as if he knows I'm up to something. "What?"

"Love you," I tell him honestly because, in this moment, it's painfully true.

Even as I attack the next instant.

I close the distance between us in two steps, moving quickly into a front, then a round kick combo that I know is going to drive him backward and put him off balance. It all happens in the space of barely two seconds and I watch as he reacts out of instinct, leaning back with surprise flashing across his face. Lining himself up perfectly for me to strike at him with my elbow, using all that built-up momentum as I pivot out of the kick. I aim for his shoulder instead of his face, trying to be nice because I do love him, but he recovers quicker than I anticipated. Reacting to the incoming hit by blocking it with his forearm and reaching down in the next breath to snag me behind the knee.

Pulling me completely off balance as he brings it up to rest on his hip, aligning our bodies in all the right places and leaving me to grip his shoulder in order to stay upright as he smirks. "Much better." He drops his head closer to mine, pulling my leg tighter around him. "Wouldn't you agree?"

"Possibly." I try and fail to keep the moan from my voice, going wet at that hardness I can feel in his sweatpants as our eyes spark against one another along with every other part of our bodies. "Want to know something?"

"What?"

I use both his and my leverage then, quickly grabbing his other shoulder and lifting myself just enough to bring my free knee up to his stomach with a hard hit. Making the air leave him in a whoosh and his hold on my leg slackens enough that I'm able to pull out of it. Jumping back a few steps before he can recover and grab for me again.

He leans over just the slightest bit, rubbing at his stomach once before looking up at me through narrowed eyes and rising back up. "That was dirty."

I tip my head to the side with a careless shrug, fighting a smile. "All's fair, as the poets would say."

"Right." The word leaves him in a short burst of air and he starts to circle me slowly then, but I opt to stay where I am, pivoting to keep him in sight as his eyes run down me with a sharper look than before. "And I see the fighting style is genetic along with the sparkling personality."

"Ha. Ha," I drone sarcastically, reminding him. "First hit, first question."

His eyes come up to lock with mine. "And what would you like to know?"

"Did you sleep with that Sour Patch–eating annoyance?"

His lips twitch. "I thought you didn't want to know?"

My lips part in surprise and I suck in a breath to tell him just exactly how he better rectify that response when he *moves*, stepping right into striking distance with all that grace I somehow forget about because of his size. I bring up my arm preemptively to ward off a hit, taking a quick step back and he uses every bit of it against me. Snatching my arm out of the air and using that plant of my heel to swing me around before pulling me into him. Ending with both his arm and mine resting against my now rapidly beating heart in a tight hold as he finally answers me.

"Do you really want to know?" he asks, breath fanning against my hair. "I won't lie to you ever again, but I don't think any good can come of talking about that type of past either."

My brows drop as I think it through, but fuck, I'm already this far down the path. If I don't find out now, it's going to drive me crazy. "Yes."

"Fine." He nips at my ear softly. "If you really must know, I slept with her once."

"B-but," I stutter as my outrage launches itself through the roof. "That's disgusting!"

Coop exhales wearily as I start to struggle in his hold. "Eleanor—"

"She's fucking my brother!"

Would the horror of her never end?

I'd happily take Hannah back right now instead.

He brings his face alongside mine. "And this happened long before you."

"Yeah, right." I scoff in disbelief. "Not long before you were obsessing over me all those years! How'd the daily routine go?" An irate snort leaves me. "Stalk a little, fuck the sidepiece a little?"

"Eleanor," he cuts me off, arm tightening over mine to lock me against his body. "I slept with her once. It was nothing more than—"

"Please shut up!" I try to drop out of his hold like Alec taught me, but I'm too late, too caught up in the argument to recover, as evidenced by him quickly sliding a knee between my legs to stop me.

"Princess." His voice drops low as he slides that leg against my pussy, the friction of it making me wet all over again and sending my breath hitching. "What I was going to say is... I married you." That leg presses against me even harder and I can't help the quiet sound of need that escapes. "I fell in love with you." He slides his mouth down to the curve of my neck, nudging my T-shirt down a bit before pulling the skin there gently through his teeth. "Happily knowing that I would never fuck anyone else again."

It's sweet. I'll give him that. Yet I'm still pissed.

Probably not justifiable considering I'd had my own share of interludes before him, but still... I honestly thought he'd say no, that I was just being a little bit crazy because of my orgasm deprivation. I've never had this happen with him before, which may be why I'm overreacting just a tad.

And even with knowing all of that, I still whip my heel up, coming right between his legs to give him a light kick to the balls. Dropping him like a fucking hot potato as he immediately lets go of me and falls to the floor with a quiet groan.

"You're right, I do fight dirty," I muse, walking to the master bedroom without a backward glance. "Let me know when you're ready for the next round."

Yeah, that definitely wasn't justifiable either, but I also can't help the smile that breaks free, knowing he's probably going to be less than a minute behind me.

Chapter Thirty-Three

I'd had this whole plan to make up for the hit-to-balls thing.

I was going to take off my clothes and be sitting in the middle of the bed, waiting for him to take me whenever he eventually recovered. It was a good plan. A great plan. One that I probably owed him after that little overreaction. In retrospect, probably stupid too, because I had failed epically at it.

Sitting here instead in my leggings and oversized Aerosmith T-shirt. Verging so dangerously close to tears that I'm at risk of losing those confident pieces that I've only just started to find again. Body and mind completely in conflict with what they want, one needing him as much as my next breath while the other is trying to choke the air from my lungs with fear. So freaking embarrassed now that he's about to walk through that door, and I'm not sure if I'm really going to be able to follow through with all the big talk I had given him out there.

The door opens the next second and I look up to meet his eyes, holding there for a beat before he arches a brow at me. "Are we done lashing out now?"

"Mhmm." I drag out vaguely, looking down and sliding my hands down my leggings.

"Eleanor?"

"Yeah?"

I look back up and meet that suddenly intense gaze, his brow pulling tight at whatever he finds there. "What's wrong?"

"Nothing." I shake my head.

He takes another step toward me, eyes raking down my body in assessment before he repeats. "What's wrong?"

"Nothing." I sigh, darting my eyes down. Not wanting him to see the fear there. "I just—" Cutting myself off, I shake my head again. "It's stupid. I just lost my nerve a little, but I'm fine."

The room fills with silence then and it continues for so long that I eventually force myself to look up, needing to know what's going on inside of his head to quell some of the fears in mine. I find his eyes narrowed on me, so intense it's jolting with a million thoughts flying behind them. It makes me swallow hard at the sense that he's turning me inside out and hating that I'm not sure if I can give him this today.

"Coop, it's fine—"

He shakes his head with a sharp move, turning around and walking back out of the room so quickly that it leaves me speechless because of all the things I'd expected, it'd never been that. My lips part as the last of the air leaves me, that choking sense starting to take over with each of the seconds that pass by. Tears overflowing in my lower lids and threatening to spill right along with the rest of me if—

He marches back into the room then with my leather jacket in hand and I gasp for a breath, fingers clenching onto the burgundy bedding below me for something solid to anchor myself to as he comes to stand before me.

Dropping down onto his heels, he looks up into my eyes with a soft look and a ghost of lips. "Let's play a new game."

"What—" I swallow hard, head spinning from the mess in it. "What game?"

He looks down, lifting his hand to slowly trail his fingers down my calf, reigniting that edge of my desire. "Do you trust me?"

"Of course," is my immediate answer. No thought needed there. Not anymore.

"Then"—he looks up at me—"scoot back on the bed."

Some of that fear starts to work its way into my stomach at his request, threatening me with panic, but I blow out a jagged breath to fight it. Clinging to the absolute knowledge that Coop would never force anything before I'm ready.

"Just a game." He emphasizes in a hushed voice, bringing his fingers up to the back of my knee and giving me a gentle squeeze. "One that will be played entirely on your terms."

It takes me a minute, but I jerk a quick nod, slowly scooting myself back on the bed as he stands and opens up my jacket, quickly pulling the knife from where I left it within. His eyes come back to mine with a reassuring nod, but still, it's only when he flicks it open, quickly flipping the blade in his hand, that I finally start to get a clue as to what kind of game he's talking about playing.

"Coop," I start quietly, knowing that this has to be walking as close to the line for him as it is for me after what he went through. "You don't—"

"I trust you," he tells me, voice absolute. "You trust me." And I see the sureness in his eyes as he lifts the knife, nodding down to it. "This is just to remind you who's in charge here."

I stare up into his eyes for a moment and my resolve strengthens to battle against that unsureness. Willing to at least try because he's shirtless and sexy and I desperately want to have his body inside of mine again. To reclaim that part of myself. "What are the rules?"

His lips lift as he kneels on the bed between my feet and holds the knife out to me, making my gaze drop to the blade as I take a deep breath. Reaching out to grasp it tentatively and exhaling slowly as I slide it carefully out of his hand.

"The rules"—he starts slowly, closing his hand around mine where it's gripping the blade—"are simple."

I look back up to meet his gaze, our eyes locking as his voice drops low.

"I'm going to play."

My lips twitch up with the memory of the last time he said those words in an entirely different situation.

"Asking you the same question, over and over again."

I cock my head at him in confusion and he lets go of my hand to lower both his down to either side of my hips, caging me in as he brings our faces barely an inch apart.

"And you're going to answer me, *honestly*, every time."

I narrow my eyes at him in question because I know I'm missing something here.

"And," he continues, gaze tracing my face even as his breath fans across my lips. "You're not allowed to let go of the knife unless it's because you're screaming so hard with pleasure"—his eyes come back to mine as my own breath hitches, body going tight with anticipation all over again—"completely lost to anything else, that it drops from your hand without you even realizing it."

I suck in the breath that's fanning across my lips as the picture he's painting flashes through my mind and makes me wiggle a little on the bed. Pussy tingling with need as he lowers his body purposely to brush against mine. "So tell me, Princess." His voice comes out with quiet demand and a twitch of lips. "Do you want me to stop?"

No. Abso-freakin-lutely not. Not at this moment anyway.

So I shake my head at him and close that space between our lips, answering. "No." And the way I *need* so much more of him right then has me almost shaking.

"Good." He pulls back, sitting on his heels and putting that gorgeous body on display for me while looking down to pull one of my feet into his lap. Leaving me blowing out a deep breath of frustration as he starts to trace words on top of my foot teasingly. "What's the first thing you want to do when all this is over?"

"Uh," I start blankly, his question taking me by surprise and leaving me playing catch up. "Well." Clearing my throat, I give him the same answer

I've known for months. "After we figure everything out." Simon. Jace. "I want to go back to Cahuita. Stay there for a few months and just… be."

His eyes come back to mine, fingers pausing for a beat. "Really?"

"Really." I nod. "Are you surprised?"

"Not exactly." He shrugs, looking down and starting to move those fingers up my calf with each letter. "More pleased."

"Why?"

"It means you were happy there. Felt safe." His eyes come up to meet mine with the answer and my own heart clenches at it. "If that's the first place you want to go."

"Of course," I tell him softly. "Of course I was happy there, Coop."

"It's nice to hear"—another shrug leaves him—"that you still love it regardless of everything that came after." Those plush lips ghost up. "I am partial to it after all."

"I'll always love it there because it's the place I fell for you."

"Right back at you, Princess." His eyes spark against mine with the shared memory and the tension between us pulls tight as I notice his fingers have moved up to the inner curve of my thigh. Not quite sure how or when they got there because he's always been too good at that. Either way though, it's the best kind of tension, drenching the space between us as our eyes stay locked and those words move his finger higher and higher up my leg. And when he finally makes it up to that space where my leg gives way to a far more intimate area, I can't help the needy sound that escapes. Head tilting back as I drop back onto my elbows and clench both of my hands, the knife in one reminding me of the earlier vision he'd painted.

"Do you want me to stop?" he asks, voice dropping to a rough note and drawing my gaze back to him. "You have all the power here."

"No." I shake my head, jagged little gasps starting to escape me as he brushes his fingers directly over my pussy and moves to the same spot on the other side. "No."

My hand clenches even more tightly around the knife and I see his eyes dart up to it before that savage smirk flashes across his face again. His gaze coming back to mine as the air between us shifts even more with a deeper note starting to come to life in it even as I do too.

"Careful," he warns, voice amused as his hand trails directly over my pussy again right before he rises up to hover above me. "Wouldn't want you to damage the goods any more today."

A surprised laugh bursts from me and I see him smile in answer as he drops his lips to mine, lingering there for a precious few seconds and teetering with me on that edge of anticipation until we both plunge together. The kiss immediately turning as deep as our need for each other, echoing in the way each of our moves trails one another until they start to overlap. The way he brushes his lower body against mine, making me gasp and open farther for him, hips lifting in search of more as he sweeps his tongue into my mouth. That first language of ours finding its voice again somewhere between the blatant intimacy of our lips and all the almost touches of our bodies through my clothes.

I start to reach my hands up to wrap them around his head before remembering the knife in my hand and dropping that one back to the bed with a groan. And his low laugh sounds into our kiss as if he knows exactly what just happened as I continue with the other to grab the back of his head. Pulling him even closer and meeting his tongue stroke for stroke. The kiss deepening another impossible degree just like our need for each other until we're both left gasping into one another's mouth.

My head is dizzy by the time he breaks the kiss, looking down at me with eyes that are all dark fire as he lowers a hand to that place on my inner thigh again. "Do you want me to stop?"

"No," I breathe, lifting my hips when he moves his hand over just an inch, palm almost on my clit and making my pussy clench. "Fuck no." Needing him to move that hand over just a little bit more.

He wastes no time in dropping his head to my neck, pulling the skin there through his teeth before trailing his lips down lower and ending right above my breast. I watch as he lowers down then, pulling my nipple into his mouth through the clothing and making me buck hard against his hand as it slides over that last little bit. My legs twitching instantly as those nerves finally fire and I try to open them up even more when he starts to slowly circle his palm. Giving me steady little brushes that leave me wanting more than I can get in my current state of dress. More than I can get with the way he's still holding back.

He lifts his head from my breast, leaving my shirt and bra wet from his mouth and rubbing against my aching nipple as he kisses it softly before moving to give the other the same treatment. Making little gasps leave me as my body tightens with each pull of his mouth and stroke against my pussy. He presses down harder then, circling just a little bit faster and my head falls back at the sense of almost being close. So close but not quite able to get there that I can't help the sound of frustration escaping my lips a moment later.

His head lifts automatically, hand stopping its motion and I almost scream at the loss as he asks seriously. "Do you want me to stop?"

I squeeze my eyes shut and choke out. "No."

"Give me those eyes, Princess." I lift my head to look at him and his gaze searches mine for a minute before his voice roughens with a new question. "What do you want?"

Swallowing hard, I give him the only word running through my head. "More."

"Are you scared?"

I hesitate before shaking my head. "No. Not of you." Of myself. Of somehow failing at this and being less than I was before, yeah, that fear is still there under all my big words and inner pep talks.

His eyes drill into mine for a beat, reading the words I'm not speaking before he sits back on his heels and holds out a hand to me with the quiet order. "Come here."

I reach up to grasp his hand and he pulls me to him, putting us almost chest to chest as he lifts a hand to my cheek. "Do you like who you are today, Eleanor?" His brows drop with the question and my lips part in surprise, not having expected it.

And I don't answer it quickly. I take my time to think it over with my eyes never leaving his.

"Yes," I finally answer, face pinching up against his hand as I confess. "But I *need* this, Coop. I need to take this back for me. To feel whole again. And I'm scared that if I can't…" My shoulders lift even as I clench the knife more tightly in my hand, anger sparking at what comes next. "I'm going to feel less than in some way forever."

A beat passes before understanding starts to flicker in his eyes. "The thing about Serena didn't help, did it?"

I shrug again helplessly. "She reminded me a little of how I used to be."

"Oh, Princess." His face falls as he drops both hands to wrap around my waist, quickly resituating us and pulling me into his lap. Sliding his grip down to my legs and wrapping them around his waist before reaching back up to hold my face. "Eleanor, *this will pass*." And the way he says it with such certainty eases something in me. "Maybe today, maybe not, either way it doesn't matter to me." He shrugs, hands sliding against my cheeks a little before I feel that thumb brushing against one side. "Because you exist in an entirely different universe to me than Serena ever did or could hope to."

I blink hard to fight the tears, overcome with the sudden urge to have the heart that's bursting in my chest from his words beating against his again and choke out. "Coop—"

"Do you know what this represents?" His hand drops suddenly to mine, the one holding the knife and he raises it back up, putting that blade right up against his throat and making me suck in a sharp breath.

"Coop—" I protest.

"It's not only the power you hold today," he cuts me off. "To say no. To stop at any point if you need to." His forehead drops to mine and I feel that blade press harder against his throat. "It's the power you have *always* held over me. I told you that first night that you were dangerous to me and I wasn't lying." And with how close we are I can practically see how those night-forest eyes crack open with each word he speaks, letting me see straight into his soul too. "Any girl that came before ceased to exist to me the moment I met you because I knew I'd finally found what had always been missing." A couple tears spill onto my cheeks as he continues. "And this, right here with you. This is enough for me any day of the week. All I ever wanted was to know I'd be breathing the same air as you for eternity."

It overwhelms me, this love that's so complete some part of me can't help but feel like maybe I don't even deserve it. No, that's not right. I know I don't deserve it. I never deserved either of them. Regardless though, it's mine and I'm never letting it go. Never letting him go. So I let that love fill me, staring at his soul in those night-forest eyes and using the strength there to battle against the lingering fear, voice breaking as I tell him.

"Take my shirt off."

His eyes dart between mine even as his body tightens under me, throat bobbing under the knife I'm holding to it as he questions. "Are you sure?"

"Yes," I breathe, bringing my other hand up to his face with the same gentle hold he has on mine. "Because we don't let the fear win and while I can't..." I trail off, trying to find the right words, knowing I can't say exactly what he did to me because Jace will never cease to exist to me completely... but I can promise him this. "You will always breathe my air, Cooper Monroe, because you are the choice I will make every day. All the way through eternity."

A long moment passes, his eyes intense and continuing to search mine before he slowly lowers his hands. Giving me plenty of time to change my mind or voice hesitation as he brings them to the bottom of my shirt. Playing with the edge there for a second before moving them under to trail along my skin and making my breath hitch. Stomach twitching and legs tightening around him as he writes an *I love you* on my skin that has me brushing my lips against his with a soft kiss. He gathers up my shirt then and I pull back only enough to give him room. Keeping my gaze locked with his, wanting to see him for this. To remember who I'm here with through every step.

He starts to lift it up over my stomach, stopping only when I order him softly. "Bra too." His brow pulls tight, but I'm already answering the question even as he opens his mouth. "I'm sure, Coop."

Those fingers trail along my ribs for a moment, lingering before he eventually gives me the smallest nod and brings them up to hook underneath the bottom of my bra. I toss the knife to the floor then, the loud clang sounding through the otherwise quiet room as I raise my arms above my head.

"You broke the rules," he reprimands softly.

I snort. "Did you expect anything else?" The knife had done its job, turning the tides and reminding me of what exactly exists between us. How powerful and full of love and even a little dark this entity of us is. "This right here." I lower a hand to his heart. "Is more powerful than any kind of weapon." Breathing out a small shrug. "It was a sweet gesture, but I don't need it with you." I cock a brow. "So how about you just make me scream so much I forget my own name?"

"Fine." His lips twitch, eyes going a shade lighter with that rare show play. "But only the first."

A soft laugh leaves me and I raise my hands back over my head, the air between us going tense as he starts to lift again. Eyes never leaving mine except for when the clothes pass over my head and even then, they're still waiting for me on the other side. Not looking down once. Keeping his gaze on mine as he pulls them the rest of the way over my arms before dropping them onto the bed.

And then we just breathe together. As I finally wrap both my arms around his shoulders, my hand immediately going up to run my fingers over the back of his hair and he brings both of his hands to my waist, running his thumbs softly against my ribs. We breathe that same precious air together for those first few minutes of a whole new kind of story. One of healing. Of growth. Of a version of us that's learning to be better than we ever had been before.

"Look at me." I finally whisper, wanting to feel his eyes on me again. "Look at me, Coop."

His chest expands with a deep inhale at my request, and still, he keeps his eyes on mine for another beat before looking down. And all that air leaves him in a rush as his brows drop, his face turning almost pained at the sight of me. "Fuck." He inhales deeply, moving his thumbs up to rest right underneath my breasts and I watch his eyes go to where our words are forever inked into my skin there. His fingertips moving to trace them for a long moment before looking back up to me.

"Eleanor Monroe."

My lips twitch at the name and he drops his forehead back to mine. Letting me see all the reverence in his eyes as his voice turns rough with feeling.

"You're even more beautiful than I remembered."

I pause then, waiting to see if any kind of fear or shame rises. Testing that current between us to see if anything has changed and quickly finding that it has. It had to. We had to. After these past weeks, months, after everything we've been through, I guess I should have expected it. So no, it's not exactly the same as it used to be.

It's even better. Impossibly deeper. So much more than just that need we'd always had for each other's skin.

"Kiss me," I gasp, somewhere between a laugh and a cry.

And he does not disappoint.

Crashing his lips down onto mine as his fingers tighten around my waist and he pulls me against his chest. Finally, blissfully, allowing our hearts to beat skin to skin against each other again. Each thump answering one another's with a stronger pulse than the last as I moan into his mouth at the feel of him. Fingers digging into his skin and relishing the heat of having his body under my touch. Nipples pebbling against his chest as I bring a hand around to cup his jaw and he drops his hands to my ass, pulling me down into him. Making me moan into his mouth all over again as I feel that hard press of his cock and roll my hips against him.

Needing, wanting, living for more of this moment with him.

After I fix one thing, that is.

I rip my lips from his, gasping another demand. "Pants."

"Pants?" he repeats, voice a little unsure even as his body locks up even more underneath mine.

Nodding, I lean back in enough to bite that ridiculously full lower lip. "And so help me god, if you ask if I'm sure"—a short laugh escapes me— "I will get that knife again."

His eyes turn sharp, running over my face once more before that rare, breathtaking smile breaks free at whatever he finds there. "As you wish, Princess."

He runs his hands over my ass, sliding them up to the top of my leggings and I scoot back out of his lap, dropping back onto my elbows again. Giving him room to start to work them over my hips as I focus solely on him, reminding myself with every brush of his hands who I'm here with. He gets the leggings down to my thighs before I pull one leg out, then the other, my skin immediately chilling from the cold you can never quite escape here and making me want to be pressed all up against him again. I see his eyes dart to the black thong I'm wearing underneath before coming back up to mine with a clear question in them and I nod immediately. Having to bite my lip to keep a laugh from escaping at his immediate exhale of relief that follows.

But I want him to see all of me, to feel that worship I see in his eyes against every inch of my skin. It's healing me. I can sense it with every passing moment.

His fingers come up to the top of my thong, looping underneath the material and pulling it down slowly. Baring me to his gaze slowly, inch by agonizing inch, as my breathing picks up pace. The unadulterated look of need and awe in his eyes is everything my soul needs to stitch those last few confident pieces back into place.

He finally pulls the thong past my feet before dropping it to the bed, eyes still on the most intimate part of me and I suck in a breath, reminding myself of how strong we are together before widening my legs for him. Loving the way his eyes flare instantly as a groan leaves him and his cock twitches, the very apparent bulge in his sweatpants drawing my gaze with the movement. He starts to run his hands up my legs, moving in and lowering his head with clear intent, but I stop him quickly.

"No." I shake my head, reaching to wrap my arms around his neck again. "I want you."

"Eleanor." A pained expression flashes across his face. "You can have me all day. Any which way." I watch his eyes drop to my pussy again. "But I can see how you're fucking dripping for me and if I don't taste—"

"Coop," I interrupt him, drawing his gaze back up to me. "This first time... I want to reclaim myself with you inside me." My lips twitch and I cock a brow at him. "And then later, you can taste yourself inside me too and won't that be even more satisfying?"

"Fuck," he chokes, pupils dilating with a rough breath. "Fine. You win."

"And" —a shrug leaves me even as I fight the smile pulling at my lips—"some poetry in my ear while I'm screaming on your cock wouldn't be amiss either."

I see him fight that same smirk for a second before he shakes his head with a low laugh. "That I can do."

He reaches down for his sweatpants then and I lower my eyes to watch him push them roughly down over his hips, freeing that magnificent cock that's leaking at the tip for me. Pussy clenching at the sight of him and stark need pounding through me so intensely that my legs start to shake with it. He finishes kicking his pants off and reaches for my hips, pulling us both back up as I wrap my legs around him again. The hard tip of him teasing at my entrance and making me reach up to grab the back of his head as he holds me above him, fingers clenching as a moan escapes me at the wetness that's rubbing against me there.

He holds me there for another moment, running his lips along the curve of my cheek on his way to my ear while murmuring. "Poetry, right?"

"And screams," I gasp, trying to lower myself down.

"How about this?" he breathes, air hitting my hypersensitized skin as he gives me that first inch that has a quiet cry escaping my lips. "You saved my life." Another inch that has my fingers digging deeper into his head. "Time and again." I roll my hips on his tip, making him groan and those hands lower me another few inches. "From the start," he gasps, grip tightening on my hips. "To the thousands of steps in between." My pussy twitches around the start of fullness from him, but I need more. All of him. And I dig my heels into his back to let him know just that right before he drops me down completely, sending me screaming as he whispers into my ear. "And eventually, even after the end of everything."

I drop my head to his shoulder, scream cutting off and breath panting out of me as my pussy convulses while trying to adjust to him again. Tears filling my eyes as I drown in his sandalwood scent and that little bit of burn from the size of him. Overwhelmed in every single sense.

He thrusts shallowly, silently checking on me and a needy sound escapes me before I bite down on his skin teasingly to let him know I'm more than okay. Moving beyond words as I roll my hips, making his body shudder in my arms as his hand comes up to the back of my head. Fingers winding through the hair there and pulling gently until I lift my head, running my gaze over his face along the way and seeing how tightly his jaw is clenched.

I bring a hand up to that jaw, locking my eyes with his and lifting my hips, gasping, "I love you," before impaling myself hard on his cock all over again.

And then I do it again. And again. Over and over while reclaiming myself in the most perfect way I can imagine. And it's not just a reclaiming of me either, it's all of the things that've been stolen from us. The things we've stolen ourselves and those that have been taken unwillingly.

I do it as his cock grows even more inside of me and my pussy clenches around him more tightly with each pass. I do it as his fingers tighten to the edge of pain in my hair and on my hip. I do it as his forehead drops to mine and he starts to choke out more poetry into the air. I do it until I'm so wet for him that words become something I can't manage.

Until he starts to thrust up into me so deep that it's the pain that sends me screaming so fucking loud that the air around us resonates with it. My orgasm crashing down on me and locking my whole body up around his, mind blanking out as I see nothing but the stars in those night-forest eyes. Nothing existing beyond his skin against mine and his cock still pumping inside of me.

Only then does he drop his lips to mine, devouring me as if he wants to take the sound inside of himself before pulling my bottom lip through his teeth roughly. His pace faltering and cock twitching inside of me for a few more thrusts before he slams home. Sending me screaming all over again into his mouth as he fills me up and another orgasm crashes through me, making me push down onto him. Wanting more of him than I could probably ever physically get.

We stay that way for a long time, no words passing between us, just gasps into each other's mouths that eventually turn into another slow kiss.

And then we do it all over again.

Reclaiming each other in every possible way for the rest of the day.

Absolutely forgetting about the groceries.

Chapter Thirty-Four

I wake up early the next morning, every inch of me aching and deliciously sore from the man who held me in his arms all night. Even through the little jolts of his body that'd woken me throughout those hours. The ones that had me tightening my own arms around him and whispering in his ear that we were safe now. Pressing my lips to that brow until it had eventually relaxed again.

And this morning, under the softest light of the earliest part of the day, there's not a trace of tightness to be found in his body, no lines marking that forehead that speak of any inner unease. It makes me smile, running my fingers up his side and over his ribs while pressing my lips directly over that long scar on his chest. Lips twitching up even more as the skin there jumps under my touch and he lets out a sleepy moan, arms tightening around me in what I'm guessing is an order to go back to sleep.

I laugh softly under my breath, rolling in his arms and snuggling my ass right up against his already hard cock. Knowing that the position plus the fact we never put our clothes back on yesterday is going to have him waking me back up again soon in exactly the way I want. Smile still in place and heart bursting as my eyes start to drift closed, staring at the icy world that's just starting to dawn outside of the window. Finally finding that peace I've been searching for so desperately.

It hits me then, in that moment right before my eyes close completely. It hits me that it's dawn. That the sun is rising while I'm lying here happier than I can remember being in… so very long. That I'm allowing myself this peace while he's lying trapped in his body thousands of miles away. And fuck, but the guilt that comes next rises so fast that it steals the air from my lungs for a minute. Has me sucking in shallow breaths next as my eyes fly wide, finding that first bit of snow that's glittering under the rising sun and knowing exactly what I need to do next.

So I wait another few minutes to make sure Coop is good and asleep before sliding out of his arms, trying not to jostle him as best I can. Walking over to the closet holding the clothes we've acquired over the past couple weeks and grabbing the hoodie he dropped into the hamper yesterday morning. Purposefully choosing the one that I know is going to smell like him so that I can keep the comfort of him close at least. Tiptoeing out of the room, I pull the door closed softly behind me before turning to the kitchen.

I walk immediately to the fancy chrome machine on the counter beside the fridge, grabbing the coffee from the cabinet above before stepping back and trying to figure out how to operate it. Eventually getting the gist enough to start going through the motions. Dumping some of the ground-up coffee beans into the metal cylinder at the top before turning some of the knobs that control heat and other things that I'm still not totally sure about. When the machine starts to whir though, I figure that I did something right and grab one of the mugs sitting on the counter next to it.

Hastily putting it underneath where I'm pretty sure it's going to drip down before opening the fridge up to grab the milk someone had thankfully remembered to put away for us.

A few minutes pass as the coffee slowly drips down before eventually cutting off and I add that splash of milk to it, trying to do it just like he always did before setting it on the counter for whoever comes next. I grab my mug and turn around, eyes quickly finding that first sliver of the sun that's waking my corner of the world. Rising above the barren branches of the trees sitting on the other side of the lake and making my heart turn so heavy that I'm pretty sure the bottom is about to give out. Unable to hold against the tide of how fucking horrible it is for me to be this happy when he can't be.

I push through it enough to walk to the couch that's still at the very edge of the living room, figuring it's better to collapse there than on the floor. Plus, I can still see the sun out of the windows and that's really all that matters. Taking a seat on the couch, I bring my legs up to curl beside me, fervently wishing that there was some kind of fire burning in that big stone fireplace.

Instead, it sits empty of anything but ash, the room eerily quiet as I cup the mug in my hands and blow on the coffee before taking a small sip. And I sit with him then, silently staring at that ever-rising sun while sipping my coffee. Trying and failing to figure out what to say. Eventually, coming to the horrifying realization when I reach the bottom of my mug, and I still haven't uttered a word that there's nothing. Nothing adequate, that is. Nothing that will make this better or easier.

But I still try because I owe him that. I owe him everything in such a contrasting way to the man I'd let help me put myself back together yesterday.

"Hey, Dawson," I whisper, the crack in my voice almost making me jolt in the silent space. "You know…" I trail off lamely. "As fancy as it is, this coffee is still shit compared to yours."

I swallow hard in the silence that follows, swearing as that first tear falls that it's like he's sitting right there on the couch next to me. And it's so real, that almost-there presence, that I bite my lip hard, trying to ground myself.

"I'm so sorry," I gasp out as my face crumbles, like the reality of him somehow being here. "I'm so so sorry, Jace," I mumble through the tears. "I shouldn't be happy when you're—" Another breath rips from my lungs, cutting me off and leaving the only certainty I have. "I don't know what to do now." And a sob comes then, its familiar wrenching at this point almost comforting. "I don't know what—" Fingers clenching around the mug as I bring my knees up and curl in on myself. "I don't know how to—" And then the inevitable truth behind all the guilt comes. "How am I supposed to save him and not you?" I rip my next breath back from the air with a sudden burst of anger. "How am I supposed to allow myself to be happy if I let you go?"

You already did though, didn't you, El?

Not like this. Never like this.

He isn't supposed to want this. He's supposed to… what?

Do what I want? What I need to be happy?

"Fuck," I curse, dropping my head down to my knees and squeezing my eyes shut. Wondering if my most selfish act isn't loving him but the one I'm committing now by not letting him go. Really go, in a way that I haven't had to face before. If why I'm holding on to him so tight is because of the guilt I'll never escape at his passing. Doomed to always know that his last reality is not the love he deserves but that of his heart breaking.

And now I don't even know what to say to him because I can't act like I'm fighting for him when the truth is, I'm fighting against him.

The mug in my hands is pulled away then and I jerk my head up to see Coop standing there in the same pair of sweatpants he was wearing yesterday. Worry clear on his face and his eyes reflecting the same pain racking me. He sets my mug down gently on the ground before sitting down on the couch and pulling me into his lap. Cradling me in his arms and bringing a hand to the back of my head, engulfing me in the comforting heat of his body as he breathes roughly. "Eleanor."

I lay my head on his shoulder, giving voice to the terrible thoughts in my head as they start to rush through my lips. "How am I supposed to let him go"—I hiccup—"when the last thing he ever knew was me breaking his heart? How can I ever not feel guilty—"

"Because," he interrupts, hand starting to run over the back of my head. "As much as I love you, would give you anything, this…" His arms tighten around me. "This isn't about you." My breath stops as his voice drops even lower. "Or me."

Understanding hits me and my breath starts again with a name. "Jace." I swallow through the tightness any thought of him brings. "It's about Jace."

And that right there is all the confirmation I need that all the horrible things I've been thinking about myself out here are probably spot on.

I tilt my head back to look at him, whispering hesitantly. "Do you think that's why he won't wake up? Because of me?" Needing to know if some part of him blames me as much as I do myself.

"I think…" His jaw clenches hard for a second before he finally looks down at me with tears filling his own eyes. "That if anyone failed him here, it's me." A deep breath leaves him. "I took the person that was meant for him, Eleanor, and as much as I love you" —he shakes his head—"I'll never forgive myself for it."

His obvious pain hits me hard and has his name falling from my lips instantly. "Coop."

"I can't change it because I would never change you, but—" His mouth snaps closed, jaw clenching again and when his chest shakes under my head this time, I know it's because he won't let his own cries free. He inhales a deep breath through his nose before unclenching his jaw and finishing in a voice that's breaking and absolute. "I failed him completely when it came to the one thing he needed me not to." That hand on the back of my head stills, fingers winding through the hair gently as he clears his throat. "But you…" His lips lift the barest hint with a sad smile. "He loved you so much, Eleanor." My heart gives a hard tug at the reminder, bottom lip trembling. "And I think deep down you know he wouldn't begrudge you a moment of happiness." His hand slides up to the side of my face. "In fact, I'm pretty sure that's all he ever wanted for you."

Promise me.

I break our gaze as his voice rings through my head, more mouthing than speaking my answer against his skin. "Maybe."

It doesn't take the guilt away though. It doesn't lessen it. Maybe it never will, and maybe that's the way it should be.

"Now." He exhales the word roughly and tightens his arms around me even more, bringing his hand to the back of my head again. "Let me take your self-destructive shift this time and talk to my cousin for a bit."

I hesitate for a second, awkward at sharing my intimate ritual with anyone else, before remembering that he's just as entitled to it as I am because of the love we all shared in equal measure. So I nod once against his chest, and after a beat, he starts slowly. "Hey, little cousin." His voice comes out hushed. "I've been thinking about the waves lately. Missing being out there with you. Remembering that time you came down to Cahuita for a week"—shock fills me, unaware that he'd ever been there—"and you bet me that I wouldn't get a tattoo because I'd always been so fucking terrified of needles before that." A quiet laugh leaves him, rendering me even more speechless as my heart twists at the memories tumbling from his lips. All the little pieces of their puzzle that I'd never gotten to see the completion of until now. How intertwined we all really were. "But I wasn't about to lose that bet, considering what the stakes were for you."

He speaks for hours, voice never faltering as he tells their stories to me and the rising sun before us that will always be Jace. From the one about when Jace convinced him to try and steal his dad's boat to go fishing at ten to the ones about when they got involved with the Morrisons as teenagers. Stories of love and laughter and even dark times. An entire life they lived together before me. And somewhere among it all, that twist in my heart starts to ease at the happier memories I can't help but smile at hearing. Remembering the guy I'd met in the bar that had teased me over a vodka soda with two limes with eyes that'd struck me hard because of my own memories. My eyelids start to drift shut as Coop's stories meld with the ones living in my head, leaving me with the last one where I'd promised to always keep chasing the sun as they close.

Hoping that maybe this will heal the cousin that I'd chosen in some way and allow him the same thing.

***

"Does it bother you?" Alec's quiet voice is the first thing I hear, his next words dragging me back to alertness. "That she loved him?"

I keep my eyes closed, some part of me wanting to hear the answer and a beat passes before Coop's chest lifts under my head and he answers with equal quiet. "It bothers me that my actions drove her to anyone else, but if it had to be someone"—he exhales a deep breath—"I'm happy it was him." His hand starts to rub the back of my head gently again. "I can understand it at least because some of the things that make her special are the same ones that made him that way too." *Made*. "So no, it doesn't bother me that she loved him because I loved him too." He pauses. "The only part of it I'll never get over is that I was the cause of it all." I sense his eyes on me then, that voice dropping even lower as he chokes out. "That will never stop killing me."

I fight against the way my face is trying to pinch up as Alec retorts with quiet sarcasm. "Do I need to be worried about you?"

"No." Coop laughs shortly, that hand pressing into my head a little more. "No, I'd never leave her willingly." He pauses and I'm guessing it's because Alec is giving him one of those asshole looks. "You know what I mean." That demanding voice drops low again. "Not now."

"How's she doing? Besides that?"

"Better," Coop answers with clear relief. "Much better, I think."

"Good," he grunts, almost grudging as he finishes. "I love her even if she is fucking migraine inducing most days."

"Oh, I know," Coop retorts and I can hear the smirk in his voice. "Pretty sure I knew that before you did."

"Yeah, yeah," Alec drones, surprising me a few seconds later when he taunts. "Ready to join us, Helen?"

I snap my eyes open, turning my head to where he's sitting on the floor in front of us and giving him a wide smile while singsonging like a five-year-old, "You love me."

Getting one of those sibling moments I've always secretly wished for when he narrows his eyes at me warningly and grumbles, "Doesn't mean I like you."

"No." My lips pull up even more and Coop's chest shakes with laughter and I start again. "But you loovee—"

"Do you want to hear what Serena said or not?" he interrupts, cutting me off and killing my mood instantly.

"No." I sniff haughtily, narrowing my eyes at him in turn. "I'd rather you refer to her as she who must not be named." He rolls his eyes as Coop's laughter starts to grow louder and I slap his chest without looking up at him, making the sound cut off quickly. "Fine," I grumble, even if his chest is still shaking a bit. "What did Voldemort have to say?"

"Serena"—he emphasizes, making me roll my eyes right back at him— "said that Bainbridge is incredibly unhappy with the information they've been able to unearth about Simon and his ties to Novikov and, by extension, to them."

"Nothing she didn't already tell me," I retort, bored.

"And," he continues loudly. "That his illegal activities go even deeper than we originally suspected. She said the money laundering is just the tip of the iceberg and that he has his fingers into pretty much everything. Including human trafficking, which she has a particular hatred of." He stops as if waiting for me to ask why, which I most certainly will not be doing, and when my silence continues he sighs. "Bainbridge wants to meet in a few days to discuss a deal."

"Again"—I snort—"not much more than she already told me."

"The meeting will take place two hours from here at a neutral location and two of the senior heads of Bainbridge will be there."

"Great."

"Along with Serena."

"Better take your wand, Harry," I quip.

He gives me a long-suffering look before that icy smile starts to spread in a way I don't like one bit. "She said Coop was invited but that you'd already declined the invitation on his behalf."

My mouth pops open at the betrayal before I gather myself enough to shoot him a look of absolute loathing. "I don't like you."

"I don't care," he retorts, smile growing as I try to lunge for him, only to be restrained by Coop's arms tightening around me.

He dips me right back into the cradle I was in before Peter Pettigrew over there went running his mouth, amusement clear in the way his voice comes out all low and teasing. "Princess?"

"Mhmm?" I blink up innocently.

His eyes spark. "Did you take it upon yourself to decline the Bainbridge meeting for me?"

"Maybe?" I drawl, tilting my head up at him like I'm guessing.

"Eleanor." And even though his tone is all reprimand, the tightening of his lips is telling me he's fighting a smile.

"Okay, yes," I mutter. "Honestly, I shouldn't be blamed for my actions around that woman."

That smile finally breaks free as he laughs softly, leaning down to nip at my bottom lip and whisper, "Brat."

Our eyes lock for a beat and I see the way his darken with the memories of yesterday. Making me sigh and tip my lips up before Alec so rudely interrupts. "Which is…" he grits out, regaining both of our attention. "Exactly why you won't be coming."

"Cool with me." I scoff.

"But I think Coop should be there." He holds up a hand when my mouth opens in protest. "They have, uh…" His gaze drops to the ground with a flash of guilt and my stomach follows, suddenly knowing I'm not going to like what comes next. "Sensitive information pertaining to you and I'd like him in my corner in case negotiations need to be made or things go south."

Coop's body goes tense as Alec's eyes finally come back up to meet mine. The hesitancy in them causing anxiety to flood through me because I can't imagine many things that would make my brother nervous.

"What?" I press. "What is it?"

"Serena didn't know for sure until she met you in person." He sighs. "Or, I guess, more accurately, who you are to me, us, but…" His hands clench in the pause that follows, but he doesn't break my gaze this time. "There was a video."

I blink slowly at him, hoping I'm wrong. "A video?"

"Of that night." He nods once. "In Simon's library."

Coop's chest goes still, his arms giving a little tremble around me before he bites out. "How?"

"I don't know." Alec shakes his head. "It's possible he had cameras in there himself and they got the footage somehow. You know them, Coop." He leans back, planting his hands. "The resources they have. That's why I think you should be there."

"Yes."

I shoot him an irritated look, but his face is all hard lines letting me know I'm not going to get anywhere with him right now. So I try to push away the sense that the ground is falling out from under me, looking back at Alec and questioning sharply. "What use is the video to them? Why not just destroy it or give it back?"

"Leverage." He shrugs. "Bainbridge has never been known to give up leverage on anyone. Plus, Serena said that…" And that damn hesitancy again just about kills me. "While you might have, uh…" He winces. "Done what you did. It was clear that your actions weren't exactly of your own volition to anyone watching."

Great. Voldemort had seen me in my birthday suit.

Multiple people had probably seen what happened in that room.

Seen me. Without my permission or knowledge.

And I'm not sure how the fuck I feel about that besides not great at all.

"So we go to the meeting," Alec hedges. "And we see what they have to say."

"Well…" I clear my throat, reminding myself of all the parts of me I've reclaimed that nobody can touch now without my permission. Looking up at the way Coop's face is screwed up, knowing that this is pushing him right over the edge because he can't stand not being able to protect me. So I reach up with a finger and bop him on the nose, startling him into looking down at me. "I wouldn't exactly be mad if you casually mentioned to Voldemort that you're married now"—my brows drop down as I think through my words and tack on—"and not in any open kind of way." He arches a brow at me with a clear message that has me snapping, "You know what I mean!"

Chapter Thirty-Five

Jace

Somewhere In Between

Why am I still here?

I stare at Coop and her on the couch, not knowing why the fuck I'm still here.

They're happy. They made it back to each other. Choosing one another just like they always do while I'm stuck watching it all play out, being dragged from what had been a dream before compared to this nightmare. It isn't that I'm not happy for them in some way for beating the odds, even if it is only temporary.

I just can't take watching it play out anymore.

Because the truth is, I'm not necessary to her, not like he is.

What had once been a reprieve when she talked to me has now just been turned into another form of torture because I love her so fucking much, but seeing them together… seeing the way they always come back together leaves me wanting to shout at her in frustration to finally let me go. To let herself have whatever short moment of happiness she's being allowed before it all comes crashing down again.

To let me go so that I won't have to witness it.

I can't do this anymore. Life after life, never knowing if there will be an end to it. Betting there isn't because she always keeps choosing him.

And then, when Coop had joined her today and opened his mouth... I felt a pulse in the air because I couldn't contain it. The hurt and the rage that came from hearing him. I didn't want to hate him. I *didn't* hate him, but now that he's alive and well, it's harder to look at him. Even if I know it isn't technically his fault, there have been plenty of lifetimes where he didn't steal her from me outright, but they had still been drawn to each other somehow.

It's all just too much. The reality is that they will always repeat this. That my life will always end in heartbreak even though I love them and they love me. And I can't take it anymore. Can't take being in this fucking place where those terrible whispers I can't understand are never too far from my ears.

What if I have to spend years like this? What if this is how they want the story to play out this time? What if I have a lifetime of this torture to live through? Watching their lives play out from the outside looking in.

Fuck. I can't do that. Can't exist like that. I can't—

It has my hands going to my head with a long, gutted shout, trying to let go of something pulsing down in the depths of my chest. Knowing I need to not be here. Willing to do anything to not be here anymore. I never want to live this life again.

"Come."

My head jerks up at the sound of a voice that sounds like the purest form of music I've ever heard, seeing nothing but a faint green light emitting from across the room that hadn't been there before.

"Let go and come."

The voice echoes around in my head, letting me know that whoever is speaking to me is doing so from somewhere more on my plane than theirs.

"Come to peace."

It could be a trick, some worse form of torture than what I'm already living… it could be. But the voice doesn't sound anything like the horrific whispering songs I've been hearing in my head. It sounds more real, a touch more human and pure. Right now though, I'm so desperate for some form of escape beyond this that I'll cling to whatever they're offering, even if it's one of those haunting whispers tricking me.

So I turn my head, looking at Coop and Ellie on the couch one more time and try to memorize their faces. Try to just remember the love I have for them and let go of the rest. And then I blow out a breath and walk toward the light without hesitation, knowing I don't need to say goodbye because they wouldn't even hear it.

"Come."

Chapter Thirty-Six

I roll over in bed and reach out an arm, trying to figure out where my space heater went. Grumbling under my breath about how I warned him against leaving me alone in this arctic tundra of a place when we were sleeping. It's just plain cruel, even if he has to pee occasionally. I flop my arm around the bed with increasingly demanding hits as my irritation grows before hitting something hard that has me cracking my eyes to the sight of a camera very much like the one I'd left behind in Landing Point. Except for the white bow tied sloppily on top, that is. It makes me blink a couple times, double-checking that I'm not still asleep before lifting up onto my elbows to reach for it.

Carefully wrapping my fingers around the camera, I sit up and pull it into my lap, rubbing the white ribbon between a couple of fingers with a sleepy smile pulling at my lips, knowing exactly who left me this gift. Tugging on the end of the ribbon and pulling it loose before seeing a note tucked underneath has my heart swelling with happiness. I let the ribbon fall away and snatch the paper up, wide awake now and eager for whatever words he's left me. Opening the note and scanning it even as that swell in my heart clenches when I remember why exactly he's not here keeping me warm this morning.

Princess,

Wanted to make up for those birthdays and Christmases I missed... and I do remember how much you love surprises.

Sneak some pictures for me while I'm gone this morning and reclaim some more parts for yourself. I'll miss you with every breath.

Always,

Coop.

PS: Alec says he wants credit for mentioning the birthdays and Christmases thing

PPS: You're right, he's a fucker.

I snort a laugh, the note easing some of my anxiety at the fact that they're probably meeting with Bainbridge right now. Refolding it carefully, I set it on the nightstand before picking the camera up to examine it. The present makes me all kinds of warm and fuzzy inside and turns that sleepy smile silly the longer I look at it, turning it on and pointing it out the window to check the views. I can tell he took his time selecting it because of the fact it's almost identical to the one I had in Costa Rica. Except for a few features that are newer than the ones I'd had before.

And fuck, but Cooper Monroe definitely knew what he was doing because my fingers are itching to try it out. To find the peace I used to get while searching for that elusive perfect shot. It even makes the cold outside seem not quite so daunting. So I smile once more before throwing back the covers and taking his advice, setting out to reclaim some more parts of myself from the past while holding the future in my hands.

***

My fingers went numb over an hour ago, but I still can't seem to make myself go back inside. As if with each click and refocus of the lens, my understanding of the universe has grown clearer. Like the shots of ice sheets jutting up along the banks of the lake and water dripping from the icicles along the trees have somehow made the world right itself. Stopped it from turning for millisecond after millisecond until eventually, all that time accumulates into a knowing of my place in it again. Centering the soul in my chest until it's this almost unbearable sense of wellness.

Because this, out here only a couple of miles down the shore from the house in this tiny little section of the earth made up of as many million pieces as I myself am... This is just me, finding my way again. Like for the first time in years, and if I'm being honest, maybe ever, I'm exactly where I'm supposed to be. No urgency or need for more. Just a blissful kind of lonesomeness. And I know deep down that what I've finally found is something that can never be given, it's the kind of peace that only comes from within.

From accepting all the pieces of myself again without any of the posturing or hiding that I used to cling to. In a way that you can't until you've grown into them and understand how far you can fall and rise again. The past months, years really, have stripped me of that anyway. Both literally and metaphorically.

I blow out a deep breath, that heaviness in my heart still there but no longer as daunting and refocus my camera to look at the house across the lake. Zooming in and seeing the family who owns it heading out for the day by way of the back door. Mom, dad, and two little girls that chase after each other through the snow. The smaller of the two falls about halfway to the car and I can see the instant wailing that transpires even if I can't hear it. The way her sister stops to look back with wide eyes while their dad sweeps her up, tossing her into the air and turning the tears into laughter. Making my heart swell another inch even as the guilt tugs because I want that.

I want that normalcy that was stolen from me before I even had a chance.

Alec's and Coop's words echo through my head as I drop my camera, looking across the water and hearing them ask about what I want at the end of this and suddenly, I know exactly what that is. Had even contemplated it once when I'd picked up my first camera in high school and felt something within me right itself.

I want to open up a place to give kids that have suffered trauma like I did a chance to work through it. To see life through the simplicity of a lens that allows them to make sense of it all. Bringing the scope of the world down to a bare few inches that's more manageable until they're ready to tackle the big stuff. I want to be there to help them through it. Call them on their bullshit like I'd eventually been called on mine and watch them grow.

And what I really want is that. I want my little mishmash of a family to grow. I want laughter and holidays and teasing, just like we've always talked about. Just like Coop and I had fought about once when he'd asked why wait late into our last night together in Costa Rica.

And for once, it doesn't scare me. My biggest fear is no longer becoming my mother or even being a bad one myself but simply wasting more of this precious time I've been given. Because if there's anything I've learned, it's that nothing is guaranteed. Not even today. Not for anyone.

I blow out a deep breath and look to where the sun sits on my right, the guilt that lives in his piece of my heart giving a little pulsing ache. Still there. Always there. Along with a little bit of heaviness. I squint at that bright orb in the sky, its rays shining down with the only kind of warmth out here… realizing that it probably never will go away completely. And standing out here staring at it, finally finding my peace again, I don't think I want it to.

Because if I let Jace go or even if he finally wakes up like I've been ordering him to, either way, if that guilt and pain go away… what have I really learned? If that feeling disappears, what reminder do I have to be better? To never make the same mistakes again? Not that there's a chance of that, but still, it's the losses that teach us even more than our victories. And Jace… to lose him.

To lose him after breaking his heart. I'll never escape that and don't ever want to. I want everything about him and everything he taught me to stay forever. Even the pain and guilt because it reminds me of how much I'll always love him. But I also know he would want me to have the life I've been too scared to claim at times.

I used to think letting go and holding on were mutually exclusive things, but staring at that sun, I now realize that they can live side by side. Because life is messy and so is healing. The happiness that comes from growth, in a thousand different ways, because of what I learned from the guilt that lives in the ache of my heart, that's him. Knowing he would want me to have everything I want at this moment and knowing I should have been better. And knowing regardless of all of that, the love we share is real, forever cherished in my memories.

All of it existing somewhere in between everything.

So I blink once more, lips lifting up into a smile as I tell him goodbye for today, remembering my promise to chase the sun as I turn away. Pulling my phone out of my jacket and unlocking it quickly before dialing the number of the person whose help I need.

The line picks up and I sigh in relief at the news I can finally give her. "Hey, Yvie." The problem of Simon would be wrapped up soon, with or without Bainbridge's help, and then… decisions would have to be made, but one way or another. "I'm coming home soon and I need your help with a couple of things."

The shouting hits me as soon as I come within earshot of the house, sending my brows dropping down as Coop's enraged voice fills the air. I pick up my pace and bypass the deck leading to the back door, heading straight for the source of the commotion at the front of the house. Picking up little bits and pieces along the way that have my shoulders tightening with every step.

"I don't care, Alec!" Coop shouts. "I will burn that place to the ground before we agree to that plan and you can tell Serena she'll be included in that if she doesn't help us!"

Alec's voice is calmer, harder to hear, but I still pick up "You sound" and "Eleanor," enough to piece together that he's probably chastising him for sounding exactly like I had at the start of this.

I can't pick up the rest of what's said over the snow crunching under my boots, but when I'm about to turn the corner, I hear Coop again, voice all kinds of violent as he warns. "I'm not having this conversation, Alec." Rounding the corner in time to see the door slam and Alec lowering his head, shoulders hunched up just like mine as he blows out a deep breath.

"What happened?" I call, making his head snap toward me and taking in the uncomfortable look there while finishing closing the distance between us.

"Oh," he starts, sarcasm in full force. "You could say the meeting went a little south, is all."

"What happened?"

An irritated scoff leaves him. "Probably would have been better if I left Cooper at home actually."

"Alec," I snap.

"It was all going fine." He sighs. "They were offering great terms, especially once they found out that Cooper was being held by the psychotic piece of shit for half a year—"

"What terms?" I can't help but interrupt, wanting to know every little detail and in the silence that follows, I can see by the look in his eyes that he doesn't want to get my hopes up before whatever this is leading to dashes them. "Tell me, Alec."

"They were offering to let me head up a new branch they're opening that's more focused on security and information gathering." My eyes widen in surprise as he finishes. "North American operations that would be based in the US."

"But that's, that's—" I sputter.

"Yeah." He nods, lips tipping up with a humorless smile. "Even wanted Coop to join me and, after hearing about his captivity, said we could base it wherever we wanted."

That's everything. Our whole life. Right there.

For all of us really. Because although Alec is a fucker, he's my family now too, and I'm not about to go back to a life without him. The sibling I'd wished for when I'd been so alone in my tragedy as a child before the guys had come along and adopted me as one of their own.

"And then"—Alec's eyes drop from mine, voice quieting a bit—"Coop asked what the price was."

My stomach tumbles over itself as I ask. "What is it?"

His gaze comes back to mine, the ice in it telling me everything I need to know really. "Their plan," he spits out, "was to release the video of you."

"What?" I breathe in shock. "Why?"

"It would create a media circus that would at least warrant government officials looking into Simon." He snorts with disgust. "Bainbridge would make sure they found the truth on his business dealings while keeping their hands clean and he would end up in jail." His hand shoots to the side in frustration. "All of it tied up nicely and no one ever the wiser to how Simon Taylor went undiscovered for years."

I let the information sink in for a minute before shooting him a confused look and asking, "Are you sure you want to work for these people?"

"Ha!" He dips his head to the side with a shrug. "The whole industry is gray, Helen. Out of all of them though, Bainbridge is one of the better options." I watch his jaw work for a second before he finally looks out to the forest surrounding us and admits. "If it weren't for the fact you're my sister, I'd even say their plan was a good one."

A long moment passes as I watch him continue to move that jaw. Unable to shake the need to know something I'd worried would come up in their meeting today. "Did you see it?" I force out quietly. "The video?"

I watch his shoulders tighten even more and know he has to be getting those painful little lightning bolts before he finally looks at me with eyes that are completely iced over. "Enough." His face is devoid of anything, letting me know just how fucking pissed he probably is. "I stopped it before…" he trails off and I give him a nod of understanding. We don't need to actually say it.

I swallow hard, wincing at the next question. "Coop?"

"Took it into the other room." He looks back out to the forest while blowing out a breath. "Came back ten minutes later and told them to fuck off to hell along with some threats if it ever came out."

"Right," I mutter, leaning up against one of the wooden posts spaced out on the porch and turning my head to look at that same forest. Trying to make sense of everything flying around in my head.

It's all there, right within reach. That entire beautiful life we'd imagined together and so much more than I'd ever expected. The answer to taking Simon down without any risk to the people I'd almost lost already.

"Can you tell?" I finally ask, looking back at him, the next words out of my mouth making his head whip toward me. "In the video, can you tell it's me?"

"Not if you didn't know you." His brows dip inward, understanding passing between us. "But people do know you, Helen. You announced your presence there. It won't take long to connect the dots."

I jerk a nod at him, figuring that was the case, but still, a girl could hope. "So I'd have to make some kind of statement."

His mouth pulls tight. "Yes, most likely to the Canadian authorities."

Inhaling a deep breath, I look back out to that forest and blow it out slowly, stomach tumbling over and over again. "And you can tell," I swallow hard, not knowing why this part is so important really, but it is. "That it wasn't..."

"Yes." Alec's voice answers me with that careful note. "There's no audio but the look on your face." He clears his throat. "The way it went down tells the whole story."

And I'm not sure why that makes me happy, but it does.

So I stare at those trees, trying to see the forest for them and figure out why the idea of this doesn't scare me half as much as taking off my clothes for Coop the first time did.

Is it because I've already ripped the Band-Aid? Faced what happened with the person whose opinion I cared about most? Is it because I've reclaimed that part of myself now? My power and choice?

I'm not sure, but somehow the idea of making him pay publicly, stripping him of that mask he'd worn for years just like he'd forced me to strip... it holds just as much if not more appeal than stabbing him in some dark corner of the earth. One allows him to be martyred like a saint, while the other reveals him as the devil he's always been.

And then it hits me. It's validation.

Even if it means casting myself in the fires to do it too. Still, I'd rise. I'd always rise while he would burn, just like I've always wanted him to. He'd burn by my choice and my skin that I'd reclaimed from him.

"It's fitting." The words leave me with a sigh of relief at how that peace is still in my soul. "That what he forced me to do is what finally takes him down." Looking at Alec, I see his eyes widen with surprise. "Not that I'm his worst crime by any means, but…" I give him a small shrug. "Still, it's an ending that seems"—my lips twitch—"poetic, almost."

His eyes narrow on mine, flicking between them rapidly before he shakes his head. "Coop will never go for it."

"Did they promise he would stay in jail forever?" I press, ignoring his worry for now. "Never get out?"

"Yeah." He nods reluctantly. "There's more than enough to ensure it once the right people start looking."

Yvie would find out. My heart clenches at the thought. She's the one person I've been determined not to drag into this but, fuck, it is all right there. And Yvie wants me home more than anything. Plus, it isn't like she is going to let this whole thing go forever. Keeping this story from her indefinitely would do just as much damage to my relationship with her as it had started to do to mine and Coop's before I came clean. I can talk to her. Make sure she knows this is not her fault.

"Do it," I order softly. "Call and tell them we have a deal."

His brows lift at me and again, there's that flash of admiration in his eyes. "And Coop?"

"Leave Coop to me," I answer, lips pulling up with a hint of a smile. "He just needs to be reminded of a few things."

Chapter Thirty-Seven

I find him in the master bathroom we've been using with his head bowed and hands clenched on the edge of the double vanity. His back is toward the doorway, but still, those night-forest eyes snap up the second I come within a couple steps of it, meeting mine in the mirror with pain and fury in them that brings me to a halt. I lean against the doorjamb and run my gaze over him, taking in everything from the sharp rise and fall of his chest to the severity with which his jaw is clenched. The way he's trying to drop his shoulders and make his body relax, like he can somehow hide the pissed-off energy filling the space.

And that right there pisses me off because I know that for a second, he considered not telling me about the deal.

I cock a brow at him, making sure my voice stays calm despite the spike in my temper. "I thought we didn't keep secrets anymore?"

His nostrils flare, body tightening right back up before he loosens his jaw just enough to confirm. "He told you?"

"Mhmm," I drawl.

"I didn't." The words come out in a sudden burst of air and his eyes drop back down to the counter. "I didn't want you to worry about it. That"—his jaw clenches again for a beat before he grinds out with deathly quiet—"video will never see the light of day."

Ease or rip? Ease or rip? Ease or rip?

Rip, definitely rip.

He kind of deserves it anyway for even considering keeping this from me, but… I do understand the reaction too. Know he's a mess right now.

So I clear my throat and lay it out there bluntly. "I told him to make the deal."

His eyes snap back up to mine and a beat passes as the air between us teeters on the edge of a fight before that demanding voice fills the space. "You did what?"

"I told him to make the deal," I repeat, crossing my arms defensively. "It's my body in that video, Coop. It was my call to make."

"You think—" He shakes his head with a short laugh as if I've just said the most ludicrous thing. "You think this is about me not wanting people to see you in the video?"

"Do you?" The words pop out before I can stop them, making me wince internally as he pushes off the counter, spinning around and taking a step toward me.

"Fuck no!" he shouts, face screwing up as the breaths start to heave out of him. "No, I don't want anyone in the world to be a few clicks away from seeing you that way!"

I wince, unable to help it when he lays it right back out there like that before trying. "Coop—"

"It fucking kills me—" His voice cuts off with a break and my stomach twists with it because I might have underestimated how hard this would be for him. "You're mine, Eleanor. Mine to protect and you shouldn't have to—" He shakes his head, stopping himself and clenching his hands. "We'll find another way."

"We could." I nod, giving him that. "We could probably find another way." Taking a slow step toward him, I press. "But at what cost? What further risk?"

His eyes drill into mine for a beat before he snaps. "It doesn't matter. You're not doing this."

I tip my chin up at him, not backing down and reiterating quietly. "I am."

His eyes narrow on me, body going that scary still and I take another step toward him while dropping my arms.

"I am doing this, Coop. So talk to me. What's killing you about it?"

"You mean besides the obvious?"

"Yeah." I exhale. "Besides that." Because I know you, Cooper Monroe and while you are a possessive bastard... There's something much deeper at play here.

A beat passes before his lips purse, words seeming to work their way up his throat until breaking free. "Do you know what I dream about?"

I swallow hard and give him a shake of my head, staying silent as he works through it.

"I don't dream about the torture, Eleanor," he finally admits on a jagged breath, shoulders dropping an inch. "I don't dream about any of the things he did to me."

It takes me a moment, but when I finally get there… damn. "Me," I guess softly. "You dream about how he taunted you."

"Yeah," his voice grates out. "And watching that video, what he did to you." He shakes his head, eyes closing for a minute and when they open again, I can see the way this is eating at him from the inside out. "It was like watching my nightmares play out."

My heart pounds with a physical ache because I understand. I do. "Coop—"

"No," he cuts me off, body starting to tighten up again. "He needs to pay, Eleanor. If it was just about me, I wouldn't give a fuck," A vicious sound leaves him. "But he needs to pay for what he did to you."

I close the distance between us with quick steps, reaching up to grasp his face and tilting my head back to look up at him. "Do you know what I just did before you got back?" His brows drop with confusion and my lips lift. "I called Yvie and asked her to put an offer in on a house for me." His face goes slack, eyes widening on mine. "For us," I correct, unable to help the short laugh that follows. "It's honestly kind of a piece of shit because it's sat vacant for a few years, but it's only a couple houses down from her and Stef, so…" I trail off with a shrug.

His face screws up again. "Eleanor—"

"I also," I interrupt, talking over him because he needs to understand, "asked her to go to Stef, her law firm, and some other locals I know would be interested in the idea of opening a new arts center for children that have been affected by trauma." Running my fingers over his face, I take a deep breath before finishing. "I want to be there to help and tell them of all the good that's waiting on the other side of whatever they're going through." My voice cracks at the end and he reaches out, wrapping his hands around my waist.

"Princess." He pulls me in, voice going low as the shadows in his eyes clear until I see nothing but love. "You continue to amaze me." His thumbs trail my ribs, lips twitching with his next words. "A house?"

"Yeah," I breathe, another small laugh escaping at the dream so close I can practically see it all. "But between the house and the center, I'm probably going to be broke by the end of the year, so I kind of need you to have a job."

Not exactly true, considering the nice little income I'm getting from the club now, but still. A girl has to make her point somehow.

That anger sparks deep in his eyes again as he lets loose a breath. "Eleanor—"

"The house needs some work," I add, trying to distract him and work up the courage to tell him about the promise I made him. "But I figured we could work on it ourselves too."

And I can see how he's trying to hold strong, to fight the pleased smile tugging at his lips before he finally gives me "I could see the appeal of that."

"This." Wrapping my hands around the back of his head, I pull it down until his forehead rests against mine. "*This* is how we win, Coop," I rasp softly. "By dragging it all into the open and then moving on with our lives."

His arms wrap around me fully, putting us right up against each other and I can see how he's struggling in the way his eyes narrow on mine. "You shouldn't have to," He pauses as if choosing his words carefully. "Sacrifice anything else. You've already given enough."

"That's funny." I flash him a grin and run my fingers over the back of his head. "Because I was going to say that lately, it feels like you've been the one doing all the giving to help my traumatized ass."

His face goes hard. "Eleanor—"

"Let me do this," I whisper. "Let me be the thing that finishes him."

He wavers in the silence that follows. I can see it in the way his eyes start to give, softening just a little like his body is starting to do around mine.

"Do you know why I made the choice I did in that room?" I push the reminder on him, twisting his earlier words as I do our bodies. Tugging on his head to make him follow me until our positions are completely flipped and I'm the one with my back toward the mirror now.

"Yes." He chokes, that pain suddenly plain as day again in every part of him, including his voice. "To save me."

"Yeah," I agree, nodding with the word that's barely loud enough to be heard and letting my arms fall from around his neck. Trailing them down his arms and snagging my fingers through his, taking him with me as I back up to the bathroom countertop. "Because there was no life I wanted to imagine without you."

"You're not going to lose me, Eleanor," he argues, chest rising with a breath that I know holds more arguments. "We can find a way that doesn't cost you—"

"Cooper Monroe," I snap, finally giving in to some of my irritation and hopping up onto the counter before he can get another word out. "Stop fighting with me." Shooting him an exasperated look, I drop my eyes to our hands and pull him between my legs, finishing quietly. "I'm trying to give you everything here."

Silence falls for a long moment before he reaches with our entwined hands and tips my chin up, making me look back into his eyes that hold a sharp kind of curiosity. Another beat passes before his lip twitches. "Use your words, Princess."

I roll my eyes at the playful jab. "I didn't go through all of that to hide out in Canada forever and plot more violence and bloodshed." A snort leaves me, and I clarify. "I mean, don't get me wrong, if Simon dropped dead or the opportunity presented itself I'd probably throw a party but—" His lips twitch again and I stop myself, seeing the humor in his eyes "Not the point," I grumble, shaking my head and tugging our hands down to my lap. Looking down and playing with his fingers nervously as I continue. "I want a *life* with you." My brows drop and even I can tell that what I'm saying still kind of sounds like a prayer. "We've wasted so much time and had so much stolen from us." I look back up to find his eyes are rapt on me, something in the back of them starting to slowly unwind as if he can sense some of what's coming.

"I want a life with you," I repeat softly, squeezing his hands probably harder than necessary but it's like all of the sudden my heart is beating too fast. "I don't want to waste any more time. I don't want to take a single day for granted. I want all of the things we've always dreamed about together and I want them now." Sucking in a deep breath, my voice goes soft as I finish. "So let Simon go, Coop. Let him go and let it be the start of our everything."

His face draws in harshly and I can see the war playing out, the struggle in his eyes as he stares into mine. And so I push at him, so different than before and yet still the same, encouraging. "Let it go, Coop."

The breath leaves him in a whoosh and he looks down at our hands, running his finger over the one of mine he put a ring on once, questioning slowly. "This is what you want?"

"Yes."

I'm ready for everything life has to give now.

"Okay," he agrees reluctantly, squeezing my hands and looking back up to me with narrowed eyes. "But if I get even an inkling that he's up to anything again," Another deep breath leaves him. "I will gut him where he stands even if it's in a jail cell," he warns. "Deal?"

"Deal." I try to fight the smile wanting to break free for a couple seconds before giving in with a laugh. "Deal."

His lips tighten for a beat before he shakes his head to hide the way they're twitching up. "Brat."

"Hmm." I smile up invitingly, lifting my feet to loop around his legs and pulling him closer. "Know what else I've been thinking about?"

"I can guess."

And the dark arrogance playing out in his eyes has me rolling mine again, debating holding out on him before I taunt him. "Actually, I'm not sure you can."

Letting go of my hands, he reaches for the counter on either side of me and lowers his head while arching a brow. "Care to enlighten me?"

"Maybe," I muse, taking far too much satisfaction in the way his eyes narrow on me for a second before letting loose a dramatic sigh to cover up the fact that my heart is racing again. "Fine. Remember that fight we had?"

That brow arches higher, humor peeking out from the back of his eyes. "Which one?"

"Ha. Ha," I mock, looking down and reaching out to play with the edge of his gray Henley. "The big one before I left for the volcano trip in Costa Rica." Inhaling a deep breath and finishing quickly. "Later that night after the ring and everything."

A beat passes before he gives me an answer that sounds more like a question. "Yeah." He clears his throat. "Yeah, I remember."

"I used to think maybe that's why you left." I lift my eyes back to his with the quiet confession. "Because I wasn't ready for that."

His brows draw down. "Eleanor—"

"Don't. It's in the past." I shake my head. "Honestly, I said some terrible things during that fight but I was right about it not being the right time." Wrapping my arms back around his neck, I follow it up with a pointed look. "Especially with the secrets you were keeping." I scoff. "Now that would have been a shit show."

"I know." He sighs. "And you're right, but I already told you." His hands go to my hips and he pulls me against him as if worried I'm about to pull away or something. "You were the most impulsive thing I'd ever done but don't ask me to be sorry for it."

"I'm not," I snort softly. "Do you remember what I promised you to finally get you to wake up?"

His eyes narrow for a second before flying wide. "Everything?"

"Everything," I echo. "More specifically, that you would win."

"Eleanor," he breathes quietly, face carefully blank. "Don't do this to make me happy—"

"I'm not." And I make sure to emphasize each word, tightening my arms around his neck. "I'm asking if you still want that."

He pauses, no trace of an expression on his face and I know it's because he doesn't want me to be swayed by him. Not this time. Not after how far we come. But he still can't hide the way the answer explodes out of him.

"Of course." His forehead lowers to mine on the rush of breath, eyes lightening enough to let me see all the happiness he's trying to keep in check. "Of course, but only if you do too."

"I'm not saying we like *try*," I blow out a breath, trying to make sensible words come out and dropping a hand from his neck to reach over and dig in my toiletry bag. Fingers closing around the plastic of what I'm looking for as I lean back, holding it up in the air for him to see before tossing it in the direction of the trash can and surprising myself when I hear it clatter within. "I'm just saying we don't not try either."

His mouth opens in shock, eyes raking my face with a thousand thoughts flying in them for a good minute before that rare, breathtaking smile breaks free. "Always so eloquent."

"But…" I hold up a finger between us in warning. "You should know if it does happen, I'm probably going to be ten times the bitch I currently—"

And then I don't even have time to get another word out before his lips silence me with a hard kiss. One that he's smiling into as his hands drop to my hips and pull me against him. My own going straight for the bottom of his shirt and tugging it up even as my legs tighten around him. He breaks the kiss suddenly, reaching down to rip the shirt over his head before bringing his lips right back to mine and tugging at my boots next. I wrap my arms around him and laugh into the kiss, struck by the sense of how right this is, knowing we were always supposed to end up here.

Life would never stop throwing stuff at us just like the world would never stop turning. We would always have something to figure out or work through. And yeah, the next couple things were huge ones, but I've never wavered since that day I chose him and this… This is our next step.

I drop my arms and shrug out of my jacket, reaching for the bottom of my thermal as he finally gets my boots off and lifts his lips from mine to lean back. Moving onto the button on my pants while I tug the shirt over my head and he pulls me off the counter to push the pants down over my hips. Our breaths already panting over each other as I reach for his pants, the hardness I can see making me want him inside of me right the fuck now.

I barely have time to get the button on his jeans undone before he shoves my underwear down hard enough that I'm pretty sure I hear something tear and spins me around. The reflection of us in the mirror making my breath stop, watching him reach up for the back of my bra and undo the clip there. His eyes finally come up as it falls to the floor, gaze trailing over my body and leaving no part untouched as he pulls down the zipper on his pants. Finally letting them join the rest of our clothes on the ground before his hands start to trail over my hips, eyes locking with mine in the mirror and making my pussy clench.

The possessive look in them unmatched by any other time I've been with him.

I narrow my eyes at him. "You better not get all crazy."

"Me?" He arches a brow, lips ghosting as he lowers his head to nip at my ear, whispering. "Never."

"I mean it—"

One of the hands on my hips starts to trail down over my pussy while the other goes in the opposite direction, moving up to cup my breast at the same time he runs two fingers through my slit. Making my head fall back onto his chest as a needy moan rips from my throat and I close the rest of that distance between us, pushing my ass right up onto his cock. He chuckles against my neck, grip tightening on my breast as his fingers continue to play, sliding slowly back and forth through my pussy. Pausing every couple of times to swirl around my clit before going back down to spear up into me the nearest bit again.

Shocking me with the sudden change of pace now that he has me naked and in his hands. The delicious laziness ramping up my need even more.

He lifts those lips to my ear. "You were saying, Princess?"

Right. I was saying… I was saying… "Huh?"

Another low laugh leaves him, breath fanning against my neck before he lets go of my breast and pulls back. His other hand pinching my clit and making me gasp before he moves it to my hip, encouraging me to tilt forward and arch my ass for him.

And lucky for him, I'm totally on board with this plan.

I grab the counter in front of us and raise my ass high into the air, going up onto my toes to help make up for the height difference. Watching in the mirror as his eyes drop and turn dark at the sight of me practically splayed out for him. His hand moves to grip his cock, pumping it hard as he lines us up and teases my entrance with that first inch of him before gripping both my hips tight.

Giving me a shallow thrust as his eyes meet mine again, the dark flecks in them sparking. "I will be a little crazy, Eleanor."

His lips twitch then and it's the only warning I get before he slams home with one powerful thrust. Ripping the air from my lungs and making my back bow with the shock of it. My mouth opens as I gasp for breath and he lowers his chest down onto my back, cock moving inside of me with the move and making my pussy tighten up around him.

He lets go of my hips and reaches forward to wind his fingers through mine, keeping our eyes locked in the mirror as he kisses my back, whispering. "I will always be a little crazy when it comes to you." Trailing his lips up my shoulder as he continues. "And if it does happen, I will probably check on you so much that you'll threaten me with bodily injury." I squeeze his fingers in reprimand, still beyond words and trying to adjust to the sudden intrusion of him. "But"—he presses a kiss to my neck that's nothing but care, reverent eyes on mine and words that follow filled with infinite tenderness—"I'll also go out in the middle of the night to get you whatever you want. I'll be there to help make your dreams come true as you bring ours to life. And"—that first soft thrust has me gasping again, heart swelling just like his cock is inside of me—"I'll never stop looking at you, holding you, and loving you through every second of it." A little cry leaves me as he thrusts harder, my eyes starting to prick even before he finishes. "Always."

He slams home again then and a scream rips from my throat as he rises to stand, pulling my hands up as he does and wrapping them around his neck, my eyes immediately devouring the erotic visual of us in the mirror. The way my breasts are lifted high and his body is dwarfing mine as he slides his hands back down to rest on the inside of my legs, trailing his fingers around my entrance that he's filling and making me gasp.

"Spread those legs for me, Princess." The order comes out rough as he drops his mouth to my ear and pulls the lobe through his teeth before whispering. "And don't you dare move those hands."

I dig my fingernails into the skin at the back of his neck hard enough that I see him fight a wince. Mustering myself to push back against all that demanding dominance he's throwing around and check him a bit. "Oh, you mean these hands?"

His eyes narrow on mine in the mirror for a second before that savage smirk flashes and he brings his fingers up to my clit and pushes down on it hard. "Such a brat."

"Fuck," I gasp, legs starting to wobble and open for him anyway as he lowers his hips to thrust up into me from below.

Squeezing my eyes shut when he repeats the motion, the sudden visual of us almost too much with the feel of him moving inside of me. Little bolts of pleasure shooting out from where he's playing with my clit and making my inner muscles clench around him with each pass as needy moans start to pour from my mouth. And when I feel his other hand lower to my breast a second later, fingers rolling my nipple between them, I have to lock my hands together to keep them from dropping from his neck.

"Open your eyes," he demands, pinching my clit again and shocking me into obeying as he picks up his pace. "I want you to see how fucking stunning you are when you're coming on my cock."

My chest starts to heave with gasping breaths, breasts lifting and falling in the mirror as I do exactly that. Eyes running along my body and seeing everything from how my inner thighs are glistening, so wet from what he's doing to the flush coloring my cheeks. The way both of our bodies are strung tight, teetering on a whole new edge and the contrast of his dark-olive skin against my light gold where his hand is on my breast. I lower my eyes back down to where he's still playing with my clit and am rewarded with little teasing peeks of his cock that have my pussy spasming around him with each one. Legs no longer wobbling but full on shaking as my calves start to cramp, leaving me practically hanging from my hold on his neck.

And all of it, the visual coupled with reality I can feel on and in every intimate part of me, is undeniably the most erotic thing I've ever experienced.

He runs his lips over that favorite spot of his at the base of my neck and I bring my eyes back up in time to lock with his right before he sucks it into his mouth. Dragging the sensitive skin through his teeth and making instant goose bumps erupt over my skin. Every part of me from the top of my head down to my arched toes tingling like there's too much blood rushing around under my skin as the gasps leaving my lips turn into soft screams and my legs give out. Feet hitting the ground and making my pussy drop down onto his cock as he thrusts up before clamping down hard around him.

"Fuck." The harsh curse leaves him and his hands instantly go to my hips as he groans. "Grab the counter." I drop my hands from his neck to grab at the flat surface of the counter, not arguing for once because of the ecstasy that's barreling down on me. Watching him now as he runs his hands down to the tops of my thighs before lifting me right into the fucking air with the low order. "Wrap your legs behind my back."

And again, I do, barely able to lock my feet together behind his lower back with the angle but still... holy shit. Who the fuck wouldn't? We're quite literally reaching whole new heights and I'm most definitely here for it.

I catch the way his night-forest eyes flash with that little bit of arrogance right before he lowers his mouth to my ass cheek, nearly pulling out of me with the move and making a sound of protest leave me. Taking his time and running his tongue over the skin under his lips, never breaking our gaze as he bites it hard enough to leave a mark. Turning that sound of protest into a moan as he finishes it up with a soft kiss before lifting up and breaking our gaze to look down in admiration with a twitch of his lips. "Think that might have to be your next tattoo."

My mouth drops open in shock, moan ending with a sound of indignation. "Cooper Mon—"

He thrusts back into me before I can get another syllable out, cutting off my rebuke by impaling me with his cock. Fingers tighten on my legs as he unleashes an almost punishing pace that sends me locking right back down around him and screaming gasps escaping from my lips. Each one holding his name as I reach up and plant my hand on the mirror, finally getting the leverage I need to push back to meet him thrust for thrust. Our eyes meet somewhere between my fingers as the universe seems to spiral down, centering around this new magnificent unification of us. Time stopping for a miraculous moment in which nothing exists but endless possibilities.

The start of that infinity I had dared to dream for the first time with him.

The little part of everything that really would exist past the end of it all.

Every muscle in my body tightens up then, fingers curling into the mirror and mouth parting with a silent scream as the orgasm crashes through me right down to my bones. Leaving me unable to move an inch as every nerve in my body screams with the pleasure I can't and my pussy clamps down, gushing around his cock. And I fight against the urge to close my eyes, wanting to see him as his cock grows harder, continuing to slide through my inner walls that are pulling at him. Watching as his face draws tight a few seconds before he groans my name and thrusts hard. Hitting me so fucking deep it sends another orgasm hurtling through me right on the heels of the last as his cock jerks inside of me and he spills a part of himself there.

And in the instant that follows, I know that it's the end of another part of my life too. The closing of a chapter by the necessity of the one my heart wants to start next. And it's there, the guilt, but I don't shy away from it. I don't apologize for the ache in my heart that comes with keeping my promise to drag all of the happiness out of this life that it has to give.

I take a deep breath, and I let it go, finding the rhythm in the air again. Finding the sun that I've become to myself today.

Coop's hands slide up my legs, letting them lower to the floor and I blink a couple times to drag myself back to the present while dropping my hand from the mirror. Finding his intense gaze still on mine as he brings his hands around to rest on my stomach with a ghost of lips. "There she is."

My lips twitch. "You better hope so." The last thing I need in my life is more testosterone. I pull a disbelieving face though, wanting to mess with him a bit. "Pretty sure it doesn't work like that though."

He ignores my witty remark, laying his chest down on my back and pressing a soft kiss to my shoulder with the quiet question. "You okay?"

And looking into his eyes, I can see that he feels it too. The finality of it all.

"Yeah," I tell him softly because it's true. "I'm perfect."

Exactly where I'm supposed to be and with exactly who I chose to be with.

Our gaze holds for a moment as his eyes drill into mine, checking on what he sees there before I cock a brow and try to lighten the mood. "Feel like letting me up anytime soon?"

"Figured I'd stay here for a bit." He shrugs casually, lips tightening. "Try for a Maddoc."

I reach back, trying to slap his ass at the audacity. "You arrogant bast—ah!"

My words are cut off by a squeal as he pulls back and out of me suddenly before swooping me up into the air and walking over to the shower. Not even giving me a second to recover before he turns it on high and blasts us with icy water that has me screaming at him.

"What?" He shrugs, still holding me captive in his arms. "This was my part of the ritual, right?"

Chapter Thirty-Eight

The next few weeks pass quickly as I sit back and watch the machine that is Bainbridge make the dominoes fall one right after another and leave me second-guessing every scandal and conspiracy theory out there. They had released the video of what happened in Simon's library the day after we agreed to it and even though the news networks had blurred out my intimate areas, I was still happy to be safely tucked away in Canada. At least for a little while longer. Not needing the front-row seat I would have gotten in LA to the speculation that had followed over whether I had done it willingly or not. Especially after I had been identified and the shit show had really begun.

Eventually though, enough of a public outcry had been raised that the Canadian officials requested an interview with me via my aunt and I'd only been too happy to agree to it. Meeting them halfway between Lake Rosseau and Montreal and walking them through what had happened with the exception of one caveat Bainbridge had set. None of it could be traced back to them. So instead of threatening Coop and being tied to Novikov, I'd painted Simon as an obsessed stalker who had dated and then threatened my aunt to get me to comply. And I hadn't lost a second of sleep over it. His actions had been the same in the end regardless of who had been threatened.

After that, I'd gotten to watch Coop and Alec really work for the first time in my life with all the resources they'd needed behind them. Including Serena much to my displeasure even though she never came to the house. They'd assembled a team within that first couple of days and started systematically stripping Simon of any ties to Bainbridge. From networks to deals that'd had Novikov attached to them too. All the while leaving his major crimes right there for the taking when warrants had been issued to dive deeper into what exactly was going on at Taylor International. And when my statement had become public, all of Simon's political friends condemned him on TV for the world to see as they washed their hands of him.

Even Mac's father, the senator, had released a statement of outrage that his son's guest at a political event had been assaulted so grievously, whipping up the scandal to the international level.

It was a masterpiece of synchronicity that had me narrowing my eyes at both of them with a whole new level of suspicion about what they were truly capable of together. Muttering as I was going to bed at night about how tricking a poor innocent girl in the bar in Costa Rica must have seemed like cake after toppling regimes while Coop just chuckled. I could tell he loved it though, being back in the thick of it and working again, and that made me happy too. Further solidifying in my mind that I'd made the right decision for everyone, especially at the look of horror on Alec's face when I'd told him that the home I bought came with a pool house that I planned on renovating for him.

Gotta love family.

I'd only made one request of Bainbridge through everything, that I wanted to be there when he was arrested. To see the look on his face as he goes down because of what he'd done to me, what he'd tried to do to all of us. And they'd agreed, saying it was the least they could do after the enterprise that had been able to fester right under their noses. To which I replied thank you very much and if they wanted to express that apology in another form I'd take a check for my arts center opening up next year.

And today is that day.

Alec got the call in the middle of the night that the warrant had been issued for his arrest and that they'd be taking him into custody. All of his avenues to escape the country had been blocked off weeks ago, with both the public and authorities keeping such a close eye on him. And the underworld, well, they didn't like anything that shined a light on them, so Simon had officially been labeled as persona non grata. Meaning he was trapped with nowhere to run as time ticked down... and wasn't that just a bitch.

So here we are. Alec in the driver's seat of the Suburban while I'm ducking low in the passenger seat, tapping a steady beat against my knee. Mac sitting behind me, complaining every now and then about *why* we can't just stop at a bar on the way home so he can get laid. And Coop... Coop had opted not to come, saying that if he laid eyes on him after watching that video, he wouldn't even make it into the cop car.

I get it, I do, but it still sucks.

"Want me to pull up some color schemes for you to pick from for the pool house while we wait?" I toss out casually, purposefully not looking toward the driver's side of the car and deciding the best thing to curb the underlying anxiety thrumming through me is, without a doubt, to get under his skin. "I was thinking some bright-coral colors would go perfectly with how it's situated right next to the pool."

A beat passes before he answers with equal disinterest. "I really don't like you."

"It'd be such a shame." I sigh. "If only I cared." My eyes trail the elegant steel-and-glass structure of the building housing Simon's main office while tacking on. "Yvie is excited to meet you though so at least someone there will be happy to see you."

That icy laugh fills the car for a second. "My adopted parents have requested to meet you as well even though I tried to dissuade them."

I whip my head toward him in surprise. "Say that again?"

"I told them you were annoying, like some giant gnat, but..." he continues, still looking out the front window and scanning the street. "They insisted on it at some point."

"Uh." I swallow, not quite sure where to start. "You're still close with them?"

"Close probably isn't the right word." He shrugs one shoulder. "The Winslows were good to me though and I'm grateful."

Silence fills the car for a second as I try to figure out what the heck that means before giving up and questioning. "Good to you?"

He had only ever mentioned them in passing and I hadn't wanted to pry into what could possibly be a wound or even grief if they had passed, but now… well, cards on the table, big brother. These people want to meet me, and from here on out, I'm maintaining a high suspicion of anyone who wants that privilege.

"I wasn't the easiest child to connect with by the time they adopted me." His eyes flick to mine with a look before he shrugs again and looks back out the window. "Never fully adjusted to my new environment."

Well, that sounds like the kind of therapist speak that I'm intimately familiar with. So I don't push for more, curbing my natural desire to mess with him and instead blurting out the first thing that pops into my head.

"What the fuck do they think you do for a living?"

Because I'm betting it isn't the truth.

A long silence fills the car and I can practically feel Mac straining his ears behind me before Alec sighs. "International investment banking."

I choke on the scoff that tries to escape, fighting against the instant laughter at the idea of Alec passing himself off as a part of everyday corporate America but Mac does no such thing. Roaring with it behind me and eventually working his words out between breaths. "They—" He laughs harder. "They think you're a-a…" Another round of gasping ensues as he tries to contain himself, making me lose the battle too and dissolve into giggles as he finally finishes. "A banker?"

"It was a logical choice." Alec snaps icily, making us laugh even harder while arguing his point. "Long unusual hours, lots of travel, not a lot of—"

"It-it's not that," I gasp, stomach cramping and making me double over with effort to get the words out. "It's just," My eyes meet his brown ones for a second and I manage to contain myself before looking down at yet another all-black outfit he's wearing today. "Look at you!" I bust out finally on another round of giggles.

Mac laughs hard again behind me as Alec rolls his eyes and grumbles. "They've never questioned it."

"Right." I manage to nod, pressing my lips together in an attempt to regain control.

"Oh fuck," Mac exhales deeply. "That's the best thing I've heard in weeks."

"So glad I could be of use," Alec drones sardonically.

Mac laughs once more from the back seat before calling to me, "Els."

"What?"

"Can we please go to the bar after this to celebrate?" he pleads. "Maybe even invite Jane Bond to—"

"No," me and Alec interrupt at the same time, making him let loose an exasperated sound.

"I don't understand—"

"It's happening," Alec interrupts, hard tone leaving no question as to what exactly it is as my gaze snaps back to the window in time to see agents dressed in black enter the building. The holstered guns at their sides leave little question as to what exactly they're here for and make my spine tingle with anticipation. "Won't be long now."

No one in the car says a word while we wait. The anticipation palpable, with the only sounds being our breaths layering over each other's and the occasional honk of a car or the rumble of an engine going by outside. I keep darting my eyes to the time on the dash, wondering how long it's supposed to take to arrest someone but not being able to force the question out. Like any kind of interruption out here could somehow disrupt the events happening within.

It takes twenty minutes and I'm sweating by the time the first agents come back out the front doors of the office building. Holding my breath until I finally see two of them march Simon out with his hands behind his back. The expression on his face weirdly aghast, like he can't believe what's happening, but I know it's all for show. All a carefully constructed act to hide the absolute psychopath within. One that he'll probably continue on with through endless appeals until his dying day.

I blow out the breath I'm holding and push open my door suddenly, ignoring Alec and Mac's shouts of protest, shutting it before they can stop me. Darting across the street as quickly as I can without drawing attention and aiming for the sidewalk where the police cars are lined up. Eyes running over my surroundings quickly and taking them in before choosing a tree that puts me perfectly within sight of where he's about to be ducked into the first cage of many to come. I lean against the tree and cross my arms over my jacket, waiting for the moment as my body thrums with anticipation. Knowing it's coming and trying to slow down everything in my head enough to savor it all as he's walked closer and closer to those cars.

"Look at me," I whisper into the air, brows dropping with the intent of my demand. Relishing the power pulsing under my skin as I recognize how free of him I am standing here. "Look at me, you piece of shit."

And the thing is, it has nothing to do with the fact that he's about to be locked up and everything to do with who I am standing here today.

"Fucking look at me."

It's like he hears me then, head turning slowly my way with searching eyes as he continues in the direction the officers are pushing him.

It doesn't take long for him to find me.

I can tell the second he does and not just because of the way my spine tingles with warning when his gaze lands on me. It's in the way he almost stumbles a step, that perfect facade slipping from his face before the desolate evil inside flashes for the world to see, coming out and taking over now that he's backed into a corner with the prey he played with just out of reach.

I cock a brow at him, letting every bit of viciousness the sight of him incites play across my lips for a second, pulling them up into a smirk before speaking into the air between us the one thing I want him to remember. "I win." Making sure to emphasize the movements of my mouth so he can see and willing my message to reach his ears.

I see the instant rage shoot straight to the front of his eyes, the same kind that I had clung to before to keep going. That's the difference between me and him though. I'm capable of letting it go because of the capacity for love I'd turned the page to cling to in the end. The endless capacity that I'd learned from the sun who'd been the first person to really teach me how to let something go.

And isn't that irony for you? That the very thing he taught me to do might be what lets me be selfless enough for one of the first times in my life to respect his wishes in the end.

So I raise my hand and give Simon a salute that holds all kinds of attitude before turning and walking away. Letting it go for good and blowing out a breath as I stroll back across the street, in no rush or hurry to do anything but just breathe in the new day.

There's nothing left to do here. No more running or hiding to be done.

Now it's just a matter of making that journey home, and for some of us, that journey might be more final than others.

***

Something is up.

I narrow my eyes at Alec as he gets back into the car after about the fifth stop on our way back to Lake Rosseau and snap, "What are you doing?"

"What?" He scowls at me.

"You used to get pissed at me if I had to even pee while we were driving around Europe and now we've stopped twice for you to do the same along with the store and—"

"Well excuse me for taking advantage of our newfound freedom," he interrupts, backing out of the gas station down the road from the lake house.

"I'm with Els," Mac chimes in. "It's sketchy. Especially when you were against the bar."

Alec snorts in response before droning, "Calm down, Watson. We're almost back."

"Joy," Mac shoots back sarcastically before asking me, "Have you booked the flights yet?"

I search Alec's face for another moment, looking for any clue as to what's really going on before shaking my head. "No, Coop and I were going to book them when I got back today."

"To Landing Point?" Alec asks, tone the slightest bit softer because everyone knows what's coming when we get there.

"Yeah." I swallow, looking back to the road and repeating it more to come to terms with it myself. "Yeah." He turns onto the road leading up to the house and my brows drop down with a thought. "Are you coming with us?"

Mac has already committed to it, says he wants to see where I was born, but not Alec.

His eyes slide over, meeting mine for a second. "Do you want me to?"

"It's up to you." I shrug, ignoring the weird sense that comes with the thought of not being together after all these months. "Where would you go instead?"

"To LA." He pulls up in front of the house and brings the car to a stop before looking back at me. "Go ahead and start scouting locations for the Bainbridge office there."

I stare into his eyes and one of those moments of understanding passes between us, allowing me the insight to guess that the place where Nadia died might be a mountain he's not ready to climb yet. So I give him a slow nod. "Sounds good to me." My lips twitch. "You'll miss me though, and you should know Coop won't be back to work for a while still."

"What?"

I push open my door while Mac laughs, tossing out over my shoulder. "I'm taking him back to Cahuita for a couple months."

"What?!" The shout makes it out before I slam the door, cutting off whatever else he's saying and running for the house.

Laughing under my breath as I shut the front door quickly and lean back against it, my eyes rolling over the living room. Brows lowering when I come up empty in my search for Coop because I'd expected him to be waiting at the door. I take another couple steps into the house while calling out. "Coop?"

My stomach drops when nothing but silence answers me and for a second, I'm right back in Cahuita. The past holding me captive until I shake my shoulders, shrugging off the sense and forcing myself further into the room with the reminder that it's never happening again. I make it past the edge of the living room and come to an abrupt stop as sound starts to filter through the air to me. Cocking my head to try and figure out where it's coming from because that sound…

I'd recognize it anywhere.

I scan the space again, searching desperately for the source of it and landing on something through the back window that has me wondering for a second whether Alec's drugged me again. Blinking a few more times to make sure I'm not actually hallucinating before the music and the fact that he's pacing finally convinces me that I'm not. I still pause to take it in though, trying to figure out what the hell is going on before slowly starting to walk to the back door. Cursing Alec the whole way because I knew something was up, but I can't deny the excitement either as I open the door and step out onto the deck.

He comes to an instant halt at my entrance, quickly turning to face me from where he's standing on the deck about ten feet away as "Just Like Heaven" by The Cure fills the air. The sand that's been scattered all over the deck a direct contrast to the surrounding snow, while the tiki torches lit around it look like they're barely hanging on against the wind. But what really gets me is the journals. Stacks and stacks of them scattered high around the deck and looking like they've never even been opened with how untarnished they are, from browns to blacks to greens and reds and everything in between.

I finally drag my gaze back to him and he flashes me that breathtaking smile that's a little less rare these days. Standing there in a freaking suit and making my lips twitch up despite how utterly confused I still am. So pulled in by him that I take a few more steps without even realizing it before the wind gusts, blowing the sand around and making me laugh. "What the hell is this?"

He shrugs, lips still left with a ghost of that smile. "It's the first time we met."

"What?" I shake my head at him, getting it but still not getting it. "What are you talking about?"

A beat passes and I see those plush lips tighten before he starts to slowly walk my way. "I had been watching you since you came into the bar," he starts. "From the back corner where you couldn't see me yet."

"Stalker." I snort, unable to help the tease because it's absolutely true too. "You were already obsessed with me."

"Brat." A low laugh leaves him as he continues to close that space. "I'd been pretty much set on just watching you at that point, knowing I should just leave you be. But then that guy bought you a drink and"—he arches a brow and comes to a halt right in front of me—"I knew in the five minutes that followed how screwed we both were."

I fight against the smile trying to break free, cocking a brow right back at him. "Confident were you?"

"I knew you were my missing piece." He shrugs as if it really is that simple, finishing with a quiet scoff. "And I wasn't about to let someone else take what was mine."

I bite my lower lip for a second, but even that doesn't work to stop the lift of my lips while admitting. "He never stood a chance."

"Good to know we were on the same page." His eyes drill into mine and the air between us goes taut, reminding me of this morning and how he'd said goodbye to me with what he considered to be his new mission in life. He blows out a breath then, making me fight to hold a laugh in because I know he was just thinking about the same thing. "As much pain as we've gone through… I wouldn't change a thing about us, Eleanor." He shakes his head. "Because it's all led us here."

"To a beach in the snow?" I quip.

A beat passes before he closes that last step between us while answering quietly. "To everything." His night-forest eyes lighten a shade as he continues. "But if I could go back to that night and know that we would still end up here… I would change it to go a little something like this." He drops his head closer, making me have to tilt mine back to keep our gaze locked as that damn presence explodes out of him, brushing against my skin like a caress. "Hello, Eleanor Delacroix." His lips twitch. "My name is Cooper Monroe and soon yours will be too."

"Ha!" I scoff, so past the point of fighting the silly smile on my face that I don't even try, but that doesn't mean I can't still play along. "And how exactly do you know my name, Cooper Monroe?" Trying for a suspicious look despite the smile.

"Because." He exhales a deep breath, a little bit of the humor falling from his face. "We had the same tragic start."

"Care to explain that?"

"Of course." He nods seriously. "You see, our parents fell in love, and that's what forever changed the course of both our lives by ending theirs."

It takes me a second to recover from the sudden levity, knowing that it's my turn to say something so I clear my throat. "And you think we should be together because of that?"

"No." A single shake of his head is all he gives me before following it up with the proclamation. "I think we should be together in spite of it."

"In spite of it, huh?" I question with mock seriousness. "Thought about this a lot, have you?"

A low laugh leaves him. "Endlessly." He nods his head toward the first stack of journals on my left. "You see, these right here are for those first years together. The ones filled with the house and the babies and the craziness that comes with trying to keep our heads above water during it all."

"Awfully confident," I tease, the break in my voice giving away how much this actually means to me though.

"And these." He looks to the ones on my right and reaches out to wind a couple of his fingers through mine. "These are for us to fill with all of the dreams you make come true for yourself. The Center just being the start of all the incredible things I know you're going to achieve."

And I can barely get the next words past my heart with how full it is. "Such pressure."

"No pressure." His fingers squeeze mine. "Just possibility." He nods back over his shoulder to the left as if he doesn't even need to look while continuing. "Those are for all of the summers we're going to spend in Cahuita." His lips ghost up as he moves his head to the right. "And those are for the teenage years and all the headache that comes with that, along with the good stuff." He steps slowly around me, keeping his fingers in mine and stopping at my back with that almost-touching move that kills me. Pointing with both our hands to a small black pile between the two on my left. "Those are for all the time we've spent apart." I let him move my finger to the next, slightly larger red pile as he drops his lips to my ear. "Those are for all of the date nights and vacations we're going to take, just the two of us. The... intimate"—his voice drops low with the word—"moments together we never want to forget."

A beat passes then before I feel his hand on my hip and he turns us both around to face a large blue pile I hadn't seen at first, set a little bit apart from the rest but still just as tall as the largest of them. "And those"—he sighs, wrapping his arms around me and fully entwining our fingers—"those are for Jace." My heart stops with a crack, throat tightening up as the tears start to slide free. "Because I don't ever want you to think that I want you to forget him or love him any less than I do too." He pauses to

422

clear his throat and when he continues I can hear how much this is affecting him in the rough cadence of his voice. "Whether he's here or gone, Eleanor. He will always be a part of our story. One of the best parts for both of us and I don't ever want either of us to lose a single memory we have of him."

He doesn't move for a long moment, taking in those journals with me as we both remember him. And then eventually, he lets go and walks slowly back around to face me. Keeping a little bit of space between us as his eyes lock back with mine, standing in our little world of feeling as he tells me softly. "A lifetime's worth of memories, Eleanor. The start of everything that matters to spite anything that stood in our way. A lifetime to live on forever so that people can read about it and fall in love right along with us one day."

I press my lips together to keep the cry of happiness from escaping as he reaches into his pocket, pulling out a small black velvet box that I remember vividly and dropping slowly down onto one knee. His lips ghosting as he opens it and reveals the Toi et Moi ring that I'd left on the bed in Cahuita years ago. The one that's the dark and the stars and everything in between.

"This little ring"—he looks down at it and swallows visibly—"has been through quite a journey. Just like us." A breath leaves him as he pulls the ring from the box and sets it down before taking my hands in his again. "It kept me company during that year apart when I was looking for you and it sat in Tommy's apartment waiting while you were searching for me."

His face screws up, remembering his friend, and he squeezes my hands. "And this time, I wanted it to come home to where it belongs the way it should have all along. Without any secrets between us and ready to face whatever comes next." I loosen my lips, sucking in a deep breath. "So Eleanor Delacroix, who might already be Monroe," His lips twitch as he finishes. "Will you do me the very unforgettable honor of being mine again?"

I drop to my knees right there in front of him, ignoring the ring for a moment and wrapping my arms tightly around his neck. Whispering with the same word we'd given each other over and over again through a choked breath. "Always."

Struck by the sense that it really is the same answer I've been giving him throughout eternity.

Chapter Thirty-Nine

A harsh ringing fills my ears, rattling around in my head and interrupting the wonderful nap I'd been taking. Dragging me awake and making me blink to clear the blurriness from my eyes while trying to figure out where the hell it's coming from. My gaze lands on the phone next to me. The screen is lit up with an incoming call and I sit up with a sigh, looking down at it while forcing my brain to actually process what my eyes are seeing. Reading through the number a couple more times because I still haven't gotten around to saving anyone's number yet, before I realize who it is.

Tiff. It's Tiff.

My stomach drops instantly and I pause, heart racing with equal parts fear and hope of what news might be on the other end of that line because Tiff never calls me. She's talked to Coop since we got him back and I've talked to her a couple times to check on Jace too, but... she never calls. We always call her.

I reach out for the phone quickly, knowing it's about to ring through to the end and not wanting to miss it despite the little bit of fear filling me. Swiping my finger across it and bringing it to my ear while rushing out. "Tiff, what's up?"

Nothing comes over the phone for a beat except scattered breaths before a sob breaks through the line, making my anxiety shoot through the roof as she hiccups through more cries. "Is-is Coop there?"

"No, he went to a meeting with Alec before we head back tomorrow," I answer quickly before offering. "I can conference him in though—"

"No!" she shouts, making my brows shoot down, now confused about what exactly is going on here because if it's anything to do with Jace, I assume she'd want him to hear it too. "No," she repeats more quietly and I can hear the way she's holding back more cries. "I wanted to talk to you."

"What's wrong?" I ask her, trying my best to be gentle because something is obviously very wrong. "Are you okay?"

"I don't—" she cuts herself off and a few deep breaths come over the line before she admits quietly. "No, I don't think so." Another breath that holds a sob echoes and her voice breaks all over the next part. "I don't know where it all went so wrong."

"Where what went wrong, Tiff?"

"Jared." She cries openly, the rest of the words tumbling out between them. "He ask-asked me to move in after you left and—and Jace happened."

My brows drop further, chest tightening at the direction this story is going. "You've been living with him?" She never told me that.

"Y-yeah," she stutters out and my mind automatically snaps to the memory of the morning I'd called her and she'd been at the hospital with Jace. In the middle of the night when she should have been home. "At first it was f-fine…"

I know by the way she trails off that I haven't just been hearing things these past months, that her voice has been lost for a reason. So I finish for her softly, guessing and hoping I'm wrong. "And then it wasn't."

Her cries cut off at my words and after a moment, she repeats them with equal quiet. "And then it wasn't."

I want to ask her why the hell she didn't call me before now, but that won't do her any good right now, so instead, I try to focus on what can be done now and what I need to know. "How bad is it?" Correcting myself because whatever this is, it's most definitely past tense. "Was it?"

She pauses before pleading. "You can't tell Coop. Please, El, he'll kill him or—"

"No, Tiffany," I cut her off because while I would do anything to help her right now... that, I won't do. "We don't keep secrets from each other anymore."

Heavy silence comes through the phone and I know we've reached somewhat of a stalemate which is the last thing I want when she's finally talking to someone. So instead, I tell her, "But I can promise to intercede and make sure he doesn't do anything that would have any permanent kind of consequences."

Because the arrogant bastard is not allowed to leave me again.

Especially now.

Her silence holds and I blow out a breath, knowing that even if she won't talk anymore... I can still be there for her. Give her the same thing that had been given to me when I was at one of my lowest points. "What do you need, Tiff?" Because she's family too. "What do you need right now?"

And that seems to be the question that finally breaks through her resolve, making her answer back. "To not be here." She cries again, words that follow breaking her voice and my heart for her. "I tr-tried to stay for Jace, but I just..." A weary breath flows through the phone. "I can't be here anymore, El. I can't face him." She hiccups. "Or my mother."

"Okay," I answer quickly. "Then I'll get you out of there."

"To where?" she asks in a small voice.

My lips lift with a small smile because I know just the place. "There's a house in LA with an empty room that used to be mine."

"I can't just take your—"

"You can. It's the safest place for you, I promise," I insist, emphasizing the next bit, so she knows there's really no argument to be had here. "And you will." Standing from the bed, I walk straight to the closet while continuing. "I'm already on my way. We'll get you out of there."

A relieved breath flows through the phone before her voice tightens up with trepidation again. "And Coop?"

"Ah," I tease, trying to make it seem like everything is going to be alright and that I might not have to tie her brother to the bed depending on how bad of shape she's in. "Leave him to me. Plus, he's about four hours away currently, so if I leave now, I'll be at the airport before he even realizes." My lips twitch at the idea even as I pull the duffel I'd already packed this morning and sling it over my shoulder. "You'll be gone before he gets there and I can deal with the fallout."

"Okay," she finally accepts. "I just… I don't want him to freak out after everything this year—"

"Don't worry. I got it," I reiterate confidently. Hoping like hell that's true. "Where are you?"

"At your house." The answer comes out with a little bit of shame I recognize all too well now. "I used the spare key you told me about."

"Perfect. Stay there." I swallow down some of the anger sparking in me. "I'm leaving now. Text you when the plane takes off."

"Okay." And I can hear the nervous breath she inhales before telling me. "Thank you, El."

"Of course," I answer softly, walking to the door and pulling it open. "See you soon."

"See you soon."

I hang up the phone then, sliding it into the back pocket of my jeans and continuing to the kitchen where I left my camera while screaming at the top of my lungs. "Macallan!"

Something thuds loudly onto the ground upstairs as if he just fell off something, making me laugh under my breath as I snag my camera off the counter. Turning back just as his heavy footfalls start to pound down the stairs and his panicked face comes into sight. Chest heaving as he scans the space tensely like we're under attack.

"What?" He continues to hurry toward me before the clear amusement lifting my lips stops him. "What's going on?"

"Time to go." I laugh again at the nervous look on his face. "We're needed in Landing Point."

He hesitates for a second and I think he's trying to figure out how to approach this delicately when that's not exactly our forte. "Shouldn't we wait for Coop?"

"Nope." I pop the *P* on the word and drag it out while walking toward him. "Tiff needs me and it'd be best if I beat him there."

I see his sapphire eyes spark at the game that's afoot, knowing he wants to play, but still, his face draws in. "Tiff? The sister?"

"Yeah." Sliding the strap of the camera over my head with a nod. "She's in a rough spot." I shrug as if it's no big deal. "So I figured she could take my room in LA."

His eyes shoot wide with horror. "A girl?"

"Yes, Macallan." And the way he says it like he's never heard such a preposterous thing has me rolling my eyes. "Same as me."

"Uhh—"

"Go get your bag!" I order with exasperation. "We have to hurry to make it there before he gets back!"

"Fine." He pouts sullenly. "But Satan's going to be pissed."

I cock a brow at him with a smirk. "And think about what fun that'll be."

***

We've already checked our bags and made it through security at the airport in Montreal by the time my phone rings, making my lips twitch with all kinds of exhilaration I probably shouldn't be feeling under the current circumstances… but still, I've learned to take the good stuff whenever it comes. Even if it is side by side with the bad. And this is going to be a fun little distraction followed by some hard truths, so I might as well make the most of it.

I slide my finger across the screen and press the phone to my ear, greeting him airily. "Oh, hello, Mr. Monroe. How can I help you today?"

The twitch of my lips lifts into a full-blown grin at the pause that follows because I can practically see the way his eyes are narrowing, trying to figure out what I'm playing at.

"Eleanor." His tone is carefully tight as if he doesn't want to assume but knows something is off. "Where are you?"

The speaker in the airport blares in the next second and the tension on the phone ratchets up a degree before I answer casually. "The airport."

"And where exactly"—his voice drops low and my skin practically fucking tingles at the grating reprimand I can hear in it—"do you think you're going, Princess?"

"To Landing Point." I sigh, taking up that haughty tone that drives him crazy. "My presence was needed there before yours."

"By who?"

"Wouldn't you like to know?"

"*Eleanor*—"

"Calm down." A soft laugh leaves me with the order and Mac shoots me a look like I've lost my mind. "I'll tell you all about it when you get there."

His breathing echoes through the phone for a moment, all kinds of tense and just inciting me to push him a bit more. Really wanting him to throw that pissed-off energy right at me in the best kind of way when he catches up.

"Come on, baby." His breathing stops completely and I have to bite my lip to keep another laugh from escaping. Knowing the nickname he'd expressly forbidden at the start of us would topple him over that edge for me. "Or have you forgotten how to chase me?"

I grab Mac's arm and point to the restroom we're passing, wanting to use it before the flight because the bathrooms on airplanes never quite feel clean to me.

He gives me a nod of understanding and I break off just as Coop finally answers through the phone. "Oh, Princess." That demanding voice roughens with all kinds of intimacy, making my breath hitch even in the middle of a crowd. "You better hope that ass of yours remembers how to run fast because when I get my hands on it—"

"Oh, Coop," I interrupt, pushing open the bathroom door and laughing a little more huskily than I probably need to. "Don't forget. You have to catch me first before you can make me scream."

I pull the phone away from my ear and hang up before he can get another word out, laughter falling openly from my lips as I scan the space and notice a girl standing at the sink that's looking a little worse for wear. Well, a whole lot worse for wear actually. She's dressed in what I'd say is a gorgeous gold evening gown, except for the visible tears and burns on it. Remnants of what looks like a fire clinging to her from the smudges of ash scattered across her light-brown skin. The waterfall of black curls falling down her back is all kinds of askew and her fingers are trembling where she's clutching the sink.

And maybe it's because she only looks a couple years younger than me, or maybe it's that lost look in her eyes… but something about her pulls at me. Reminds me of the same instant draw I've only ever felt with two other people in my life.

It makes me take a hesitant step toward her, calling out softly. "Hey."

Her head turns toward me in surprise, large clear crystal-blue eyes widening on mine as I try for a nonthreatening smile. "So"—I walk to the sink next to hers and lean up against it—"I've had a hell of a couple years and you look like you've had a hell of a night." Her face turns perplexed, looking at me like I'm the strangest person she's ever encountered and while that might be true… I shrug. "That's my way of asking if you're okay."

Her mouth parts in surprise, painfully delicate features blanking out for a second before laughter falls from her lips that strikes deep at me, the sound like… I don't even know. Tinkling bells or something. Like all the joyous and mournful notes in the world have come together seamlessly. I've never heard anything like it. Not even Jace's melodic voice comes anywhere close to the sound of this girl's laughter.

If gods sing though, I'd like to think it sounds like that.

"No." She shakes her head with the answer, fingers trembling again on the sink as her throat moves. "I don't know what I am."

"Been there," I mutter, sighing deeply and trying to ignore the fact that I really need to pee. "Piece of advice if you want it?"

Her eyes move slowly between mine for a minute before she asks in an almost scared voice. "You can really see me?"

"Um." My brows drop as I pull a face, looking around the bathroom before answering with what sounds like a guess even to me. "Yeah?"

"Then yes." A smile finally lifts her strong, full lips that contrast all the other soft features making her up. "I'll take your advice..." she trails off questioningly.

"Eleanor"—my lips twitch with the next part—"Monroe."

She holds out a hand to me. "Beatrix."

I take her hand, intending to shake it, but that same... something pulls tight between us and her eyes widen on mine as if she can sense it too. Leaving neither of us moving an inch and I swear the air starts to pulse around us, making every hair on my body stand on end. Her lips part again and I suck in a breath, to do what I'm not sure but the energy filling me is about ready to burst and—

"Beatrix?" a very male voice calls, bursting the bubble we're locked in and making both of us drop our hands. "We need to go now."

Her throat moves a couple more times before she swallows and calls. "Coming! Just give me a minute more!"

Neither of us moves as someone grumbles, obviously not happy, but the door closes a moment later and she lets loose a breath. "You were saying?"

I'm not sure what the fuck I was saying.

"The advice?" she reminds me with a small smile.

"Oh, yeah." I shake my head, trying to press through whatever the hell just happened and yet still feeling it like a charge on my skin. "Just..." I shrug, finally remembering the words I was going to give her. "No matter how bad things seem, you can always find your way back from it, you just have to dig deep enough to find what's always been there."

She pauses for a long moment and by the end of it her eyes are shining with unshed tears.

"Are you okay with that guy out there?" I tack on casually, wanting to check without raising alarms because you never know what kind of situation a girl is actually in.

"Yeah." She nods seriously before stepping away from the sink and giving me another smile that's a little stronger than the ones that came before. "Thank you, Eleanor. I'm happy we met."

"Me too." I shoot her a wink while backing up toward the stall because I *really* need to pee now. "And do me a favor, don't let whoever that growly bastard is order you around, okay?"

"I'll do that." She laughs again, striking me silly for a second before I shake my head and she nods goodbye as I close the bathroom stall, both of us ending what was probably one of the strangest bathroom encounters of our lives.

At least you didn't pee in front of her, El. Now that would have been strange.

True. I should probably figure that out soon.

Chapter Forty

I step out of the Uber we'd taken from the airport in front of Gram's house just as the sun is starting to set and am brought to a halt as the memories flood. Gripping me with the same tightness that's working its way up my throat as I stare at the porch that's empty of the person who will forever live in his piece of my heart. I had expected coming back here would be hard, knew it would be, but this… this reminder of how he's absent in a way I'd never expected him to be is brutal. Not out there living his life but locked inside his body in a hospital bed a few miles away from here.

It guts me, plain and simple. Staring at that front porch where he'd been waiting for me time and again. It'd be too much to bear if I didn't already know that this pain is a part of life that I want. The reminder of how much I love him. Never fading, simply grown around.

And me… fuck, but it feels like I've lived a whole other life in the time that I've been away from here. Come so far that the girl who first stepped out of her car here wouldn't even believe who I'm standing here as today. It has me blowing out a slow breath and taking that first step on the final part of this journey with a bittersweet ache in my heart. Lips lifting a bit as I come alongside Franny, where she sits side by side with Tiff's small sedan, giving her an affectionate pat. "Missed you, girl."

"So, uh," Mac starts, voice a little off and making me look back at him as the Uber pulls away. "This is it, huh?"

437

"Don't be a snob." I laugh. "I told you it was small-town America at its finest."

"No, no," he rushes out, walking to catch up with me on the way to the front porch. "It's nice."

I shoot him a disbelieving look and he shrugs. "Normal, I guess."

"I'm sure you're so sad now that you can't stay long," I joke, rolling my eyes.

We decided on the plane that he would take Tiff to LA, much to his continued horror. But she needs to leave and I get that with a painful familiarity. So does Mac, even if he's still bitching about me making them live with an actual girl. Imagine that.

And I... I need to stay.

To figure out for sure why that boat exploded. To say goodbye one way or another. To finish this part of the story and tuck the journal away.

I'm reaching for the handle to the front door when it's flung open, revealing a breathless Tiff standing there. Face red and splotchy like she's been crying most of the day, but that's not what has my mouth falling open. It's the way those pinup-girl curves have fallen away to reveal a gauntness to her face that makes it look like she's had the life sucked out of her. That hyper energy gone from her right along with it, leaving nothing but a blankness that rivals even Alec's. The split lip and the fresh bruise on her cheek standing out even more because of the obvious pain in her eyes. Auburn waves framing it all like a picture and falling loosely past her shoulders.

I should never have left her. She was supposed to be safe here. Cared for by the doting boyfriend and the mother who, while I hate… is still the fucking sheriff. But still… I should never have left here. She's Coop's sister, Jace's cousin. At the very least, I should have sent someone to check on her.

"How the hell did this happen?" I breathe out, thoughts escaping through my lips.

Her face pulls in with a shrug. "I don't know."

I drop my duffel onto the porch quickly and step forward with outstretched arms. "Come here." Wrapping them around her tightly as she collapses into me with a sob. "Shhh." I bring a hand to the back of her head, rubbing it across her hair, making those same soothing noises for a long moment that she'd once made for me. "It's all going to be okay now. I promise, alright?"

"Okay." She wobbles through another cry before stepping back and sucking them down while wiping at her eyes. "How much time do we have?"

"Not long." My face pulls in with worry and I try to convince her. "You should stay, Tiff. At least to see him and say hi. He's not going to lose it and like go kill him or something."

"Seriously?" She scoffs in a very un-Tiff-like way but then again… I guess she's grown too, just in a different way.

"Okay." I'll give her that. "He might want to, but I'll stop him and he's missed you," I tell her honestly, knowing it's the truth as I reach out to

439

grab her hand with my best pleading smile. "Please." Making sure to drag out the word.

Her expression drops along with those blue eyes that used to be so bright and she whispers, "I don't want to be here, El. I can't."

"Okay." I suck in a deep breath and exhale the word again. "Okay. Well then, let's go in and catch up before you leave, yeah?"

"Yeah." She nods, looking back up with a little bit of guilt. "You'll tell him I'm sorry, right? That y'all won't be able to get rid of me when you get to LA?"

"Of course."

Her eyes move past me then, brow tensing instantly and reminding me of her brother as I look over my shoulder and realize she must have spotted Mac where he's hanging back on the bottom step of the porch.

"Oh," I start as he starts to climb the stairs. "That's—"

"Macallan Astor." He flashes that troublemaker smile, hooking one thumb underneath the strap of his bag on his shoulder. "Chauffeur extraordinaire."

I look back at Tiff to see the look on her face hasn't changed, not even when he holds out a hand a second later and her eyes just drop to look at it before she asks quietly. "Aren't you the one who downloaded that thing onto her phone?" Her eyes come back to his with a little bit of anger in them. "The one that kept him from calling her?"

Oh well, there is that.

"Uh." Mac's hand falls from the air and I dart my eyes to him, watching that smile fall with a rare falter of his confidence. "Yeah, but that was, well." He shoots me a look like he's wanting to be saved but no freaking way. I'm having too much fun with this. "I thought I was protecting her."

She just looks at him then for a long minute before nodding slowly. "I understand." But the tone she uses makes her disapproval of him clear and has me fighting a damn cackle. "Want some wine?" She turns to me with the question. "I could use a drink before the plane."

"Oh." I pause, taking a quick step forward and looping my arm through hers. "Not tonight. Flight gave me a headache." Cringing openly and jerking a nod over my shoulder. "Gotta make sure this one stays sober enough to drive you both to the airport too." I peek back in time to see the aghast look on his face at my words before whispering loudly. "He really does have such bad habits. Maybe you can help him with that."

And then she shocks me even more by saying, "No, thank you."

Using all that Southern decorum for an absolute dismissal of him.

***

I feel the bed dip next to me in the middle of the night, rousing me just enough to crack my eyes and make sure it's who I suspect. The dim light in the room allowing me to make out the arm planted next to my head with our words winding up it. His breath at my ear the next second dragging

441

me back to alertness and making me arch my ass in search of where he's holding himself above me as he rumbles out. "You are in so much fucking trouble, Princess."

"So?" I mumble sleepily, finding what I'm looking for the next second as my ass hits his cock. Grinding against it with a happy sigh and stretching my hands up above my head.

"So? Huh?" He laughs dangerously, trailing his lips down to my neck and biting down hard on his favorite spot. Hands gripping my hips the next instant and holding them still as he snaps out in a low voice. "No cock for you."

"Wh-what?" I stutter, fully freaking awake now thanks to that asinine declaration. "The fuck?" And I know that I'm not really making sense but whatever, it still pretty much sums up my opinion.

"That was a long, long flight," he starts, voice going deep and fingers moving to the top of my underwear, starting to work them off while continuing. "It gave me plenty of time to think up all kinds of ways to make you pay for giving me a fucking heart attack." His hand comes down on my ass with a light smack before he grabs the cheek roughly, making me moan and try to widen my legs against the underwear still halfway down my legs as he finishes. "But I finally decided a simple apology would do just fine."

"An apology?" I scoff, trying to lift my hips further but his hold on me tightens. Not allowing me to move an inch and making that innate defiance spark, stomach flipping at the prospect of this game. "Oh baby," I breathe out, hiding my smile in the covers as his fingers tighten on my ass to the point of pain before looking back over my shoulder and meeting his night-forest eyes. "Do your worst."

His gaze darkens a shade and all that demanding dominance of his pushes against my skin as he reaches down to pull my panties the rest of the way down my legs roughly.

"Stubborn," he taunts darkly, arching a brow.

And my lips twitch up into a smirk as I toss back. "Ass."

The low laughter that falls from his lips next is practically the only warning I get before he drops down onto the bed and switches his hold on me to one where he's reaching up from below. Still keeping me completely immobile as he scoots up until his mouth is directly underneath my pussy, making my spine tighten with anticipation as I push up off the bed and look down at him.

"Not really seeing how I'm losing here."

"Oh, you will." He lifts his head and licks me from my entrance all the way up to my clit before smirking up at me savagely as I gasp. "Because you can ride my face all night long, Princess, but I'm not giving you my cock until you're sobbing for it."

My mouth pops open and I barely keep the "*Oh*" from escaping, lodging it in my throat instead before he pulls my hips down and it turns into a moan. His mouth lands directly on my clit and he sucks it into his mouth deeply, not even giving me a second to catch my breath before he starts to roll his tongue over it. Pressing down harder with each pass and sending my hips bucking, or they would be if not for the iron grip he's keeping on them. Those damn fingers digging into my hips with answering reprimand the more I try and driving me crazy already.

I drop my hands down onto the bed in front of me, collapsing as he chuckles before pressing lips against my intimate skin again. The new angle just allows him better access to rake his teeth over my clit and rip a crying kind of breath out of me. His hands move around to cup my ass and he pushes me up until his tongue finds my entrance, spearing up into me to lick at my inner walls and making them quiver. Trying to tighten around something that, while amazing, is not exactly what it needs to fill it.

He slows down the pace then, turning lazy with it as he licks at me over and over again to the point where I'm about to scream with frustration. My entire body one right push away from falling blissfully into the kind of ecstasy I need to break me right now. Needy little sounds escaping from my mouth with every touch of his mouth against me as he slowly nudges his way back up to my clit. Moving his hands back to my hips and holding me up as he rakes his teeth over it with a barely there pass that has my whole body jolting. So freaking close before he lowers his head back down to soothe the edge I'm trying to jump off with a slow, open-mouthed lick.

I try to reach for his head, needing him to finish it but he lifts a hand to give my ass a hard smack. Making my back bow as blood rushes to the area, pussy spasming with need so severe that it finally sends that scream of frustration from my lips.

Arrogant fucking bastard.

I lift up to look down at him again, chest heaving as I blink a few times before finding night-forest eyes as he kisses his way over to my thigh. "Apologize for making my heart stop today."

"No," I snap through another gasp.

His shoulders shrug between my thighs. "Have it your way."

And then he does the whole thing again, and again, and again. Ramping me up with hard, fast touches before backing off right before I reach that euphoric peak and bringing me back down. Leaving me fucking twitching and shaking like some kind of feen by the time he does it again and makes an actual sob escape from somewhere in my chest this time. My eyes screw shut, trying to block out the way everything is too much, my skin too tight, knowing I can't take a single touch more except for the one that's going to send me over the edge. Wanting him to fill up the place that's pushing me to give him what he wants with increasingly desperate demand.

He flips me over the next instant and my eyes snap open as my head hits the pillow, watching as he strips off his shirt before dropping back down. Crashing his lips down onto mine and letting me taste every bit of myself on his tongue as we still fight for dominance, even in the kiss. My legs finally free to wrap around him and dig my heels into his ass, dragging him down to press against where I need him most of all now. Grinding against him as another little sob escapes me into our kiss and he lifts his lips enough to breathe against mine.

"Come on, Princess," he encourages, pressing all that hardness into me and taunting me with his cock. "Say the words."

I open my eyes to find his, seeing how hard the need is riding him too in the way his pupils are practically blown before gasping out on a choked breath. "I fucking hate you."

A low sound leaves him that sounds suspiciously like a laugh and he drops his forehead to mine. "I fucking love you."

"No more than I do." I reach up to hold the back of his head, not giving him an apology... but somewhat of an explanation instead. "Someone needed my help and it couldn't wait, Coop. Trust me on that." Lifting up to brush my lips against his. "I'll tell you the rest after." I roll my hips against him again and his hands go to them with a groan. "And wasn't it a little fun today?"

His lips twitch. "Maybe."

"You loved it." A wide smile breaks free on my face and I drop my hands to the waistband of his pants, quickly shoving them down. "Now would you please make me come"—finally freeing his cock and feeling it brush against my pussy, quickly making me gasp out the rest—"pretty please because I'm about to die of—"

He thrusts hard, powering into me with a move that has my pussy locking down around him instantly after all of that torturous buildup. A scream leaving my lips that he swallows by bringing his back down onto mine and kissing me deeply as I finally start to come apart under him. Not needing much to push me over that edge. His hard cock prolonging it with powerful strokes that have me an incoherent mess as he brings his arms up and grabs my left hand from behind his head. Caging it between us and pressing a kiss to the Toi et Moi resting there, whispering over my cries while grinding against my clit. "You and me, Princess, not only always but endlessly."

I dig my heels harder into his ass then as the orgasm crashes through me, making me want to hold him there so that he can feel every bit of it. Until our cells remember exactly how to do this forever and we're nothing but dust on the wind that the heavens collect together into their grip. Infinitely together. I want this dance of ours to echo even then. Whatever we're made up of in this moment forming new constellations for people to marvel over for thousands of years to come. I want them to look up and see all the love we hold for each other, just like he said... endlessly loving and yielding and fighting and crashing back together over and over again. Everything that he does to me and gave for me and everything we became together living on through this miraculous story of us. Falling through time together, forever.

And when he follows me a few seconds later with a groan, I lift my lips back to his with my own whisper. "Never stop chasing me, Cooper Monroe. Right on through eternity."

Chapter Forty-One

"How are they?"

Coop takes a bite of the eggs I made after a trip to the store this morning that had come on the heels of me talking him off the ledge all night and chews for a long moment before swallowing. "They're uh…" He swallows again. "Good."

I narrow my eyes at him. "Shut the fuck up."

"How the hell are they watery and burned?" He chuckles, setting down the plate and snagging my arm when I turn to march away. Pulling me against his body and trapping me there as he smirks down at me. "It's a good thing we got muffins too." His brows drop, eyes raking my face with a question in them. "You need to eat."

I shrug. "I'm fine." Just nervous about everything this day holds.

He raises a hand to my face, thumb caressing my cheek as he asks quietly. "You want some time with him first?"

My face pinches up at the question and I blow out a breath. "I don't want to keep you—"

"You're not," he interrupts, shaking his head with that thumb on my cheek again. "I'll go look at what's left of the boat and poke around town a bit. See what I can find out about the explosion. I need to call Tiff and check on her too." His lips ghost up with a sad smile. "It'll give you two some time before I come up there."

I jerk a nod. "Okay." My voice hesitant because of the pit growing in my stomach, but knowing that it's not going to get any better.

"You are the person he would want there more than anyone else, Eleanor."

"I know," I choke out. "But I left him—" My throat tightens up and I suck in a breath, trying to push through it. "I left him."

There's nothing more to it. Nothing more to say. It's all just those three heartbreaking words I can never change. I left him.

I broke myself in two to keep the part I chose beating.

"You love him too," he reminds me softly. "Go see him. Tell him everything just like you did with me." Wrapping his arms around me fully, he pulls me in and tucks my head under his chin. "Because you've always been his too."

***

I'd done okay on the way here. I really had.

Drowning in my oldest and favorite Guns N' Roses concert tee I'd found in the back of Gram's closet and tucked into a comfy pair of leggings. Converse-clad feet not faltering once. Not while I'd driven Franny here with the windows down, breathing in the ocean air I'd missed so much. The one that smelled like him and made me smile to myself from all the memories it brought to mind. Not when I'd asked the receptionist what room he was in, telling her that I was family when she'd asked. Not when I'd navigated the winding hallways to the back of the hospital where he was with the long-term care patients.

But the sight of that dirty-blond hair lying against the pillow through the open door of the room right around the next corner. Room 323. The room they told me was his. It stops me in my tracks, freezing me completely and leaving me unable to take one more step.

Eyes stuck on that long, messy hair on the pillow I'd recognize anywhere and the little bit of the well-defined jaw visible from where I stand. Remembering the first time he'd stepped through the door at the bar and how struck I'd been by those firework eyes that I might never see again. My face crumbling and eyes instantly filling with tears at the little glimpse of the tube disappearing into his mouth, chest starting to rise and fall rapidly with staggering breaths. Heart folding in on itself from the pressure increasing on my chest by the second. That pit in my stomach turning inside out until I'm sick from guilt that seems boundless in this moment. The one I'll never escape by the continued choice to remember everything he is to me.

I stand there for so long that my feet start to tingle, like maybe if I wait long enough, he'll move. Roll over and ask where the hell I've been. Tell me that I better never bitch about his cousin brooding because I could have laughed forever with him.

I stand there, wanting to go to him but so fucking scared to take another step because I know it's one I'll never be able to take back. It will alter everything, just like the choice I made before. It will change what in some small way has only been a bad dream before this moment into the painful reality of the nightmare waiting to welcome me into that room.

It makes me want to call Coop and tell him I've changed my mind. Not wanting to face this alone. But I can't… I can't do it because he deserves for me to give the best of myself to him just like he gave to the lost girl who showed up broken in a bar. Forever changing both of our lives.

"Can I help you?"

I'm so lost in my head that I jump at the voice, completely unaware of the doctor who stops beside me with a curious look. Blinking at her for a minute as I try to remember how to talk again. "Um, no." The words come out as a mutter as I blink a few more times to try and get rid of the tears. "I'm just here to…" I trail off, nodding toward Jace's room.

"Oh, Jace." She smiles kindly with a look toward his room. "Yeah, he's Mr. Popular around here. Lots of visitors." Her eyes come back to me with a curious look. "Did you know him well?"

I look back toward his room, eyes finding that little bit of him and rasping quietly. "Yeah." My mind a mess as the reality of it all falls closer, dropping from the sky at her casual words. Mr. Popular… lots of visitors…. Fuck.

What have I done?

Move your mouth, El. You already look like a mess, no need to act like one too.

"Can you—" I try to start, unable to get the question out while looking at him and dragging my gaze back to her before starting again. "Can you tell me how he's doing?"

Her face turns apologetic. "We can't give that information out to anyone besides—"

"I'm family," I interrupt, voice breaking—and heart along with it because of the meaning—as I repeat it for the second time today. "Please. Tell me."

She pauses, as if not sure whether to believe it or not, before stepping in closer with a shrug and speaking gently. "Overall, his condition isn't terrible. He has a physical therapist that comes in and works with him to make sure his muscles don't atrophy completely. He receives his meals through a feeding tube and fluids through the IV to keep him hydrated. Bedsores are a reality for anyone in long-term care but…"

My gaze strays back to where his head is lying against the pillow then and my mind checks out in a last-ditch attempt to escape the horror falling kindly from the doctor's lips. Overcome by the pressure on my chest, sucking in shallow breaths as every part of me mourns in apology to him for letting him lie here and continue suffering like this when it was never his wish. Never my wish for him, I just…

Couldn't let him go.

Couldn't stop loving him.

Didn't know how or when to stop fighting for him.

The silence hits me then and I look quickly back to the doctor, finding the sympathy on her face clear as she stares at me.

"Wh-why?" My mouth moves around the word a couple times. "Why won't he wake up?"

I'd heard it before. I'd heard it dozens of times at this point.

But in this moment, I need to hear it again, right here with him.

"He took a traumatic hit to the back of the head," she sighs. "To the area called the thalamus in particular." I watch her raise her hand, my eyes tracking it with the sense that everything's moving in slow motion as she points to the area on her own head. "When he came in, the hope was that we could stop the bleeding and give his brain time to heal. So when the swelling went down and the bleeding stopped a few days later we found that he still had some brain activity. So we weaned him off the anesthesia in hopes that he would start breathing on his own again and wake up but he…" I press my lips together, trying to keep it together and not have a full-on breakdown right here in the hallway but obviously I don't do a good enough job because she reaches out a hand to rub my arm in a way that reminds me of Yvie. "You're the girl, aren't you?" She smiles sadly.

"Excuse me?" I choke out. What girl?

She nods toward his room. "The one who brought in all the other doctors to see him. The one who pays for his care."

It takes me a minute and a few more hard blinks to get out. "Yeah." My voice cracks again on the confirmation. "I'm the girl."

"Sometimes." Her voice softens, words seeming to come carefully. "No matter what we do, they just…" she trails off with another sigh. "Can't find their way back."

I breathe out jaggedly. "Or they don't want to."

"Maybe." She tilts her head at me with a curious look. "But I think it's much more complicated than all that."

"Thank you." Nodding at her suddenly, I wave a hand toward the room and suck in a deep breath. "I think I'm going to, uh…" The words die in my throat for a moment as I gather up all that love I have for him in order to face it. "Go in now."

She pats my shoulder consolingly. "Take all the time you need."

I force my feet to move again as she moves away, face falling a little more with each slow step that brings me closer to his room. Making it to the doorway as the tears that I've managed to hold at bay break free at how close I finally am to him again and yet wondering if he would really want me here at all. I'm not sure now because despite what Coop said, despite how much I will always love him…

There is no getting away from the fact that I broke him too.

I gasp for a breath as he finally comes fully into sight, quickly ducking inside to lean against the wall and stare at him. Taking in all the stark changes that I've missed these past months. The way his skin is a few shades lighter, no longer holding that suntanned color that came from endless hours surfing under the bright Alabama sun. How his hair lies a little more limp than ever before with no more days on the boat to give it that messy, windblown look that used to drive me and every girl around crazy. That muscular swimmer's body now a little more slight, not quite as wide in the shoulders and the lines of his arms less defined.

In that last moment, he'd told me he wasn't sure it was actually okay and seeing him now... I know it's not. None of this is okay because this isn't supposed to be his story. He isn't supposed to be here. He isn't supposed to waste away like this. He isn't supposed to be the one to pay. To suffer like this.

Fuck. What have I done?

What the fuck have I done to him?

It sends me sliding down the wall, hitting the floor with the words I can never say enough. "I'm sorry." They rip out of me in a sob so deep that I know it comes straight from my soul. "I'm sorry," I continue, gulping to try and get them out. "I'm sorry, I'm s-sorry, I'm s-so-sorry."

I raise my hands the next instant, covering my mouth to silence the cries and bringing my knees up to my chest to hold it all together. Knowing that if I keep carrying on like this, I'll attract the attention of someone passing by and that's the last thing I want. Suddenly incredibly grateful that I'm alone and didn't call Coop.

Because this damnation of me is a private one.

Just between me and Jace as I stare at him, jaw switching between quivering and locking with each breath against my shaking hands. Tears falling in a torrent down my face and a pounding pulsing through my head with each explosive beat of my heart. Staring at him and recognizing that peace that still sits somewhere in my chest even with how I'm falling apart. The peace I learned from him first and then found again in myself somehow. Filling me with life and light even as it fades from him.

It's not right and it's not fair.

That I should grow as he withers a little more with each sunrise.

And I know then what I have to do. How I can repay everything he's given me, because regardless of anything between us… No matter whether he hates me as much as loves me in the end. *This* can't be his end.

I have to let him go.

I have to let him go because lying here in this bed as the world passes him by… is a betrayal of everything he is.

My heart struggles with every beat that's bringing further sureness, not wanting to accept what I'm forcing it to endure. A world without him. A world where I won't let go of the love and the guilt even during this. But this… it has to stop. Even if it means that his story continues without us ever existing together again. And I hope by some miracle there's so much more out there, after this, waiting for him.

A world of his own filled with endless sunrises and music that might meet mine of eternal stars and poetry for a few precious seconds one day again.

A moment in time when all of our twisted stories come together once more.

So I push up off the floor and walk slowly to the other side of the bed on aching legs. Struggling heart becoming a ravaged thing barely capable of another beat as I finally see his face and my own collapses at the sight. Because even now, he makes me smile smally through the tears. Some part of him still reaching out to soothe the desolation of my soul in this moment and nurture the peace he's taught me.

And seeing him now… I don't even hesitate. I can't.

Maybe it's selfish and if it is, I'll gladly take all that damnation down into my soul to rest with all the guilt that's already there. But I don't falter once, choking out the same words I've spoken to him with every sunrise for so long as I've tried to anchor him here. "Hey, Dawson." Reaching for his hand and pulling it gently to the side before lying down right in the crook of his arm, just like I have so many times before. Resting my head on his chest and breathing in the sea-spring scent somehow still clinging to him while whispering the rest. "I've missed you."

And I tell him everything too. All the life I've lived since he's been asleep, even the thing I suspect but haven't told Coop yet. I ask him to forgive me for living the life that might've been his at another place in time. I ask him to forgive me for fighting for him when he didn't want to be fought for anymore.

I tell him I love him… Will always love him and then I fall asleep in his arms for what some part of me knows is the last time.

***

My eyelids flutter open to see the sunlight streaming through the window, completely bathing the bed in light as if it misses him just as much as I do. I look up to see that his face is still unchanged, those rose-colored lips contrasting against the tube coming out of his mouth and expression empty of the mischief it always held even in sleep. It makes me squeeze his fingers that are wrapped up in mine with apology again, even as I realize someone else is holding my other hand. Turning my head, I find Coop in a chair next to the bed, brows dropped low with worry and grief etching deep lines into his face.

Still though, he tries to ghost those lips up for me. "Hey, Princess."

My lower lip trembles for a second before I'm able to answer with one of the only things left in my head. "We have to let him go."

It's a long moment before he nods, fingers that are full of all the life missing from my other hand tightening around mine. "I know." He sighs. "I've known."

And then comes the next. "I think I'm pregnant," I whisper on a choked breath, giving voice to the other thing as fresh tears start to fall from my eyes again.

His face screws up and he scoots his chair close to the bed, wrapping an arm around my legs and laying his head on my stomach. Night-forest eyes locking with mine and filling with his own tears. "I know." He echoes, voice rough with feeling as his body trembles against me.

Because he knew before I did. Just like always.

And so I squeeze his hand tighter and press my face back against Jace's chest, crying with him for everything we'd lost and gained in the end.

Chapter Forty-Two

Vanilla, chocolate, strawberry, cookie dough, mint chocolate chip, rocky road, rainbow sorbet…

Where is the freaking dulce de leche?

I want the dulce de leche and I want it now.

My eyes scan the ice cream selection again at the Local Mart before I sigh, finally accepting that there's no dulce de leche to be found. Maybe I could make some. Ice cream couldn't be that hard to make, right? Maybe I'd finally find my niche with it. And dulce de leche is just… what exactly?

"Fuck." I sigh out loud this time, reaching out to open the freezer and grabbing some chocolate and vanilla so I can at least mix them together.

Maybe it'll taste something like dulce de leche in the end.

I start to walk to the checkout before looking down at the pint-sized ice creams in my hands and deciding that just won't do. Quickly turning back around to switch them out for gallons because I'm definitely going to need them with everything the next few days would hold. Tomorrow is the day we're supposed to say goodbye to Jace. We discussed it with the doctors yesterday when we left and they agreed that it's time. After that, it'll just be the memorial to say goodbye.

We'd been working on the logistics of it all morning. The first order of business being a trip to see Jack and ask his permission even though Coop didn't strictly need it. And while it hadn't exactly been a smooth conversation, in the end he had come around, saying that he knew his boy wouldn't want to live like that either. Needless to say, I'd been a sobbing mess by the time we'd left and when we'd gotten back to the house to start working on the arrangements for it… I'd needed a breather.

So I'd come to the store to get ice cream before diving back into it all again. Coop had mentioned casually that I should pick up a pregnancy test on the way out the door just so we knew for sure. I had told him I didn't want the universe to know yet because it'd probably jinx it.

It'd be par for the course at this point, really.

I'm in the midst of switching out the pints for gallons when I hear a voice from the next aisle over that freezes me instantly. Stomach bottoming out and adrenaline rushing suddenly as his rasped words make their way over to me. That same chaotically cruel voice that threatened Jace and me in the bar before I'd fought back with the threat of equal violence for one of the first times in my life.

"You need to get your son under control, *sheriff*," he threatens. "He was poking all around town yesterday asking about the explosion."

My heart stops before my mind even catches up to the meaning behind what he's saying. Then the next voice chimes in, sparking that almost forgotten rage.

"Don't talk to me about this here," she snaps sternly, the undertone of disgust clear.

I set the ice cream containers down as quietly as possible before quickly digging my phone from my back pocket and pulling up a message to Coop.

Texting him with shaking fingers as Kyle continues, completely unaware that I'm listening in.

"We had a deal. You get me and my brother out of jail for that little misunderstanding at the bar and…" he trails off nastily. "I help you out with making that little present for Jace Dawson."

Morrison and your mom are at the store. Get here now.

Holy shit. They're talking about the explosion at the boat. They have to be.

"I held up my end."

I slide the phone back into my pocket, listening to her angry whisper of a reply as my pulse starts to pound in my ears. "Now get out of my face and talk to me about this at a more appropriate time."

"Funny thing." He laughs. "There never seems to be an appropriate time for you these days."

My phone starts to buzz in my back pocket then and I wince, mouthing a curse and reaching back to silence it immediately but I'm too late. The sudden quiet coming from the next aisle tells me everything that I need to know. They know someone's listening. I turn and start to walk back down toward the front of the store as quickly and quietly as possible, fighting against the demand in my heart that they pay because there's nothing I can do right now.

I don't have a weapon or the means. I'm outnumbered. I'll be lucky to make it out of here without being spotted.

And I have more than myself to think about now most likely.

I need to get out of here and to safety. Call in the cavalry.

Fuck. I need to—

I'm almost to the end of the aisle when Kyle Morrison appears and makes me halt in my tracks. His eyes land on me and a smile starts to spread slowly across his face, making the breath leave me in a panicked whoosh and sending me backpedaling hurriedly. Trying not to trip over my own feet as I keep him in my sights, noticing that he hasn't changed one bit. Scar on his face still standing out with the bad dye job framing it and all.

Guess there's no question that he recognizes me too.

"Well, well, well," he starts with that cruel delight clear in his voice. "Eleanor Delacroix as I live and breathe."

His eyes move over my shoulder and I chance a peek behind me, seeing Leah Reynolds peering down at us from the other end. Her eyes moving between us with a detached look for a couple seconds before a hate-filled expression twists her face.

"All yours," she states quietly. "She knows too much now."

No. She can't do this. I try to plead with her using my eyes, knowing if I say the things I'm thinking out loud, it will only give Kyle more fuel. *I'm your son's wife. I'm pregnant with—*

"I spared you once when you were a child, Eleanor." She tilts her head at me, eyes moving quickly over my body before coming back to mine. "You should have stayed gone."

What the fuck? Did she just—

And then she turns and walks away, quickly moving out of sight as my mind struggles to comprehend what she just said. Leaving me staring at her with an open mouth as my heart thunders louder and louder, every beat unleashing a wave that moves through my body. Drowning me in pain and grief and fury, not only unlocked from the small child living inside of me who'd stared at the starry night-light on her ceiling as the police officer carried her away but triggered by the loss of Jace too.

She doesn't get to walk away.

Fuck no. She doesn't get to just walk away after taking—

I go to take a step after her, but a rough arm comes around me, the distinct metal of a gun pressing against my back and making me freeze as Kyle whispers threateningly. "Not so fast. You and I have some catching up to do and Jacey boy ain't here to save you now."

Fuck.

Fuck, fuck, fuck.

I forgot about him, just like Alec warned me never to do. I let my emotions run wild and take control, blocking everything out and allowing him to sneak right on up to me. But I'm not the same girl he'd scared to death in the bar once. I've survived greater monsters than him by now, and more importantly, I've learned to fight back.

The gun is my biggest problem. The risk that it will go off if I make a move is all too real. I have to do something though, because if he gets me out of this store… If I go with him now and don't make any kind of scene. It'll be over.

Alec's voice rings through my head as if he's right next to me, warning me that if anyone ever tries to take me, the worst thing I can do is allow myself to be moved to a secondary location. Better to be shot where I'm standing than disappear without a trace, he always said. Make it a bloody fight because at least then there's some kind of trail to follow. Some mark of where I've been.

I just have to pick my time now.

"Walk to the exit." He moves up to walk beside me, resting his arm across my shoulders and digging his fingers into my arm with enough force that I feel it right down to the bone. A quiet cry escapes my lips at the pressure and he slides the gun between us, pressing it harder into my side with the order. "And don't make a sound."

Coop is on his way, I remind myself, taking a breath with that first step and pushing back against the adrenaline urging me to do something right the fuck now. I just have to get away from Kyle and stop Leah before she gets away.

Nothing too big. Nothing I can't handle.

Right. And then the sheriff is just going to fall at your feet? Not thinking so, El.

That isn't my most pressing problem right now though, and maybe I'll make her. It's the least of what she deserves because apparently, I had been so very wrong in believing what she said at Adam's cabin. We all were.

Except for Jace, maybe. The toe of my Converse stumbles with the realization, making Kyle's fingers tighten to the point where my eyes are pricking even as my mind leaps to make the connection. The distinct possibility of what would make her go so far as to blow up his boat and me being there... yeah, that probably would have been the icing on the cake for her.

I have to get away from the bad dye job now.

We're getting too close to the exit, rounding the corner of the aisle where it leads straight to the cashiers and then to doors I can't let him take me through. My best chance of him being distracted is next to the cashiers and customers, but at the same time, I don't want to put them at risk. So it has to be before then and I have to be fast if I have any chance of catching Leah before she is gone.

And then Kurt Morrison strolls into the store, making all of my hopes disappear.

Fuck. How am I supposed to escape two of them and a gun stacked against me?

It pretty much drops my chances to nil.

Kyle keeps walking as I rack my brain, trying to figure a way out of this and Kurt scans the store before his eyes land on us, going wide with recognition as they settle on me. He starts to make a beeline to us, that stringy brown hair trailing behind him before we meet a little behind the cashiers but still too close for my liking.

"What's going on?" he demands quietly, eyes moving between his brother and me before dropping to the gun. "What the fuck are you doing with her?"

Kyle's body goes tense against mine and my brows drop in confusion. Not understanding the underlying hostility I can sense between them.

"Eleanor here was eavesdropping on me and the sheriff," Kyle drawls with equal quiet, but still, the cashiers and customers a few steps away are starting to look our way curiously. This isn't going to hold for much longer. "So I'm just taking her for a little walk to teach her to mind her manners."

Kurt pauses for a moment, looking his brother in the eye as his face turns hard. "No."

Well, this I did not expect.

"No," he repeats, shaking his head. "I never agreed to your deal. To do that to Jace, and now you want her too?" He shakes his head again, more adamantly this time. "No, he loved her and you already made him pay the price for Trey that I never agreed to."

I hear his voice then, pleading with Kurt in the bar, reminding him of how they were friends once and that Kurt wasn't like his brother. That he didn't really want to hurt a girl. I hear his melodic voice and then I hear another demanding that I move *now* if there's any chance of making this all right.

And I know it's time, even more, I know how to push this all right over the edge.

"I'm pregnant." Because even worse than hurting a girl is hurting a pregnant one and right now, I'm not above using it to my advantage.

Shocked silence follows my proclamation before Kyle's fingers loosen on me and he mutters, "What the fuck?" Giving me all the opening I need.

I drop like a weight to get the rest of the way out of his hold before turning away from the gun and using the momentum to pop back up and bring my elbow right up into his throat. Cutting off his airway momentarily before spinning again to grab the back of his head and jerking it down to meet the knee I'm already pulling up. His nose crashes against my bone, spurting blood everywhere as he drops to the floor with wheezing breaths, but all I can think is how freaking proud Alec would be of me right now.

Go. Run. Hurry.

The voice pushes at me again and I turn to see Kurt staring at me with a dumbfounded look before he jerks his head toward the door. Letting me know he's not going to stop me. And I don't need any further encouragement, dropping to grab the gun that fell from Kyle's hand before launching into a sprint. Hauling ass past the open-mouthed cashiers and customers and not stopping until I've made it through the sliding glass doors.

The harsh sunlight hits my eyes, making me blink rapidly while searching for the woman who destroyed my childhood and yet gave birth to the person I love most of all. Trying to remember that in order to fight against the darkness pulling at me, demanding I make her pay for her crimes.

I spy her cruiser backing out of a spot not too far away from the door and rush toward it without any kind of fear or self-preservation. The mix of adrenaline and rage pumping through me more potent than anything I've experienced in my life. Blocking everything rational out and making me tunnel only on her. Everything but the memories pouring through my head of Jace singing me to sleep and my mother's laughter over cookies and my father tossing me into the air.

So I don't hesitate once as I come up behind her cruiser and bring my hands slamming down on the trunk while shouting. "Get the fuck out!" The car pauses for a second before continuing, backing up right against my legs and making me take a few steps back.

Fine. We'd do it the hard way then.

I raise the gun in my hands, pointing it right at where she's sitting in the driver's seat and hoping Alec's brief lesson has stuck in my brain somewhere as I order again. "Get out of the fucking car!"

The cruiser comes to a stop and doesn't move again this time, idling for a tense beat before the lights flash red, signaling that she's put it in park. Her door cracks then, making me move the gun to keep her in my line of sight but when she steps out holding her own on me… it strips some of that rage clouding my mind, leaving me with the certainty that I'm at a distinct disadvantage here. Because she has nothing to lose by shooting me, the crazy girl holding the gun on the cop, whereas I don't want to kill the mother of the person I love. Even if she deserves it. Even if I want to on some level. I still don't want to carry that. I want her to pay, but I don't want this.

Her coppery hair flashes in the sun as she moves along the side of the cruiser toward me and suddenly I'm right back at the dock again. Remembering something so small among everything else that transpired that day, it simply sank away into the gray matter of my brain until now. It strikes so suddenly and hard that I'm left with only one question.

"Why?" I heave, eyes pricking from the sunlight and the sadness in my heart. "Why did you do all of this? How?"

Because if I'm going to die, I at least want to know that.

How did my parents really die? Why did she come after Jace?

Couldn't she have found a way to let go of it all like I had?

"How what, Eleanor?" she snaps coldly, gun in her hand rising and making me back up several steps. Trying to distance myself from it as much as possible while still being able to keep her here.

"How—" I swallow down the dryness in my throat, trying again. "How did you kill my parents?"

A beat passes before her eyes scan the parking lot, checking to make sure there's no one within earshot before coming back to mine with a simple word. "You."

My brows drop, head pulling back because I don't— "Me?"

"You were all the leverage I needed." Her lips lift the barest hint with a disdainful smile. "Just had to wait over you with a gun until your father checked on you before he went to sleep and then outline exactly what he was going to do to save you."

I blink, lips parting to ask something, but all I'm left with is, "I don't understand."

"Stupid girl." She continues with disgust, words rushing out next like little hits to my heart. "When I told Cane about the affair, all he had to say was that he and Nadia would figure it out. Even if she chose someone else in the end, and that just wouldn't do. So I went to your house that night and held a gun to your head. Told Cane if he didn't cooperate and kill Nadia that he'd never see his baby's eyes open again."

The world starts to tilt and sway around me, making it hard to speak. "But…"

"Then Nadia just had to keep screwing me over right up until the end by calling Adam when Cane started to lose it." Her words are nothing but bitterness as she spits them out into the air. "And I got to watch my boy *comfort* the daughter of the woman who'd stolen everything from me." She scoffs coldly. "Luckily, no one knew he was there until Adam came back out and took him. Never seeing where I was hiding in the closet."

"My-my father," I stutter.

"Loved you," she snaps hatefully. "Enough to kill your mother and then himself when he couldn't live with what he'd done to save you."

Oh god. How had I missed it? How had I assumed he had—I should have known, suspected something. He had never shown any signs of violent tendencies before. He had never—

"So you see, Eleanor. I didn't lie when I told you what happened that night at all."

Fucking monster. I knew it in that cabin and I should have pushed harder then.

The gun in my hand shakes as I press now instead. "How did Jace find out?"

"Adam's crash," she answers, voice quieting a bit as her eyes take on a faraway look. "He must have not bought it completely and started looking into Adam's crash. That was the one thing that night I hadn't planned."

"What hadn't you planned?" I demand, voice trembling as tears fill my eyes at everything she's done.

"I stood there"—her eyes clear, coming back to mine—"after I left your parents and drove back down the road. I came across the crash and I just"—a weary sigh leaves her and the gun in her hand drops an inch—"stood there for a while, wondering if he would ever let it go after seeing her die or if he'd come clean in the hopes of giving you some closure one day. Dragging our dirty laundry out for the whole town to see and ruining me." She shakes her head. "And then the next thing I knew, he was dead."

"How?!" I shout. "What gave it away?!"

"Because a mother loves her child more than anyone. Even me. It's biological." The gun in her hand rises high again and all of a sudden, it's like all I can do is stare the barrel down. "I took him from the car and dropped him at the hospital. Told them he fell down the stairs when Adam dropped him off after practice and wanted to make sure he was alright…

and then I went back to your parents." A hate-filled expression fills her face and she shakes her head again. "Jace got the police report about the crash that night from an old Navy buddy working as a police officer in Mobile. Figured out Coop wasn't in the car when someone found it. The stories didn't match."

She takes a step closer to me and all of the sudden... I'm terrified. The adrenaline fading rapidly at the absolute certainty in her eyes and the reminder that I'm very possibly almost a mother now too. I start to shuffle my feet back, not wanting to alarm her but wanting to put as much distance between us as possible. Because it wouldn't just be me dying here. It'd be her grandchild. Nadia's grandchild. The final chapter of a tragic tale that defies it with new life and hope, and I can't let her take it from us like she has everything else. And staring at her now... I know she wouldn't care, it would just antagonize her further.

"I knew it was only a matter of time before he told you both." I hear a car screeching into the parking lot and tighten my grip on the gun. Fuck, I don't want to shoot her. I don't want to kill anyone. I'd let it all go. I'd clung to the light and the peace— "Just like it would be with you."

BANG. BANG.

Two shots happen in rapid succession and my body jerks in surprise, eyes going wide as I stare into Leah Reynolds's that are suddenly missing that hate-filled life. The hole in her forehead perfectly centered and bleeding a thin line down for a split second before she drops to the ground. A kill shot. It was a kill shot. She's dead.

The final monster gone from my life. Only the one inside me remains, the one I can choose to release if need be and I'm strangely okay with that, because I'm in control of it. But my hand is still raised without a finger on the trigger. So if I didn't fire it, if I didn't unleash that monster today to protect those who matter most to me... who did?

I move my head from side to side, sweeping my eyes across the parking lot as my arm drops to my side with the weight of the gun that's so incredibly heavy now.

"Eleanor!"

The panicked shout comes from behind me, and I turn around, feet stumbling a bit as the entire world seems to slow down. My eyes find him immediately, that singular entity of ours pulling tight across the space, and I can almost see the way our souls seek out one another desperately. Winding through the air and reaching out between us. I exhale in relief, lips pulling up into a smile despite it all because he's here now and everything's going to be alright. We're going to be alright.

And then I cough.

My brows drop down in confusion because the air in my throat suddenly feels wet, but that makes no sense. Air couldn't be wet. Am I throwing up?

I cough again and try to raise a hand to my mouth at the wetness that seems to splatter across my lips, but I can't. It's too heavy and I don't understand. Why can't I move?

I look back to Coop for an answer as to what's happening to me because he always knows before I do. He knows everything before I do. Us. Our love. Our sins and secrets. The end of the person we both love. The new life we're going to bring into the world. The entire story of our eternity. I'm the one that's always playing catch-up. It takes me longer because I'm always so scared to lose it all. To believe in it.

But I'm not scared anymore. So why does he look terrified?

Horrified as he sprints to me and I drop to the ground.

Landing hard on the concrete and still not feeling it. Why don't I feel it?

The only thing I feel is… cold.

Oh shit.

"Fuck!" he shouts, hovering over me suddenly with a face that's nothing but pain and fear. Pressing his hands hard to somewhere above my left breast and making me wince because it fucking hurts when he presses on it. "Call 9-1-1!"

I see Alec then, face appearing above me with a phone pressed to his ear and devastation clear in every hard line of it but that doesn't make sense. He wasn't here.

He must see some of the confusion in my eyes because he drops down to his knees next to me. "Why the fuck didn't you shoot her, Helen?" he snaps, rattling off something into the phone that I don't catch before he seems to force his lips up. "Stopped by to finally admit I missed you and you just had to make me do the heavy lifting, huh?"

A laugh tries to work its way up my throat but it just comes out as a cough again and this time, I see the blood spurt into the air.

Fuck. This isn't good.

Come.

My brows drop at the sound of that voice again and for the first time I start to wonder who the hell has been in my head all these months because that… it isn't my mother anymore. It isn't me.

"Eleanor!" Coop's shout makes my eyes snap back open, and it's only then that I realize they closed at some point. That Alec is the one pressing on my chest now with a fear in his eyes that scares even me while Coop's hands are wrapped around my face. Something wet on his thumbs as they caress my cheeks. "Princess," he chokes out, eyes bleeding tears just like my body is life because that's what's happening. I understand now. "Don't you dare leave me," he orders through a clenched jaw that I know is holding in cries. "You hear? I won't allow it."

I try to nod. I really do. But I can't.

All I can do is keep my eyes on his.

"You listen to me, Eleanor." He sobs openly now. "I told you before that if you leave me, I will chase you even there. Wherever there is." I never thought it possible to love like this. Didn't think it existed. This love where two people could complete each other so perfectly. "But it's not our time yet." His voice is trying for an order, but I hear the rough plea in it. "We have so much life left still. So many journals to fill with stories of every kind." He drops his forehead to mine and I struggle to keep my eyes open, to keep them locked with his because he's forced me to believe it. Over and over again. "So I need you to hold on, okay, Princess?" And I want to tell him that he is the best first and last part of my life. "I need you to fight for that life of endless poetry and the house with the—" A gutted sound explodes out of him, cutting off his words. "All the good you're going to do." I breathe in some of his sandalwood scent then and am so grateful for it because if there's one thing I want to smell last, it's him. "You're my home, Eleanor," he whispers brokenly, tears dripping down onto my face. "Don't you dare leave me because my life didn't start until you walked into that bar and this isn't how it ends."

Someone touches his shoulder then and he shoves them away with a shout I can't make out anymore. I watch Alec get right up in his face then, pushing at his shoulders to force him away as some vaguely familiar faces appear above me. Where did I know them from? They put something on my heart, mouths moving rapidly as they shine something in my eyes and it hits me then, they're the same paramedics from the dock. The ones who'd taken care of Jace. I can see the moment it hits them too in the look they exchange before diving right back in and starting to assess me with frenzied moves.

All I care about is Coop though. I want to know where he went.

And like he can hear me, his face appears above mine again, upside down but there as his hands come up to cup my face. Those tear-soaked night-forest eyes rise to the paramedics long enough to tell them something that, while I can't hear, am able to make out perfectly.

"She's pregnant."

Alec appears behind him then, face going about five shades whiter and nearly matching his hair as he looks down at me with a sick look.

Come.

I don't want to though. I want to stay right here. I have to. He needs me and I need him.

So I blink slowly and look back into Coop's eyes, trying to anchor myself to him just like I'd held them both here for all those months. I try to fight against the heaviness pulling at my cells, forcing my eyelids to stay down a little longer each time they close. The strangest sense taking over a little more with every shallow, gurgling breath as the world starts to flash in and out, changing from the night-forest one I see in Coop's eyes to a place of real stars and shadows that are tinged in green light.

Eventually though, I know that I'm going to lose because his eyes start to come less and less often compared to that other place. So I dig deep, past the blood and the air rattling in my lungs, and try to make my lips move enough to give him one last word. *"Endlessly."*

And I'm still trying to figure out whether I got it out or not when my eyes close again with his scream echoing through the air, reaching me even here.

Wherever here is.

Fractured

Chapter Forty-Three

El

Hidden In Between

I open my eyes to a place that stuns me, gaze immediately going to the star-filled sky hanging overhead and the moon eclipsing the sun there.

All of it colored with hues of the green-eyed boys that made up my life.

The shadows and light playing and warring throughout the sky, giving and taking as one cedes ground to the other before overlapping again. Stars twinkling as if they're shooting fireworks even as the darkness swallows them up. I turn slowly in place, head tilted back and trying to take in the infinity of it all. Yet somehow knowing that no matter how long I stare, it'll never be enough to truly grasp what it is I'm seeing.

The eclipse snags my gaze again as I turn back toward it, dropping my eyes down to examine it more closely and gasping at what I find there. The entirety of the sky that's reflecting back in the gentle sway of the ocean and making it seem like I'm somehow hanging right between it all. Completely awestruck and left staring at the last sliver of the eclipse disappearing beyond the horizon. My eyes trace the way the sun is fighting behind the moon to cast streams of light across the water that make it all the way to where I stand. It's mesmerizing, all-consuming, and painfully heartbreaking.

Just like our love for each other.

Standing though. I'm standing… on what?

I look down and find planks of wood under my feet that I recognize, ones that make my heart jump violently and send my eyes running up to find the metal railing at the front of the boat. The one I know somehow will be there, just like the white paint and blue trim that make my mouth open with a cry because this boat… it doesn't exist anymore. I reach back for something to steady myself, knowing my legs are about to give out at what my mind can't comprehend.

So I grab hold of the first thing I find, not noticing that it's warm under my fingers until I hear his voice. "Ellie?"

I freeze instantly, not moving an inch as my heart thunders and my lower lip starts to tremble. Unable to make myself move because if I turn and he's not there…

"Come on, Blondie." That melodic laugh fills the air. "You're not really going to make a guy wait on you, are you?"

I spin around so fast that it's like the world around me blurs, taking a second to reorient itself when I stop and find myself looking up at him. Meeting those firework eyes that have another cry escaping and a smile breaking free on my face right before the breath whooshes out of me. Head pounding with a rushing sense because suddenly, I remember it all.

Looking up into his eyes, I remember every time I've fallen for them, the thousands of years we've played this story out over and over again. I remember the scattered moments of happiness between all three of us that I've treasured more than any of the others. Those precious ones that we stole before the inevitable end that always followed. Before the pain and the heartbreak that came for us every time in one form or another. The loss of them both and sometimes even myself that I've lived through more times than I can really even come to terms with still.

I remember it all.

I remember breaking us every time for the love I've never been able to turn away from that wasn't his.

The choice I've always made in the end.

It sends me rocking on my feet, face collapsing with tears falling from my eyes as I look up at the ones that I've loved through time. Even if it's never been enough. Never what he deserves. It just makes me love him more though, because he's never faltered once in bringing that light to my life, no matter the cost to himself.

I see it in his eyes too, the knowledge and truth of us and it turns my heart inside out in my chest because more than that, I find the love we've always shared. Shining out and telling me everything I need to know about how it's so much more powerful than any of the pain found among it all.

And it has me throwing my arms around his neck, sobbing on scattered breaths that hold the echoes of him in my head. "Hey, Dawson."

His arms come around my waist slowly, lifting me off the ground as he lowers his head to whisper back. "Hey, pretty girl." He presses a kiss to the top of my head, breathing me in and finally answering the words I've spoken to him with all those sunrises. "I missed you too."

I lose it then, deep gulping sobs leaving me in quick succession as my fingers grasp wildly for the back of his shirt. Terrified that he's about to disappear from under my fingertips. Body trembling and chest heaving as I squeeze my eyes shut tight and hold on to him for dear life. Never wanting to let him go.

"Hey, hey, shh," he soothes me, bringing a hand to the back of my head as he walks us forward and sets me down against the railing of the boat. "None of that here."

"Wh-where"—I try to choke out, opening my eyes and having to suck in a few deep breaths before I can finish—"is here?"

"I'm not sure," he sighs, arms squeezing me tighter. "But it's better than before."

I nod against his chest, trying to get control of myself, but every time I'm close, it hits me all over again. That he's really here in my arms, talking and holding me and whole. Skin tanned once more, hair shining under a green light that matches his eyes. Holding me right on through it for what could be seconds or thousands of days scattered through time. It's hard to tell here.

But I want to remember it all, every pass of his fingers trailing up and down my spine. The way our arms are locked around each other, anchoring us against the memories filling this place even as our hearts break from them. Pressed close together and re-forming with every breath of remembered happiness too.

And eventually, my sobs quiet, turning into soft cries which ease finally to slow, stuttering breaths. Just like they always do, because no matter how deep the pain in life… there's always an end to be found, even if it's a bittersweet one.

There's a tug at the back of my hair then and I turn my head into his neck, smiling against the skin there and squeezing him impossibly tighter to let him know that I'm alright. I'm alright now because he's here. Here and dressed in the same clothes as the first time we met, full of all that life he'd held then.

He pulls back then, looking down at me as his fingers come around to play with the bottom of my hair in an absentminded move, eventually breaking the silence between us. "Ellie." His face turns pained, eyes lifting back to mine. "Why are you here?"

My brows drop and I give him a confused look. "What do you mean?" Does it matter? I'm here, and we're together now.

"Ellie." He swallows hard with an imploring look. "*Why are you here?*"

I pause, still not understanding. "I-I don't know."

"What happened?" He pulls his bottom lip through his teeth. "What happened before you woke up here?"

"I was…" I trail off, looking up into his eyes that are suddenly so sad and trying to rack my brain, willing to give him anything to take away that look. "I was at the store getting ice cream and then… I'm not sure."

"What happened next?" he prods gently.

What happened? I was going to switch out the ice cream and then…

My chest heaves suddenly as I finally remember what came next. "Oh god," I cry, swaying on my feet again and he reaches out to steady me. "She shot me, she fucking shot me. Oh my god. I can't, I can't—" The panicked words leave me in a rush before the rest of it dies out and I'm left with only one question that's twisting my face up with it. "Am I dead?"

"I don't know." His brows drop. "You feel different."

"What do you mean?" I shake my head, not understanding any of this.

"You feel more"—a beat passes like he's trying to find the right words—"urgent than anything else here."

"I can't—" My protest cuts off at the reality. At all of the reasons why this can't be. "I can't be dead, Jace."

I have to go back to Coop. I have to live so that our baby doesn't die. I can't die yet and leave him to survive an entire life without me.

So I give Jace a single nod as if that's that, and I'm in control of it all. "We have to go back. Both of us."

He looks down at the bottom of my hair with a small lift of his lips and gives it a tug. "Not sure it works like that."

"I don't care how it works," I scoff angrily, taking a step back and looking every which way in search of an exit. Not caring that we're in the middle of an ocean on a boat that shouldn't exist. "We're not staying here."

"Blondie…" he drawls as I take another step away and start turning in a circle before walking toward the back, determined to find a way out for us. "You know we're not the ones in control here. We never have been."

Right, because he was always supposed to be the one I chose, but my ass just couldn't ever seem to get it right because of the love I hold for someone else.

So what the fuck do they expect? That we'll just live in this eternal torment?

No. No fucking way. And if not for me, then for Jace because he's been the one who's lost the most through this all. I stop to meet his gaze for a moment and the pained acceptance I find there sparks every bit of defiance in me.

"No." I shake my head adamantly, looking to the sky. "Do you hear me?!" I shout, hands starting to tremble with the rage I'm unleashing. "You don't get to do this again! You don't get to treat us like we're fucking dolls!" He"—gasping for a breath to keep going, I point to Jace—"is not staying here!"

"Ellie." He takes a step toward me, voice nothing but care and gentleness. "I don't want to—"

"Don't!" I snap at him, eyes starting to leak tears again because I won't allow him to say it. So I look back to that heartbreakingly beautiful sky and continue to scream. "I will drag him out of here with me! I will become your worst nightmare to—"

"Quiet, child." The sudden voice has me whipping my head toward the front of the boat, words cutting off in shock at the woman who's appeared there. "They'll hear."

Jace swings back around, putting his back to me, and we both go still while taking her in. The black curls falling from her head, tumbling down all the way past her waist and the oversized crystal-blue eyes that are shining against her skin that looks like it's been dusted with pure gold. Staring right at me as if she's known me forever. Every feature on her face utter perfection, from the pert nose to the strong, full lips, knocking the breath right out of my lungs. The simpleness of the white dress she's wrapped in doing nothing but accentuating that she's this vulnerable kind of beauty, everything about her inviting you in. And her voice... the music of it, my heart cracks in my chest because I miss it already. Need her to speak again even more than I need to get back home right now.

"Who..." I pull a few deep breaths into my lungs and am still barely able to start again. "Who are you?"

"I've been known by many names." Her voice trails out soft, filling the air with music again and making me step around Jace even though he tries to stop me. Needing to be closer to her and knowing that I'm... I'm not quite sure. Tied to her somehow. "I'm the first," she continues, taking a step back toward me as those lips tip up the barest hint. "But you can call me Pandora."

My eyes go wide at the name because it's one that has lived on… well, almost forever. Just like I'm beginning to suspect this place has.

"Pandora?"

"One of my many names." She tilts her head at me, eyes running over my face. "Just like yours."

My mouth moves for a second before I force a question out that I can't help but already know the answer to. "Do I know you?"

"Yes." A full smile pulls her lips up with the word, making tears fall openly from my eyes as she slowly closes the distance between us and takes my hands in hers. "Yes, Eleanor. I was the first, and you were third." She sighs. "You have known me in every life because I've always been watching and waiting for you all to finally end up here."

"But—" I gasp because it's too much. Too much to process at once, so I go for the first thing that pops into my head. Just like that voice has been doing for months now, her voice. "The voice? You've been talking to me." Guiding me here. "You sounded like my mother though."

"Yes, I took the voice I knew would call to you at first." She nods, eyes moving over my shoulder briefly to Jace and going blank with a look I can't quite pin down before coming back to mine. "When he ended up in between, life hanging in the balance, it opened up a way for me to speak to you again because you three are inextricably linked, but the cost was…" A pause passes and the music of her voice threads with a darkness that eats at me. "Great."

"Why?" I shake my head at her in confusion, the word leaving me as a cry because I just want to understand. To understand my existence and why we've all been doomed to this never-ending tragedy. "Why do they keep doing this to us?"

"They didn't." She exhales a heavy breath, beautiful face pinching up to match mine. "If you want to blame someone for the pain you've endured, look no further because the fault is mine."

"Wh-what?" My brows drop at the sense of being rocked to my core because what she's saying doesn't match the certainty in my bones about her. "Why?"

"Because." Her eyes flick over my shoulder to Jace as he walks up to my side before coming back to mine. "The way he sees the world." Her hands squeeze mine, eyes blinking with tears. "The way he described it to you that night on the beach as everyone's actions and reactions building into a rippling water filled with life and endless possibility..." She sighs deeply, looking directly back at Jace while finishing. "That's the way it should be. Not this stagnant predetermination humans have."

Her gaze comes back to mine, words filling with urgency as they start to tumble rapidly from her lips. "The gods never intended for man to reach for something higher, to have free will. That was stolen for them at great cost to someone who saw everything they could be." Those delicate hands of hers grip mine with surprising strength, making me wince. "And so man was given the bright spark of a soul and the first woman was created as the gods' revenge."

"The box," I breathe.

Those crystal-blue eyes shoot up, running across the sky as if she can see something that I can't before coming back to mine. "We don't have much time." Her face falls with a mournful look. "I never wanted my fate, Eleanor. I didn't know it was even cast or what I was unleashing on the world. I just knew that I couldn't get that damn box out of my head and then one day…" A single tear falls from her eyes with a blink. "I opened it, dooming everyone I had come to love."

"I still don't understand." A gasping breath leaves me because her hands are almost rattling in mine and I know our time is running out. "Why do I matter in all this? What was in the box?" I'm a girl, a woman now, but nothing special. I'm not a god.

"Fate." The word explodes from her lips. "Fate was in the box, Eleanor. The loss of free will so that humankind would never transcend what had created them." Her face fills with disgust. "So that they would remain nothing more than playthings."

Fate. Our fates… the ones we kept defying. The exception to the doom of man.

"How?" I snap, gripping her hands with equal force at the suspicion filling me. "What did you do?"

She drops her gaze from mine. "I was so close, so close to destroying it."

"What?"

"The loom, the Moirai, everything I had unleashed." Her eyes come back up to meet mine. "And then I felt them coming and knew there wasn't time. They were going to catch me before I could finish it, so I did the same thing you have eventually done over and over again." A few more tears fall, running down her cheeks as she sucks in a breath before exhaling two words. "I chose."

"Me." I'm not sure how I know, but I do, as if her decision is right there pulling tight in my chest.

"Yes." She nods once, untangling one of her hands from mine and bringing it up to rest against the side of my face. Agony filling her face and making my heart stumble, then break. "I chose to sacrifice the soul of the child who had inherited all the painfully beautiful mortality the gods had given me so that I could hide the one that inherited all of the immortally divine gifts." A small cry of music escapes her. "I followed the voice in my head just as you followed mine and tangled their threads with yours, giving you the choice everyone else had been denied." She nods again then, seeming to gather herself as she blinks. "Knowing that your defiance of fate would keep them distracted from what I had hidden underneath."

"What?" I breathe, hardly believing the story she's telling me, if not that I feel it, having lived it countless times. "What, child—what thing did you hide?"

A small, sad smile pulls at her lips and she moves her hand to the bottom of my chin, tipping my head back. "Look up," she whispers. "And see the souls, the free souls, of an entire people that exist because of what you sacrificed for them."

And as I stare at the sky, I finally realize what it is that I'm seeing. I finally understand. The way each of the stars is exploding with fireworks that are being sucked in by those nearby. All of them pulsing together in perfect synchrony and tangled like the branches of trees against the night sky. Wild and free and full of life.

Deep stuttering breaths start to leave me because the magnitude of what she's saying and what I see before my eyes is… unfathomable.

"Each defiance of your fate allowed this sliver of a place between the gods and man to grow from that thread hidden underneath yours. Allowed its people to thrive in secret so that I wouldn't fail by standing alone again." That perfect voice turns rough in a way I couldn't even imagine possible. "And then I waited for what sometimes felt like an infinity, waited for you three to somehow end up here. Then, when enough time had passed and the situation became dire, I tried to guide you." She nods once. "Now the time has finally come for your mortal part to end."

"But…" I drag my eyes back down to her, shaking my head. "We're not all here. Coop isn't here."

"Blood is a magic all of its own." She tilts her head at me again, eyes dropping purposefully down. "Enough of him is."

My lips part as I stare at her, filled with relief because that means— "What is she talking about, Ellie?" And just like that, the relief is gone,

492

my face crumbling as Jace steps around to stand by her side, grabbing my arm with a fierce look. "What the fuck is she talking about?"

"I'm—" A sob leaves me, cutting off my words because I can't... I can't say it here in person to him.

"Jesus Christ," he mutters, eyes widening with horror before he turns to Pandora and demands. "Send her back. Send her back right now."

I shake my head at him adamantly. "I'm not leaving without you!"

"Yes, you are because I don't want to go!" His shout echoes back, reverberating around us and making me pull it back. "I don't want to go," he repeats, face falling to match mine. "I will always love you, Ellie. It doesn't matter whether she says it's by choice or fate. You were always meant to be mine." I press my lips together, but it does no use to keep the sob coming up my throat inside. "Knowing what I do here..." He shakes his head sadly, but there's a resolute look in his eyes. "I don't want to go back."

"You promised," I protest, grasping for anything to not lose him after I've finally found him again. "You promised me that you'd keep chasing that sunrise, same as me."

"And I will." He nods, pulling me into his arms as I grasp desperately for him again. Not wanting to accept what he's saying. "Just not where you are." That melodic voice roughens, rumbling out from his chest. "I'll find new sunrises to chase somewhere beyond all of this."

I sob into his chest before turning my head and looking at Pandora, barely able to cry the words out. "Wh-what comes after?"

"That." She pauses. "Not even the gods know. When a life comes to an end it goes somewhere beyond them."

"Let me go, Ellie," he whispers, arms tightening around me despite his words. "You have to let me go."

I pull back to look into his eyes and argue. "What if there's nothing?"

"There is." That playful grin lifts his lips, the same one I've fallen for time and again. "There has to be." He reaches up and tugs on my hair, calling me out. "You know that."

"I-I can't lose you." Every part of me hurts with the thought.

"Yes, you can." He raises a hand, eyes tracking the movement as he pushes the hair behind my ear while speaking. "I have watched you become so incredibly strong these months, Eleanor. I have watched you survive day after day. Survive things that would bring other people to their knees." And when his firework eyes come back to mine, they're filled with tears. "I have watched you become the sun and stars, creating an entire universe within yourself to weather it all. And the truth is," he sighs. "The truth is, you don't need me or even Coop now because you can stand all on your own." A sad smile pulls at his lips. "Not that you'd ever choose to stand without him."

I stare into his eyes then, shaking my head in refusal but knowing that there's something in his words that I can't deny. And maybe that's the truth of it. That after all these thousands of years together, something of all of us has soaked into one another.

"No." I breathe raggedly, trying once more. "No, please."

"You have to," he whispers, pressing a kiss to the top of my head. "Just like you need to go back to him."

A sob bursts from me, and I throw my arms back around his neck, squeezing as hard as I can.

"Would you tell him something for me?"

I nod against his shoulder, body shuddering with cries.

"Tell him... that I forgive him. Tell him that I heard him too." He pauses then as my sob turns into something like a mourning keen, clearing his throat. "Now go, Blondie, before it's too late."

"He's right," Pandora interjects, drawing my gaze as that musical voice fills the air with a hard note. "I can sense them searching for you now. They know something is wrong." She takes a step back closer to us with a look of encouragement. "And without you fracturing this fate, all is lost." Jace puts his hands on my shoulders, gently pushing me back as she continues. "You're the linchpin for everything."

I look back up to Jace and find his eyes, trying to memorize them desperately while asking her. "How will it happen?"

"You'll take my hand and open your eyes," she tells me softly. "Nothing more is required of you."

"And you?" Because I understand now why that connection exists between us.

Just like it had with that girl in the bathroom in Montreal.

"I..." she trails off with a sigh. "Will finally pay my own price to rectify what should have never been."

My eyes go to her instinctually, wanting to make sure of what she means. "Will you die?" I whisper, needing to know.

"No." She gives me a small smile. "At least not at first." Another step brings her right next to us and her face falls with a tortured look as she raises a hand to my face. "I chose to sacrifice you because you were the ordinary one, a great beauty but entirely mortal…" Her fingers trail down. "Never knowing how in awe of you I would stand one day after watching everything you endured at their hand. I was with you every time. Every time they captured your soul and cast it back out in a new form." Her eyes fill with tears as they stare into mine, letting me see all the wonder and love there. "I owe you everything, Eleanor. An entire people do for the part you have played in their stories. Never forget that." She raises a single finger to the side of my temple, pressing down hard while humming under her breath, and I know that somehow she's making sure I'll remember it all. "Now go. Go and be happy in this last life, knowing that you are forever beyond their reach now."

She holds her hands out then and I hesitate for a moment, not wanting to leave either of them. And then Jace places his hand in hers, making me look back at him. That playful grin spreads across his face and makes my lips twitch in spite of everything.

"Name the kid after me, yeah? Just to piss Coop off a bit." A tear-filled laugh escapes me and his face falls into a pained look again. "I'll always be there, Ellie. Right there in your heart where you can feel me just like I can you." A rough breath leaves him. "And know that wherever I am, I'm loving you."

"I know," I rasp back quietly, keeping my eyes on his and placing my hand in hers. "I love you too, Dawson." She starts to hum then, filling the air with music laced with power that hits my skin like lightning in a storm and leaves me fighting a sob to tell him. "Always have, always will," I choke out. "And I promise that I'll see you again."

Even if it's only for a few fleeting seconds when a world of endless sunrises and music meets one of eternal stars and poetry. A twist in time where we come together once more, chasing each other's tales with new stories of our own.

Laughing together again.

"Promise." He smiles.

The final version of this forever fractured story.

My eyes grow heavy then, closing as every memory of us flashes through my mind, from this life and all the ones past. Water drops on my skin at the beach as he tackles me into the sand. Meeting for that very first time in a village that fell through the cracks of time with a reluctant smile sparked by the charm he always had. Laughing on the boat as he chased me through the cabin, catching me right as I stepped onto the deck. Riding through fields of wildflowers with the cool mountain air hitting right before I met his most trusted friend. Loving through the birth of our children who'd gone on to rule kingdoms after we both fell.

Kissing with the ocean all around.

Healing somewhere in between it all.

Finally letting go of the fate that should have never been.

And I know that as I open my eyes, somewhere else in another room not too far down the hall, Jace Dawson's heart just gave out.

Because all he'd been waiting on was me and to finally say goodbye to everything we've shared.

And then I blink, seeing another part of almost the same sky, eyes that are a shade darker than the ones I just left looking down at me.

"Hey, Princess." His night-forest gaze fills with tears that are already falling from mine too. "Just so you know," he chokes out, bringing his hand up to rest on my cheek as the steady beep of machines sounds in the room. "We're officially pregnant and I'm never letting you out of my sight again."

The future I've chosen over and over again, echoing through that thumb on my cheek with all my memories of him. The love that brought on great wars and ended kingdoms. That baffled the gods and defied every power that tried to pull us apart time and time again. The love that tangled itself so deep in my soul that he became my heart and I became his, bringing us together over and over again. Right through all of the first times that he had me. Because we've chosen each other in spite of it all. Finding, chasing, loving, and fighting for it.

And this time, we get to be happy.

Finally, endlessly happy.

"I know," I rasp, ignoring the pain radiating from my body to ask the one question left. "Can we go to Cahuita now though?"

"Of course." The breath leaves him in a rush as he drops his forehead to mine and I feel it tense there. "There's just a little bit of cleaning up I'll have to do when we get there."

Chapter Forty-Four

Pandora

She had finally done it.
Her and the mortal girl who'd once been hers.

And for the first time in eternity,
Three threads snapped on the loom.
The ones she had tangled at the end,
Before they'd locked her away in this tomb.

The Moirai screamed and the mountain shook,
As the fracturing took place,
The eyes of all turning toward the hall of fates.

And the gods felt something that they had forgotten,
As they finally saw what she'd hidden underneath,
The one bright and fateless thing,
Right before it disappeared again from their gaze.

And all the while she hummed,
A song without words that most had forgotten,

Fractured

As the ground cracked under her feet.

Revealing a boat sitting on a glass sky,
And the man still standing within,
The place in between now held by him as the binding thing.

And Pandora smiled,
Because while the first part was done,
She knew this was only the beginning.

Epilogue

Seven Years Later

I watch Maddoc playing a game of tag with the waves, lips twitching as he shouts and makes a run from the one barreling down on him. The boy makes my heart stop in my chest most days, but damn if I'm not impressed with how fearless he is too. And right now... well, this is tame compared to most of the games he likes to play.

Especially in Cahuita, ironically.

He's a fish. Has always loved the water from the time he was born nine months to the day after we left Canada. Coop taught him to surf when he turned six on this trip and the next morning, we woke up to find him sitting on a surfboard out in the water. It made us both stop in our tracks for a moment, remembering with equal parts heartbreak and joy another boy who'd loved to surf just as much.

And then I'd sent his daddy out there to get him and drag him back inside our little home away from home. Watching him complain all the way about *why* he was grounded from surfing for the rest of the trip when he was *perfectly fine* on his own. That same daddy had arched an amused brow at me while walking by that I'd chosen to ignore because we'd had that conversation before. A few times.

I'm well aware that the little tyrant is all me on the inside. On the outside though, he's all Coop, with floppy dark-chocolate hair and olive skin, almost an exact replica of every feature. Except for his eyes, those huge gray orbs are mine too.

Coop likes to say that's how he knew that Maddoc was going to be hell on wheels. It's the devil in his eyes. I then like to remind him, not so subtly, which one of us is still called Satan.

Maddoc wades out a little farther than what we typically allow and I shake my head, fighting a smile while shouting, "Not one more step, Maddoc Monroe!"

"Ah, Mom!" he yells back. "Let me live a little!"

"That's exactly what I'm doing!"

I can see the annoyed shake of his head from where I'm sitting in the sand, but I let it go because I get it... I really do. The girl who jumped from waterfalls and roofs shares a kinship with him. Even if I only ever jump from them now when he isn't looking and Coop is waiting underneath to catch me. I even strip naked on the beach still, once in a blue moon, it took me a few years, but I got there eventually.

Maddoc moves back into more shallow water and my eyes drift to the sun for a moment, Jace coming to mind and making me smile just like always. And I know he's with me by how his place in my heart is still full of my memories of him... in the way I can sense him with every sunrise. Hoping he's found whatever more he went in search of out there, maybe even a new love and a whole story of his own too.

I'd been right when I woke up in the hospital that day. He'd died at the same moment that my eyes had opened, much to the doctor's consternation. Coop and I spread his ashes in the Alabama waves he loved almost more than anything, surrounded by family and friends. I'd told Coop everything too. Everything I remembered from that place in between it all. And while some of the memories have faded, I still remember the important stuff.

Even when a girl I'd met randomly in the bathroom had come knocking on my door later that same year asking about it.

I haven't seen her since, but I'm strangely okay with that too, because my part in all this… it's done. I'd given enough. We all have.

The only thing Coop said about it was that he didn't care as long as they kept their hands off of us now and through whatever eternity came after. That one lifetime of happiness with me was all he'd ever wanted. Anything more was extra, but he had every certainty that we'd be together forever, just like we were meant to. No matter what that after was. He'd tagged on later that night that I was his and he'd gladly fight a god any day of the week over that.

He'd also been oh so conveniently inside of me at the time and marking up that favorite place of his on my neck.

Possessive bastard.

"Hey, Princess," his voice calls out quietly, drawing my gaze to where he's walking up behind me with a tiny pink bundle held close to his bare chest. "I think someone wants Mama."

"Hmm." I narrow my eyes at him teasingly. "Are you trying to pass the Kraken off on me?"

"Maybe." His lips twitch. "She told me that Daddy's poetry was getting old."

I gasp dramatically. "Blasphemy."

"I know." He kneels down next to me. "But then she promised to never date, so we called it good."

"Fair, fair," I agree, holding out my hands. "Hand over my girl."

He passes her to me and we both look down to see her blinking up at us with those serious night-forest eyes, forehead tensing a little under a sprinkling of platinum hair.

"Hi, Stella-della," I coo, bringing my knees up and laying her on my thighs to rest. "Needed some girl time, huh? I get it." Making sure to whisper loudly as I continue. "Don't worry about that no-dating thing, by the way." I lean down and rub my nose against hers, breathing in the bliss of her baby smell. "You need your own stories to tell and what Daddy doesn't know can't hurt him."

"Not funny," Coop chokes, leaning in to look down at her as I pull back. "She's just so perfect. No one could ever possibly deserve her."

"Ah." I smile widely at her and see those tiny little lips ghost up just a bit before looking at him with a cocked brow. "I'm sure someone will come along who's worth falling for one day."

His brow tenses, perfectly matching hers for a moment before he grumbles. "Maybe."

Fractured

A soft laugh leaves me. "Don't worry. You'll survive it."

"Maybe," he repeats in a low voice, darkness in his eyes sparking as he leans in and brushes those full lips against mine. "With lots of distraction."

"Lucky for you." I kiss him back slowly before whispering, "I know a game or two."

He rests his forehead against mine then and we just breathe together for a moment, eyes locked in our own little universe that had created a place greater than anything else. The love we've bled for and even died for by choosing each other right on through it all. I see it all in his eyes too. Even if he doesn't remember it like I do, it's still in the soul-deep love there.

"Love you, Princess," he whispers roughly. "Endlessly."

My lips twitch as I brush them against his again. "Endlessly."

He arches a brow. "I'll show you endlessly later tonight."

Another laugh leaves me and that savage smirk flashes across his face as he stands, hollering out to the beach. "Maddoc Jace Monroe!"

I turn to see Maddoc freeze instantly, eyes going wide as he stares at his dad before Coop yells. "Run fast!"

They both take off a beat later, Maddoc sprinting as fast as his little legs will carry him, while Coop flies down the beach after him. Eventually catching up and throwing him over his shoulder before wading out into the water to toss him into the waves while Maddoc screams with delight. I watch it all happen with a wide smile splitting my face, heart so incredibly full that I still wonder sometimes if it'll just burst from happiness one day.

Until then though… I'm going to soak it all into my soul and cherish every moment I'll take into whatever eternity comes after. Because I can finally see it all, the life we imagined on this very beach once, right here playing out right in front of me. All because of the love we share.

Because love at its core is a defiance of reason, and if you dare, even a defiance of fate itself. It's greater than any powers that may be. It's life's greatest mystery. The way it can span across time and space, across universes, and through lives. Changing histories and inspiring the most epic of stories. Drawing two people together when everything in existence is trying to tear them apart. Entangling you with another down to the very matter of your soul. Powerful enough to shatter the heavens, to defy the gods, and to even fracture fate itself.

So I watch them laugh and chase each other through the water, trying to remember every moment to make Coop write down later. This final version of us that I want to outlast all of the others. The one with the happily ever after.

But really, once is all you need when it comes down to it.

One extraordinary lifetime of love to overcome all the other stories.

END OF A TWISTED TALE

Follow R. Phillips!

For the latest updates on future books.

@rphillipswrites

www.rphillipswrites.com

Facebook

Rachael's Tangled Readers

Instagram

TikTok

Goodreads

Amazon

An Open Letter About A Twisted Tale

I'm going to be real with y'all… I wrote those last words and SOBBED.

This was my first book baby. These characters will forever be the first ones I brought to life and I think they'll always be a little more special because of that. I'm almost four weeks out and I'm still getting these little pangs in my heart when I remember that I'll never write from El's POV again. And I've had people tell me that their story doesn't have to be over, that I could write as them again one day… but that's not true, because they earned it. El and Coop earned their happily ever after and I am so incredibly honored that I could give it to them.

Fractured was a book that pushed me beyond what even I was expecting it to. There was no gray in Fractured. No more choices or maybes, everything was final. I think the hardest part was continuing to tell a different kind of love story between these three people even after that choice had been made. But there was always going to be a choice, there's no getting around that, and it was always going to be Coop. The story they'd been robbed countless times whether it was Helen and Paris, Isolde and Tristan, or Guinevere and Lancelot. But El and Coop, yeah, I got to

509

finally give them the ending they deserved. A purpose to everything they had all been through, including Jace.

And yeah, I know… You get to the end and realize this entire time you've really just been reading the heartbreaking prequel. The first mortal and arguably most important part to a far greater story.

Now let's get into the mess of it and try to find our way out, yeah?

First, Jace Fucking Dawson. Jace broke my heart from the first moment I wrote him and a little more with each one that followed as I fell in love with him right along with El. He was honestly the hardest to write because I always knew how this story was going to end. I always knew that while he played such a big part in it and while the love that he and El and Coop shared was so valid… this was never his story and it wrecked me for him at times. But just like El said, he deserves so much more. A whole love and life of his own for once. And as for his ending in this story… I'll just say this, energy cannot be created or destroyed, but it can be transformed.

Second, El. To me, El has always been a lot of the things I think we all wish we could be at times. She's brave and bold and doesn't give a fuck, to a fault yes, especially at the start of Entangled. And yeah she can be a brat and annoy the shit out of even me at times… but damn, don't we all wish sometimes that we had the audacity she does? To walk up to the guy in the bar and throw caution to the wind? Again, granted, not always the smartest move, but El is all of the things we're sometimes too scared to do come to life. She reminds us to be a little more brave, I think, and I freaking love her for that because she reminded me to be brave too. Writing El reminded me of a piece of myself that I had hidden away during a time when I had been told it was wrong and then we kinda found that piece together again. I'll always be grateful to her for that.

Out of all of the characters in this story, she grew the most. She realized that she could be everything she needed to herself and that she didn't have to fear all of the good life had to offer. She chose and fought and learned how to finally let go. She grew into herself and I am so incredibly proud of her. She'll never not be in my head and heart.

Third, Cooper Monroe lol. And yes, there has to be a lol because Coop was one I didn't have to work too hard at. Coop came to me as naturally as writing poetry in my journals always had. He just… was, if that makes sense? I never had to work at Coop, we understood each other. Coop is demanding and he'll push and he can be selfish and even manipulative at times. But his love is also so pure in its own dark kind of way because it is the embodiment of that raw poetry you write in the wee hours of the night when the deepest truths slip through. It demands honesty, it demands bravery, it never wavers and that's why his love made El so much stronger too. He took every piece of El exactly as she was and loved her anyway, letting her do the same. And he grew in Fractured too, they both did. They recognized how one another had changed and grew stronger together. In my head they'll always be doing that, tucked away on a beach in Cahuita watching their kids splash in the waves.

That was the only thing Coop had ever truly wanted in life.

Now onto the most important part.

Thank you, thank you, thank you to all of my readers! Y'all are everything. Every page you read, book you buy, quote you love, message you send and just general love for my books you express means the world to me. I wouldn't be able to do what I do without y'all and please know how incredibly grateful I am.

Ellie, I'm keeping you forever too. Thanks for cleaning up all my grammatical messes in this one. I wouldn't have been able to do the story justice without you.

Clarissa, thank you for bringing my visions to life and designing the most beautiful covers for this trilogy. Also thank you for dealing with everything bringing my visions to life entails, I know it can be painful at times lol.

To my mini. You are the only thing I love in this world more than telling stories and I hope you get all the happily ever afters that life has to offer. Always know that being your mom is the greatest story of my life, and my favorite one too (and this one will always be your green book).

To my mama. Thank you for being such an incredible mom to me. Thank you for supporting me in this career even though you don't like to read lol. Thank you for letting me live my life never doubting for a second that I am so loved by you. That's all a kid really needs in the end.

To my sestra, Morgan. If only they knew the crazy author moments you had to deal with throughout this whole trilogy and how many times you saved so many characters from dying lol. Thank you for dealing with it all and reading these stories probably a dozen times before they were even done. I'm not sure I would have made it out of this sanely without you.

To my sister. Thank you for reading this one even though you were scared too. Thank you for being my biggest cheerleading and always letting me know how proud you are of me. It means everything. You are the best big sister I could ever ask for.

To Lauren. Thank you for putting up with all the torturous texts before I let you read this book and for everything you help me with (and for being such an amazing friend even though I kicked you off my arc team lol). Love you girl and am so grateful I met you through this.

To Steph. Thank you for answering all of my questions about Canada's geography and political system! You have officially replaced google for me when it comes to all things Canadian.

To all of my day ones. I sent probably hundreds of emails and messages asking people like you to read and review Entangled at the start of this journey. And y'all were the ones who answered. You were the ones who took a chance on a first time author and I will always be grateful for that. You got the word out there about my books so please know, that I know, how big a part y'all play in any and all (hopeful) success I have from here on out. Each and every one of you has joined me on this emotionally traumatic journey and I thank you from the bottom of my heart.

It's been a wild ride, the end that's really the start of everything, but that's life isn't it?

Can't wait for all the stories to come.

XO,

R. Phillips

About the Author

R. Phillips loves to write romance stories full of angst, plot twists and a generous sprinkling of salacious scenes. Playing with timelines is one of her favorite things to do in her writing along with including a dash of mythology. She's also a big fan of leaving your jaw on the floor.

Rachael is a native Texan, reader first, and frequently imagines her book scenes to songs. She is a lover of coffee, tex-mex, and is probably too particular when it comes to her choice in red wine. She credits any success to the long line of strong women she comes from who gave her a steely spine, taught her to know her mind, and to always rise.

Made in the USA
Middletown, DE
13 October 2023

40514085R00289